TEMPERING STEELE

Cover photo by Vincent Ledvina, Unsplash.com

Published by History of the Saints Inc., Sandy, Utah

Cover and interior design by Susan Lofgren and Anna Oldroyd
Interior photos by Glenn Rawson, Depositphotos.com, and Unsplash.com; sketches by Kelly Donovan

Copyright ©2021 History of the Saints, Dennis C. Lyman, Glenn Rawson

All rights reserved. No part of this book may be reproduced in any format or medium without the written permission of the publisher, History of the Saint's Inc. 1785 East Sunrise Park Drive, Sandy, Utah 84093. This work is not an official publication of The Church of Jesus Christ of Latter-day Saints. The views expressed within this work are the sole responsibility of the author and do not necessarily reflect the position of The Church of Jesus Christ of Latter-day Saints, or any other entity.

Printed in the United States of America
First Printing: December 2021

ISBN 978-1-7355962-3-5

History of the Saints

TEMPERING STEELE

GLENN RAWSON
PUBLISHED BY GLENN RAWSON AND DENNIS LYMAN

Prologue

LEMHI, IDAHO, DECEMBER 24, 2006

Frigid arctic air meets warm water at the Aleutian Islands, located in the northern Pacific, making the island chain one of the major storm capitols of the world. Just days before Christmas in 2006, a massive low-pressure system was created in this desolate vortex and sent spiraling on a south-easterly course toward the North American mainland. The ferocious storm slammed ashore at the mouth of the mighty Columbia River near Astoria, Oregon. Rain fell in record amounts. As though being guided by an invisible hand, the storm then barreled its way east through the mountains, maintaining tremendous power as it approached Idaho. The polar jet stream dipped south, drawing down frigid arctic air, while the subtropical jet stream rose north, laden with tropical moisture. In a rare occurrence, the two met in a wide convergence zone directly over central Idaho. The result was a storm to be remembered—the storm of the century.

Darkness came prematurely over Idaho's Lemhi Mountains as a thick cloud mass slowly swathed the rugged range like a heavy, wet blanket. Stiff breezes that had swept through the area that morning rose to gusts of more than fifty miles per hour. The fresh powdered snow of the previous week's storm was blown into the air, churning with the new snowfall. By late afternoon, the full power of the storm stalled over Idaho's River of No Return Wilderness. Snow fell so heavily, and winds howled so fiercely that drifting snow overwhelmed roads, power lines, homes, and any unfortunate man or beast caught out in it. To face the storm would have been akin to being attacked by a rogue sand blaster loaded with grains of dry ice. As the defeated sun set behind the western mountains, darkness deepened, and the storm raged with no visible signs of abating. It would not relent for two days.

Families up and down the Lemhi Valley had stocked supplies and prepared for the worst. In home after home, the occupants gathered around warm fires and watched constantly updating news reports of the storm's progress. Soon tiring of the drama, they turned to drinking Wassail and singing traditional Christmas carols. The spirit of the holiest night of the year replaced their worry and filled their hearts with peace and joy. The Spirit of Christ once more worked its power, and the world—even with its storms—became subdued with the realization that God was with man again.

Far off the main road, partially sheltered by tall cottonwoods, stood a rustic ranch home. Fragrant pine smoke rising out of the chimney was caught by the wind and whipped into oblivion like a bird in a gale. Saddle horses stood in the pasture next to the house, facing away from the wind, their backs humped against the cold. The ferocious wind covered them and their last feeding of hay with a blanket of white.

The first thing that would have impressed a visitor who walked through the antique front door of the Steele home was its warm, inviting atmosphere. A fire crackled in the fireplace in the corner, emanating a reassuring warmth that tamed the thick frost framing the corners of the large picture window. The smell of cinnamon and Christmas potpourri filled the air. A large, ornately decorated pine tree stood in front of the window, its lights twinkling and reflecting in the iced glass. Traditional Christmas music wafted like a gentle breeze through the house. Even a total stranger would have felt like he had come home.

The festive aura of the home made the tragedy playing out in the master bedroom especially poignant.

"Joseph."

Joe Steele, barely able to lift his hand from the bed, reached out for his oldest son, Joseph Orson Steele. J.O., as everyone but his father called him, came forward, fighting valiantly to hold back the tears. The lump in his throat threatened to cut off his breath completely. Even as he clasped the bony hand in a grip that was now as weak as that of an infant, the lad sensed that these would be his father's last moments in this life.

"Joseph," his father said again, his words not much more than a whisper. J.O. leaned down to hear his father's words.

"This is it, Son. I'm leaving. Take care of your mother and your brother. They are everything to me. Please do for them as I would have."

"I will, Dad," the boy said as he tightened his grip on the frail hand. "I will!"

Joe Steele settled back into the pillow, closed his eyes, and seemed to relax. Then, as though someone had spoken to him, his eyes opened and fixed on something to J. O.'s left. His countenance brightened perceptibly, becoming almost radiant. J.O. turned to see what his father was looking at. He saw nothing there but an empty room.

"Yes, I'm ready," Joe said in voice noticeably stronger and infused with pure joy.

The smothering blanket of gloom seemed to momentarily lift, as though a summer wind had carried in the scent of mountain wildflowers. But J.O. was so consumed by grief that he took little notice of the change in his father's countenance. In fact, it would be many years before the heavy curtain of pain would be drawn back enough for J.O. to reflect on this moment.

Across the room, Ruthie Steele's stoic reserve crumbled. She pulled her younger son to her bosom and began to sob, burying her face in his tousled, blond hair.

Joe Steele looked at his older son for the last time on this side of the veil. His gaze was intense, his face almost aglow with an unearthly light.

"Find Him, Son. Find the Pole Star!" The whisper trailed off. Then, with a faint sigh, Joe Steele closed his eyes and departed this life.

J.O. lowered the now-lifeless hand onto the bed and looked at his mother and younger brother, who were sobbing unrestrained. Tears welled up in his own eyes, and this time there was no stopping them. He bolted through the open door of the bedroom and passed the brightly lit Christmas tree. As he jerked open the front door, the ferocity of the storm hit him directly in the face but slowed his steps for only a moment. Plunging through the snowdrift at the door, he began to run.

Within seconds, the darkness swallowed him. Plunging into the storm, he wished with all his soul that he could die and go with his dad. Wind-driven snow and ice stung his cheeks and caked in his hair, yet he felt nothing but the pain in his wounded soul. He ran into the darkness until his lungs burned and his clothes were covered with snow and ice. Finally, he was forced to stop. Exhausted, his chest heaving, he dropped to his knees in the snow. Great racking sobs punctuated with a profusion of tears split the blackened air.

"Heavenly Father," he started to say, but then suddenly stopped.

His head came back up and his eyes opened into the darkness. For months, he had prayed every day—constantly, in fact—that his father would live. Those prayers had been as sincere as any eleven-year-old could utter. Yet they hadn't worked. His dad was dead! Bitter anger welled up inside him. J.O. set his jaw and defiantly stood. No loving God could be so cruel.

"There is no God," he muttered through clenched teeth into the wind, "and if there is, He doesn't care!"

He brushed the icy tears from his cheeks. He was through praying, through crying. His mother and brother would need his strength now, not his weakness. The promise he had made to his dad to care for the family solidified in his young soul and would become one of the driving values of his life.

An involuntary shudder spread through his body and brought him back to dangerous reality. The wind-driven temperature was far below zero. He looked down. The snow had already buried his feet up to the ankles. If he didn't get back quickly, his unprotected body would freeze in a few more minutes. He looked into the storm for the lights of the ranch house, but nothing was visible. He looked up into the heavens for the North Star, as his dad had taught him to do, but saw nothing more than a dizzying swirl of white. His father's last words came to his mind: *Find Him. Find the Pole Star.* What could that mean?

He shook off the thought, set his jaw with determination, and began to run through his anger and grief, not knowing for certain where he was going. He had only instinct to follow.

That night—that painful moment—defined the next fifteen years of J.O. Steele's life.

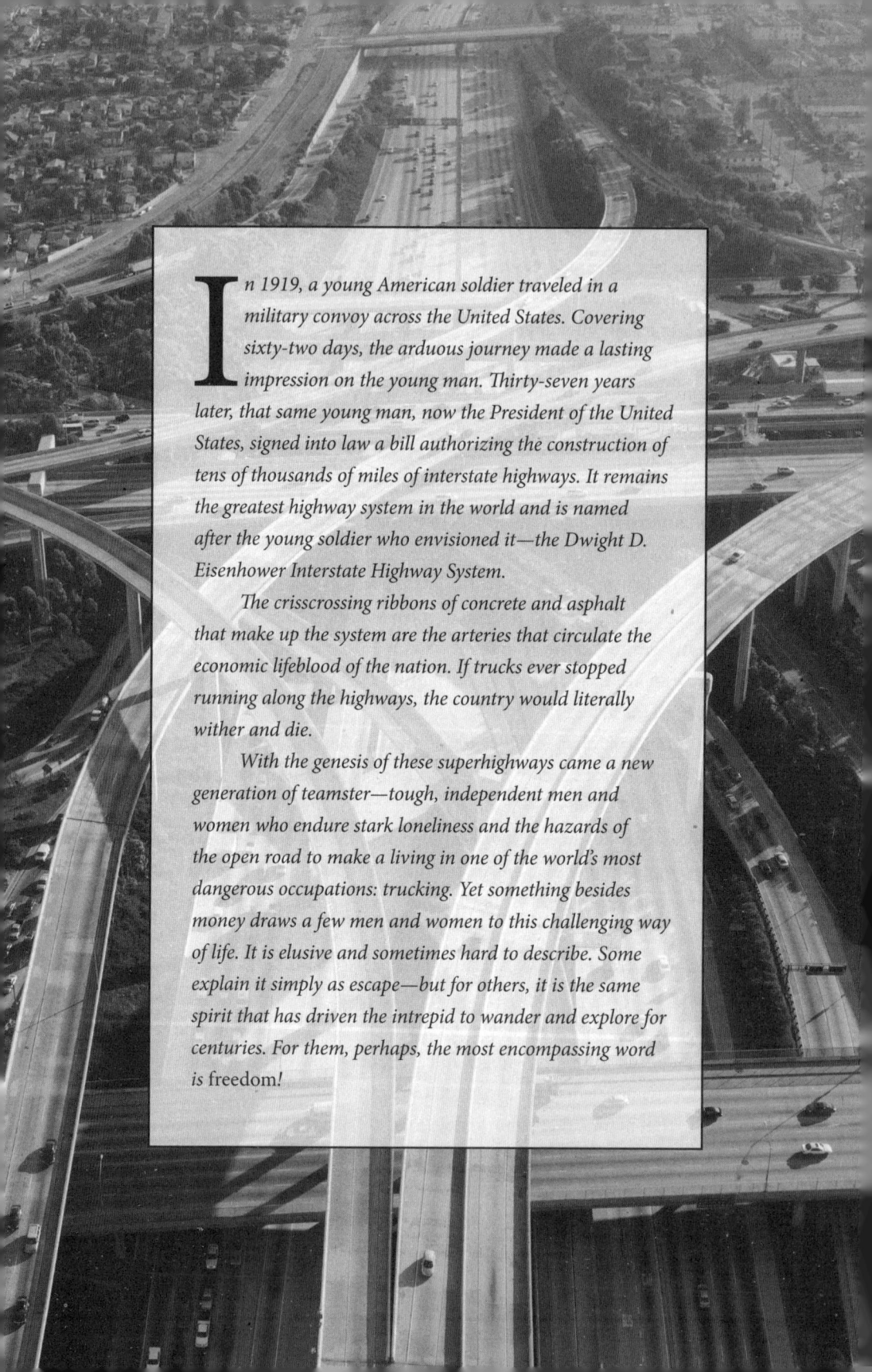

In 1919, a young American soldier traveled in a military convoy across the United States. Covering sixty-two days, the arduous journey made a lasting impression on the young man. Thirty-seven years later, that same young man, now the President of the United States, signed into law a bill authorizing the construction of tens of thousands of miles of interstate highways. It remains the greatest highway system in the world and is named after the young soldier who envisioned it—the Dwight D. Eisenhower Interstate Highway System.

The crisscrossing ribbons of concrete and asphalt that make up the system are the arteries that circulate the economic lifeblood of the nation. If trucks ever stopped running along the highways, the country would literally wither and die.

With the genesis of these superhighways came a new generation of teamster—tough, independent men and women who endure stark loneliness and the hazards of the open road to make a living in one of the world's most dangerous occupations: trucking. Yet something besides money draws a few men and women to this challenging way of life. It is elusive and sometimes hard to describe. Some explain it simply as escape—but for others, it is the same spirit that has driven the intrepid to wander and explore for centuries. For them, perhaps, the most encompassing word is *freedom!*

PART ONE:

Just Before Dawn

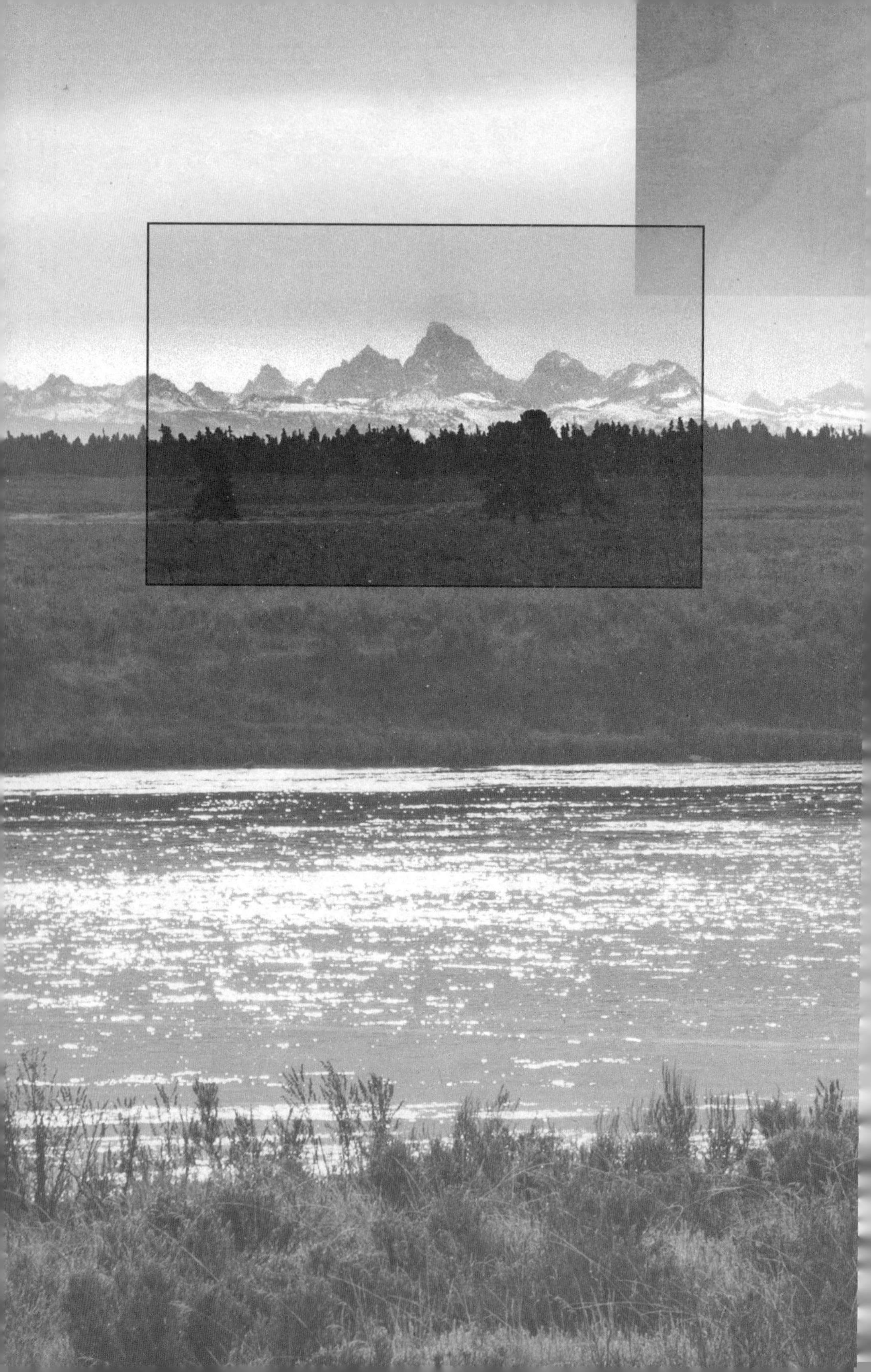

Chapter One

ISLAND PARK, IDAHO, EARLY SUMMER 2021

J.O. Steele glanced quickly at the highway in front of him before looking away. The road was clear. His new W900 Kenworth with its eighty-thousand-pound weight negotiated the narrow two-lane highway as though it were open freeway. J.O. turned his gaze from the road to the southeast horizon. It was a gorgeous early June day with an azure blue sky. On this scenic byway between West Yellowstone, Montana, and Idaho Falls, Idaho, the magnificent peaks of the Teton mountain range can be seen through the lush pine and fir forests of Island Park—but for only a fleeting moment. J.O. had traveled these roads hundreds of times, and he knew just where to look.

Suddenly there they were, shattering the monotony of the alpine horizon like the caw of a crow on a still morning. The jagged peaks of the Three Tetons rose nearly fourteen thousand feet above the surrounding Snake River Plain, a distinct landmark to any traveler. Visitors from all over the world came to experience their rugged beauty, some to climb and others to simply stare. In 1880, an English traveler had aptly captured their unique profile when he declared the Tetons to be "the most perfect example in all the world of how mountains should appear on the horizon."

As he stared through the opening in the trees, J.O. experienced the same feeling he did every time he looked at these mountains. Two years earlier, he had fulfilled a lifelong dream by climbing to the summit of the Grand Teton, the highest of the three peaks. The peaks were ruggedly beautiful from any perspective, but the vistas that had opened to him during the two-day climb had taken his breath away. Staring at them now, even from fifty miles away, he relived those memories.

J.O. glanced back at the road to make sure it was still open in front of him. After all, a fully loaded eighteen-wheeler can't stop on a dime. The road was clear. He leaned forward slightly, rested his forearms on the padded steering wheel, and turned his attention back to the peaks. They seemed massive, as though they were only a few miles away, yet he knew they were far off in the distance. He had experienced that same sort of sensation when he had climbed them; all sense of dimension and space had been skewed as he stood among them. Rock outcroppings that seemed so close took many hours of rigorous climbing to reach. Distances that seemed so small were gigantic in reality. It didn't take long to lose trust in one's sense of perspective in the Tetons.

Driving down the highway, J.O. recalled the late afternoon of the first day of their climb. His party made camp in a place called the Petzholdt Caves, named for the famous Teton explorer, Paul Petzholdt. They were high up in the mountains just below the Lower Saddle. As the others in his party rested from the long trek to the caves, he was too excited to sit still. For several hours, he explored the landscape like a man taking a last drink before he crossed the desert. Tiny, stunted mountain flowers, few and far between, caught his attention, and he studied them curiously. He found caves where remnants of the winter snows remained, even though it was the end of August.

The real experience of that first afternoon in the mountains came when he sat down on a massive rock that was too big to be called a boulder and too small to be called a mountain. It was high on the side of the mountain and overlooked the trail they had climbed earlier. J.O. was awestruck with the grandeur of it all. Below him lay the vast bowl that was formed by the convergence of the three peaks, strewn with rocks and boulders that had shattered away from the vertical rock walls over centuries of time. Just to look across that bowl distorted all sense of space and distance. It didn't seem all that far across, especially with the huge peaks looming thousands of feet above him, yet he knew it was. It had taken hours to hike across only a small part of it.

But the real shock came when he saw something moving near the Meadows in the bottom of the bowl. Squinting, he looked more closely, barely able to see a man setting up a tent for the night. From where J.O. sat, the man looked like an ant on a gravel-strewn sidewalk. Holding up his thumb and index finger, he gauged the man's height from that perspective to be less than an eighth of an inch. An overwhelming feeling of smallness and insignificance came over J.O. His eyes lifted to the sheer, jutting rock column of the east face of the Middle Teton with its stark black stripe. It loomed over him like a summer thunderhead. Its immensity was incomprehensible. He had once heard that no one *conquered* mountains like these; the mountains let them pass. It was true! Man was puny and insignificant when compared with this enormity. Where did such beauty and power come from? Was its magnificence and bulk an accident of some nebulous force called *nature*, or did it have a creator? And if there was a creator, who was He—or it?

Before J.O. could ponder any more questions, a rapid movement caught his peripheral vision, pulling his eyes back to the highway in front of him and launching his heartrate into orbit. As he rounded a bend in the road, an old station wagon was puttering down the highway in front of him. He was bearing down on the decrepit jalopy so rapidly that he knew he would never be able to stop in time. He stomped on the brake with all his power, but the fully loaded rig scarcely slowed. If he hit that car at the speed he was traveling, it would be a deadly disaster.

In a millisecond, J.O.'s trained mind processed his avenue of escape. In less time that it takes to tell what happened, he checked his mirror and cut the wheel to the left. The truck veered sharply into the other lane, and J.O. stomped the accelerator to the floor. A pickup truck pulling a large camp trailer was coming toward him. It would be close. J.O.'s knuckles whitened as the distance narrowed. A quick glance at his right-side mirror told him that the back of his trailer was just past the front of the old car. He flipped the turn signal and cut the wheel hard to the right, just clearing the old station wagon. The oncoming driver had slowed and moved onto the shoulder of the road to avoid a head-on collision, passing just as J.O. got back in his lane. J.O. was sure he could see the angry look the man shot him as he went by.

Relieved, J.O. sagged back into the seat, blowing out a thankful breath. That was close, too close. He was certain the guy in the pickup was giving him what his mother used to call a "scotch blessing." Maybe he deserved it. He had been foolish. *No piece of scenery is worth killing someone for.*

Suddenly a brown blur appeared out of the corner of his eye. That same old station wagon went roaring past as if his truck was parked. J.O. glanced down at his speedometer; the old car had to be doing at least ninety, disappearing down the road in a cloud of blue smoke.

"*Now* he decides to drive," J.O. muttered.

He watched as the old car disappeared around another bend in the road. Gradually, J.O. calmed and adjusted his position in the air-suspension seat to get more comfortable. The view of the Teton mountain range was gone now, obliterated by the endless walls of evergreen trees that lined both sides of the highway. J.O. rolled down the window and welcomed the sudden blast of warm air laced with the scent of fresh pine. He drew several deep breaths, letting them refresh him. He had been on the road since before dawn, and he was starting to feel the effects of the miles and hours.

J.O. dragged his fingers through his hair. It was his father's hair, thick and full, reaching just to the top of his ears. No one was ever quite sure whether to call it red, blond, or light brown—but whatever it was, the slightest breeze picked it up and scattered it like straw, giving him a restless, carefree appearance. He arched his back and stretched, extending his long legs as far as he could to restore the circulation.

Standing six-foot-three and weighing about 190 pounds, he was not built like most truck drivers. His body was lean and hard from hours of exercise and running. His shoulders were broader than his hips, and the muscles of his back and shoulders were well-defined and toned. He wasn't a body builder, but it was plainly obvious he wasn't a beer-bellied couch potato, either. If there was one thing J.O. Steele was addicted to, it was exercise and feeling good. There weren't many opportunities for trips to the gym when he lived on the road, so he compensated by a daily workout of running, pushups, and lifting weights wherever he happened to be. It was likely that he had run in more cities and out-of-the-way places in the United States than any man alive, and the eighty-six-inch studio sleeper on his truck was a combination home and workout gym.

Big trucks had been a part of J.O.'s life from the time he was a small boy on the ranch. He remembered sitting by the side of the road that ran down the valley through the ranch with his dog, watching as the big logging trucks rumbled down the mountain road with their engine brakes rattling. From the time he could remember, he had been captivated by the sheer size and power of big trucks, and he started driving professionally as soon as he was old enough to get a job. In some ways, it was a lonely, disreputable life; in others, it was very rewarding. Open spaces, new scenery, and continual adventures had captured his heart, gotten into his blood, and kept him on the road most of the year. Opportunities had been handed to him to do other things, but the lure of the big trucks and open roads kept him coming back. He drove a truck not because he had to by occupational default, but because he chose to as a way of life, and he prided himself on being a professional.

Being on the road worked out too because there was little reason to go home. His mother and younger brother were comfortably situated in the townhome he had purchased for them in Pocatello, Idaho. His mother worked as an elementary school teacher, and his brother, Tate, was a business and finance major at Idaho State University. They led busy lives and got along fine without him. Because he never stopped working, he made more money than he could possibly spend. He used his money to support his brother in college, and he sent his mother on vacations abroad every year. His cell phone bill attested to the fact that he kept constant contact with them. They were a close family, even though he was always gone.

Tate enjoyed school and had big plans. His mother, however, was another concern, and she occupied his thoughts constantly. Since selling the ranch at auction eleven years ago and moving to the city, she had never seemed content or settled. Part of that was due to living in the confines of a city, but most of it was due to missing her husband. When Joseph Steele died of cancer, he left his thirty-four-year-old wife a widow with two sons and a large cattle ranch to manage. She and her boys had tried valiantly to keep the ranch going, but in the end, bad markets and crooked men took it away from them. They sold it for enough to clear the debts and get a fresh start elsewhere.

It was hard at first, but Ruthie Steele was a strong woman. She squared her shoulders, faced forward, and went on to build a new life for her and her sons. When the boys enrolled in school, she went back to school herself, eventually obtaining a teaching certificate. From that point on, she lost herself in the lives of her sons, her students, and every other struggling waif that came under the sprawling shelter of her huge heart. If there was a person more loving and giving than his mother, he didn't know who it was.

A quick glance at his watch revealed that it was approaching 5:30 p.m. His mother would just be getting home. J.O touched a button on his steering wheel that activated his Bluetooth connection to his cell phone. "Call Mom," he intoned, and the call went through.

When she answered, he greeted her cheerfully.

"J.O., where are you, Son?"

It was the first question she always asked when he called her. The places he traveled always seemed to fascinate her. The interest she had taken in what was important to him had kept him close to his mother all through his teen years. Many kids rebelled against their folks, but the idea had never crossed J.O.'s mind. How do you rebel against a friend? Last summer she had even gone on a few short runs with him. Occasionally, she asked him to pick up souvenirs for her students.

"I'm in Island Park."

"Great! Then you'll be home tonight." There was no mistaking the excitement in her voice. Her enthusiastic welcome caused him to look forward to those times when he was home.

"I will. I won't deliver the load I'm bringing in until Friday around noon. I'll be home all day tomorrow. After I deliver the load on Friday, I'll head south."

"Well, at least I'll get you for one day," she said, laughing. "Would you like me to save you some supper?"

"No, it'll be late by the time I get there. I think I'll just stop here in Ashton at Big Jud's and get a hamburger before I go on. I need to stretch my legs anyway."

"Okay, Son. Hurry home."

"I will," he said warmly. "I love you. Bye."

Just as he hung up the phone, he couldn't believe his eyes. That same old brown station wagon was once again crawling down the road in front of him, once again going at a snail's pace. This time, however, J.O. had plenty of warning. He eased off the accelerator and flipped on the engine brake, letting the eighty-thousand-pound rig slowly rumble to a mere thirty-five miles per hour. As he came up behind the old car, he saw that the bumper was wallpapered with religious stickers. J.O. felt a brief flash of annoyance. Everywhere, even on the paint, were sayings, slogans, and decals praising God and calling upon whoever was reading to confess and be saved. J.O.'s irritation deepened. Somehow the idea of getting one's salvation off the rear end of a car didn't seem plausible. *Probably some zealot on Bible vacation*, he thought with growing disdain.

Slowly, a mischievous smile spread across his sun-tanned face.

Obviously, this cleric in a clunker had a stunted attention span. Maybe it was time for a little *revival!*

J.O. eased the large truck forward until it was only a few feet behind the plastered bumper of the car. When he was sure he was close enough that the only thing the driver would see in his rear-view mirror was a huge grill, he reached up and jerked the air-horn cord. The twin chrome horns emitted a piercing blast only a few decibels below that of a train whistle. J.O. leaned forward, every muscle tense and ready for whatever might happen. He mentally pictured the man's startled face appearing in the rear-view mirror and nearly laughed aloud at the hilarious image. The man's panic would be consummate at the sight of the chrome grill of a mechanical monster about to crush him into a dirty brown grease spot and propel him into eternity to meet his maker.

J.O.'s grin turned to outright laughter as a cloud of blue smoke again belched from beneath the car and it shot forward, leaving him in the dust.

Serves him right, J.O. thought to himself, still smiling.

He had no more time to concern himself with the old car as the warning sign marking the steep descent of Ashton Hill came into view. J.O. slowed the truck, geared down the transmission, and set the engine brake for the descent. A fully loaded eighteen-wheeler can be pulled down a steep hill with greater force than the brakes can withstand, causing the brakes to overheat and become ineffective. It had taken only one experience with a runaway truck on a steep mountain pass to scare J.O. enough to never forget again.

Just beyond Ashton Hill is the tiny village of Ashton, Idaho. The town's claim to fame are snow machines and potatoes, and most people know it as a few buildings and a reduction in the speed limit on the way to Yellowstone. J.O. knew it for another reason: Big Jud's, a small diner with a big reputation on the north end of town that served the most massive hamburger he had ever seen. It was a full pound of meat and filled a regular-sized dinner plate.

He pulled off the road and parked his rig. As he walked in, he noticed a dirty, beat-up, brown station wagon parked at the front door. Incredible—it was the fickle-footed zealot he had nearly run over. He smiled to himself and walked in. Now he would see the man behind the bumper stickers.

J.O. took a seat at the end of the counter nearest the cash register. The young waitress gave him a welcoming smile. He returned the smile before turning to survey the dining area. There were a few people scattered through the area, but no one stood out to him. The waitress came and took his order, pausing once on her way to the kitchen to glance appreciatively at the handsome young stranger. Just then, the door opened, and a man walked in. His appearance immediately interested J.O. His hair was long, reaching down the better portion of his back and pulled into a frizzy ponytail that was as tangled and unkempt as the rest of him. A long, straggly beard resembling a sparse patch of summer-burnt grass hung down his front. The man gave J.O. a bloodshot stare as he sauntered to the dining room and took a seat at a window table. A faint, bemused smile spread across J.O.'s face. *There he is—the zealot*, he thought.

Soon his order was delivered, and he forgot all else. While he ate, he mentally ran through his schedule and calculated the days ahead. Professional drivers are limited by law in the number of hours they can work in a day and a week. J.O. was scheduled to take the load of mining machinery he carried now up to a gold mine that was above the Yankee Fork of the Salmon River. Before that he could enjoy a welcome night at home with his family.

The sound of raised voices interrupted his concentration, and he turned to see the source of the commotion. The zealot had moved over and sat down across the table from a grizzled old gentleman wearing bib overalls. From all appearances, J.O. guessed he was a local farmer having supper. The rising intensity in their voices indicated that their conversation was anything but friendly.

"Mister," the old man said, "I don't need your hi-falootin' preachin'. Why don't you go back to your table and let me eat my supper in peace?"

At that, J.O. spun around on his stool and watched the exchange with open interest.

"You can't be saved without confessing Christ," the zealot said. His voice was surprisingly shrill and nasally. "Have you confessed Jesus?" he whined.

The old man leaned forward, real anger now showing on his face. "That, Junior, is none of your business. Who gave you the job of saving the world anyway?"

"I was visited," the zealot answered, placing his hand on his chest, "by the in-filling of the Holy Spirit."

"That's all fine and dandy for you, Mister, but the only thing you're filling me with right now is heartburn. Now, if—"

"But you need to be saved, man. I want to save your soul."

The old man dropped his fork on the plate with a clatter. He leaned forward again, his eyes narrowed to wrinkled, weather-beaten slits. "Are you saved? Are you going to heaven?"

"I am," the zealot answered proudly. "I've confessed Jesus and I'm saved by His grace."

J.O. sensed where the conversation was going, and he unconsciously smiled.

"Then I don't want to be saved," the old man continued. "I would rather be in hell than spend forever in heaven with a mule-headed fool like you." The old man leaned back, a look of triumph on his face. The zealot sat with a befuddled expression, momentarily stunned into silence by this unexpected twist in the conversation. J.O.'s grin deepened. The old man was a lot quicker and sharper than he looked.

For a moment, the zealot sat shaking his head with a dazed expression. Then he went on as though he hadn't heard a word the old man said. "But you need to be saved, man."

J.O. felt his own ire rising. More times than he could count, people had tried to cram religion down his throat. If there was anything that peeved him, it was unbridled religious bigotry. He had heard enough. The old man needed help. Standing abruptly, he walked the five steps to the two men and slammed both hands down on the table so hard that the old man's plate jumped. Startled, both men lifted curious eyes to J.O., who now leaned down and let his eyes bore into those of the zealot. "Do you believe that your God is a loving, gentle God who looks out for and protects His people?"

It took a moment to process, but the zealot nodded his head. "Yes, I do," he said matter-of-factly.

"Do you believe that he is fair and just?" J.O. pressed.

There was another nod.

Then J.O. bored in. "Then how do you explain to me that this loving God allowed six million of His chosen people to be slaughtered in a Nazi holocaust? How do you explain the millions of children and innocent people who are starving to death as you sit here and fill your filthy face? Tell me, where is God when terrorists slaughter thousands? Explain that to me, if you can!"

The zealot's mouth dropped open. He stared at J.O. After a moment, his jaw began to work, but no sound came out. He looked back and forth from J.O. to the old man, who was now grinning wickedly. Suddenly, the zealot stood up so rapidly that his chair shot back and fell to the floor.

"You're—you're—you're going to hell!" he cried, shaking his finger at J.O. His voice was shrill to the point of sounding hysterical. With that, he spun on his heel and stomped out of the restaurant. Every head in the place turned to the window as the zealot climbed into his car and roared out of the parking lot in a cloud of dust and smoke. As he disappeared, the curious patrons looked back to J.O. and the old man. Slowly, J.O. raised himself up to his full height, his features softening into a warm, lopsided grin.

"It's okay, folks," he drawled for effect. "I'm really not going to hell. I'm actually just headed for Pocatello."

Relieved laughter rippled through the diner, and everyone turned their attention back to their food. J.O. walked back to his sandwich, but he wasn't hungry anymore. He dropped a twenty-dollar bill on the counter and told the smiling waitress, "Keep the change."

The young waitress looked up with a startled expression. "Thanks!" she said.

He had just reached the door when he was stopped short. "Just a minute, young feller." It was the old man.

J.O. turned back and faced him. The look in the old man's eyes was intense. This man had something to say. "I appreciate what you did back there, getting rid of him and all that, but I have a question." He paused, waiting for a sign to continue. J.O. nodded. "Do *you* believe in God?" the old man said, staring hard at him.

The abrupt question caught J.O. off guard, but he quickly recovered. "No," he said with a smile, "I don't." He turned and started through the door. "I outgrew that years ago."

The old man's voice barely reached him as he stepped off the porch. It sounded strangely sorrowful. "Yeah, that ya did, Boy. Grew right out of your own britches, ya did."

With the old man's words still echoing in his ears, J.O. walked across the road and climbed into his truck.

What was that supposed to mean? he thought as he started the engine and released the brakes. Whatever it meant, there was no mistaking the rebuke in the old man's tone. J.O. felt suddenly defensive. *How could I believe in God? If there was a God, my dad would still be alive.*

Painfully, J.O. let his mind drift back to the last time he had ever sympathetically entertained the idea of the existence of God. All the ache of that long-ago Christmas came back in an instant.

J.O. reached inside his shirt and retrieved a small, steel medallion that hung around his neck. On one side was the inscription, *The Polar Star*. On the other side were the Big Dipper and the North Star against a mountain relief.

"There is no God," J.O. said with bitter finality. He dropped the medallion back beneath his shirt and swallowed the lump that rose in his throat. This was the very reason he never expressed his feelings on this subject to another living soul. Those who knew him knew better than to bring it up. Not even his mother had been able to penetrate his emotional armor.

A loud splat on his windshield suddenly grabbed his attention. A huge raindrop splashed across the glass, followed by another, and then another. J.O. leaned forward and peered through the windshield up into the sky ahead of him. He had been so engrossed in his own thoughts that he had failed to notice that he was driving into a massive thunderhead. It seemed to be rolling toward him like a giant, blue-black tidal wave less than a mile in front of him. Rounded, sagging bottoms hung beneath the leaden clouds. Lightning pierced the sky, and the rain was so heavy that it hung in a long, grayish curtain in front of him.

The rain and wind slammed into him as if he had driven into the roaring surf. It came in such ferocious horizontal sheets that his windshield wipers couldn't keep up. The temperature instantly dropped by twenty degrees as the sun was darkened. J.O. slowed and turned on his lights. Squinting into the darkness, he leaned forward and concentrated on the road in front of him.

He had seen many summer thunderstorms, but this one was worse than most he could remember. To the side of the road the trees whipped violently in the wind, reminding him of scenes of hurricanes he had seen on television. Though he was tense and ready, he wasn't terribly worried. Summer microbursts could be dangerous, but they usually didn't last long.

A blinding flash of brilliant white light, accompanied by a thunderous explosion, startled him. He cried out and reflexively jerked the steering wheel hard to the left. The loaded truck careened wildly on the slick pavement and started to slide. His instincts took over, preventing panic. Steering into the slide, he finessed the rig with the brakes and accelerator until it straightened out. Once under control, J.O. let the rig roll to a stop on the shoulder of the road. He set the parking brake. For a moment he sat unmoving, his heart pounding so hard it felt like it would erupt out of his chest.

Opening his door, he stepped to the ground and walked back to see what had happened. As he cleared the end of his trailer, the sight that met his eyes so stunned him that he stopped in his tracks and stood gaping. The top forty feet of a huge cottonwood tree, with a trunk some four feet thick, lay on the side of the road with its uppermost branches just touching the asphalt. A bolt of lightning hotter than the surface of the sun had struck the tree, vaporizing the sap and causing the tree to explode as though it had been hit by some gigantic weed-whacker. The part of the tree still standing was split and splintered almost to the ground. Clouds of steam emanated from its ruined core. Cautiously, J.O. drew closer. Despite the torrential downpour, the blackened portion of the tree still smoldered and sizzled. He stared in open wonder, oblivious to the driving rain that was soaking him. Lightning had never come so close, nor had he ever imagined that thunder could be so loud. Only when the rain finally blurred his vision and a chilled shiver ran up his back did he turn and walk slowly back to the truck. He paused once and looked back at the jagged, blackened trunk, marveling at how close he had come to being incinerated.

He was almost back to the truck when the rain suddenly let up and settled into a light drizzle. Sunlight broke through the clouds to the west and dappled everything with a peculiar golden glow. A strange peace settled over the scene. It became as beautiful and tranquil as it had once been violent and dark.

J.O. reached the cab of the truck and stood for a moment on the running board, staring at the eerie landscape. It was unique and beautiful, a rare scene to see. Reluctantly, he climbed up and settled into the driver's seat. In deep thought, he tipped his head back and pondered what he had just seen. Strangely, not a single car had passed in all the time he had been stopped there, which for this stretch of highway was unheard of. After a few minutes of sitting there, he released the brakes and shifted the transmission. As the truck rolled forward and picked up speed, he cast one last glance in his mirror at the shattered tree. At that moment, a thought—or maybe it would be better described as a voice—came into his mind with such force that it seemed to slap him. *There is no God*, it said in a tone of mild, but unmistakable, rebuke. J.O. straightened in his seat. The voice seemed to almost mock him, yet he recognized it.

The voice was his own from just minutes earlier at the diner.

26

Chapter Two

TETON VALLEY, NEAR VICTOR, IDAHO

Shawnee James made one last check of the worn leather cinch on the old rough-rider saddle. It had been her father's when he was a boy, but since he didn't ride much anymore, she had taken it over. With its light weight and high cantle and swells, it was her favorite saddle.

She tucked the end of the cinch away and stepped to the horse's nose, rubbing her hand from his forehead to his nostrils and back again. The large buckskin leaned his head into it, enjoying the attention.

"You ready, old man?" she said, coaxingly. "I need a good run today."

She stared for a moment into the large, intelligent, brown eyes of the best horse she had ever ridden. He was an eight-year-old quarter horse and Arabian cross, and he was masterfully trained. He nuzzled her as if to say, *Let's get on with it.* Gathering the reins, she picked up her stirrup and stepped onto the horse with a practiced grace. Immediately, he began to prance and ask for his head. Shawnee turned him toward the west gate and the mountains.

Her grandparents' ranch was one of the last ones that had escaped the urban development of Teton Valley. It lay nestled against the mountains south and west of Victor, near the mouth of Pine Creek Pass. With its rolling, green hills and fields of alfalfa surrounded by pine-covered mountains on three sides, it was the most heavenly place on earth to Shawnee. For as long as she could remember, her parents had brought her here every summer. They said it was for a vacation, but now she knew it had been to teach her how to work and to love the land. Under the tender care of her grandfather, a tough old cowboy, she learned to irrigate the fields and work cattle and horses. Her mother and grandmother had taught her how to cook and keep a home. She was at home in both worlds and moved back and forth with ease and confidence. Shawnee was brought up to spend the day driving cows with the best of the men, then come home, clean up, and be every part a woman of grace and finesse.

Now twenty-two, Shawnee was a skilled registered nurse at a hospital in Pocatello. After graduating at the top of her class, she was offered the opportunity to work as part of a helicopter life-flight team. The work was intense and exciting, keeping her so busy she had little time for herself. The coming of spring had stirred a yearning to be outside and away from the city. This was, and always had been, her place of first retreat, her connection to heaven.

The adrenalin coursed through Shawnee's veins as the horse pranced through the gate. He had done this before and knew what was coming.

Minutes before, Shawnee's grandmother knew what her oldest granddaughter was going to do to and had warned her against it. "What if that horse stumbles or steps in a hole and you get hurt?"

Shawnee gave her a big smile and then a tight hug. "I love you, Grandma," she said lightly, as if to say *I'll be fine*, and turned toward the barn.

"Oh, you!" her grandmother grumbled. "You're just like your dad. He never listened either." Grandma's words sounded stern, but the twinkle in her eyes told Shawnee that this was all part of a ritual that had been going on since her father was a boy. It was Grandma's job to worry and warn the kids away from trouble, while Grandpa, on the other hand, always pushed the kids to try new things and let nothing scare them. Shawnee and her father had always listened to Grandpa.

Teton Valley

    Now clear of the gate, Shawnee threw her weight from side to side to test the tightness of the cinch. It was adequate. She looked to the west where the foothills of the ranch gave way to the more vertical slopes of the mountains. Off in the distance a hawk was circling, riding the updrafts. He was exactly where she wanted to be. She stood up in the stirrups, leaned over the horse's mane, and loosened up on the reins. At the same time, she touched her spurs lightly to his ribs. The gelding shot forward, his powerful hindquarters propelling him into an all-out run. She let him go. This was the moment and the feeling she had repeatedly rehearsed and imagined all winter. The wind in her face picked up her long, thick, blond hair and whipped it behind her.

    "Go, Duke!" she cried in his ear. The horse responded with more speed. The first five hundred yards were open pasture with no obstacles, but then a five-foot-wide irrigation ditch appeared. Without breaking his stride, Duke leaped and cleared it easily. Shawnee put her hands on the big horse's neck, feeling the rhythm of his stride. This was the embodiment of freedom to her—open country, no fences, beautiful scenery, and the wind in her face. It was all she could do to keep from shouting in exultation.

After the ditch, the terrain changed from pasture to open foothill country covered with sagebrush and trees. This is where a rider's skill was tested, and this is where Shawnee most enjoyed the ride. At that instant, Duke leaped over a sagebrush rather than go around it. His front feet landed; he cut hard to the left and vaulted over another one. The move would have unseated most riders, but Shawnee held to the saddle like it was a part of her body. Her joy increased another fraction as she felt that familiar feeling of being able to anticipate the next move of her horse. Nimbly, Duke cut from side to side or jumped the obstacles in his way, all the while maintaining a hard gallop.

Duke was her horse. From the time of his birth, she had worked with him; under her grandfather's watchful eye, she had trained him and come to love him. As Grandpa got older, he sold off most of his stock, but he kept Duke, just so his oldest granddaughter would come to visit. The horse was as nimble and agile as any cutting horse and had the most heart of any horse she had ever known. The quarter horse blood in him made him strong, while the Arabian blood gave him incredible stamina. He would go hard all day and still be asking for more at the end. In many respects, this horse had taught her some powerful and important lessons for life. If you love what you do, then you can do more and never give up.

Shawnee marveled at the power that emanated from this animal. It never ceased to amaze her that she could control him. He outweighed her twelve to one, yet he was responsive to her every command. Maybe that was part of the reason why she loved this experience so much. Whatever it was, she couldn't get enough of it.

The foothills faded and the climb became steeper. She pulled Duke up and let him find his own trail. Several times, Duke lunged up steep slopes. She threw herself down the left side of the horse's neck as Duke passed under the low-hanging limbs of a Lodgepole pine. Duke suddenly broke through the trees into a small mountaintop clearing about fifty feet across that opened on the east to a breathtaking view of Teton Valley. Shawnee reined the sweating horse to a stop, but he pranced around as if asking for more.

"Easy, Boy," she soothed as she patted his neck. "Just relax. This is as far as we go for now."

Duke seemed to understand and immediately quieted. Shawnee slipped out of the saddle and dropped the bridle reins to the ground. A well-trained cow horse never runs with the reins on the ground. Duke had long ago earned her trust, and now he stood still as she turned her back to him and walked away. After a moment, he dropped his head and began grazing on the lush mountain grass.

Shawnee walked around the clearing, taking it all in. It had been more than a year since she had last been here. Wild geraniums were coming out in full bloom, their red flowers decorating the floor of the meadow like a delicate pattern in a fine carpet. The big, yellow blossoms of arrowleaf balsam root were beginning to wilt and fade, their season coming to an end. She stooped down and plucked a small, blue flower the color of summer sky. Her fingers lightly caressed the petals, soft as goose down. She drew in a deep breath, savoring the rich smell of pine. This was as heavenly a place as any she knew.

Turning to the east, she walked over to a rock that rested on the edge of the meadow where the slope dropped away to the valley. She stepped on top of it, and with her hands on her hips drank in the view that her imagination had replayed all through the long winter. A warm breeze moving up the mountain ruffled her hair and caressed her face. She closed her eyes for a moment and enjoyed it. Her senses were attuned to every sight, sound, and smell of her surroundings. She opened her eyes. Teton Valley lay spread out before her in its early summer greenery. Shadows were deepening across the valley as the sun dropped lower in the sky. No painting or photograph could ever do justice to this scene. Far below, she could see the ranch house, and she thought she could even see her grandmother puttering around in the yard, probably in her flower gardens. Farther to the northeast, the towns of Victor and Driggs shimmered in the heat of the late afternoon sun. The valley resembled a patchwork quilt in earth tones.

Shawnee's eyes scanned the horizon. The peaks of the Three Tetons were plainly visible, their gray granite accented by the last of the winter snows. After a few seconds, she realized she was holding her breath. This place always seemed to have that effect on her. Grandpa had first brought her here when she was barely twelve to show her the view. She had returned every year of the ten years since then. When she was just a girl, she came for the climb and the adventure; later, in her teens, she came for the view. But now, as life's challenges became heavier, she came for a deeper reason. This place had become sacred to her. It was her place of retreat where the world couldn't find her. It was where she had first learned for herself that God loved her and answered prayers. It was here that she had discovered that she did not have to walk alone. Her life had been changed here, and those moments were indelibly etched on her mind and soul.

Oh, how she hoped He would be here for her today. She needed answers. A proposal of marriage was not a matter to be taken lightly, especially from a man like Justin. What was wrong with her? The man was everything she had ever wanted in a husband. He had so many good qualities. In fact, everything was right about the handsome, young pre-med student—everything, that is, except being her husband.

Shawnee's mind raced back in time to a day earlier.

||||||||||||||||

It was late in the evening under a full moon on the banks of the Snake River across from the Idaho Falls Temple. After eating dinner at her parents' house, Justin suggested they go for a walk on the green belt. The evening was lovely. The moonlight reflected off the water as ducks quacked near the bank. They walked hand in hand, talking; occasionally, joggers or people on roller blades passed them, but for the most part, the walk was peaceful and comfortable.

Justin and Shawnee had known each other for about three months. During most of that time they had been friends, but lately, almost imperceptibly, things between them had become more serious. At first, Shawnee had welcomed the change, but she had felt strangely unsettled during the previous few days. She chided herself that she was just being foolish, experiencing little-girl jitters, but that didn't make the feelings go away. Worst of all, her feelings weren't consistent. Most of the time she was comfortable in the relationship and where it was going; other times, she felt uneasy. She kept telling herself that time would smooth things out and she would feel differently. But that hadn't happened.

As they came to the area in front of the temple, Justin stepped off the path and sat down on the thick grass. "Let's sit down for a while," he said, reaching for her hand.

She took his hand and sat down on the grass beside him. Damp and cool from the dew that had already begun to settle on it, it felt good. For a few minutes, they sat in silence looking at the temple. When Justin finally nervously cleared his throat, an impression slammed into Shawnee. The time, the place, his nervousness—he was about to *propose*. Her heart leaped and threatened to choke off her breathing. Justin turned to face her and got up on one knee. She thought her heart would stop.

Justin took her left hand in both of his. "Shawnee James, will you marry me?"

She was speechless. Her eyes searched his as she took inventory of her heart. Did she love him *that much*? Was this *right*? She waited for a confirmation. Nothing came. Instead, a sick feeling of dread washed over her.

"Justin, I . . ." Her voice trailed off. Tears welled up in her eyes, and she brushed at them angrily. This would be hard enough without that.

"I—I don't know," she managed finally.

"What do you mean?" he asked, pulling back and releasing her hand.

"I don't know what to say," she said. "I wasn't expecting this."

That was certainly true. She hadn't been expecting this. In truth, she had hoped this wouldn't come up at all until her feelings were more settled.

A glimmer of hope came into Justin's eyes, and he drew even closer, taking her hand again. "Will you think about it?" he asked earnestly.

When she said she would, a large smile broke across his face. She knew at that moment she had made a mistake. The answer should have been no, but she just couldn't bring herself to say it.

There had been practically no rest for Shawnee since then. Justin drove back to Pocatello, and she stayed in Idaho Falls at her parents' house. She wrestled with herself every night until the wee hours of the morning. It was not until she resolved to come to the mountain for help that she felt any measure of peace. With that decision made, she finally drifted off to sleep around five in the morning. Now here she was, her head still wrestling with her heart.

||||||||||||||||

She sat down on the rock at the edge of meadow and pulled her knees up under her chin. After a few minutes she was staring, but no longer seeing the scenery, her thoughts having taken over. Duke drifted across the clearing, still grazing, and the sound momentarily pulled her out of her thoughts. A faint smile graced her beautiful features as she studied the horse. Then she turned back and looked once more at the peaks. A tortured sigh escaped her lips and she slid off the rock to her knees in the soft grass.

"Heavenly Father, please...." There was no difficulty in finding the words. Her thoughts tumbled out in a stream. There were times when she struggled to focus while praying, but this was not one of those times. It was as though Heavenly Father was right there next to her, listening to her every word. Tears coursed down her cheeks as she unburdened the cares of her heart. Justin was everything she had always thought she wanted in a husband, but there was just one problem. She didn't love him. She didn't consider herself an expert on love, but she was certain it had to be more than what she was feeling now. It had to be. And somehow that seemed very important if she was going to make such a commitment.

After some time praying, a warm glow began to fill her. A familiar feeling of love and acceptance settled on her like morning dew, and she found herself openly weeping. Finally, when she knew she had said all that needed to be said, she started to close her prayer when another thought suddenly occurred to her. In her mind she weighed the words. They were not to be uttered lightly, but they were the heart and soul of this prayer. Could she say them and mean them? She raised her head and opened her eyes. A gasp involuntarily escaped her lips. The setting sun had bathed the Teton mountain range in a brilliant, flaming orange. The Tetons glowed with warm light as though they were illuminated with floodlights. The emotions she was feeling intensified. It was enough. Closing her eyes, she finished the prayer. "Father, Thy will be done."

She stopped speaking, letting the quiet and peace of the mountains speak to her. As she listened, a peace filled her heart that was accompanied by an unmistakable impression. There was no doubt in her mind what now needed to be done. Justin would always be a friend, but nothing more. Rising to her feet, she stood and looked across the valley, her stance set as firm as the mountains she had grown to love.

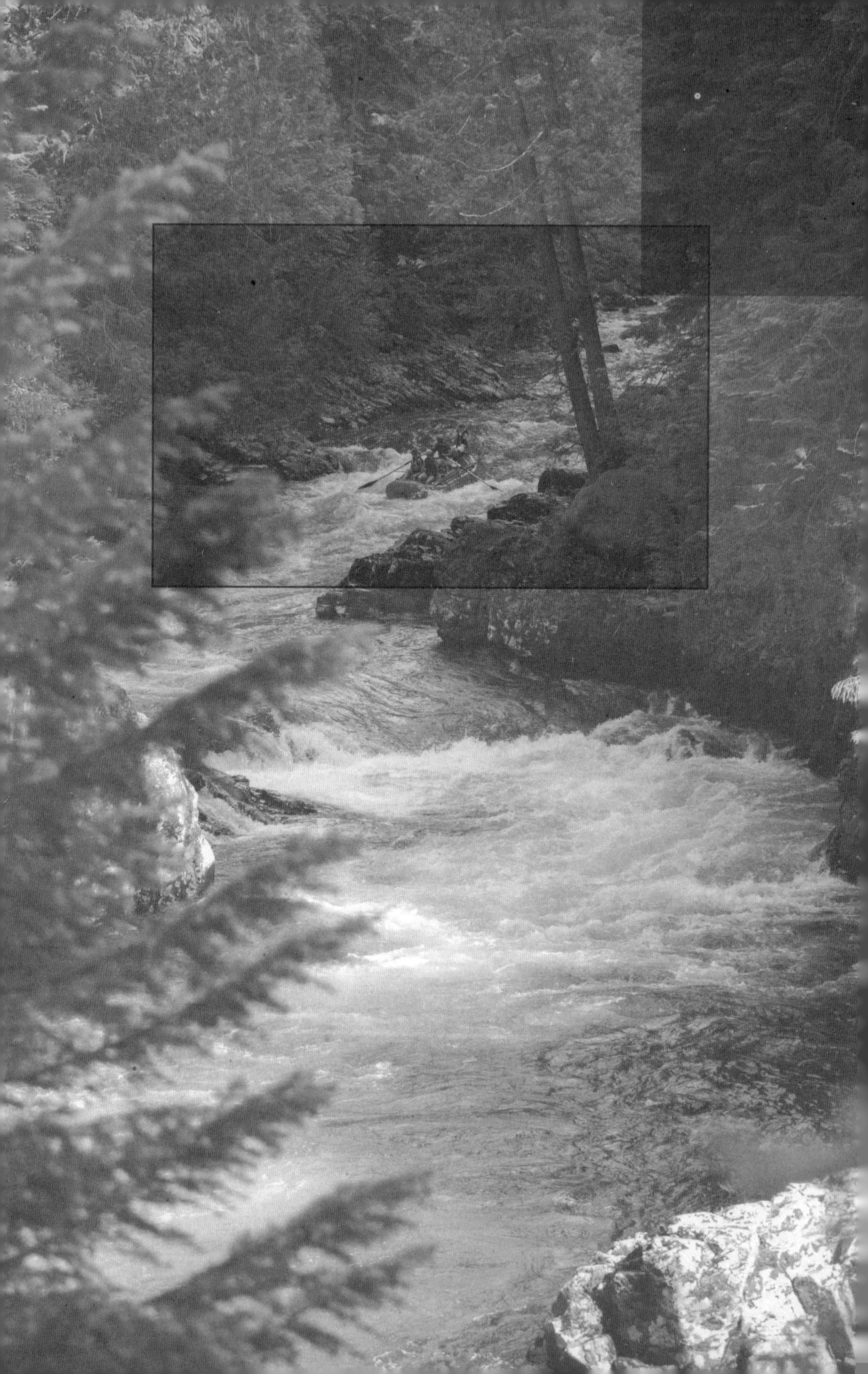

Chapter Three

NEAR CLAYTON, IDAHO

The sun shimmering on the surface of the water resembled millions of dancing crystals in a light parade. The Salmon River was as beautiful as it was mysterious. It traveled its life within the borders of the state of Idaho. Originating high in the northern Rockies near the city of Sawtooth, Idaho, it gathered spring runoff through some of the most rugged and beautiful wilderness in the world. It moved so swiftly that once a boat traveled downstream, it couldn't return unless powered by a motor—thus earning it the name *River of No Return*. All his life, J.O. had heard stories about this river and the wilderness through which it passed. This time of the year the river still ran high and was very dangerous to all but the most experienced river runners. He glanced once more at the river and then at his watch—10:35 a.m., plenty of time to reach his destination before 1:00 p.m.

The day at home with his family had been wonderful. With school out for his mother, she had lavished her attention on him, and he had appreciated it. Tate was enrolled in summer classes at the university, so J.O. had seen him only briefly.

After a hard early-morning run and the kind of breakfast that gave new meaning to the words *home cooking*, J.O. had accompanied his mother to her school to do some redecorating. They had spent a wonderful day together talking, laughing, and working in the world of small children. She was animated and a joy to be around. He noticed that she seemed especially happy in this environment, her classroom.

He had determined to find out why. "Mom, why do you teach school?"

She had thought about his question for a moment then her eyes glistened as she spoke. "I love the children, Son. I can't explain why, but other than you and Tate, there are none in this world more important than my children, and no work as important as preparing them for the world ahead of them."

The intensity of her feelings had impressed him, especially when she referred to her students as *my children*. While he was contemplating that, she had asked a question that seemed to come out of the far-left field.

"J.O., how much longer are you going to drive a truck?"

He had stared at her and for a moment said nothing. Then almost in defense, he had said, "Mom, I thought you liked what I did."

"I do, Son."

"Well, then—"

"I don't know," she had gone on, picking up a large alphabet letter. "I've just been feeling that there was something else you need to be doing."

"Like what?"

"I don't know. How am I supposed to know? It's your life!"

He had laughed, stood up, and walked over to wrap her in a big bear hug.

"Mom, I love you."

"See that you do!" she had said with mock sternness.

Glancing back at the river now, J.O. noticed some river-rafters making their way through a strip of white water. For a moment, he wished he were with them. Maybe Mom was right. Maybe it was time for him to hang up his keys and do something else, but what? He let the thought run through his mind, but nothing came to him. Maybe she thought he ought to be a teacher. The idea seemed almost laughable. *Me, a teacher? That'll be the day* he thought before dismissing the idea.

If there was something different he was to do with his misguided life, he had no idea what it was. Nothing interested him other than open roads, new sights, and big engines. He did know one thing: It would take something significantly important to persuade him to give up driving.

Just then a sign that said *Yankee Fork* stood at the side of the road. He did a quick check of his delivery instructions. This was it. This was his road. He made the right-hand turn and climbed the steep hill past the quaint little country store nestled in the pines.

||||||||||||||||||

"Oh, this is beautiful!" Shawnee exclaimed as her white Toyota crested central Idaho's Galena Summit and started down the north side.

"That it is," Lisa said. "Almost makes up for the time of day that you woke me up."

Shawnee laughed and looked at her close friend and roommate. "How long are you going to hold *that* against me?"

"Forever!" Lisa returned with a laugh.

Lisa and Shawnee had met about a year earlier when they had become roommates. Lisa was from Wyoming and, like Shawnee, was studying to be a nurse. The two had become fast friends, as close as sisters.

Suddenly, Lisa sobered and looked intently at Shawnee. "You ready to tell me about it yet?"

"About what?"

"C'mon, you came in last night crying, then you spent more than an hour on your knees, and this morning you were standing by my bed before the sun came up, all of a sudden wanting to take off and get away for the day. Doesn't that all sound just a little out of the ordinary?" Lisa paused for a moment, watching the cloud of emotion darken her friend's face. "This wouldn't have anything to do with Justin, would it?"

Shawnee turned her face to the window and wrestled with her emotions, not wanting to speak until she was in control. After a moment

39

she turned back. "I ended it last night."

Lisa looked startled. "You did? Why?"

"Well, that's kind of hard to explain, but the whole thing just wasn't right."

"Shawnee! Justin Rence is just about the most perfect man that ever walked the earth. Every girl I know wants him, *and you don't?*"

"I know. I know." Shawnee didn't even try to hide her anguish. "Don't you think I've thought about what I'm doing?"

"Then why?"

Weighing her words carefully, Shawnee related her experience with prayer on the mountain. Lisa had not been raised in a religious home, and Shawnee didn't want to say anything that would tip her friend's world on end.

"Are you sure that it was God?" Lisa asked.

Shawnee looked at her sharply. Seeing the expression on her face, Lisa quickly went on, "All I'm saying is that it's an awfully important decision to make strictly on the basis of a feeling. I hope you're sure."

Shawnee tried to think of a profound way to respond to that, but nothing came, "Me too," she finally said with simple honesty. Then wanting to change the subject, she said, "Shall we stop and stretch our legs?"

"Great idea," Lisa said. "I'm starting to go numb from the waist down."

Shawnee quickly pulled off onto the Galena overlook. They stepped out of the car, stretched, and walked to the edge where the majesty of central Idaho's Sawtooth Mountains was laid out before them like a gallery panorama. The two young women stood in admiring silence. After a moment, Shawnee spoke.

"Lisa, why are you taking the missionary lessons?"

Lisa seemed to be caught off guard. "You know the answer to that. We've talked about it before."

"I know, but I want you to tell me again."

"Well," Lisa said, seeming to reach for words, "I don't know how to describe it. There's something there that I like. I like the people, and I like what the Church teaches."

"How do you know you like it?"

Lisa stared at her for a moment. "That's kind of a dumb question, don't you think?" She had her hands on her hips and was smiling faintly. It was clear she meant no offense, and Shawnee took none.

"No, I'm serious. How do you know you like it?"

"Well, I don't know. I guess because it all makes sense, and it makes me happy."

"There! You see!" Shawnee said triumphantly.

"See what?"

"You like The Church of Jesus Christ of Latter-day Saints because it makes sense and *it makes you happy*. What is happy if it's not a *feeling*? Based on a feeling, you're investigating something that could radically change the course of your life. Based on a feeling I had during prayer, I made a decision that radically changed the course of mine. It's no different."

"Hmm." Lisa seemed deep in thought as she turned to look over the vista again.

Shawnee let her mull that over as they got back in the car and continued driving. After a couple of minutes, Lisa spoke again.

"I guess I've never thought of it in quite that way," she said. "Still, though, how do you know that those feelings and that answer came from God? Maybe your own emotions gave you the answer you wanted. How can you be sure?"

Shawnee started to answer then stopped. Behind Lisa's words was the unspoken question, *How can I be sure that what I'm feeling about the Church is from God?* Shawnee finally answered, "I guess if I were to be totally honest with you, I'd have to say that I'm not absolutely certain, beyond any shadow of doubt. I think that's why it's called *faith*. I don't know everything, yet the Lord is asking me to trust Him and follow Him."

"But that's just it," Lisa said. "How do you know that it was the Lord talking to you? If I knew how to recognize when it was God talking to me, I'd do what He says with no questions asked."

"Even be an active Church member for the rest of your life?" Shawnee asked.

"Even that!" Lisa said firmly.

"Have you prayed?"

"Of course. But nothing happens."

"I thought you said you got a good feeling when you thought about the Church and all that it teaches."

"I do." After pausing briefly, Lisa continued, "Are you telling me that those feelings are how God answers prayers?"

Shawnee felt suddenly unsure. *What am I doing? I'm not a missionary. I don't have all the answers, especially to these kinds of questions. What if I say something wrong and it winds up hurting Lisa? I wish Dad was here. He would know what to say.*

Heavenly Father, she said, offering a silent prayer, *I don't know how to answer her. I don't know what to say. Please help me.*

Suddenly getting an idea, Shawnee said, "Let's think about this. Is it reasonable to expect that whenever one of God's children prays, that person should expect to hear God's audible voice?"

"No, of course not," Lisa said.

"Well, then, is it reasonable to think that whenever one of us prays we should get our answer by seeing an angel or a vision?"

Lisa thought for a moment. "That happened all the time in the Bible—but no, that doesn't seem logical either. If that were the case, there would be a lot of people talking about angels and visions."

"Then what's left?"

Lisa pondered for a moment. "I guess that leaves only two alternatives: either God is not answering anyone today, or He is talking to them in a way that I don't understand . . . maybe through feelings, I guess."

Lisa looked out the window; deep emotion seemed to pass over her. Shawnee sensed it and spoke softly. "Do you really think your first alternative is the right one?"

Lisa turned her head back and looked at her. There was an unmistakable sheen in her rich, brown eyes. "I hope not. Oh, I hope not! I have to know. All my life I've wondered about God. It never seemed to matter all that much to me, until now. Now for some reason, I have to know." She looked out the window again. "I just have to know!"

"I want you to know too," Shawnee said gently. "And I think you are going to discover that if you listen to your heart, it's there that you'll find God talking to you."

Lisa's emotion seemed to change abruptly, and she slapped her hand on her leg in apparent frustration. "That's what's bothering me about all this. My *heart* is about as stable as blowing wind. It changes direction all the time. Sometimes I feel so strongly about the Church, and other times I just don't know. I feel so confused."

"Which feeling do you like the best?"

Lisa looked at her sharply. "What do you mean?"

"You said that sometimes you feel so strongly about the Church, and other times you feel so confused. When you feel strongly about the Church, what does that feel like?"

"I don't know," Lisa said. "I guess I *feel* good, I *feel* like it's right, like I need to be there."

"How does it feel when you're confused?"

"Oh, you know. I get all . . ." Lisa hesitated, struggling for the right words, "mixed up inside. Nothing makes sense. Sometimes I feel like I just want to cry."

"Kind of a dark, heavy, depressing sort of feeling?" Shawnee prompted.

"Exactly!"

"I know the feeling. It's exactly what I felt in my relationship with Justin. I kept trying to tell myself I should love him and marry him, but

43

it never felt right. There was always that confused, mixed-up feeling that left me feeling horrible. Like I wanted to cry. For a while, I ignored the feelings, hoping they would go away. They never did. Finally, I couldn't take it any longer. I had to settle my own heart once and for all. That's when I went up on the mountain and prayed."

"What happened?"

"I got on my knees and told Heavenly Father my feelings."

"That's the part that's so hard for me," Lisa interrupted. "I just can't seem to talk to someone I can't see—at least not like that."

"Oh, He was there," Shawnee went on quickly. "I didn't see Him with these eyes," she said, pointing at her eyes; "I saw him with these." She pointed at her forehead. "It was like I could sense His presence, like I could see Him in my mind. I poured out my heart to Him, as if I was talking to my dad. I told Him everything I felt."

"What happened?" Lisa repeated.

Shawnee drew a deep breath and exhaled. "I don't know how else to say it. He was there. It was like I was connected to Him. Suddenly, all my doubts and confusion were gone. I knew what I had to do. I knew that I had to break it off with Justin and get on with my life."

"How did you know?" Lisa asked, still seeming frustrated.

Shawnee thought for a moment and then looked intently at Lisa. "One minute I was depressed and confused, and the next I was calm and at peace. I knew what I had to do. All the doubt was gone. It was the most wonderful feeling I have ever felt. I just felt—" she stopped, struggling for the right word. "I felt loved! Like He was right there with me."

She stopped again, studying Lisa's reaction. When Lisa stared out the window and didn't answer, Shawnee continued. "I followed those feelings, and I broke it off with Justin last night. I know it was the right thing to do!"

"Then why were you crying last night?" Lisa asked.

"Because it hurt. It hurt him, and it hurt me to hurt him. I didn't want to do it, but I knew I had to." She paused for a moment and then added softly, "I still know."

She glanced over at Lisa and saw the tears running down her cheeks. She gently placed her hand on her friend's arm.

"There really is a God, Lisa, and He loves us and talks to us. Down deep inside there is probably a very tiny, little voice that's telling you that what I've said is right and that you should listen. You probably hear that voice most when you are at church with me, or when you're reading the scriptures. When you can hear Him, there's a feeling of rightness and peace, but later there is this other voice that seems to shout in your head, telling you not to listen and that it's wrong. If I'm not mistaken, you probably get all confused and dark inside when you hear that voice."

Lisa looked over at her, the tears still streaming down her cheeks. She nodded.

Shawnee placed her hand on Lisa's and squeezed it gently. As Lisa's eyes met hers, she felt the tears well up in her own eyes. For a moment neither spoke. Finally, Lisa broke the silence.

"I have to know, Shawnee. I can't keep feeling this way. I never used to care, but now it's like the most important question in my life. I would give anything to feel the way you do."

Shawnee thought for a moment, wanting to say something, but realizing that nothing needed to be said. The moment was over. The rest was up to Lisa.

A few minutes later they saw a sign that read *Yankee Fork River*.

"Hey, this is where that ghost town and museum are!" Shawnee said with excitement, hoping to lighten the mood.

"Let's check it out," Lisa said.

Shawnee signaled left and turned the little Toyota up the road along the river.

J.O. downshifted as the truck began climbing the last steep hill to the Cougar Mountain gold mine. The truck lurched forward when the eight driving tires bit into the hard-packed dirt road. The truck was only moving about ten miles per hour, yet the five-hundred-horsepower Caterpillar engine was roaring at full tachometer. As the truck topped the hill and eased onto level ground, J.O. backed off the accelerator and shifted to a higher gear. In his mind, he rehearsed the directions given by the dispatcher.

Top the hill, turn right, and go straight through a series of offices and shops. Go to the end, and you will run right into the mill.

Outside the offices on his left was the muddiest collection of white, four-wheel-drive pickups he had ever seen, all lined up in a row. To his right were the shops with the huge, ore-hauling trucks parked around them in various stages of repair. He leaned forward and stared at one of the monsters as he drove past. Though they were shorter in length than his truck, their overall bulk made his truck look like a Matchbox truck in a sandpile full of Tonkas.

A man suddenly stepped in front of him and waved for him to stop. J.O. braked, and the truck rolled to a stop. He opened his door.

"Can I have you hold up here for a moment, Sir?" the uniformed guard said politely. "It won't take very long."

"Sure. No problem."

The man stepped back a couple of steps and turned his attention to some activity about a hundred yards in front of them. J.O. followed his eyes. A ring of men surrounded an armored truck parked near the front of the building. They appeared to be loading something into the truck.

"Gold shipment?" J.O. asked, noting the weapons all the guards were carrying.

"Yes," the guard said tersely.

Knowing perfectly well that he was treading in forbidden waters, J.O. asked tentatively, "A big one?"

The guard turned and looked at him, seeming to size J.O. up. J.O. realized he must have passed the inspection when the guard stepped closer to the truck and answered, "No, not that big. Only a few bars."

"How much are those bars worth?" J.O. asked, still not sure whether his question would be rebuffed.

The guard's features relaxed even more, indicating that he didn't perceive the curious truck driver as any kind of a threat. "The bars are about the size of a loaf of bread and weigh about eighty pounds apiece. Each one is worth about a quarter of a million dollars."

J.O. let out a low whistle.

The guard leaned in closer. "That's nothing compared to the shipment that's expected to go out of here in a few weeks. They're projecting that it could be as much as twenty million dollars' worth of ore."

The guard looked like he was enjoying impressing this naive stranger with his knowledge.

"Wow!" J.O. said, demonstrating that he was duly impressed. *But if I owned a gold mine, this man would be the last person I'd want as a security guard.* "Anyone ever tried to steal it before?"

"Nah," the guard scoffed. "No one would be that crazy. The security here at the mine is airtight." He gestured toward the guards surrounding the truck. "And besides, if they did steal it, how would they get it out of here? There aren't exactly a lot of roads where they could escape. Nah," he said with a shake of his head, "no one would be stupid enough to attempt such a thing."

At that moment, the guard's radio came to life. "Okay, Monte, send him up."

The guard grabbed his radio off his belt. "Roger!"

The guard waved his hand nonchalantly. "You can go up now. Have a nice day."

"Thanks," J.O. said, smiling to himself.

Renchard Johnson stood in the mill doorway as the last bar of ore was transferred from the safe to the back of the armored truck. He watched with curious interest as the guards used their special keys to secure the gold and then open the doors into the cab of the truck. He smiled to himself, knowing that those guards would choke if they knew how much he knew about the special codes and keys used to gain access to that very truck. As the armored truck drove away, the mine's security guards began to disperse.

"See ya' later, Ren," one of them called over his shoulder.

"Yeah, see ya', John."

Johnson was just turning to go back into the building when he saw the beautiful blue-and-white truck with the tall twin exhaust stacks coming toward the mill. He knew that it carried the replacement conveyor equipment the mine had ordered. Turning to one of the mill employees standing nearby, he said, "Tony, go get the lift truck and unload that stuff, will you? I need to check the mill."

Tony grunted and nodded as he walked away.

Johnson cast one more look at the polished truck and turned back into the plant. Minutes later, sweating from exertion, he stopped and leaned over the steel rail that protected the catwalk three stories up. Roiling beneath his feet, not more than ten feet down, was a series of huge vats containing solutions that stripped the gold and silver ore out of the cyanide suspension that carried them. This was the heart, soul, and nerve center of the Cougar Mountain mine. Gold was mined in these mountains in open pits. The rock was blasted from the mountain; hauled to a gigantic crusher, where it was ground into a fine particulate; then heaped in mountainous piles on top of a waterproof pad. Sprinkler pipes that sprayed a cyanide solution over the ore were run over the piles. As the cyanide leached down through the pile of ground aggregate, it chemically bonded with the gold and silver ore, pulling it free from the rock. The ore-laden cyanide suspension then drained to the bottom of the pile and was captured in runoff pipes that carried it to the mill, where it was extracted and formed into raw ore bricks called doré.

Johnson stared for a moment, lost in thought, then continued walking, making his routine visual inspections of the tanks and the numerous gauges and dials that monitored the chemical extraction process. He descended the catwalk stairs and walked into the mill office. Picking up his foreman's clipboard, he made the usual notations, unable to restrain his smile as he did so. The mill was running at peak efficiency, and the ore flowing through it was the richest in years. By his calculations, the next shipment would be the richest in the mine's history. He was foreman of the mill; who would ever suspect him? His round, sunburned face almost erupted into full-blown laughter at the thought. It had all come together so neatly that he could scarcely believe his luck. Finding Trent at the last minute had been the capstone of the operation. The man's expertise and access to the same armored trucks with which the mine contracted made the operation fail-proof. Then there was the mysterious French woman with money and a penchant for dangerous adventure. He didn't yet know what to make of her, but no matter. She had proven useful and resourceful.

"Hey, Ren. You want to sign this guy's bills?"

Johnson turned to see Tony approaching with a tall, clean-cut young man. Absently, he reached for the proffered clipboard and scrawled a lazy, illegible signature across the papers. As he handed them back, he looked up into the blue eyes and broad smile of the young driver.

"Thanks," the young man said, cheerfully.

Johnson grunted and watched as the young man walked away and climbed into the cab of his truck. He strolled over to the door and watched as the truck started down the road that led off the mountain. His eyes followed the truck, but the expression on his face was blank. His

Yankee Fork Dredge

mind was thousands of miles away on a resort beach in Europe, enjoying a well-deserved, early, and permanent retirement. Even Christmas as a child hadn't been this exciting. Christmas! *A perfect analogy. Santa Claus is about to give me the gift of a lifetime—several million dollars in gold.* He could hardly wait.

⁂

J.O. stared curiously at the large, odd-looking structure in the creek bed. He had seen it on the way up to the mine and wondered about it. It looked like a floating three-story house with conveyors coming out of it. He had never seen anything like it. He glanced again at the sign. *The Yankee Fork Dredge.*

He looked at his watch. *I've got time. I've got to check this out.*

"Would you like to take a tour?" the elderly host asked.

"I would."

After paying the fee, J.O. was led inside the bowels of the huge marvel of machinery. The guide who had met him at the entrance was at his side, explaining the development of the dredge and the process by which it had dredged gold for several miles up the Yankee Fork.

"So that's why this valley resembles a moonscape," J.O. exclaimed, "It's the tailings of this dredge."

"That's right, Sir," the guide answered. "It's one of the unfortunate side effects of this remarkable era in Idaho's mining history. There wasn't much concern for the environment back then."

As he had come up the valley, J.O. had noticed the ugly trail of tailings and had wondered at its cause. Now that he knew, the remarkable engineering of the dredge and its revolutionary techniques seemed less impressive. He wondered how much longer this tour would take.

The sound of feminine voices caught his attention. In front of him, evidently also taking a tour, were two young women. One of them was quite animated, talking, laughing, and asking lots of questions. She was pretty with shoulder-length, dark-brown hair. His attention, however, was drawn to the other young woman, who now had her back to him. She was taller than the other girl, lean and well-figured, probably between five-eight and five-ten. Her hair was long and blond, falling thick and full down her back. She seemed to walk with the casual grace of a dancer. Her shoulders were carried high and her back was straight.

Even at the angle she was standing, J.O. noticed the sculptured and refined lines of her face. Everyone has his own idea of what's attractive, but even without seeing her face in full light, he could tell she was strikingly beautiful.

The women began walking toward him, their tour finished. J.O. tried not to stare. She was beautiful! Strangely, he felt his pulse rate quicken slightly. His guide was talking, pointing out some arcane detail of the dredge, but J.O. wasn't hearing a word of it.

As she passed him, their shoulders touched slightly on the narrow, grated catwalk, but J.O. was still unable to get a good look at her face. Her head was turned, and she was saying something to her friend. Her voice was pleasant with a rich, lyrical quality to it.

Two steps beyond her, he stopped and turned around to look after her. The faintest trace of a sweet perfume was in the air behind them.

Then, before he could turn back around, she stopped and looked back over her shoulder, directly at him, catching him in open appraisal. The exchange of glances was brief, only a moment, yet something powerful and familiar passed between them. She smiled slightly, as if embarrassed, and then turned back and rejoined her friend. J.O. hesitated only a moment longer before turning and following his guide.

||||||||||||||||

Shawnee turned away from the tall, rugged young man in blue jeans and quickly rejoined Lisa. The feeling that had passed between her and the stranger had stolen her breath. And that smile . . . had she ever seen him before? No. Of that she was certain. But she still felt as though she knew him from somewhere.

"Shawnee, what's wrong?" Lisa asked.

Shaken out of her thoughts, Shawnee answered, "Oh—uh, nothing. I'm fine. I was just thinking about something, that's all."

As they exited the museum, Shawnee looked back over her shoulder one more time, hoping to see the tall stranger. He was nowhere in sight. With a mild pang of regret, she climbed into her car and started the engine.

||||||||||||||||

When J.O. emerged from the dredge, it had begun to rain. A quick glance in all directions revealed that the two women were nowhere to be seen. A little disappointed, he climbed into his truck and started down the valley. The rain was coming harder now. The dirt road was muddy and slick. Just to be safe, he slowed down. Rolling down his window, he let the rain-washed mountain air fill the cab. It was refreshing.

It wasn't long before he reached the main highway that paralleled the Salmon River. Doing some quick calculations in his head, he should be home by 6:00 p.m., barring any difficulty. There would be enough time for dinner with his family and a quick shower before he hit the road to Denver. He had to be there in a little fewer than forty-eight hours. There was plenty of time.

As he rounded a corner, he came up behind a white Toyota that was traveling about ten miles per hour slower than he was. The road ahead was curved and uneven, not to mention slick and wet. There was no way he could pass safely, especially along the river. He would have to wait. He slowed his speed and backed off.

Scarcely had he restored a safe following distance between him and the car when a movement high on the mountain to his left caught his attention. Rocks and mud dislodged by the abundant spring rains were tumbling down the steep mountain toward the road. Glancing back to the road, he realized the huge rockslide was going to bury the car. J.O.'s muscles went instantly rigid; there was no way to warn the driver of the other car in time.

With helpless dread, J.O. watched the rocks land on the road not thirty feet in front of the little Toyota. There was an instant flash of brake lights as the car went into a slide. At what he gauged to be forty miles per hour, the car slammed into a boulder twice its own weight and ricocheted to the right, toward the river. J.O. rose up in his seat and watched as the car plunged over the embankment and disappeared.

Desperately, J.O. slid to a stop across both lanes of traffic, a few feet short of the rocks. Throwing open his door, he vaulted to the ground and ran to where the car had gone over. It had rolled several times down the steep bank and was upside down in the river, going under quickly. Throwing himself over the bank, he rolled and slid through the mud and debris to the edge of the river. The battered car had landed in a river eddy on the edge of the current, where the water was deeper than normal. In fewer than thirty seconds the car dropped beneath the water's surface in a muddy foam until only the tip of the rear wheels could be seen. J.O. took two steps into the frigid, glacier-sourced water and waited, holding his breath. No one came up. There was no sign of survivors.

J.O. sucked air into his lungs and dove into the water, ignoring its icy bite, and swam down to the driver's door. It was hard to see in the murk. He found the handle and yanked with all his strength, but it wouldn't open. He pulled himself around the front of the car, feeling more than seeing where he was going. The windshield had been forced out, but the opening had been crushed down. He couldn't get in that way, either. His lungs were starting to burn. He found the passenger's door and planted his feet against the side of the car and yanked. It opened, but not enough to squeeze through. It too had been jammed. He pressed his face into the small opening, attempting to see the occupants through the murky water. He could make out a figure struggling inside the cab. Adrenalin surged through him as he realized that someone was still alive.

But time was running out—if he didn't get into the car in the next few seconds, someone was going to drown.

He pulled himself around to the rear of the car and discovered an opening where the back window had been. As he propelled his body through the opening, a foot hit him squarely in the face with such force that he felt his lower lip begin to fatten. A terrified young woman appeared out of the murk, grabbed his clothing, and screamed something at him that he couldn't understand. J.O. wrapped his hands in her jacket and roughly shoved her toward the opening. Strangely, she fought against him. Thinking she was in a state of panic, J.O. wrapped both arms around her and using the front seat for support, propelled himself through the opening, taking her with him. At the surface, she choked and tried to scream, but J.O. cradled her in a rescue carry and pulled her to shore. As he dragged her up on the beach, the young woman found her voice.

"Shawnee," she screamed in a choking sob. "She's still in there!" Her trembling finger pointed to the river.

"What?" J.O. yelled. "There's someone still in the car?"

"Yes!" the girl said, sobbing.

J.O. spun around and dived into the water, no longer conscious of its forty-five-degree chill. Seconds later, he was back inside the car. Feeling his way through the murky water, he found another woman hanging upside down, still seat-belted into the driver's seat. She wasn't moving. Deftly, he unsnapped the seatbelt and allowed her body to settle into his arms. Quickly but carefully, he worked her limp body through the back window, being careful that a shard of glass didn't slice her. As he did, he slipped against the window's edge and felt a sharp pain in his left hand. The water around him swirled muddy red. Ignoring it, he wrapped the woman in his arms and pushed off the bottom with all his waning strength. With his own vision blackening and blurring from lack of oxygen, he broke the surface, gasping for air and clutching the woman to him. He swam a few strokes when a burly man in miner's clothing, waded into the water, reached out for them, and pulled them onto the bank.

    The man released his grip. J.O. remained half in the water on his hands and knees, gasping for breath. There was no time to think of his needs. The woman was probably already dead. He scrambled onto the sod bank; as he rolled the woman onto her back, three things slammed into his consciousness simultaneously. One, there was large purple lump on her forehead over her left eye. Two, she wasn't breathing. And three, it was the same beautiful woman he had seen back at the dredge.

Chapter Four

"I'll radio for an ambulance," the miner called out as he ran for his truck.

J.O. began forcing the water out of the unconscious woman's lungs. He was barely aware of the sobbing young woman at his side as he began to administer CPR and mouth-to-mouth. Desperate seconds ticked by, and J.O. continued to work over her. Still there was no response. A yearning gut-level panic grabbed him as he racked his brain for everything he had been taught about first-aid so many years earlier. She couldn't die, but what could he do? His anger and desperation increased by the minute.

"Please," he blurted out without thinking, pumping her heart again.

After two more thrusts of chest compression, her body suddenly jerked, and she began to choke and cough as the other woman's sobs changed to joy. For several seconds, her body was racked with violent coughing as she tried to expel the water from her lungs. J.O. cradled her head carefully as she regained consciousness. Finally, weak and barely coherent, her tear-filled blue eyes opened and she seemed to focus. Weakly, she smiled up at him.

Relief and elation swept over him.

"Oh, Shawnee. Are you alright?" the other woman asked as she moved to Shawnee's side and threw her arms around her.

"I think so," Shawnee said weakly as she attempted to sit up. "What happened?"

"Rockslide," J.O. said. "You didn't have a chance. It forced you off the road and you rolled down into the river."

Shawnee jerked as if startled. "The car—"

J.O. caught her by the shoulders and held her. "It's totaled!"

She sagged against him for a moment and then looked at Lisa.

"Are you alright?"

"I got some cuts on my arms, and my knee is bruised, but I'm okay, thanks to the seatbelt."

At the sound of sliding rocks, they turned around. The miner was sliding down the bank toward them.

"I reached the mine on the radio," he said. "They've called Challis for an ambulance and the State Patrol. They'll come from the other side of the slide. That's the closest hospital. They should be here soon."

"We need to get you out of this rain and somewhere where it's warm and dry," J.O. said. "Can you stand?"

"I think so," Shawnee said.

With J.O.'s help, she struggled to her feet, but as she attempted to take a step she fainted and collapsed. Catching her, J.O. scooped her into his arms and started up the hill to the road. She regained consciousness partway up.

"What . . . ?" she mumbled groggily.

"It's okay," he soothed. "You passed out. We're getting you up the hill. Just relax and let me carry you."

Strangely, she did relax, her head against his shoulder next to his cheek. A couple of times, he slipped in the muddy, slick soil and nearly fell with her. Finally, he reached the road, where anxious hands from motorists who had stopped guided him to the open door of a travel trailer. J.O. carried her inside and placed her on a bed.

"At least this will keep you dry and warm until the ambulance gets here," he said, brushing a wet lock of hair out of her face.

"Thank you," she said with a faint smile, settling wearily into the pillow.

Two women he didn't know rushed to attend to her. He smiled.

"I'm going for your friend. I'll be back in a few minutes."

Outside the trailer, the crowd of onlookers was growing. Already the traffic was backed up several hundred yards around the corner and out of sight of the accident. Curious people were walking toward the scene. People stared as he slid down the riverbank to where a couple of men were helping Lisa to her feet.

"I have to get to Shawnee," she said.

J.O. could tell that shock from the accident was setting in, and he detected hysteria in her voice. J.O. took her hands in his and spoke directly into her face.

"Shawnee's okay," he said. "We made a bed for her where it's warm and dry. We'll take you to her right now. Don't worry, an ambulance is on its way. You're both going to be okay."

His words seemed to penetrate her frenzied state of mind, and she nodded. She took a step to start to climb the bank, but as the weight came down on her right leg, she gave a sharp cry of pain and slumped to the ground. J.O. scooped her up and began struggling up the hill a second time. Two men rushed to his side and helped him scale the hill.

"It hurts!" she cried, wrapping her arms around his neck and squeezing it. She buried her face against his neck. "Oh, it hurts. I've never felt pain like this in my life!"

"Hang on," he said. "We're almost there."

J.O. had been injured enough times in his life to know that pain is always worse after the initial shock of the accident passes.

Reaching the top of the embankment, he carried the woman into the trailer and placed her on another bed. The women inside tried to place blankets over her, but her agonized writhing made it impossible. She continued to sob from the excruciating pain.

"Lisa!" Shawnee threw off the blankets covering her and came toward her friend. "Oh, Lisa. I'm sorry. I'm so sorry."

"It's not your fault, Shawnee," Lisa choked out, her face twisted in pain.

"You need to stay down," J.O. said to Shawnee, as he caught her by the shoulders and stopped her. Shawnee reeled with dizziness.

"No!" she said fiercely. "She's hurt. She needs help. Can you give her a blessing?" The beautiful blue eyes seemed to bore into him with an intensity he had rarely ever seen.

Seeing his blank expression, Shawnee looked to the small group of people crowded inside the trailer.

"Can anyone here give her a blessing?"

When no one responded, her blue eyes returned to J.O.'s face.

"Please!" she pleaded. "Doesn't anyone in here hold the priesthood?"

J.O. felt helpless. What was a *blessing?* If he had known at that moment what it was, he would have walked on hot coals to get it for her, but he had never heard of such a thing.

The paramedics arrived a short time later and immediately set to work on the two stricken women. J.O. hovered as close as possible and listened to the preliminary diagnosis. Lisa had a severely sprained right ankle and a torn right knee. She would need stitches in several cuts on her arms. Shawnee had a concussion, a broken thumb, and a separated shoulder. Both women were in extreme pain, and Shawnee lost consciousness several times. J.O. watched as the paramedics worked to stabilize the two women. An Idaho State Trooper arrived on the scene and began asking J.O. questions. He answered as best he could but was anxious to get back to the two women.

When the patrolman moved away to question other witnesses, J.O. returned to the trailer. The ambulance personnel were just bringing the two injured women out on stretchers. J.O. fell in step beside Shawnee's stretcher. Through the fog of what must have been a blinding headache, she recognized him and lifted one hand to him without speaking. He took her hand and held it.

It was a challenge for the paramedics to carry the two women on stretchers over the treacherous rocks and mudslide to the other side. J.O. helped steady Shawnee's stretcher, never letting go of her hand. Shawnee seemed to drift in and out of consciousness through most of the ordeal. When they reached the ambulance, their hands broke apart as the paramedics loaded Shawnee's stretcher into the ambulance. At that moment, she regained consciousness and struggled to sit up. The restraints on the stretcher prevented her. She reached out toward J.O.; he stepped closer and took the outstretched hand. A weak smile graced her pale features.

"Thank you," she whispered, "for all your help."

He smiled widely. "Anytime!"

With that, the doors slammed shut, and she was whisked away in the direction of Challis, lights flashing.

|||||||||||||||||||

It was some time before crews were able to clear the narrow road of the rocks and dirt from the slide and retrieve the totaled car from the river. J.O. gave a more detailed account of the accident to the Idaho State Police, anxious all the while for the road to be cleared. He had already made up his mind to go to whichever hospital the women had been taken to. He had to know if they were okay.

"Excuse me, Officer," J.O. said, as he concluded the interview, "but how do I find the hospital they were taken to?"

"Depends on how serious the injuries were. There's a smaller hospital in Challis, but if it was something really serious, they would probably have gone on to Idaho Falls or maybe even Salt Lake City."

"Thanks. Is it okay if I go now?"

"Soon as that road is clear, go ahead."

|||||||||||||||||||

J.O. walked resolutely through the emergency room doors of the Custer County Hospital and went straight to the desk. A tough-looking nurse built along the lines of a farm tractor greeted him with a cold stare as he walked up. It scarcely registered to him that his clothes were a wrinkled and matted disaster. Mud streaked his face as though he had been wrestling with a pig. It had now been almost six hours since the accident.

"Were two young women brought in here by ambulance a while ago?" he asked the woman at the desk. "One was named Shawnee, I think, and the other was named Lisa."

The woman looked down at her book. "Yes, they were here, but they were treated and released."

J.O.'s questions tumbled out. "Do you know where they went? Do you know where they live? Could you tell me their full names?"

"I'm sorry, Sir, but I can't give that information unless you're family."

J.O. looked at the woman's hard face. It was evident in her expression that when she said the information wasn't available, it wasn't available, and arguing with her was going to go nowhere. Frustrated, he turned his back to the woman and ran his hand through his hair. A glance at his watch made him realize he couldn't search any longer. He had deadlines to meet, and he needed to be on the road.

"Thank you," he said politely, and walked resolutely out the door to his truck.

∥∥∥∥∥∥∥∥∥∥∥∥∥∥

"How are you feeling, Dear?"

Shawnee felt the gentle caress on her cheek and opened her eyes, trying to focus on her mother's face. Her only response was a groan. It was dark outside. The faint glow of a small lamp was the only light in the room, for which she was grateful. She couldn't remember ever having a headache as bad as this one.

"How's Lisa?" Shawnee asked thickly as her mother placed a cool cloth on her forehead.

"Sleeping. I think the painkillers finally took over. She's out cold."

After treatment at the hospital in Challis, the doctors had released Shawnee and Lisa into the care of Shawnee's parents. They had insisted on bringing the two home with them to Idaho Falls rather than letting them return to their apartment in Pocatello fifty miles away. Both would be in sore need of tender, loving care for the next several days.

Shawnee struggled to prop herself up on one elbow, momentarily forgetting her wounded shoulder. As the fiery pain blurred her vision, she dropped back in the bed, gasping for breath and fighting against the pain.

"I feel so bad," Shawnee said after a moment. "If only I hadn't suggested that we take that trip."

"Honey, listen," her mother said firmly, "there was no way you could have prevented that or foreseen it. It was just a freak accident. It's not your fault."

Shawnee turned her head into the pillow and closed her eyes, squeezing out the tears the pain had caused. Slowly, she nodded. "I guess you're right. I'm just glad we're both okay."

"You almost weren't," her mother said. "Has anyone told you what happened?"

"Other than how we wound up in the river, no."

"According to the police report, the car rolled three times down the embankment. You were probably knocked out when the car hit the rock. The car came to rest upside down in the river, underwater. Lisa said she tried to open the door but couldn't. Then some guy came out of nowhere and dragged her out. She said she fought him as he tried to pull her out, but he was too strong." Her mother smiled wryly. "Probably a good thing, too, or both of you would have drowned instead of just one."

Shawnee's eyes widened.

Her mother continued, "Lisa said when he pulled you out of the car, you were limp and blue and not breathing. He performed CPR. She thought they had lost you, but suddenly you came out of it."

Shawnee stared at the tears that trickled down her mother's cheeks. All she could remember was hitting the rocks and then waking up cold and wet on the bank of the river.

"You don't remember any of this?" her mother asked.

"No. I remember coming to and some guy carrying me up the hill. I think he was the same guy we had seen earlier at the dredge museum. Everything's kind of blurry after that. I remember Lisa crying from the pain and I remember trying to find someone who could give her a blessing. No one could. Then the ambulance took us away."

"Who was he?" her mother asked.

"I don't know. I never heard his name."

"Well," her mother said, leaning over and embracing her gently, "as soon as you are back on your feet, we'll find him and thank him for saving your life."

Released from the embrace, Shawnee settled back into the bed, an unexpected emotion suddenly welling up in her. "I love you, Mom. Thank you."

"I love you too, Dear." And with that, her mother closed the door.

Shawnee smiled, closed her eyes, and let her head sink back into the fat pillow. She hadn't told her mother everything. This part of her memory was clear. From the time she woke up until the ambulance took them away, the young stranger had never left her side. Several times she had looked up during the horrible pain and had seen his face looking down. His eyes were a clear blue, but that wasn't what stuck with her now. She had seen blue eyes before. No, it was the expression in those eyes and the way it had made her feel. Even as she thought of it, the warmth returned. There was only one other man on whose face she had ever seen such an expression of caring and concern for her—and it was not Justin. It was her dad. Quietly, there in the dark of her room, two things solidified in her mind. One, she had done the right thing with Justin. And two, she would find the mysterious stranger who came out of nowhere and, if nothing else, thank him.

|||||||||||||||||

"Are you sure you have to leave tonight, Son?"

J.O. looked down from the running board of his idling truck into the concerned face of his mother. He stepped to the ground and took her in his arms.

"I'm afraid so, Mom. I had planned on bedding down in the sleeper over near Little America in Wyoming by about 9:30 p.m., and it's after 11:00 now. I'm way behind schedule. I have to make up the lost time."

"But it's so late, and after that accident—"

J.O. grinned at her. "Mom, I'm a truck driver, remember. I'm used to running on no sleep."

"Are you sure you're okay?"

"I'm fine, Mom. Don't worry!" He bent over and kissed her on the forehead.

|||||||||||||||||

She sighed deeply as her oldest and most independent son turned away and climbed into the cab of the truck. He waved one last time and then eased the truck into gear and pulled out onto the highway. Within minutes, all she could see were the taillights of his rig as he disappeared into the night.

Ruthie Steele knew her son well. There was something J.O. had not told her about that accident today. He had tried to hide the injured hand, but she had seen it and insisted that he let her dress the wound. He was just like his dad. Joe had never wanted her to worry either. And that was exactly what worried her now. Something else had happened at that accident that had really upset him. Something he hadn't told her. It was in his eyes.

She turned to cast one more look at the red taillights as they vanished. A lump rose in her throat. He was so much like his father—kind, gentle, good-natured, and tougher than iron nails. Losing her husband at such a young age had scarred her. He had been so strong, so powerful. She had never felt safer than when she was with him. When he died, she was crushed. For months after that, living had been little more than wandering in a numbed daze. Finally, when she had come out of it, her life became her two sons. In every way, she had tried to teach them to be like their father. Her gaze turned away from the black ribbon of highway that had swallowed her son. She had succeeded. J.O. was so much like his dad. Would he also be taken from her before his time? The thought was too much to bear, and she shuddered involuntarily.

Then Ruthie did something that had recently come to seem so natural and feel so right, especially when J.O. was on the road. She uttered a small prayer in her heart.

"Oh, God, watch over my boy until he's home again."

Chapter Five

IDAHO FALLS, IDAHO

Trent Lawson set his lunch pail on his toolbox and slipped his lanky frame into his filthy work coveralls. A quick glance around the shop told him no one was paying any attention to him. The other technicians were occupied with projects of their own. Reaching into his lunch pail, he retrieved two small electronic devices and eased them into his pocket. Johnson had given them to him only moments earlier.

The armored truck that made the regular run to the Cougar Mountain gold mine sat in his work bay, needing a minor repair and a lube and oil change. Trent whistled as he worked to keep up the appearance of nonchalance, but inside, his heart pounded like a jackhammer. He hadn't felt this kind of excitement in years. Finally, he was going to get out of this dead-end lifestyle and do what he had always wanted to do: see the world. He was still amazed that Johnson and the French woman had shown up to talk to him on the very day that his wife Joanie had kicked him out of the house. Joanie had been angrier than he had ever seen her. Impending divorce was a sure thing; he had already been served with the papers. Money had been a major reason. There had never been enough. He smiled to himself. *There will be enough now, and she will never see a dime of it. Maybe I'll send her a postcard from the Caribbean, or maybe a photograph of me with some beautiful women on an exotic beach somewhere far away.* He relished the thought of seeing her squirm with regret.

Still reveling in his thoughts, he lifted the hood of the truck and refilled the engine with oil. After another glance around the shop, he deftly reached over and disconnected the coil wire. It took only seconds to attach a small, rectangular, black box to the coil and reconnect the wire. He started the engine and checked for oil leaks. Another glance told him he was still unobserved. Inside the secured cab, he retrieved from his pocket a small aluminum cylinder about the size of a long hot dog. He looked at it carefully. Johnson had cautioned him, "Whatever you do, be careful. That cylinder contains enough pressurized gas that if you rupture it, you could put yourself and most of the guys in your shop in la-la land for the rest of the day."

His hands shook and beads of sweat broke out on his forehead as he carefully attached the cylinder under the truck's dashboard.

Trent didn't understand how they worked, but supposedly both of these devices could be remotely activated from several hundred yards away. The plan was beautiful. The more he thought about it, the more foolproof it seemed. A smug grin spread over Trent's hawk-nosed face. With these two devices and the codes and duplicate keys to the truck sitting at home, they were set. They couldn't miss. Soon he would be a rich man in another part of the world.

Trent finished attaching the gas cylinder and cleaned up his tools from around the truck. It was finished. More than that, his part of the preparation was done. Now it was up to Claude.

|||||||||||||||||||

"It is arranged."

"Give me the details," Johnson requested, pressing the cell phone closer to his ear.

"I've arranged for a pilot, who'll ask no questions," Claude stated matter-of-factly. "He'll bring the chopper in just about sunrise and secure it in the clearing. Once we've landed at the ghost town, he'll fly out and disappear."

"Good! I'll have a vehicle waiting at Gilmore that will transport us from there. Now, what about the charter?"

"All taken care of. It will be waiting at the Jackson airport, fueled and ready to go."

"Claude, you're beautiful!" Johnson said. "You've made this operation come together flawlessly. How did I ever get so lucky as to team up with you?"

"Guess you just played your cards right, Darling."

Johnson laughed. "Guess I did at that, didn't I?"

On the other end of the line, Claude laughed along with Johnson, but the mirth went no further than her voice. Her eyes and mouth were set in a hard, determined line. Soon this peevish charade would be over.

////////////////

Somewhere in the desert north of Las Vegas, J.O. rubbed his eyes and yawned. *Tired* didn't begin to describe how he felt; *wrung-out* might be closer to the truth. As much as he wanted to keep driving, he knew that if he didn't find a place soon and stop for the night, someone would have to scrape him off the road.

The whirlwind trip to Denver had been bad enough, but no sooner had he unloaded than a load was waiting for him to deliver to the east coast. From there he had taken load after load and worked his way west. There had been grinding deadlines and little sleep. Finally, he had reloaded in Phoenix for Salt Lake City. After more than four weeks on the road, he was going home for a few days off. It had been a long time since he could remember being this tired. Only part of his fatigue had been caused by the hectic schedule, however. The other part baffled even him. It was that young woman, Shawnee. Those eyes, the pleading. She

69

had needed him, wanted something from him, and he had no idea what to do to help her. Her face, her words, and, most of all, a feeling echoed in his soul like distant thunder in the mountains. He knew the feeling would pester him until he settled it.

Can you give her a blessing? What did that mean? And what's more, why was it so important to know? Just then a reflective green sign appeared in his headlights, marking an exit. *Perfect*, he thought.

Snapping on his turn signal, he rolled off the exit to the bottom of the underpass, crossed the highway, and stopped partway up the on-ramp. He turned off the ignition. As the big engine lurched into stillness and the lights went out, an engulfing sense of solitude and peace came over him. The crowded truck stops back in Vegas and at other points along the interstate were fine for some drivers, but not him. He preferred places like this, out in the middle of no-man's land, where it was just him and open country. There was, of course, a considerable danger from the criminal element that ran the freeways, but the peace and quiet were worth the risk.

J.O. leaned back in the seat and put his hands over his face, pulling down, as if trying to pull off the fatigue that was etched in his features. A deep sigh escaped his lips. His hands dropped to his sides. He thought again of the accident. The day after it happened, he called the Idaho State Police on his cell phone, requesting information, but was tersely informed that such information was not available pending completion of the accident report. He called back later only to be told that the information was not to be released.

As he thought about it now, maybe it was just as well. What was he going to say if he found her? "Uh, sorry about your car?"

He waved his hand in front of his face as though to brush the whole affair away once and for all and opened the door to step out. He did a walk-around inspection of his rig. His stiff muscles caused his first few steps out of the truck to resemble those of a duck. A cool night breeze bathed his face and seemed to wash the fatigue from his eyes. He pulled the fresh desert air deep into his lungs and felt invigorated. Just beyond the fence that paralleled the interstate he could see the outline of a small, brush-covered hill, barely discernible in the faint light. It looked inviting enough that he crawled over the fence and walked the two hundred yards out to it.

From the small promontory he could see the lights of Las Vegas shimmering in the darkness to the south. Even from this distance, they were a fantastic sight. The lights of the huge city illuminated the entire southern skyline like some gigantic forest fire, and the glow reached up into the heavens in a surreal way. J.O. stood for a time admiring the view, then squatted down near a large sagebrush. Stripping some leaves off the sage, he rolled them between his fingers to crush them and then lifted the aromatic leaves to his face and breathed deeply. It was a smell that took him back to his childhood in the Lemhi Valley.

The stress of the long day seemed to dissipate like morning fog as he let his eyes drink in his surroundings.

After a few minutes, he sat down on a thick tuft of desert bunchgrass. Overhead, the night sky was brilliant and clear. The Milky Way, so often obscured by city lights, was prominent and breathtaking. Instinctively, he located the Big Dipper, and then, following the outer two stars of the cup, he located the North Star. A gentle tinge of longing came as he stared at the star. It never moved. It was constant and consistent. Just like . . . his mind suddenly filled with poignant memories of a hunting trip with his dad years before in the mountains of central Idaho.

"Joseph," his dad had said, "if you ever get lost, look for the Big Dipper and the North Star, and you'll find your way."

It was one of the clearest and fondest memories he had of his father. The Polar Star had evolved into a symbol of his dad's love for him. J.O. reached inside his shirt and pulled out the small medallion. He ran his fingers over the engravings. He had made it while in high school and had worn it on a chain around his neck ever since. Each time he looked at the night sky or felt the medallion under his shirt, he was reminded of his dad and of the quest his dad had left him with.

Off in the distance, a coyote howled. Another answered.

"Where are you, Dad?" J.O. heard himself say. "Are you out there? Do you even still exist?" J.O.'s eyes swept over the massive expanse of the heavens. "I miss you, Dad. I really miss you, and I need your help."

For the next few minutes, he sat staring up into the endless, blue-black of the heavens, pondering life and its purpose and meaning. *Is there life after death? Is my father still out there somewhere? Why are there so many questions and so few answers on things that matter so much?*

Frustrated, he abruptly stood up, dusting off his jeans. Hundreds of times he had asked these same questions, and he still had no answer—probably because there was no answer to be had. His dad was gone, forever! Just like the beautiful woman he had met weeks ago.

Picking up a rock, he flung it with pent-up frustration. It sailed out into the darkness and disappeared, followed moments later by a faint thud as it hit the ground. *Where did this earth come from? Why was there so much order that governed the movement of the earth and the stars at night, but no order on earth? Who or what planted the North Star in place when all around it was in a state of constant motion? Was the profound beauty of a mountain wildflower an accident of nature or the design of some Supreme Being? Was the absolute complexity of the physiological systems and the perfect symmetry of the human body no more than an accident—a result of the evolution of electrified swamp scum?*

All through school, J.O. had been the one to argue the point of evolution. Recalling how he had won most of the debates against the creationists gave him no satisfaction now. The strategy had always been the same: cite the fossil records and ridicule the Christians' simple faith and lack of answers. It was always so easy to portray them as blinded simpletons and their faith as passé. Tonight, however, a gnawing little voice inside chided him for his dishonesty. Evolution, at least as far as the creation of man and this earth was concerned, was not true. Even if one did not accept the creation story, it still seemed more honest than the transparent theories of scientists trying to validate their own intellectual existence. But that did not excuse religionists; he had often been frustrated with church people for their blind faith. Just *poof!* and God created the earth with His magic wand, and no more answers were needed? Maybe that was good enough for them, but certainly not for him. There had to be more than that. There had to be answers. Surely if there was a God, He did not mean for His children to be standing in the midst of so much beauty and wonder and not know anything about how it came to be, why it was there, and its destiny. And what of man? Was he really the end-product of some haphazard evolutionary journey, a half-breed chimpanzee at best?

A slight stab of pain in J.O.'s head caused him to shake off the mental reverie. It was always the same, a million questions and no answers, nothing but a headache whenever he thought about it.

"Dad," he said, looking up at the Polar Star again, "if you're out there somewhere, help me. I don't want to live like this anymore. I want some answers."

J.O. grasped the medallion as the tiniest whisper of peace crept into his soul. He closed his eyes and savored it. Opening them, he glanced once more at the North Star then turned and went back to his truck to sleep.

|||||||||||||||||

"Don't forget to call me on Monday so I can line you out for the next day," the company dispatcher said.

"Sure thing," J.O. said and closed off the call. Four weeks on the road was long enough. He was ready to go home.

Quick as he could, he placed a call on his cell phone.

"Tate?"

"Yeah!"

"I'm on my way home."

"Great! It's about time. Where are you?"

"I'm just leaving Salt Lake. I should be home in about three hours."

"Okay," Tate said. "I'll tell Mom. By the way, do you have any plans for the next couple of days?"

"Besides sleeping around the clock tonight, no. What've you got in mind?"

"How about if we do that Teton climb we talked about?"

There was not the slightest hesitation with J.O. "Count me in! That's just what I need. When are you leaving?"

"Whenever you want, I guess, but Friday would probably be the best day for me."

"That sounds good. That'll give me some time to rest up and get some supplies for the trip. How many are going?"

"Probably just you and me, if that's okay." Tate's voice mellowed a bit as he continued. "I just need a break from the rat race and a really good work-out! You okay with that?"

"More than okay, little brother, I'm looking forward to it."

J.O. closed the call and placed the phone back in its holder. He felt excited. Finally, the last peak of the famous Three Tetons was going down. By this time next week, he would have stood on top of the world, or at least as close as he was going to get in this life. He couldn't wait!

||||||||||||||||||

Renchard Johnson kicked at the pile of rusted cans at his feet. They were more than one hundred years old, remnants of the wild days of Gilmore, Idaho. Once the site of a thriving lead mine, Gilmore was now one of the many ghost towns that peppered the mountains of central Idaho. It was also the perfect location for his plans. His eyes scanned the desolate valley spread before him. Gilmore was close to a state highway that carried a minimal amount of traffic. There was good, quick access in and out of the town, making it perfect for a transfer site. Since there were no permanent camping facilities in the ghost town, there were very few, if any, people in the area. Which was all the better for him. On the ghost town's western edge, he found a meadow in the pines where the chopper could land.

He surveyed the range of mountains towering above him. Between here and the Cougar Mountain Mine, there were two rugged ranges of mountains he would have to cross. If they got the chopper as far as Gilmore, chances were slim to none that anyone would connect it to a gold heist.

He had met with Trent and Claude that morning. They had reviewed every facet of the plan. Everything was set. It would be flawless. No one would get hurt. No one would ever know who did it until it was too late. Now it was just a matter of waiting until the right moment. Johnson smiled to himself. It had been years since he had enjoyed anything this much.

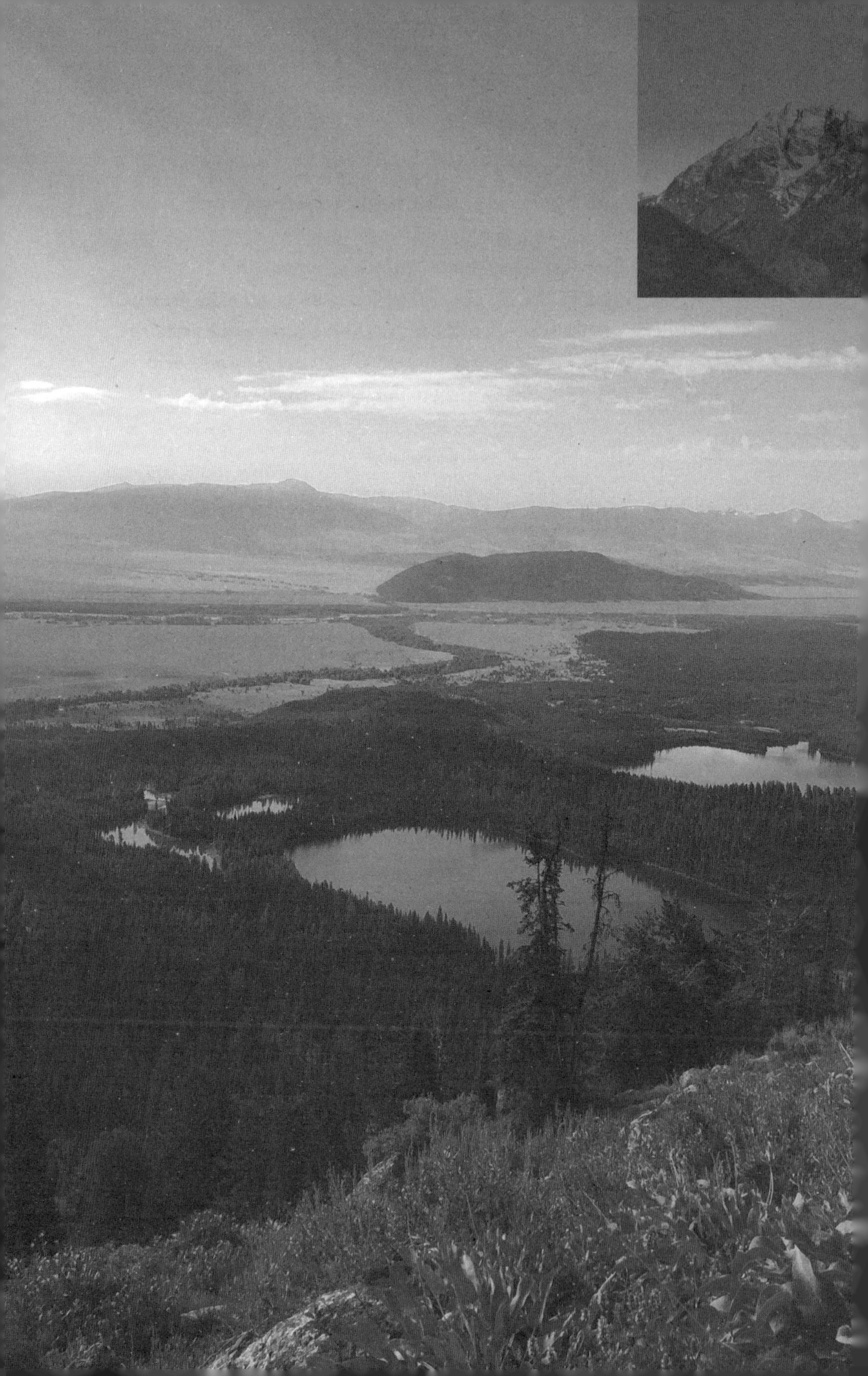

Chapter Six

GRAND TETON NATIONAL PARK, WYOMING, LATE JULY 2021

J.O. stopped abruptly and turned his face to the east. Tate, walking behind him with his head down and deep in thought, nearly bumped into him.

"Check it out, Tate."

Tate stopped on the narrow trail and followed J.O.'s eyes to the east, where the rising summer sun was only seconds from breaking the horizon. The underside of some lazy cumulus clouds blazed crimson in the light of the coming dawn. A slight nip in the air had kept the two brothers moving at a vigorous pace. They had left the Lupine Meadows trailhead around 5:00 a.m. and had climbed steadily through the trees and up the mountain trail. They were above the foothills now and almost into Garnet Canyon.

J.O. was well rested. A soft bed and his mother's cooking had restored his vigor in a short time. He had been eager for the long-awaited climb and wanted to miss nothing. Sunrise was his favorite time of the day. It was an awakening, a renewal. He had always found vigor and energy first thing in the morning. It probably grew out of doing early-morning chores with his dad as a boy. Now he stood riveted and gazing east, not wanting to miss the first light to break over the mountains.

Suddenly, brilliant, piercing shafts of light shot over the Gros Ventre mountain range, striking J.O. full in the face. The contrast startled him. He had thought his alpine world had been beautiful before, but under the illumination of a rising sun, it was breathtaking. Golden light bathed Jackson Hole. Shadows stole away, and topographical details seemed to rise out of a darkened mist even as he watched.

"It's awesome! Isn't it?" Tate said.

J.O. sighed deeply, then filled his lungs with the mountain air. "I'll say."

Both brothers closed their eyes and let the sun's warmth flood their souls. After a moment, J.O. spoke. "Have you ever noticed how much difference the sun makes?"

"What do you mean?" Tate asked.

"Well, look at it. Did you notice that we had plenty of light just before the sunrise? We could see well. Everything seemed pretty clear, but when the sun came up, it all changed."

"I'm not sure I'm following you," Tate said.

"Look at those lakes down there," J.O. said, pointing to the valley floor. "An hour or so ago you would never have been able to pick them out of the forest from right here. As the light increased, they became open black patches in the pines, but look at them now. The light's beginning to reach them, and you can see the blue of the water and the shoreline all around them. If all you ever saw was this world before sunrise, you would think you really had something—until you saw it with the sun shining on it."

Tate put his hands on his hips and cocked his head to one side. "I think you've been alone in your truck too long, J.O."

J.O. laughed. "Ah, admit it. I'm right. You could go through your whole life looking at this world with predawn light and think it was pretty neat and never know what you were missing until you actually saw the sun come up and recognized the difference."

"If you say so," Tate said, laughing, "but I still think you've been smelling too many diesel fumes. What brought on all this philosophy?"

"I don't know. I guess it just came to me as I watched the sun come up. It occurred to me that I'll bet 90 percent of this world has never watched a sunrise. They have no idea what they're missing."

"Probably not," Tate said quietly as he turned and followed J.O. up the trail.

They had walked only a short time when Tate spoke again.

"J.O., Can I ask you a question?"

"Sure!"

"What happened at that wreck a few weeks ago?"

"I told you what happened. A rockslide forced some people off the road and into the river. We fished them out."

"Uh-huh. Is that all that happened?"

J.O. stopped and turned around to face his brother. "Okay, what is this—an interrogation?"

Tate shrugged. "Mom talked to me. She thinks something else happened that you're not telling her."

J.O. laughed. "Not much gets past her, does it?"

"No. I expect not."

J.O. and Tate had always been close, best friends since the very beginning. It wasn't that they worked hard at getting along, it's just that they had never had a reason to fight. Nothing had ever come between them that had been worth a fight. Once in a while they had disagreed, and Tate had gotten angry, but he could never stay that way for long with J.O. always cracking jokes and laughing. How do you get mad at a guy who isn't angry himself and who is always making you laugh? There was a bond of trust between the brothers that was rare and satisfying.

"So, what happened?" Tate persisted when J.O. didn't answer.

As they walked up the trail, J.O. told him about meeting Shawnee at the dredge and about seeing her again at the accident on the river. He concluded his narrative by telling him of his futile attempts to find out if the two women were okay.

"Have you tried to find out who she is?"

"Yeah, but there's not much I can do. No one will tell me anything. I'm not *family*," he said with a sardonic twist in his voice.

"So, what are you going to do?"

"Nothing." He shrugged his shoulders. "Let it go, I guess."

Tate said nothing for a moment as they continued climbing. Then in an offhanded sort of way he said, "Hmm, too bad."

J.O. shot him a questioning glance but decided to let it go.

The exertion of the climb caused them to stop talking so they could save breath. They were setting a fast pace. It was their goal to be up and well off the mountain before 3:00 p.m. As they hiked, J.O. retreated into his thoughts. *Should I tell Tate about the mysterious experiences I had? Tate is no more religious than I've ever been. How can I tell him about something I can't even figure out myself? I really would sound like a moron. The old saying, "Better to remain silent and be thought a fool, than to open your mouth and remove all doubt" seems applicable here.* He said nothing, but it gnawed at him. He needed to discuss it with someone, just to get it off his chest.

Sometime around 8:00 a.m. the two brothers arrived at a fork in the trail in a place called the Meadows. The right fork of the trail led to the Lower Saddle and to the top of the Grand Teton. However, if one crossed the small stream and went left, the routes led to the summits of the Middle and South Tetons.

After filling their water bottles at the stream, J.O. and Tate crossed the stream and continued toward the top. It was a considerable distance to the top of Garnet Canyon and the saddle between the Middle and South Tetons. The hike was steep and mostly a scramble over loose rock and boulders.

"Looks like we may have company," Tate said as he sat down to rest on the side of the trail.

J.O. dropped beside him. They were at more than ten thousand feet in elevation now. It was not wise to push too hard from this point on if they wanted to avoid altitude sickness.

"Yeah, kind of looks like it," J.O. agreed as he studied the climbing party several hundred yards up the trail ahead of them. "I wonder if they are heading up the South or the Middle."

Tate only grunted as he took a long drink from his water bottle.

After a few moments, J.O. spoke again. "You know, this really is deceiving up here."

"How's that?"

"Well, look at where we've come from. When you're walking up that trail you walk so slowly that it hardly seems as though you are making any forward progress at all. But when you stop and look back, it's amazing how far you've actually come."

"Yeah, I see what you mean. How far do you think we've come since we left the Jeep?"

"I don't remember exactly, but it will have been about eight to ten miles by the time we reach the top."

"It seems like a lot farther than that," Tate said with a distinct note of weariness in his voice.

J.O. laughed. "What's the matter, old man, getting soft and flabby in that classroom?"

Tate snorted. "Soft! Look who's talking. I'll bet I get more exercise typing a paper than you do driving that truck. How hard can it be to shift a gear and turn a wheel?" He reached over and poked his fist into J.O.'s belly. "Don't call me soft, blubbergut!"

"Blubbergut!" J.O. said with mock indignance. "On your feet, Boy, and let's climb. We'll see who's the blubbergut here."

Tate grinned as J.O. pulled him to his feet and shoved him up the trail in front of him. He shouldered his pack as he stumbled forward and said, "Just holler when you need a rest, old man."

"Walk!" J.O. commanded from behind him.

Tate enjoyed the banter. He missed it. It had been his tendency to take himself too seriously when he was younger. School, grades, friends, girls, and life in general always seemed to be weighing him down. During those years, J.O. had teased and prodded him incessantly, trying to loosen him up and help him see that there was a lot more to life than being constantly stressed out. He was grateful now that his older brother had never given up on him. It was indeed a lot more fun to laugh and joke than to worry and fret. Still, he sensed that all this ribbing was not breaking through. J.O. seemed uncharacteristically tight. Something was on his mind. Maybe it was that young woman he spoke of, but likely it was not. Girls had never been a worry to J.O. He was comfortable with them and they with him. There had to be something else.

They walked a few hundred more yards when J.O. stopped and stood for a moment with his hands on his hips. He inhaled several long, deep breaths of the thin mountain air and let his eyes pan the vista before him. There it was again, that feeling that had nibbled at his consciousness since sunrise. What was it? Probably the closest word he could find for it was *awe*. He felt awestruck and overwhelmed by the vastness and beauty of what lay before him.

How could it all be an accident? It couldn't. There is just no way!

||||||||||||||||||

"How far do you think we are from the top?" Tate puffed, arching his spine to stretch.

"Probably less than forty-five minutes. How are you doing?"

"A little light-headed, but not too bad. I can make it."

They had reached the saddle between the Middle and South peaks and stopped briefly for lunch. After what seemed like a barely adequate rest, they turned north and resumed the climb toward the summit of the Middle Teton. The trail led precariously along a razor-sharp ridge. To the east the trail sloped gradually toward the meadows, but to the west, the ridge fell away abruptly for about a thousand feet. The cliff was a sheer drop and left no room for stupid antics and recklessness. They picked their way among the rocks with great care. Before long, the trail led across a more gentle, open slope. From there it entered a nearly vertical chute that led to the top. Because of the steep grade and loose, sliding rock under their feet, this was, by far, the hardest part of the climb.

J.O. kept looking up at the sky. The clouds were gathering and darkening at an alarming rate, which heightened his sense of urgency.

"Are we going to make it?" Tate asked, glancing at the sky.

"I think so, but it's going to be close."

J.O. looked again at the gathering clouds and made a calculated guess. He knew the horror stories about thunderstorms in the Tetons, and he had no desire to get caught in one. It was obviously going to rain. Clouds had been gathering, thickening, and darkening since midmorning. Even so, J.O. hadn't been too concerned until the massive darkbottomed thunderheads shrouded the peaks and hid them from view. They were running against time. J.O. wrestled with himself. Should he do the safe thing and turn back, or should he keep going? Common sense told him to go back, but. . . .

There was no way he was going to come all this way just to turn around. He looked one more time at the clouds and quickened his step.

||||||||||||||||

The sound of voices reached J.O. before he could see anyone. He and Tate were negotiating their way over some boulders when they came upon the other party of climbers sitting and resting about thirty feet away. There were four—at first glance, it looked like two men and two women. J.O. glanced back to see if Tate was still with him. Tate caught his eye and grinned slightly, the signal that said, *I'm alright, let's keep going.*

As J.O. approached with the intent to pass the other climbers, a man who looked like he was in his mid-forties glanced up and smiled a weary smile. The teenage boy beside him scarcely even looked up.

Looks like he's had all the fun he can stand, J.O. thought wryly as he studied the weary boy.

The thought had barely registered in his mind when he heard a distinct gasp. A dark-haired young woman with a baseball cap pulled low over her eyes shot to her feet. In that same moment, the other climber, a blond woman who had been digging in her pack, stood up and turned to face him. J.O. stopped in stunned amazement. It couldn't be. Standing directly in front of him, not five feet away, was Shawnee.

She reacted first and crossed the distance rapidly. Her hand was extended toward him as she approached. At the same moment, the other woman reached his shoulder and grabbed his arm excitedly. J.O. looked down into her face and recognized her. It was Lisa.

"You—what are you—I can't believe this!" Shawnee stammered as she grasped his hand and shook it firmly.

"Dad, you're not going to believe this," she

said to the middle-aged man as he stepped up beside her. "This is the guy who saved Lisa and me—the one who pulled us out of the river."

The man's face split into a wide, handsome grin as he extended a large, well-muscled hand.

"Well, I'm glad I finally get to meet you," he said, shaking J.O.'s hand. "My name is Rick James."

Never one to be slow on the uptake, J.O. recovered quickly and extended his hand. "I'm J.O. Steele. It's good to meet you."

"You've already met my daughter, I guess," Rick said, laughing.

"That I have," J.O. said with a chuckle. He turned to Shawnee. "But I never knew your last name. I tried to get hold of you after the accident to see if the two of you were alright, but no one would give out any information."

"We're fine!" Lisa said. "Still a little tender in places, but almost as good as new."

J.O. noticed the cast on Shawnee's thumb and the wrap on Lisa's ankle.

"We tried to find you too," Shawnee said. "The Idaho State Police gave us your name and your number in Pocatello, but every time we called there was no answer."

"That figures," J.O. said with a wry smile. "My mother is a busy schoolteacher and my brother—" He suddenly remembered Tate and pulled him to his side.

"I'm sorry. This is my brother, Tate, Tate Steele. Tate, this is Rick James, his daughter Shawnee, and this is Lisa . . ." He paused, waiting for her to supply her last name.

"Banks. Lisa Banks."

"Nice to meet you." Tate shook hands around the group.

"This is my son, Brian," Rick said, completing the introductions. "He's fourteen, and not so sure right now that he should have come with us."

A wave of laughter swept the group Brian raised himself off a rock and came toward them. He fulfilled the obligatory handshakes and sat back down heavily, looking like a runner who had just finished a marathon.

"We've tried several times to get in touch with you," Lisa repeated, "but—"

"We're never home," Tate interrupted. "I'm always in school. J.O.'s always on the road. And Mom, who knows where she is?"

"We wanted to thank you," Shawnee said, her voice dropping slightly.

J.O. couldn't be sure, but the way she dropped her gaze and looked away made it seem she was embarrassed by her emotions.

"For saving our lives," Lisa said, jumping in quickly. "It was incredible! We didn't find out until later all that you did. Thank you."

"Yes, thank you," Shawnee said, looking up into his face, "especially me. There was no way I would have gotten out of that car if it hadn't been for you."

"You're very welcome," J.O. said, beginning to feel just a bit uncomfortable. "I'm just glad I could help."

Rick entered the conversation again, sensing J.O.'s discomfort. "I take it you're going to the top," he said, as he gestured up the mountain.

"That we are," J.O. said, glad the attention was elsewhere.

"Do you mind if we climb with you?" Rick asked. "We've never been up here before."

"That'd be great!" Tate said. "We'd be happy to have the company."

J.O. smiled as he perceived his brother's quick glance at Lisa and the lightning-fast acceptance of the request. It was also fine with him, though he couldn't help but cast a glance at Shawnee to see what she thought of the idea. She met his eyes. The ready flash of her smile gave him the answer he needed.

"Well, we'd better get climbing," J.O. said matter-of-factly. "That weather isn't looking too promising." He nodded his head toward the menacing, dark clouds above them. A feeling of dread once again passed over him. They were really going to have to hurry now.

||||||||||||||||

J.O. stood and watched as Shawnee, standing on the sloping rock of the highest point of the Middle Teton, pulled off her hat, shook out her long, blond hair, and rose to her full height. Instantly, the powerful winds picked up her golden hair and whipped it in undulating strands behind her. Her slender feminine form was silhouetted against the backdrop of roiling thunderheads that were close enough to touch. Beyond her to the north, barely visible in the dark clouds, was the summit of the Grand Teton.

J.O. took it all in. It was a singular moment and breathtaking—the kind of scene one sees only once in a lifetime. Reaching for his cell phone, he dropped to a crouch to catch Shawnee's silhouette against the dark storm clouds. He snapped off two shots, but not before she caught him in the act. A pretended pout of disapproval crossed her face, making it even more appealing. He snapped the shutter again, catching the expression.

"Gotcha!" he said, smiling up at her.

With a laugh, she tossed her hair in the wind and offered him a hand to step up beside her. He accepted the hand and jumped up next to her. As she lifted him to his full height, a heady feeling, almost a momentary wooziness, came over him. He was once again standing on top of the world, but this time, beside the most beautiful woman he had ever met. She took his arm as though to steady him. He looked out over the world spread before him, and even though he couldn't see the valley below, he knew it was there. That familiar warmth of soul that he had felt before in these mountains glowed anew within him. It continued to grow until it felt like a burning fire. His breath was short, and his heart pounded. Something was happening to him, like it had when the lightning had downed the tree. He looked over at Shawnee. She still held his arm, but her eyes were closed, an enraptured expression on her face. Was she feeling it also? He looked away toward the Snake River Plain to the west. He could see nothing but clouds.

"Look!" Shawnee said suddenly, pulling him out of his thoughts.

Looking where she pointed, J.O. watched as the massive clouds to the east rolled back and opened, like God parting the sea, exposing a breathtaking view of Jackson Hole, some six thousand feet below.

"Oh, wow!" J.O. said, breathlessly.

Now both of her hands clutched his upper arm in a tight grip. "Look at that, J.O. Look at it! It's incredible. Have you ever seen anything like it?"

J.O. shook his head, unable to speak. There was simply nothing he could say that would do justice to what he saw and felt. How often does one get to see the world like this?

Shawnee turned and stood face-to-face with him. The intensity in her eyes surprised him.

"J.O., I don't know anything about you or what you believe or even why I'm saying this, but I want you to know with all my soul, *there is a God, and this—*" her hand swept over the panorama—"is only the beginning of

His gifts." She stopped speaking, but her eyes, shining and blue, held his.

J.O. couldn't look away. Something in those eyes captured and held him. Her words cut to his soul like a knife. Slowly, almost unconsciously, he nodded in agreement. She was right! There was no explaining it, but he knew unequivocally, she was telling the truth. There *was* a God! It was as though he had always known and there had never been so many years of doubt. He looked away toward the clouds. The gap in them closed as quickly as it had formed, shutting off all view of anything beyond more than a hundred feet.

Together they stood reveling in the moment. Then something jolted J.O. An innate sense sounded an alarm, and he once again became acutely aware of his surroundings. The hair on the back of his neck began to stand up, and a peculiar fuzziness charged the air. He paused for a moment, sensing, listening, then he caught it—the hum and crackle of static electricity. Adrenalin hit him like a sledgehammer.

"Get off," he shouted at the others as he jumped off the summit rock. "Get off, now!"

They all looked at him in confusion. He jumped off the rock and reached behind him for Shawnee. Seeing her bewildered expression, he thrust his arm to the sky and shouted, "Lightning! We've got to get down, fast! Any second this mountain is going to start popping like the Fourth of July."

Spurred to action, they grabbed their packs and began scrambling over the rocks as the wind increased to gale force. The first drops of rain came moments later and hit their faces like the sting of bees. They had only gone about two hundred feet down when the first bolt of lightning flashed, followed by the simultaneous crack of deafening thunder. It was right on top of them. J.O. wiped the rain out of his eyes and spotted a grouping of large boulders against the rock face of the chute about twenty feet down and off to the left. He yelled over the howling wind for the others to follow him. Jumping and sliding through the loose rock

89

Lightning in the Tetons

with reckless abandon, he dove into a crevice between the rocks. One by one the others plunged in after him.

"If you have rain suits, put them on," J.O. barked. "Put your pack on the ground and sit on it. Don't let any part of your body touch the ground or the rocks above us. Keep as low to the ground as possible." As he said this he crouched on his pack, wrapped his arms around his knees, and tucked his head.

As they scrambled to obey, the clouds seemed to burst. The rain pounded down in a blinding torrent, obscuring anything and everything beyond a range of more than a few feet. Those parts of their bodies not shielded by the waterproof suits were instantly soaked. It became as dark as the late stages of twilight, which only added to the terrifying effect of the lightning.

J.O. looked up into the storm. The flash of the lightning and boom of the thunder were continuous. The rain came in sheets that obscured all visibility. He knew only too well how dangerous their situation was. They were human lightning rods. Any second, their lives could be vaporized in a flash of white light.

He looked over at Rick; his head was down, and his arms and upper body were wrapped over Brian to protect him. The boy whimpered in terror as each thunderous crack seemed to shake the ground beneath them. Lisa was next to Tate. A particularly brilliant flash and an ear-splitting explosion struck. Lisa screamed and shot upright; Tate reached out and pulled her down. She threw her arms around him and buried herself against his chest. Finally, J.O. looked at Shawnee. Seeing the terror in her eyes, he reached for her and she moved to him, pressing herself against him.

The storm raged around them, fulfilling every awe-inspiring story J.O. had ever heard about the fury of Teton storms. In fact, what they were experiencing was much worse than any story had detailed. Lightning seemed to explode directly over the top of them at the same moment the thunder crashed. He had never been in a war under mortar fire, but he couldn't imagine that it could be a whole lot worse than this. Another terrifying explosion that seemed to shatter the rocks around them brought Shawnee's head up with a jerk. The look of panic in her eyes caused J.O. to hold her more tightly. The pressure seemed to momentarily calm her. Suddenly, Rick was in front of them. "We need to pray," he shouted over the roar of the storm.

Shawnee glanced quickly at J.O. and then was instantly out of his arms and kneeling beside her father. Lisa joined her. Tate followed Lisa and knelt beside her. J.O. hesitated, momentarily bewildered. He wanted to shout at them to knock off the nonsense and get back on their packs, but instead, he slid off his pack to his knees on the outer edge of the small group. The others bowed their heads and closed their eyes as Rick began to pray, shouting to be heard over the howling wind.

"Heavenly Father, we're in great danger. We place ourselves in Thy hands and ask that Thou wouldst temper the elements and, if it is Thy will, that Thou wouldst calm the storm around us. Help us, O Father. There's nothing we can do. Thy will be done, O Father."

He closed the brief prayer with an "amen." J.O felt a hand clutch his and squeeze tightly. He opened his eyes. Shawnee was looking over at him, a smile on her face. He smiled back, uncertain what he should say or do next. They returned to their positions on their packs.

The storm continued unabated. On his pack, J.O. rolled into as much of a ball as he could to keep the rain from running down his neck or soaking his feet. Shawnee sat close to him, taking shelter against his body. J.O.'s thoughts became lost in Rick's prayer. Questions pelted him like the driving rain. *Is there a God? Does prayer really work? As recently as a few days ago, I would have said no, but now I'm not so sure.* His gut knotted as the confusion increased in his mind. *What kind of a woman is this? What kind of a family is this? Blessings! Prayers to stop storms! Do they really think that something as pitifully weak as a prayer was going to stop something as powerful as a storm like this?*

Doubts and questions pounded his mind like the storm ravaged the mountain. Rick's sincerity in the prayer was admirable, but J.O. couldn't help but feel that the man was deluded. *If there was a God, why had He allowed the storm in the first place? Why didn't He just divert the clouds before all this happened? Why hadn't this God—this* Heavenly Father— *been there when Dad needed Him? Why wasn't He there now when so many thousands of His children were suffering and dying all over the world? Why? Why?* The questions howled at him louder than the wind.

J.O. was startled out of his thoughts by movement when Shawnee lifted her head to look into his eyes. When he looked down, her face was so close to his that he could have kissed her. He studied her eyes and the expression they carried. They were a deep blue with dark flecks throughout, a combination that reminded him of the deep, fathomless blue of a midnight sky. At that moment they were soft and gentle in expression. Her lips were turned up in a slight, amused smile, leaving him wondering what she was thinking.

"Are you okay?" she asked.

The question surprised him. "I'm fine," he said guardedly. "Why do you ask?"

"I don't know. You just seemed really tense. Is it the lightning?"

"Well, yeah. I suppose so. I mean, after all, we are one second away from being vaporized."

Then he paused. He had been so caught up in reflecting on the prayer that he hadn't noticed that the storm was dying down. The lightning had subsided. "The lightning's stopped!" he said.

"I know" she said softly. "It hasn't struck close to us since the prayer."

J.O. had been studying the sky, but his head came down sharply at her comment, and he looked into her face. Surely, she didn't believe that the prayer had anything to do with the storm dying out. Teton storms blew in and out in minutes. It could be a nightmare from hell one minute and the essence of serenity the next. Surely, she didn't believe. . . .

She smiled at him and stood up. Shaking off the rain, she moved over to Lisa, who also stood. J.O. stared after her, dumbstruck. She *did* believe it! Her calm assurance let him know she absolutely believed that a few words of prayer had calmed the elements and saved their lives.

"There's something I have to ask you, Shawnee, but I don't quite know how to say it."

She smiled at him. "Just out with it, J.O."

He fell into step beside her, took a deep breath, and exhaled loudly.

She laughed. "It's okay. You can ask me whatever's on your mind."

He waited for the rest of the party to pass. Lisa and Tate walked by, laughing and completely lost in each other's company. Rick smiled pleasantly as he passed. Brian plodded along behind his father, so tired he was conscious of nothing but the unending trail. Once they were all ahead on the trail, J.O. turned to her, his expression deeply earnest.

"You really do believe it, don't you?"

The question seemed to take her aback. "Believe what?"

"In God, and in prayer."

Now she looked shocked. "Of course I do. Don't you?"

A look of intense pain clouded J.O.'s features. "I—" he started to speak but stopped, struggling for words. "I . . . I used to."

Chapter Seven

IDAHO FALLS, IDAHO

Shawnee sat on the edge of her bed and slowly pulled the brush through her long, silky hair, her mind far away from the softly lit bedroom where she now sat. Over and over, she rehearsed every word, expression, and nuance of her conversation with J.O. as they had walked off the mountain. The existence and nature of God were not passing intellectual fancies for him; coming to the truth about it seemed as vital as life. He had said little of what he believed, choosing instead to question her about her beliefs, but despite his guarded demeanor, she could tell that he was as torn and confused about God as any person she had ever met. It seemed so strange to meet someone who seemed to wonder about the very existence of God and yet seemed to take the matter so seriously. It was as though he was at war with himself over an issue that the rest of the world was indifferent to. Surely, though, he must have felt something in those exhilarating moments on the summit rock.

She sighed and put the brush down. Life could be so perplexing at times. It was no accident that they had met J.O. on that mountain, of all places. Of that she was certain—but why? Why did such a man have to come into her life, especially now? After breaking off one troubling relationship, jumping into another was the last leap she wanted to make. Why not just put herself back together, physically and emotionally before she let her heart go again? That had been her determination until J.O. had come along—and suddenly, whether she liked it or not, she found herself entertaining the possibility of greater things.

Shawnee shook her head in visible frustration. That was impossible! He might as well be from another world. In many ways, he was. The two of them couldn't have grown up more differently, yet they were so much alike. Her heart felt a little like a tennis ball in a heated match. If it was meant that she was only to be his friend and help him find the truth, then she was destined for one of the greatest tests of her life. The deeper into his troubled soul she had probed, the more she was attracted to him—and all the while, her head was telling her she was crazy. In every way he was wrong for her, yet her heart was drawn to him.

Marrying J.O. was out of the question. Long ago—in fact, as a little girl—she had decided on the kind of man and marriage she wanted, and she had never wavered. J.O. Steele neither qualified as the man or the marriage of her dreams. That conclusion had cemented itself in her mind by the time they had reached the bottom of the mountain. So, when her dad had invited him to dinner at their house on Sunday night, it had both frustrated her and delighted her. Even now, she had to smile. It had been hard to tell who had been the most surprised at her father's boldness—her or J.O. And if anyone seemed excited and enthused about the invitation, it was Lisa and Tate.

"If I let you get away again without inviting you to dinner so the rest of the family can meet you, I'll be in serious trouble. They all want to meet the hero," Rick had said.

"The hero? Mr. James, I—"

"Rick. Call me Rick, and please don't argue. Just come to dinner."

J.O. had looked at Shawnee and then back at Rick. With a shrug of his shoulders, he had said, "Okay, I'll be there."

He had glanced again at Shawnee, his eyes probing hers for some sign of approval. She had not known what to do. With all her heart she had wanted him to come, but at the same time. . . . She remembered now the faint smile she had let him see. It had been enough. He had accepted the invitation.

She stood up from the bed and walked to her dresser, the frustration swelling all over again. How could her dad do this to her? J.O. and Tate would be here in less than an hour. Lisa was already here and as eager as a schoolgirl for them to show up.

Shawnee put the brush down and picked up a framed picture of the Savior. As she turned back to the mirror, she pulled the image to her chest and wrapped both arms over it. For a moment, she stood staring into the mirror at the image before her. Suddenly, like sunlight bursting through the clouds, it became clear what she would do. She would do everything she could to help J.O., to teach him, just like she was doing with Lisa, but she would not let her heart get swept away. All she would ever be was his friend—no more. And if that were not possible, she would walk away. If it came down to a choice between a temple marriage and this young man, there would be no question. No matter how much he took her breath away now, he would not take her heart away later.

The doorbell rang, and she started at the sound. There was an instant clamoring of voices and the thunder of many small feet running through the house.

"It's him! It's him!" she heard her younger siblings shouting.

Her pulse quickened as she closed her eyes.

"Oh, help me, Father, please."

|||||||||||||||||||

"I hope you're sure about this," Tate said, as the chime of the doorbell sounded inside.

"I hope so too," J.O. said, turning to his brother with an apprehensive smile.

All the way from Pocatello to Idaho Falls, J.O. had been lost in his thoughts about the possibilities of tonight and everything that could go wrong. It made him more nervous than he cared to admit. He had laid the spiritual troubles of his soul on the table with Shawnee, and even though she had been attentive and interested, he still felt like a fool for exposing his soul the way he had done. A resolution came to him in that moment between the chime and the door opening. He was going to laugh and have a good time, notwithstanding the proximity of a woman who rocked his world—and he would sidestep questions of faith like a good saddle horse avoids a snake.

The door swept open. Rick's frame filled the doorway, his hand outstretched toward them.

"Come on in," he said with a smile, taking J.O. by the hand and pulling him into the entryway.

J.O. stepped in, looking around as he did so. Instantly, he was struck by the feeling inside the home. It was like nothing he had ever felt before. Before he had time to process the thought further, his attention was drawn to what was gathering in front of him. A slender, attractive older woman walked into the entryway with a towel in her hand and an apron around her waist. She wore a light cotton dress and looked as though she were dressed for some occasion. This had to be Shawnee's mother—and it must be where Shawnee had inherited her slender build and beautiful, blond hair. The resemblance between mother and daughter was striking. The sound of running suddenly stopped as two more children who looked younger than eight skidded around the corner and into the entryway. They pulled up short at the sight of him and stopped, staring. He did a quick count—one, two, three, four, five, six. Six children and two parents. Just as he was wondering what to say, Rick came to his rescue. Taking him by the arm, he stepped to his side.

"J.O., I'd like you to meet our family. This is Emily," he pointed to a gorgeous little girl that was about four, "and this is Ben; he's six." He continued his introductions all the way up the line from youngest to oldest. J.O. shook hands with each of them in turn, stooping down for the littlest ones.

"And this is my wife, Marie."

"Pleased to meet you," J.O. said as he reached to shake hands with her, but she stepped past his outstretched hand and pulled him into a fierce embrace.

"That's for saving my daughter's life," she said, a tinge of emotion in her voice. "Thank you so much."

She held him for a moment and then stepped back. Before he could regain his composure, the littlest girl, Emily, stepped up and threw her arms around his legs.

"Thank you for saving Nawnee," she lisped.

Completely unnerved, J.O. stood there, struggling to swallow the lump that had suddenly formed in his throat. Bending over, he scooped Emily up into his arms and patted her back. She wrapped her arms around his neck like she had known him all her life. When he set her down, she stared up at him in open appraisal.

"I'm sorry," Rick said, with a sudden chuckle. "I should have warned you about this family. They're pretty open with their feelings."

His comment helped dissolve his nervous tension, and J.O. laughed. "Yeah, I noticed."

He turned back and gestured toward Tate. "This is my brother, Tate. Tate, this is . . ." and then one by one, from the youngest to the oldest, he repeated the names of each of the members of the family.

"I'm impressed," Marie said when he finished, "you remembered them all."

Just then another person moved at a stair landing a few steps above the level of the entryway. "I'm impressed too," Shawnee said.

J.O. looked up at her, as did the rest of the family.

"Hello, J.O., Tate," Shawnee said softly.

"Hello," both brothers said, almost in unison.

Shawnee descended the last few steps. J.O. felt the sudden catch in his chest. This young woman was as close to perfection as any he had

99

ever seen, and every time he saw her was like a jolt of electricity. She was wearing a soft floral-print summer dress that came below her knees and fit her lovely form perfectly. Her hair reflected the last rays of sunlight that filtered through the still-open doorway.

As she came forward and shook his hand, he sensed something about her. She seemed guarded, nervous.

"Do you really drive those big trucks?" a wide-eyed boy of about ten said.

"I sure do. Would you like to go for a ride sometime?"

"Yeah!" the little boy shouted excitedly.

"Did you really save Shawnee's life?" It was Ben, the youngest boy.

"Ah, well—" J.O. hesitated.

"He did, Ben," Shawnee said. "He jumped into that river and pulled me out of the car. If it weren't for him, I wouldn't be here."

"Wow!" the little boy said, his wide eyes looking at J.O.

"Now, don't you kids start in on J.O. already," Rick said. "After we eat, we'll sit down and ask him to tell us the story."

"That's right," Marie said, ushering Ben toward the table. "Right now, it's time to eat. Everyone come to the table."

Shawnee glanced up at J.O. as Ben scurried away.

"Come on, hero," she teased, "let's go eat."

"Thanks a lot," J.O. muttered under his breath.

She laughed then took his hand to lead him to the table.

All thoughts of guests were momentarily forgotten as the children charged for the kitchen and took their places.

Rick rolled his eyes and sighed. "Children," he said with mock gravity, "you try to teach them manners but. . . ." He let the sentence trail off unfinished.

As they took their places at the table, J.O. didn't miss that Lisa took Tate by the arm and seated herself next to him.

"This food is wonderful," J.O said.

"Why, thank you, J.O." Marie said. "It's nice to hear things like that once in a while."

J.O. finished downing another bite of chicken cordon bleu. "You should hear it more often. This is good."

"It's probably because all he ever gets to eat is truck-stop food," Lisa said. "Even dog food would taste good after eating that stuff."

J.O. laughed. "I'm afraid that is all too true. If I weren't a runner, I would probably be as round as I am tall from all the grease I've eaten."

"You're a runner?" Rick asked.

"I am."

"Well, how about that? So am I. So are Shawnee and Brian. I don't know if Shawnee still runs, but she did in high school. Brian was on the junior-high-school track team."

"I've been a little out of shape lately," Shawnee said. "Injuries from the accident kind of slowed me down, but I'm getting back in shape again now."

"How do you run when you're on the road?" Marie asked.

"I just get up in the morning and go, wherever I am."

"How many different cities have you run in?"

"I have no idea," he said, laughing, "but at last count I had run in forty of the fifty states."

"Wow!" Brian said. "That would be cool."

"How long have you been driving trucks?" Rick asked.

"About four years. I started driving just before I turned twenty-one."

As the conversation ebbed and flowed throughout the meal, Shawnee quietly watched the people at the table. All the children stared wide-eyed at J.O. He had obviously captured them with his charm and smile. Her parents seemed bent on making J.O. and Tate feel comfortable and at home. Lisa was the most transparent—and Tate was the sole center of her attention. She hung on his every word. Shawnee had no doubt that her best friend was utterly smitten, and from all appearances, Tate was feeling a bit the same way.

Of all the people at the table, though, it was J.O. who most intrigued her, especially the way he treated the younger children. He responded to any question, whether it came from the smallest child or the oldest adult, in the same way. The children were not spoken down to, but treated with respect, as equals. He was always smiling, and that was one of his most striking features. Every time he smiled, his entire countenance lit up. And for the first time, she noticed the unusual richness and timbre of his voice. It was deep and soothing. His laugh was frequent and pleasing. It was one of those laughs that is almost musical—and the more you hear it, the more you want to laugh with it. Some would call it an infectious laugh.

Tactically, she had placed herself at the end of the table with J.O. at her left, giving her the chance to study his face without him seeing her. The lines of his face were prominent and more angular than round. He had a strong, square chin and a broad smile. His eyes were a bright, clear blue, which automatically caught the eye. She noticed the laugh lines at the corner of his eyes accentuated by the deepness of his tan. Her dad had the same lines. She had come to love them on him because they bespoke cheerfulness. Short and well-trimmed, his hair was somewhere between a sandy blond and a light brown. She was impressed that he didn't seem to be into any strange or outlandish fashions; his clothes were neat and attractive without any sign of the vanity of name brands. In short, he was just about as clean, neat, and conservative as any guy she had ever met.

"J.O.?"

It was her brother Ben, trying to work himself into the conversation. An unexpected ill premonition caught her.

"Yes, Ben," J.O. said.

"Where did you serve your mission?"

Shawnee groaned inwardly and looked down at the floor. Lisa and her parents knew that J.O. was not a member of the Church, but she hadn't thought she needed to talk to her brothers and sisters about it.

J.O. froze with a fork-full of food hovering above his plate. He glanced sideways at Tate. Now everyone at the table sensed the tension and stopped eating. Even Emily knew something had changed. Shawnee opened her mouth to speak, but before she could say anything, J.O. spoke.

"I haven't been a missionary, Ben."

"Oh," Ben said, suddenly embarrassed, but not sure why he should be.

"No, it's okay, Ben," J.O. added quickly, trying to rescue him. "I'm not a member of your church. In fact, Tate and I don't belong to any church."

Shawnee was impressed as J.O. quickly reached out and placed a reassuring hand on Ben's shoulder as he spoke to him. "But I'm impressed that you would think I look like a guy who's been a missionary."

"You know about missions?" Shawnee's mother asked.

"Oh, sure," J.O. said lightly. "There's no way to grow up in this part of Idaho and not know what an LDS mission is all about. I had several friends in high school who went on missions and are back now."

"So, you know about the Church?" Marie asked.

"Of course."

"We not only know about it," Tate was speaking now, "but I have a lot of respect for the Church and what it teaches."

"So, it doesn't bother you that right now you are completely surrounded by Latter-day Saints and they are out to get you?" A slight smile started to spread across Rick's face.

"Dad," Shawnee scolded.

She almost wanted to crawl under the table. This was typical of her dad. His bluntness would offend most people if he wasn't so loving and cheerful. Some people were unsure how to take him.

"It's okay, Shawnee," J.O. said with a twinkle in his eye. "It doesn't bother me a bit. They've been trying for years, and I hope someday they do—get me, that is."

Shawnee gaped at him, not only because he had met her dad on the field of verbal battle and proved himself an equal, but because of what he had said. Her heart raced. Did he really mean that? Her dad tipped his head back and laughed. J.O. joined him, as did everyone at the table. The tension was gone.

"To be honest with you, J.O.," Rick said, "we were a little uncertain how to treat you and Tate. Shawnee told us enough that we realized you were not of our faith. We're a pretty religious family, and sometimes that makes strangers uncomfortable. As I said at the door, we're a pretty open and expressive bunch, and some people have a hard time with that."

"Well, I'll be honest with you too," J.O. said. "Religion has been a really hard thing for me. But I have to say, I like the way your family does it."

Rick smiled and laughed again. "Good. Good!" he said.

"So, J.O.," Marie broke in, "tell us about the rest of your family."

Shawnee smiled. Her mother was the perfect match for her dad. She was lively and enthusiastic and the perfect diplomat. This was her way of steering the conversation clear of potentially dangerous waters. Shawnee felt herself relax. The one subject that seemed the most unapproachable had just been safely navigated. Somehow, she felt confident they would return to these waters again. And for now, the thrill and elation she felt buoyed her up beyond belief.

||||||||||||||||

When the dinner was over, the two brothers stood and began clearing the table and carrying the dishes to the sink. They had made only a couple of trips when Marie spoke up.

"No. Why don't we put the cleanup off for a while. Let's all go into the family room and sit down." She turned her attention on J.O. "I can almost bet you're not going to like this, but before the little ones go to bed, would you mind telling us about what happened at the accident? Everybody really wants to know."

The younger children began jumping up and down and shouting,

"Yeah! Yeah! Tell us."

J.O. glanced from Marie to the children and finally to Shawnee. His gaze lingered a moment with her before returning to her mother. He drew in a deep breath and then said, "Sure. If you'd like me to."

The children began to cheer and stampede for the family room, probably as eager to get out of cleanup responsibilities as they were to hear the story.

J.O. sat on a big recliner that faced the rest of the family. Rick and Marie strategically placed each of the children. J.O. marveled in admiration as he watched these two parents shepherd their little flock. It left him with the impression that these were people who parented by plan and not by accident. As soon as everyone was ready, Rick came and stood by J.O.

"Okay, everyone. This is a special night. I think before we begin, we should have a word of prayer. Brian, would you offer it?"

All the children dropped off the sofas and chairs to their knees on the carpet. J.O. stole a glance at Tate. He was sitting on the fireplace mantle with Lisa beside him. He was already on his way down. J.O. followed suit and knelt close to Rick.

Brian offered a short, simple prayer, and everyone quickly resumed their seats.

"As you all know," Rick began, "Shawnee and Lisa were in a car accident a few weeks ago. They were almost killed. If it hadn't been for J.O., they probably would have been." J.O. felt himself squirm. This was not going to be easy. "We've asked J.O. and Tate to come tonight so we could tell them thank you and get a chance to get to know them. We'd also like J.O. to tell us what happened."

Rick stepped aside with a gesture toward J.O., and then he sat down by his wife, putting his arm around her and pulling her close.

"Well," J.O. said, clearing his throat nervously. "I guess it started just a little while before the accident when I saw Lisa and Shawnee at the Yankee Fork Dredge. I was taking a tour. . . ."

Shawnee's thoughts returned to that moment in the dredge when she had turned around and locked eyes with J.O. A warm glow gently rose as she remembered the feeling that had passed between them.

J.O. continued, telling about the rockslide. An involuntary shudder passed through Shawnee's body as she remembered her car hitting the rock. It was a sound she would probably never forget. It was at this point in the story that everyone seemed the most riveted, since no one knew what had happened next. J.O. described the car sinking into the river. He paused for a moment, seeming to relive the horror of it all. He then described diving into the frigid water and the panic of trying to find a way into the car. As he spoke of finally getting into the car and trying to get Lisa out, his narrative was interrupted by a soft sniffle. Shawnee glanced quickly at Lisa. Tears were streaming down her cheeks.

"I'm sorry," she sniffed.

Shawnee moved over and sat on the floor in front of her and took hold of her hands. J.O. continued, telling how Lisa had kicked him in the face and had been nearly incoherent with panic and fright. When he came to the part where Lisa had told him that Shawnee was still in the car, it was Marie who was now in tears. He told of diving back in and finding Shawnee unconscious and upside down in the seat. Marie sobbed outright when J.O. told of bringing her to shore and discovering that she was not breathing. He hesitated a moment, seeming to weigh whether he should go into detail about those agonizing moments when he was trying to resuscitate her. His voice strained as he described the yearning prayer he had offered on her behalf and the profound joy he had felt when she had revived. By now, every adult in the room was in tears. Tears were even coursing down Tate's cheeks, something J.O. had not seen since his father's funeral.

"I can't remember the last time I felt so grateful and happy as that moment when you opened your eyes and started coughing," J.O. said to Shawnee.

"And I can't remember a time when I ever looked up into a more concerned face," she said, laughing through her tears.

The James Home

"There is one part of the story, though, that I have to ask you about," he said, suddenly sobering.

"What's that?"

"When we finally got you back up on top, you kept asking for someone who could give Lisa a blessing."

Shawnee nodded. "I remember that."

"You even asked me."

"I remember."

"I suppose I should know, but what is a *blessing*?"

Shawnee glanced at her father. Rick jumped in. "That's probably a question I should answer. In our Church we have what is called the holy priesthood. When a person is sick or injured and has faith, he or she can call on someone who holds that priesthood authority to lay hands on the afflicted person and speak for God on that person's behalf. The person who receives the blessing can receive promises, counsel, healing, and various other blessings."

J.O. seemed to mull that over in his mind for a few moments. "I think I understand."

"When Lisa was in so much pain," Shawnee offered, "it was the only thing I could think of to help her. I hope I didn't embarrass you."

107

"No, you didn't embarrass me, but it did bother me for a few days. I wish I could have helped you."

"Help me!" Shawnee scoffed. "You have no idea how much you *did* help me. How do you say thank you to someone who's just saved your life? Even now, I have no idea what to say, and somehow 'thanks' just doesn't seem like enough."

"I remember my dad once saying to someone he had helped, 'Don't repay me, just go and do it for someone else.' I guess that works for me too."

At that moment, Emily stood up, walked across the room to J.O., threw her tiny arms around his neck again, and kissed him soundly and wetly on the cheek. "I love you, J.O.," she announced matter-of-factly.

|||||||||||||||||

Caught completely by surprise, J.O. sat stunned. Then he returned the little angel's hug. "I love you too, Emily."

Marie stood up. "I think that is a perfect conclusion to our evening. It's getting late, and it's time for family prayer."

At that cue, the children groaned, but after a look from Rick, they dropped to their knees on the plush carpet of the step-down family room. Not knowing what else to do, J.O. knelt along with them. Rick called on Lisa to offer the prayer.

"I'm still not very good at this, Brother James." There was a pleading tone in her voice.

"That's what makes you so good at it, Lisa. You pray from the heart and not the head. Please, go ahead."

"Alright," she said reluctantly.

She began to pray, expressing thanks for the love and kindness of the James family and for the chance to learn the gospel. When she began to express gratitude that she and Shawnee had been allowed to live, her voice broke and she had to pause until she regained her composure.

As the prayer proceeded, J.O. noticed the unusual feelings of calm, love, and peace that seemed to fill the room. The feeling was exhilarating and filled him with a profound sense of well-being. At that moment, he could not remember ever having felt so loved. Just as the prayer ended, he opened his eyes and took in the singularity of the scene—a father, a mother, six children, and three outsiders kneeling together in a home that felt more warm and secure than anything he had ever known. The thought crossed his mind that if he were ever privileged to have a wife, family, and home, this was what he wanted.

"I just want you all to know," Lisa said after the prayer, "I love this family and I hope someday I have one just like it."

J.O. smiled. She had spoken the thoughts of his soul perfectly.

|||||||||||||||||

"Thank you for coming," Rick said, standing in the doorway with his arm around Marie. "It was a wonderful evening."

J.O. stood just off the front steps of the large home. Tate stood near him, with Lisa at his side. Shawnee stood at the top of the steps as though she might come down.

"The pleasure was ours," J.O. said. "You have the most wonderful family I've ever met. Tell them all thank you."

"That goes for me too," Tate echoed.

"We will," Marie said.

As they turned to walk toward the Jeep, Shawnee came down the steps and walked beside J.O.

"Did you really mean that?" she asked.

"Mean what?"

"About my family."

"What, you don't believe me?" he teased. "I've never been more serious in my life."

She didn't say anything as she searched his face, trying to determine if he was really serious.

He stepped directly in front of her and looked into her face "They are awesome. I meant what I said."

Shawnee laughed at his choice of words. "Awesome, huh? I'm glad you liked them. I was afraid the James family would be a little too much for you."

"They were great, especially Emily. Give her a hug and a thank-you from me tonight, will you?"

"I'll do that," Shawnee said with a soft laugh. "Whenever I come home from college, she gives me the same kind of hugs and kisses. It makes coming home worth it. I love it."

By this time, they had arrived at the side of the Jeep, where they joined Tate and Lisa.

"Then I'd have to say you are about the luckiest woman alive to have a little sister like that. About all I get from Tate when I come home is a sour grunt and a wave."

"Hey," Tate said with pretended offense. He grabbed for J.O., who ducked out of the way. "That's because all you ever you do when you come off one of those long runs is sleep. You're more like a hibernating bear than a person."

This time, J.O. took a swing at his brother that missed by a large distance.

Shawnee and Lisa both laughed at the banter and antics of the two brothers. Shawnee sensed the bond of deep affection that ran between them.

J.O. faced the two girls and said, "I'm afraid he's right. I don't sleep all that well in a truck."

"I thought the sleeper of those trucks was plush and comfortable," Lisa said.

"Oh, I suppose you could say that, but if you can imagine sleeping on top of your washer and dryer when they are running, that is a little bit what it's like."

Everyone chuckled at the image his words created.

"Say, I have an idea," Tate broke in with sudden enthusiasm. "Why don't the four of us get together next Saturday and go to the dunes west of Rexburg for an evening of dune jumping and picnicking?"

Lisa immediately jumped in. "That sounds like a great idea." She turned to Shawnee as she spoke.

Shawnee was immediately caught. She had sensed that this moment was coming and tried to anticipate what she would say. If she were honest with herself, she had to admit that spending an evening with J.O. left her heart pounding with excitement. There had not been one time all evening that he had disappointed her. There was nothing about him that she didn't like, except one thing—religion. But even with that, there had been that moment at the table when he had admitted his openness to her beliefs. Her eyes locked with Lisa's and she read the excitement and thrill there—the open pleading. Lisa was taken with Tate and wanted to pursue the relationship. It was evident that Tate was in favor of the idea as well.

"That does sound like fun," Shawnee said, "but what is dune jumping?"

Both brothers looked at each other as if incredulous. "You've never been dune jumping?"

Shawnee and Lisa exchanged glances. "No. Never heard of it."

This time it was Tate and J.O. who exchanged glances. "Then all we can say," J.O. said, with a mischievous look in his eye, "is wait and see. There is no sport quite like it."

"Then I guess you'll just have to show us," Shawnee said, a challenge in her voice.

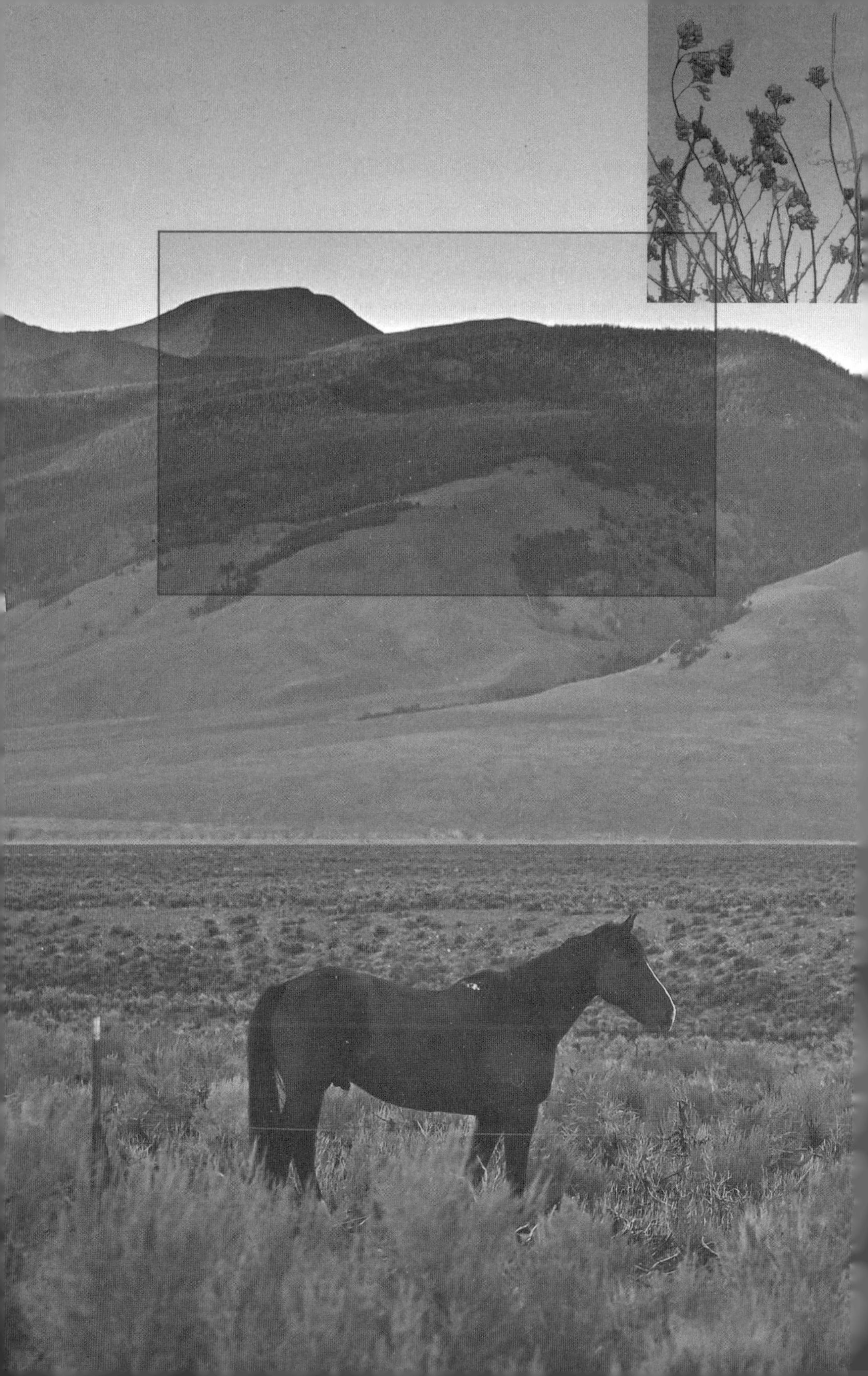

Chapter Eight

CHALLIS, IDAHO, JULY 2021

"Okay, let's review the plan one more time and see if we've missed anything," Johnson said. He slid his chair closer to the table and placed a beefy arm on it.

Trent Lawson leaned forward and listened carefully as Johnson reviewed each step of the operation. As Claude looked at the other two, she realized she was the only one who seemed bored by the tedium of plan and re-plan.

Small and petite in build, Claude stood barely five-foot-three and weighed scarcely more than a hundred pounds. Her hair was short, dark brown, and full of curls and wave. She gazed on the world through rich, brown eyes that should have been warm and attractive, but instead were cold and flat.

As she watched the two men practically drooling over the map, she felt contempt register on her face. Claude knew that her slender figure and soft features made her attractive to almost every man alive. For most of her adult life, she had studied the art of tantalizing men and manipulating them to her purposes. Her natural gifts had served her well. There had been few things she had not been able to obtain if she wanted them, which was exactly what brought her here now. Gold! Several million dollars' worth of gold beckoned to her like a siren's song. *For that kind of reward, I can endure this putrid game for two more weeks.*

Claude leaned forward to study the map, her countenance instantly changing to mirror the expression on Johnson's face. For the next several minutes, she assisted them as they reviewed every part of the plan again. When they finished, Johnson stood up and reached for her hand. When she stood, he pulled her into his arms, kissing her quickly as he did so.

"Two more weeks, baby," he said exultantly, "and we'll be the newest millionaires in Europe."

She returned his embrace, but her revulsion and disgust almost made her push him away. She bit back the retort that formed in her mind. *Only in* your *plans, you bloated tub of guts.*

||||||||||||||||||

"Going out again?" Shawnee asked as Lisa came bouncing through the kitchen of their off-campus Pocatello apartment.

"We're going bowling," Lisa answered, the excitement evident in her voice.

"You two have been together every night this week. How are you getting your homework done?"

Lisa laughed. "Concentrated studying."

Shawnee smiled. "What in the world does that mean?"

"That means make the most of every minute of the day, and don't fall asleep when you study."

Shawnee got up and followed Lisa back to where she stood at the mirror touching up her makeup. "You really like him, don't you?"

Lisa's expression sobered. "I do. I've never felt this way about anyone before."

"Are you sure he's what you want?"

Lisa looked surprised. "Shawnee, I thought you liked Tate."

"I do, Lisa. I do. It's not that."

"Then what?"

Shawnee stumbled for words. She shouldn't have said anything. It just came out. Lisa's faith was as delicate as newly sprouted corn. There was more that she did not understand about the Latter-day Saints than she did understand. This was not the time to challenge her on her interests in a man who did not share the same faith and beliefs.

"Well, it's just that—well—I don't want to see you get hurt."

Lisa studied her for a moment. Finally, she smiled. "It's okay, Shawnee. If it makes you feel any better, I'm not sure about anything at this point. I like him and we have fun together, but beyond that I'm not committing to anything."

Shawnee smiled, shrugged, and started to turn away.

Lisa's next words stopped her cold. "Do you miss him?"

"What do you mean?" Shawnee asked, turning slowly back around.

"Come on, Shawnee. Don't play games with me. I've seen the way you look at J.O. and how he looks at you. I'm no physicist, but there's some definite energy between you two. Everyone can see it. You haven't seen him since Sunday, and now he's somewhere between here and California. Do you miss him?"

"I—I don't know yet."

Lisa was an intense person. There was nothing mellow about her. She bored in. "What do you mean, you don't know? This guy makes Justin, as perfect as he was, look like a vagrant alley cat. Look me in the eye and tell me one thing that's wrong with him."

"There's nothing wrong with him."

"Then what's the problem?"

"I don't know," she said evasively. "I guess I'm just being stupid. What time will you be back tonight?"

Lisa was astute enough to recognize when she was being put off. She ignored the question. "Shawnee, he'll be here in two days, and the two of you will be spending the better part of the day together. You had better know by then what you are going to do."

Lisa's words slammed home like the coupling of train cars. She was right. "I already do, Lisa. I already do."

"What then?"

"We can only be friends," Shawnee said with resignation.

"What! Why?" Before Shawnee could answer, Lisa continued. "Don't tell me. Let me guess. Religion! Right?"

Shawnee didn't like the tone in her friend's voice, but there was no turning back now. The die was cast. Lisa may have been her best friend, but that did not negate the strong sense of justice and fairness that spawned the indignant tone in her voice now. This was not going to be easy.

"Lisa, would it surprise you to know that I have stronger feelings for J.O. than for any guy I have ever met?"

"Then why just friends? Guys like him don't come along that often."

Shawnee chuckled softly. "I vaguely recall you saying something similar to me about Justin."

"Don't change the subject," Lisa growled.

"Alright, alright. Remember Cindea Kelly, that girl at school?"

"Yeah. So?"

"You probably don't know this, but she's divorced. During her freshman year, she fell in love with a student from Germany who was studying here."

Lisa seemed genuinely surprised. "I didn't know that. What happened?"

"Well, after they got married, they moved to Germany, where they had two kids. It was hard for her. She couldn't speak the language. She didn't know the customs or the culture. He expected her to make all the changes, and—well, you can pretty well figure how well that went."

Lisa seemed thoughtful. "Divorced," she mused.

"Yes, divorced, and you should take a careful look at her. She's been through so much that she hardly looks like her old self. She's lost so much weight from the strain of it all that she's practically skeletal. If it weren't for her parents taking her in, she would be on the street as a welfare case. She's a mess—and what's worse," Shawnee bored in now with intensity, "she's a mess with two little children who will probably never know their father."

"I think I understand," Lisa said quietly.

"Do you?" Shawnee pressed, her own anguish heightening the sharpness in her voice. "Do you think I want to take a chance on doing something like that to my own life? The differences between J.O. and me run way deeper than language or customs. They're fundamental matters of the heart. We live two totally different lifestyles. I go to church. He doesn't. I love God and want to follow Him. J.O. doesn't even seem to know if He exists." Tears came to her eyes as she continued. "Do you really think I want to take that kind of risk with something so important to me?" The lump in her throat overpowered her voice and she turned away. The pain she felt seemed as though it was more than she could bear. She was surprised when arms circled her from behind. She turned and looked into Lisa's moist, brown eyes.

"You really do care about him, don't you?"

Shawnee nodded and then buried her face against Lisa's shoulder as the emotion overtook her.

|||||||||||||||||

J.O. glanced at his watch. He had been running for almost an hour now. It was time to head back, shower, and get on the road. If all went well, he would be home by nightfall. As he came to the next intersection, he turned right. By his calculations, if he went about five blocks and then right again, it would bring him back to his truck, parked at a truck stop on the outskirts of Las Vegas. Unable to sleep, he had risen at five and gone for a run to clear his head.

Within five minutes, J.O. was back at the truck. He unlocked it and had just retrieved his duffle bag from the sleeper when he heard the sound of a woman's voice from the truck next to him. As he stepped to the ground, she came across the front of his truck on her way to the casino's restaurant, swiping at her disheveled hair. He recognized her instantly. The previous evening, he had rolled into this casino/truck stop dog-tired and ready for some food and sleep. He had eaten in a daze and walked out of the restaurant. As he had passed in front of the long line of parked trucks, he noticed an attractive young woman knocking on the driver's door of a rig. He had stopped and briefly studied the situation. She was young, probably in her early twenties, with attractive features, wearing the kind of clothing and makeup that identified her occupation. The driver of the truck had opened his door. J.O. was too far away to hear what was said, but the door shut, and the woman had moved on to the next truck, where she had knocked on the door. With a sad smile and a shake of his head, he had moved on to his own truck. A prostitute. She was what the drivers called a "pavement princess." He had seen his fair share in his years on the road, but something about them repulsed him. No matter how pretty they were, there was something base and ugly about them that had kept him away.

    J.O. locked the door of the truck, shouldered the duffle bag, and walked into the casino to shower and eat breakfast. The woman catapulted his thoughts in motion. *What sort of men are attracted to such women? Do most men marry women who have the same character they do? What kind of woman do I deserve to marry? What kind do I want to marry?* The last question answered itself in a vivid mental picture of a lovely, blond nurse back in Idaho. *She's everything I've ever wanted, and more, but am I worthy of her? Am I good enough?* A pang of sadness pierced him as the sum of his self-inventory left him woefully lacking. A small voice inside spoke accusingly, "You're *not* good enough!" He shoved the thought down and headed for the showers.

Chapter Nine

THE SAND DUNES WEST OF REXBURG, IDAHO

"This is it," J.O. said.

"What? Where?" Shawnee said, sitting up and looking around.

Without warning, J.O. suddenly turned the wheel hard to the left and gunned the engine. The four-wheel-drive Jeep Rubicon left the pavement and leaped forward, its oversize tires digging deep and throwing sand high into the air. The Jeep chewed its way to the top of a small dune. J.O. spun the wheel and revved the engine. The Jeep spun in a circle, throwing sand everywhere. He then straightened the wheel and drove off what looked like the vertical edge of the dune. As they plunged over the edge, Shawnee grabbed for the dashboard handholds and screamed. From the backseat, Lisa did the same. The Jeep went down the short slope into a rocky ravine. Instead of slowing down, he gunned the engine again and grabbed another gear. Directly in front of them loomed a massive dune with a long, steep face. Shawnee's eyes grew wide and she turned to J.O.

"Oh no," she yelled over the roar of the engine. "You're not going up that?"

J.O. turned and had only enough time to grin as the Jeep shot up the slope at close to fifty miles per hour. Expertly, he controlled the wildly fishtailing Jeep, keeping its nose pointed up the slope. The passengers were thrown in all directions against the restraint of their seat belts, the open top of the Jeep letting the wind and sand blow all over them. They broke over the abrupt edge at the top at close to thirty miles per hour. All four wheels of the Jeep left the ground. The two girls

Rexburg Sand Dunes

screamed again, this time with what seemed like wild delight. The vehicle landed hard. As it did, J.O. stomped the brake and slid the Jeep to a stop on top of the dune. As it came to rest, he shut off the engine and looked over at Shawnee. Much to his relief, she was laughing. He had learned to run the dunes years earlier. It was a favorite—but expensive—sport.

Shawnee shook back her hair and unsnapped her seat belt. "You're crazy," she said with a laugh as she stood up and jumped out of the Jeep. "I think I'd rather walk."

"It's a long way" he countered.

"Yeah, but it's safer."

"Maybe, but it's not nearly as much fun."

She looked at him for a moment. His lopsided grin was showing. Reaching down, she grabbed a handful of sand and threw it at him. "I agree," she said, and took off running.

"Hey!" J.O. protested as the sand hit him.

He took up the chase. After two laps around the Jeep, he tackled her and returned the sand. They came to their feet laughing.

Lisa and Tate jumped out of the Jeep, their hands locked together as they landed.

"If you want to see fun, wait until we bring the bikes up here," Tate said. "That's when it gets really crazy."

"Oh, that's okay," Lisa said. "That was enough for me!"

"Coward!" Tate said, laughing and poking her in the ribs.

"Without a doubt," she said as she ducked away from him.

"This is pretty," Shawnee said, putting her hands on her hips and facing toward the west. "The sand looks like it goes on for miles."

"It does," J.O. said. "I don't understand the geology of this place, but it's a gigantic band of shifting sand in the middle of a sagebrush-and-rock desert. People come from all over to study it and play in it, but that's not all. Turn around and look east."

Shawnee, Lisa, and Tate all turned to the east and looked in the direction J.O. was pointing.

"The Tetons!" Shawnee exclaimed.

Off in the distance the summer haze seemed unusually light, causing the peaks to stand out clear and prominent against the horizon.

"Look how distinct they are," Lisa added. "They're beautiful!"

"And to think we were just there," Tate said.

"It's amazing," Shawnee said thoughtfully. "From here we can see exactly where we were in those mountains, but from up there we would have been hard pressed to pick out this spot where we are now."

"Kind of like life, isn't it?" J.O. said.

The others looked at him curiously.

"Say what?" Tate said.

"Think about it. Those standing on the high ground, those who are doing something with their lives, are the ones we notice, the ones we look to. They stand above the crowd, while the rest of us are just boring landscape, no one standing any higher than the other."

"Hoo, that was deep!" Tate said jokingly. "Any more philosophy, Professor, before we eat?"

J.O. grinned.

"Well, I liked it," Lisa said in J.O.'s defense. "I think he's absolutely right."

"I do too," Shawnee agreed.

"Alright, alright!" Tate said in defeat. "The groveling ignorant bow to the superiority of the intellectuals." He bowed low in mock reverence.

"Well," J.O. said abruptly, "Let's set up a quick camp and do what we came here to do."

Using wood and supplies from the Jeep, they quickly built a small fire and made camp. J.O. had driven them deep enough into the dunes that they were far from the noise of the highway and the interruptions of other dune enthusiasts.

"The food will be ready in about thirty minutes," J.O. called. "Just enough time to do some jumping!"

"This I've got to see," Shawnee said, straightening up where she was tending the fire.

The camp had been built on top of a large dune off to one side, leaving a broad, open area. On its western face, the dune dropped off nearly vertical for about ten feet and then sloped another thirty feet to a rock-strewn ravine below. J.O. trotted across the top of the dune until he was opposite the steep part. He waited while the others joined him.

"Okay," Lisa said, "show us how this is done."

"It's simple," J.O. said as he kicked off his shoes and socks. "You just run and jump for all you're worth."

"You've got to be k—" But before Shawnee could finish the sentence, J.O. took off. His long, powerful legs quickly propelled him to a sprint. When he reached the edge of the dune he leaped up, out, and vanished from sight. A banzai yell split the desert stillness, followed by a muffled thump.

"He's crazy! This guy is bonkers," Shawnee said, laughing as she pulled off her shoes and socks.

"I know," Tate said, "but at least it's never boring with him around."

Shawnee was digging in her feet to get some starting blocks when J.O.'s voice floated back to them. "C'mon, you guys, hurry up. The sand is great!"

With that impetus, Shawnee leapt forward, her feet slipping in the loose, dry sand. In seconds, she covered the fifteen yards across the dune top. As the earth suddenly fell out from under her, her scream started in one pitch and ended in terror. She had no idea it was such a long way down. The landing was surprisingly soft. Sand flew in all directions. She lost her balance and plunged face first into the sand. She came up spitting. J.O. was instantly there to help her.

As she came to her feet, she looked up into his face. "Well?" he said expectantly.

She spit one last mouthful of sand. "I thought for sure I was going to break my leg, but that was great," she said breathlessly. "Let's do it again."

They scrambled back to the top just as Tate went flying by, followed immediately by Lisa. Their yells and screams ended in gales of laughter as they landed in the sand and rolled. All four of them were laughing. J.O. and Shawnee went back to the starting area.

"I'll go first this time," Shawnee said. "I want to see how an expert does it."

"Expert! Right," J.O. said sardonically

Shawnee took off and made the leap. Without the fear of the initial experience, she ran faster and jumped harder. She landed, this time staying on her feet but sinking almost to her knees in the soft, warm sand.

"Clear?" J.O. called from up above.

"Clear!" Shawnee confirmed. "Go for it!"

Shawnee watched and waited. Suddenly J.O. flew over the edge of the dune a full ten feet over her head. The lean form in faded blue jeans hurled gracefully through the air, his legs still kicking like a trained triple-jumper. His movements were controlled and coordinated, like those of a naturally gifted athlete.

J.O. landed seven or eight feet down the slope from where Shawnee had landed.

She clapped her hands at his performance. "I'm impressed."

He extricated himself from the sand and scrambled up to her. "Come on," he said, extending a hand to her, his face flushed with excitement and exertion. "Let's do it together this time."

She took his hand and he pulled her up the slope. Clawing and digging through the churned sand, they reached the top. When he could have let go of her hand, he didn't, holding on to it until they reached the other side of the dune. As they waited for Lisa and Tate to appear, he dropped her hand and dug his feet into the sand to get ready.

Tate and Lisa appeared, laughing almost to the point of tears.

"What happened?" J.O. asked as they approached.

"I lost my balance and rolled," Tate called back. He spit and shook his head. "I've got sand in every place you can imagine."

Lisa erupted in a new wave of laughter. "He looks like a piece of shake-and-bake chicken. All we need to do is fry."

Tate pushed her gently. "You wait. Your turn is coming."

"We're coming through," J.O. called. He turned to Shawnee. "Ready?"

"Ready!"

He reached for her hand. "On three. One! Two! Three!"

At first J.O. was ahead of Shawnee, but she quickly caught up to him. By the time they left the edge, they were matched stride for stride and hand in hand. J.O. tugged on her hand as his powerful leap propelled him past her. She was literally pulled through the air, causing her to land off balance with her feet behind her. His hold on her hand broke, and she rolled wildly down the slope nearly to the bottom of the dune. By the time she stopped, he was instantly at her side.

"Are you alright?" he asked, helping her to her feet. "I'm sorry."

She came up laughing. "I'm fine, but I know what Lisa meant now by shake-and-bake. I'm okay. Really."

"I'm sorry. I guess I jumped a little too hard."

"It was fine. I'll be ready next time."

His expression changed abruptly, and a crooked, mischievous grin lit up his face. "Well, in that case we'd better hit it again." He took her hand and started up the slope. "When they put this new sport in the Olympics, we'll be ready to go."

"In the Olympics," she laughed. "And what would they call it?"

"Figure jumping!"

||||||||||||||||||

The last flame flickered out, leaving only glowing coals. A slight breeze rose out of the southwest, adding just a nip of chill to the desert air. Lisa moved closer to Tate. He put his arm around her and pulled her in. J.O. stood up.

"Unless there is another call for food, I'm going to stow the grub box."

"I'm stuffed," Tate said. "I wouldn't dare eat another bite."

"Me too," Lisa added.

"I'm fine," Shawnee said, "but I'll give you a hand."

She stood and went over to where J.O. was packing the food and gear into a wooden box. It didn't really matter where she went as long as it was away from Tate and Lisa. Their feelings for one another seemed to be growing stronger by the minute, and that was wonderful—for them. But somehow it also made her uncomfortable when J.O. was near. She wished J.O. would hold her the same way, but at the same time she was glad he didn't. They packed the gear without saying a word. When they finished with the box, J.O. called out, "How about a little moonlight jumping before we leave?"

Shawnee looked at him. "You do this in the dark?"

J.O. grinned. "Sure! It's more fun that way. When you jump, you can't see the bottom."

He turned his back and walked toward the launching area.

"You call that fun!" Shawnee called to his retreating back. "Sounds more like suicide!"

Tate and Lisa followed J.O. The sand was cooler and felt wonderful on their feet and between their toes.

"You two go first," J.O. said to Lisa and Tate.

Hand in hand, they took off.

"Let the lovebirds have their time," he said dryly, looking over at Shawnee.

"Thank you!" Shawnee said, relieved.

So, he was as uncomfortable with it as she was. Tate and Lisa leaped, but their hands broke apart as they jumped. The sounds of laughter carried on the breeze. For a moment, Shawnee wondered if J.O. was going to reach for her hand. At that moment he said, "I'll go first if you don't mind."

She smiled at him. "See you at the bottom."

No sooner had Tate and Lisa appeared on top of the dune than J.O. took off. He pushed himself hard, throwing all the power into his legs that his body would give him. All evening Shawnee had seemed tense, like she was holding back, and he thought he knew why, which only frustrated him all the more. There was something powerful between them. He felt it like he never had before, and he perceived that she did as well, but she was stifling it. That was what frustrated him.

He sensed the edge of the dune and kicked harder for speed. Suddenly the brink appeared. He leaped out and up, gravity carrying him down the slope almost to the bottom. He landed perfectly, with his feet sinking into the sand and throwing a large cloud of it out in front of him. He turned around and took two steps toward the top just as Shawnee leaped the edge. J.O. stopped and stared. Directly behind her, the rising moon caught her in full silhouette, its brilliant silver light backlighting her lithe, slender form like an actress on stage. The momentary effect created the illusion of an angel descending from heaven toward him. Her long, blond hair streamed behind her, its color a luminescent silver. It was an electrifying image he would never forget. Unconsciously, he caught his breath. He had never seen anyone or anything more beautiful. How could it be that he would see something like this *twice*?

There was not a sound as she flew toward him. She landed about three feet up the slope from where he stood. Her balance was slightly off, and her momentum catapulted her forward, nearly headlong. She threw her arms out to catch herself. Rather than step aside, J.O. squared himself and caught her by the shoulders, but her momentum carried her deep into his arms and against his chest.

"I've got you," he said, his strong grip holding her firmly.

|||||||||||||||||||

For a moment they were frozen in place. Her feet were barely touching the sand. Slowly her eyes lifted and locked with his. Even in the darkness, there was no missing the feelings she saw there. Unconsciously, she melted into him, savoring the firmness of his muscles and the masculine smell of him. Her breath caught and her heart began to race. All her resolves and frustrations seemed momentarily forgotten. It was the same thing she had felt when they had seen each other at the dredge, except more powerful. Her surroundings became a blur. The cool breeze and brilliant night sky faded into blissful oblivion. She pulled back enough to look into his face. In that suspended moment, she explored every feature of his face and every nuance of his eyes. He was so good to look at. Then, slowly, almost imperceptibly, his face lowered, his eyes searching hers. He was going to kiss her! Her arms went around him, and she found herself rising to meet him. Just as his lips began to brush hers, she caught herself and turned away.

"I'm sorry," she said in a hoarse whisper. "I—I can't."

There was silence for a moment as she looked away, fighting the lump that threatened to choke off her voice. The anguish she felt was unspeakable. She must have hurt him, but when he spoke there was no bitterness.

"I know," he said softly. "I understand. I'm sorry."

She looked at him, a sheen of tears illuminating her eyes. She saw no anger, no resentment, just a look that bespoke the silent pain of understanding.

||||||||||||||||||

"No, please," she said quickly. "It wasn't your fault. I should've never—"

He reached up and gently placed his finger against her lips. "It's okay. There are a lot of things I know I don't know," he looked up into the sky, "but there is one thing that I'm sure of." His eyes came back to hers with a quiet intensity. "I know the differences between us. I know what you are and what I am." He drew a deep breath and looked over her shoulder into the night sky. This was harder than he could've imagined. It felt like his heart was being torn out, but he was not going to play little teenage games with her. He was not going to try to manipulate her feelings. She deserved more respect than that. "Meeting you," he continued, "meeting your family and being here was no accident. I don't know why we met, especially under such unusual circumstances, but I'm sure of this, you were no accident in my life. No matter what happens now."

"J.O.—"

Tate's voice called out from above. "Everything alright down there?"

Shawnee looked startled. She glanced back at J.O., a pleading expression on her face.

"Everything's fine," J.O. called back calmly. "Shawnee and I are going to take a walk for a minute. We'll be right back."

J.O. took her by the arm and led her down into the ravine. They walked about a hundred yards to another dune and sat down in the sand.

As soon as they were seated, J.O. picked up where he had left off. "I've been out of high school long enough, Shawnee. I don't like games. I prefer to say what I feel straight out and let the chips fall where they may."

She nodded in silent agreement.

"We come from totally different backgrounds," he continued. "I know something of what you believe, and I want you to know I would never take that away from you. I wasn't even sure coming here tonight was such a good idea, but I have to tell you the truth. I've felt things for you that I've never felt for anyone else. From that first moment when I saw you in the dredge, I thought you were the most beautiful woman I had ever seen, and then we ran into each other on the mountain. It was no accident. If it were left up to me, I'd chase you like there was no tomorrow." She smiled deeply. He paused and returned her smile, but the smile abruptly went away. "But it's not all up to me. I think I know what you want, and I can't give it to you."

|||||||||||||||||

"Why not?" Shawnee asked softly. She wanted him to keep talking. It was exhilarating to talk to this man. He was composed, mature, and so frank and open that it was nearly startling.

"I've never been religious," he continued. "I think you've known that from the beginning. A lot of strange things have happened to me recently that have really caused me to wonder about what I've always believed about God. Most of those experiences involved you in one way or another. I've felt some powerful things that I don't understand."

"I can help you," she said gently, touching his arm.

"No, you can't." The sadness in his voice was evident even in the dark.

His words hurt, and she looked away. Gently, he touched her cheek and brought her back to look at him. "I wish you could, but it's your faith and my lack of it that stands between us. Your life revolves around your God, and mine doesn't. As much as I—" he hesitated, seeming to search for the right word. "As much as I care about you, I would never put you through that. What you have, you can't give me. I have to find it on my own."

Shawnee sat looking deep into his eyes, exploring their depths. Her first impulse was to protest, to argue with him, to tell him that she could help him find faith—but something told her he was right and to let it go.

"J.O.," she said with sorrow. "This has been really hard for me. I've had feelings for you too that were almost more than I could bear at times, but you're right. My religion does stand in the way. Everything that I am is centered in what I believe. I've wondered what to do, how I was going to tell you." She looked down at the sand for a moment. When her eyes came back up, the sheen of tears was there again. "I've made myself a promise, J.O., that I'll never marry outside the temple. No matter how grateful I may be that you saved my life, or how much I care for you, or for any other man—" her voice caught. "I will never break that promise. I can't!"

She finished speaking and watched him. He looked straight ahead into the night sky for what seemed like a long time. Finally, he turned to her, his face breaking into a large smile. "I hope you never do. I don't know much about temple marriage, but I hope you get it."

Shawnee stared at him, unable to believe what he had just said. Then, with a beaming smile, she threw her arms around him in a fierce embrace. He returned the embrace. He held her for only a moment, and then stood and helped her to her feet.

"C'mon, let's get back before Romeo and Juliet come looking for us."

"Speaking of those two, what are we going to do about them?"

"What *can* we do? They're big enough to decide for themselves how to live."

"Lisa doesn't feel the same way I do, J.O. She's only been investigating the Church for a short time. She thinks I'm crazy for not falling all over you."

J.O. grinned again, that crooked little-boy smile. "I like the way she thinks."

Shawnee laughed and bumped up against his side. He reached and put his arm around her shoulder, and she returned the affection. The tension was gone. It now felt right. There was feeling of peace and mutual understanding that seemed to warm her soul. As friends, they could relax.

||||||||||||||||||

As they walked, J.O. looked toward the north and saw the cup of the Big Dipper in position below the North Star. The cup was full. This matter may be settled as far as she was concerned, but the power of her faith in God left him all but trembling. There would be no peace for him until he knew for himself the truth about God. This time there was just too much at stake to brush it aside!

Chapter Ten

INTERSTATE 80, SOMEWHERE IN NEBRASKA, EARLY AUGUST 2021

J.O. shifted the transmission into its highest gear. Before him lay one of the longest and most boring stretches of road in the entirety of Interstate 80. This part of Nebraska was not known for its scenic vistas. Settling back into the custom air-ride seat, he fitted his Bluetooth earpieces and turned on his New Age classical music. The thought passed fleetingly how strange his tastes in music were for a man of his occupation. He had never met another driver who listened to his kind of music. It probably had something to do with his mother. She had kept the house filled with music when he was young. When she wasn't playing it on the piano, it was on the stereo. After some musical forays into other venues during his teenage years, he had settled with modern classical. This album was called *Mountain Symphony*, and the music was expertly mixed with various sounds of nature. He sighed deeply as the haunting sound of gentle winds set to the piano filled his ears.

He looked out the window. As far as the eye could see was nothing but miles and miles of farms and fields and interminably flat terrain. He leaned forward and glanced up at the sky. Lazy cumulus clouds floated here and there above him. It was a beautiful summer day. He enjoyed these moments when the road was no challenge, and he could lose himself in his thoughts.

Since that night on the dunes, he had seen Shawnee more than he expected—and that was because of Tate and Lisa. Their relationship grew deeper and sweeter with each day, and they usually wanted Shawnee and J.O. with them. Tate's interest had not only blossomed for Lisa, with him spending nearly every minute he could with her, but it had also grown for the Church. To J.O.'s surprise, it looked as though Tate might actually get baptized.

Tate and Lisa had met with the missionaries twice a week for the last two weeks. Lisa had already met with them a couple of times, but since Tate had joined in, they had gone back and started over. A Book of Mormon was on Tate's nightstand, and the bookmark moved noticeably deeper into the book every night. Tate had started going to church with Lisa and Shawnee and had begun going with them to other activities as well. To J.O.'s knowledge, Tate had never spoken two sentences about religion in his entire life, and now, there was no doubt he was changing.

The idea of Tate becoming a religious zealot made his stomach churn every time he thought of it. He had fully expected that Tate would come after him to proselyte him to the faith, but so far, he had never even brought it up. Only Lisa in her innocent exuberance had dared broach the subject. J.O. smiled to himself. It was hard to be upset with Lisa. She was like a volcano of enthusiasm that bubbled with the fire of life. If she occasionally boiled over where she shouldn't, it wasn't because she was intending to hurt anyone. She was just very unrestrained.

It all troubled him. *What happens to a person who is converted? What is going on with Tate? Would this ruin my relationship with him? What was it about religion, especially this one, that engenders such loyalty and devotion from such seemingly intelligent people? Rick James is no fool, no blind sheep. Neither is Shawnee. Is Tate doing what he is doing for the love of God or the love of Lisa?*

J.O.'s thoughts turned to his own experiences. Could he honestly say anymore that his own spiritual feelings were nothing more than a contrivance of the imagination? Was he going to be the blind fool he had accused all religionists of being and close his mind to what he himself had experienced in the last few weeks? Or was he going to be as honest with himself as he had always been? The core question seemed to burn into his mind: could man be happy if he ignored God? Could he ignore what was happening to him? It was as though someone or something from the unseen was trying to reach him—tell him something.

J.O.'s eyes fixed on the freeway in front of him, and all consciousness of the external world faded as his mind began to wrestle with the burning questions of his mind.

<hr>

Renchard Johnson picked up his lunch pail and left the mill. As he started his pickup and drove away, he reached for the cell phone clipped to the dash. Seconds later another phone rang in Jackson, Wyoming.

"Hello."

"Claude?"

"Yes."

"It's time. The chopper and the jet ready and in place?"

"Ready and waiting."

"Let's meet Friday night in Challis at the motel. We'll be in place the next morning. We'll proceed according to plan." Johnson couldn't resist his excitement despite the possibility that the call could be monitored. "And Baby—"

"Yes."

"It's bigger than we thought."

Claude laughed. "That just means a longer party, right?"

Now Johnson laughed. "Absolutely! I love you, Baby. See you tomorrow night." He turned his phone off and suddenly felt the urge to do something he hadn't done in years. He began to whistle in time with a popular song on the radio.

Claude Richards placed the phone back in the receiver and turned. Two men stood looking at her expectantly.

"It's time. We move into place tomorrow night."

Broad smiles broke over the faces of both men. Claude stood and crossed the room. She moved gracefully into the arms of the taller of the two men and kissed him.

"I can't wait for this to be over," she said, her voice like the purr of a cat. "But I have to say it will all be worth it just to see the look on his face."

Both men tipped their heads back and laughed heartily. Claude laughed with them, but the merriment she felt still did not soften the hardness behind her eyes.

||||||||||||||||

The road between Hoback Junction and Alpine, Wyoming, winds along the Snake River at times several hundred feet above the roiling stream. On the best of days, the road is dangerous, but today it was especially treacherous. Summer thunderstorms had left the highway nearly as slick as if it were iced over. J.O. was unusually tense and impatient. He had run against deadlines before, but for some reason, this one was the most pressing he had ever known. He pushed his rig as hard as he could on the hills and sharp corners. His frustration was heightened by the fact that the car in front of him was going at least fifteen miles per hour under the speed limit. J.O. had tried every trick he knew to let the car in front of him know that he was in a hurry. The guy seemed totally oblivious to everything but the wonderful scenery in every direction. Gritting his teeth, J.O. sweltered in his driver's seat. The only way he was going to make any time was to get around this guy. He would lose a full thirty minutes following him. But there were very few places for a rig as long and slow as his to pass.

J.O. waited and watched for his opening, following the car as close as he could. Suddenly, there it was. If he hurried, there might be just enough time to make it. He hit his left turn signal, checked his mirror, and pulled the wheel to the left. He rammed his accelerator all the way to the floor, but for some strange reason there was not the usual responding surge of power. The truck seemed sluggish. Slowly it gained on the car until he was driving alongside it. He cast a nervous glance out his left window. The Snake River was several hundred feet down a nearly vertical embankment.

The moment his eyes returned forward his heart leaped into his throat. A large motor home rounded the corner ahead of him in the oncoming lane. Its lights flashed in warning as it bore down on him. In an instant, the gravity of his situation became clear. The oncoming vehicle was not slowing down—and there was not enough room to pass three abreast, even if they wanted to. He was now going faster than sixty-five miles per hour, and there was no way to stop in time. He had less than three seconds to do *something*. J.O. touched his brakes and slowed the rig as he tried to get back behind the car he was trying to pass, but to his utter horror and astonishment, the car slowed with him. J.O. looked at the driver of the other car. The man was laughing insanely.

"What are you doing, you idiot!" J.O. screamed, waving his arm at the man. "Let me get back!"

The man only laughed harder as he made an obscene gesture.

J.O. looked forward again. Time was up. Someone was going to die if he didn't do something. At that instant he made his decision and jerked the wheel of his rig hard to the left. The rear axles of his trailer raised off the highway as the rig threatened to flip.

"No!" J.O. screamed hoarsely, as the sixty-five-foot rig left the pavement and shot over the cliff toward the roiling river below.

Slowly, gracefully, like some great juggernaut, the huge rig rolled in mid-air. J.O. watched the world out his windows go from sky to river to ground. Any moment he knew the eighty-thousand-pound rig would smash down on top of him and snuff out his life like a bug under a car tire.

"Oh Father—forgive me—" he pleaded, his eyes clenched shut.

J.O. shot up in his bed, throwing the light blanket across the truck's sleeper. His chest heaved as he struggled for breath, and he looked around wildly in the darkened interior. Disoriented, he collapsed back onto his bed, unable to figure out where he was or what had happened. Slowly, he sat back up and tried to orient himself.

The next moment his recovering senses told him that he was panting as if he had just run a sprint, and his body was soaked with sweat. Suddenly all of it flooded back. He was in his sleeper in Cheyenne, Wyoming. He had stopped for the night, eaten supper, and gone to bed unusually tired, more from mental fatigue than from physical exertion. He had had a nightmare. He would be home tomorrow.

His thoughts turned to the dream, and it came back with such awful clarity that it took an effort in the darkness to convince himself that it was not real. There are some dreams—nightmares—that are so real that it sometimes takes several minutes of battling with the senses to determine what is reality. J.O.'s hands trembled violently as he remembered the rig going over the cliff. Every driver dreads such a thing happening—and his dream had been so real it was as though he had just lived through it.

Unconsciously and unbidden, a thought formed in his mind as his eyes closed against the replaying images.

"Please, Father," he heard himself say.

His eyes shot open as the significance of the words hit him. If it was true that there are no atheists in a foxhole, had he just found his foxhole?

||||||||||||||||

"Shawnee, you in here?'

Lisa tapped lightly on the bedroom door then peeked tentatively into the room.

Shawnee was sitting on her bed in her pajamas with her back propped against her pillows for support, reading from her Book of Mormon.

"It's okay, Lisa. Come on in."

"I didn't think you'd still be up this late."

Shawnee smiled at her. "I waited up for you."

"Tell me you're kidding, right?"

Shawnee laughed. "I'm kidding. I worked late at the hospital finishing up some paperwork. I just got home."

"I wish I could say that," Lisa said, as she sat down on the edge of the bed.

"Say what?" Shawnee asked.

"That I had finished up some paperwork. I'm so far behind in school it'll take me all weekend just to get caught up."

"Those men do require sacrifices, don't they?" Shawnee teased. "I thought you were doing some, now what did you call it, 'concentrated studying,' wasn't it?'

Lisa grinned sheepishly. "I'm afraid if you concentrate it too much it disappears entirely."

Shawnee laughed lightly and then grew serious. "You're in love with him, aren't you?"

Lisa sighed. "Without a doubt. If he asked me to marry him right now, I would without hesitation. These last few weeks have been the happiest of my life. I've not only found Tate, but I've found the gospel at the same time."

"You mean—" Shawnee hesitated, not sure if she was hearing right—"you got an answer?"

Tears welled up in Lisa's eyes. She nodded her head. Shawnee stood and enthusiastically threw her arms around her best friend.

"That is so awesome, Lisa! What happened?'

"Tate and I drove to the Idaho Falls Temple tonight and walked

Idaho Falls Temple

around the grounds. We eventually wound up on the other side of the river sitting on the bank, staring at the temple as it got dark, and talking about our feelings. Oh, Shawnee, it was the most wonderful, powerful thing I have ever felt. As we talked, we discovered that we both felt the same. We both felt like it was true. Then Tate turned so that he was sitting directly across from me on the grass. He took both of my hands in his and asked if we could say a prayer together. It was the most beautiful prayer I have ever heard. He told Heavenly Father that we felt it was true, but we wanted to know more surely. As he prayed, I felt like I was on fire inside. I could hardly breathe. It was so powerful. It felt like it went through every part of my body. When he finished the prayer, I looked at him and I knew that he was feeling the same thing."

Lisa was crying openly.

"Then what?" Shawnee prompted.

"We talked about it. He *was* feeling the same thing I was. There were tears in his eyes too. Oh, Shawnee, it was so amazing. I've never felt so much love in my life, but not just for Tate. I felt it coming from God also. I know now what it means to say I am a child of God."

Lisa stopped speaking. Shawnee stared at her in open amazement. Overcome with joy, she threw her arms around Lisa again.

"Oh, Lisa. I am so happy for you. What are you going to do now?"

Lisa pulled back and laughed through her tears. "What can I do? I'm going to go with it. It's true!"

"What about Tate?"

"He's going to be baptized as soon as he finishes meeting with the missionaries."

"When?"

"I'm not sure, but soon."

A sobering thought penetrated Shawnee's euphoria. "I wonder what J.O. will think?"

The smile slowly faded from Lisa's face. "Tate and I talked about that. J.O. is his best friend. He knows how J.O. feels about religion and God, and he's been very careful to avoid the subject with him. It's tearing him up inside to think that he might lose his relationship with his brother, but after tonight, he says if that happens, then so be it. He quoted an interesting thought he had read somewhere that said, 'Be right, and then be easy to live with, but in that order.'"

Shawnee sat back against her pillow, lost in her own thoughts for a moment. "Oh, J.O.," she said aloud. "Please open your heart. Don't let stubborn pride rob you of that which is most dear and precious."

At that instant, Shawnee's cellphone buzzed on the nightstand so abruptly that it shocked both of them from their thoughts. She snatched it up before it could assault them again. As she lifted it, she saw the ID. It was J.O. "Hello?"

"Shawnee, this is J.O. I'm sorry for calling so late, but it's important. I don't have time to explain, but I need to talk to you as soon as possible. Could we get together tomorrow night?"

"J.O., are you alright? Has something happened to you? You sound upset."

"I'm fine, and yes, something has happened—something I have to talk to you about. May I see you tomorrow night?"

"Of course. What time?"

"I'm not sure. I'm sorry. I know that's pretty bad manners, but I'm in Cheyenne, Wyoming, right now. I'll leave here as soon as I can and get there as soon as possible, but it may be late."

"That's fine. I'll be here."

"Thanks, Shawnee. You're the best!"

"You're welcome, J.O."

"Okay, see you tomorrow night."

"Tomorrow night then," Shawnee echoed, "J.O.—"

"Yes?"

"Please be careful." It overwhelmed her how much she actually meant those words.

"I will. Thanks. Good night!"

As the phone went dead, Shawnee sat for a moment holding the phone in her hand, a dazed look on her face.

"Well, what did he want?" Lisa asked.

"He wants to see me tomorrow night. He wants to talk."

Lisa clapped her hands with seeming excitement but stopped in the middle of a clap at Shawnee's next words.

"Something's wrong. Something's happened to him. He wouldn't tell me what it is."

Chapter Eleven

POCATELLO, IDAHO

J.O. brought the Jeep to a stop in front of Shawnee's apartment complex. Nearly twenty-two straight hours without sleep was taking its toll. He could feel the tightness around his eyes and the bone-weariness that penetrated through his entire body. As the engine stopped, he sat for a moment without moving and took a deep breath. A light evening breeze ruffled his hair. He had come into town less than an hour before, stopping at home long enough to shower, change clothes, kiss his mother, and run out the door again. Why had he called Shawnee after that dream? He had berated himself all the way across Wyoming for that. If he was intending to put distance between himself and her, this was not the way to do it. But it had seemed like the right thing to do then. He shook his head. Who was he kidding? There was not a living soul who would even come close to understanding what he was feeling and why it was so important. Unbuckling the seat belt, he slipped out of the Jeep and walked to the front door. It was later than he had wanted. The sun was just dropping below the western horizon. His pulse quickened despite himself at the thought of seeing her again.

He reached for the doorbell but pulled his hand back, choosing instead to rap lightly on the door. It opened immediately. Shawnee stood framed in the doorway, wearing a loose-fitting white denim shirt and faded blue jeans. Her hair hung loose and natural down her back, brushed to a glossy sheen.

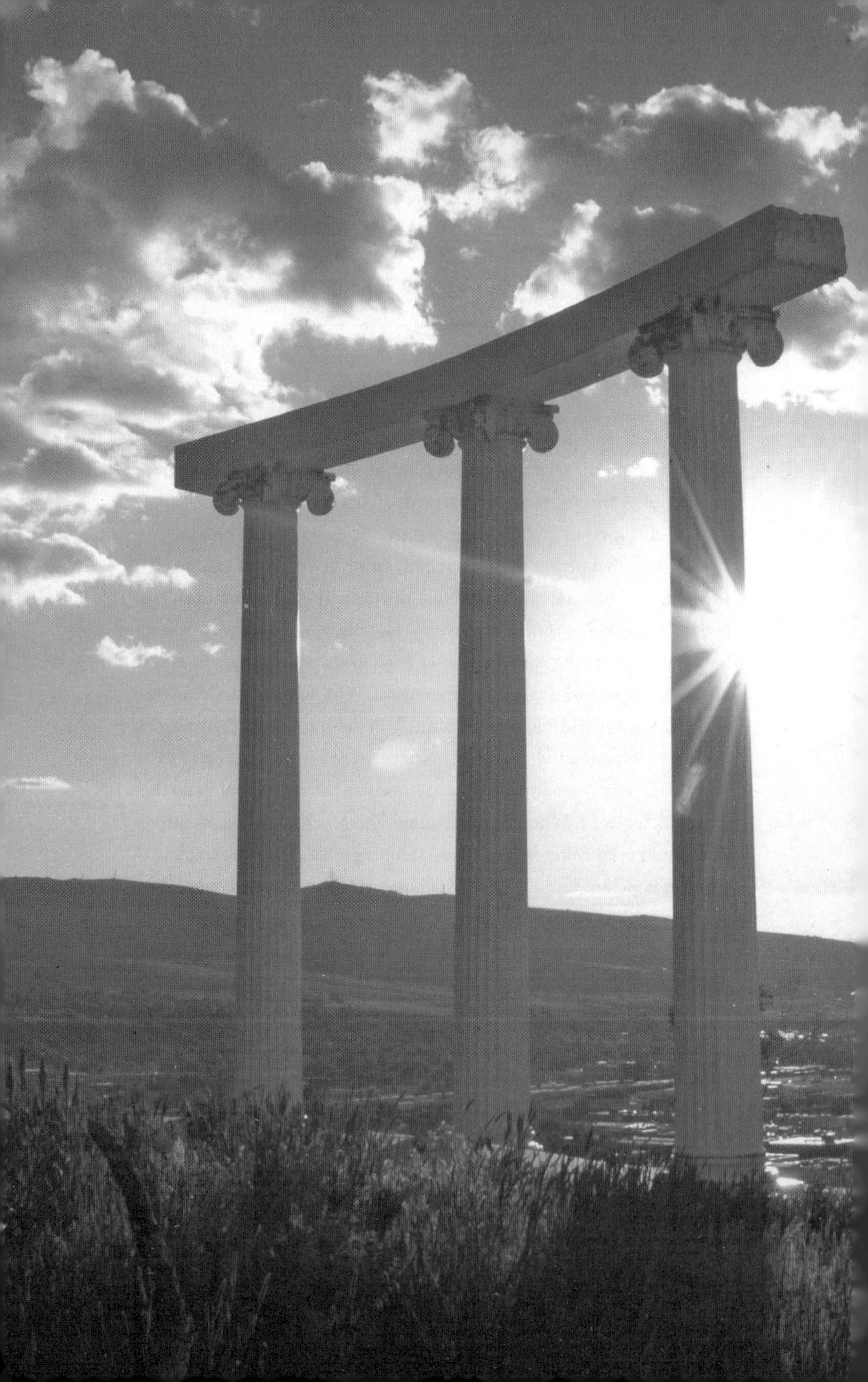

She said nothing. Her eyes were wide, and for a moment she just stood looking at him in the fading evening light. Then tenderness and compassion filled her delicate features.

"Oh, J.O.," she said, as she stepped forward and embraced him. "Are you alright?"

He chuckled softly. "Do I look that bad? I'm fine." He took her into his arms. "I'm sorry I'm so late."

"It's fine. Don't worry about it."

For a moment they just stood in each other's arms. After a few seconds, she backed up without letting him go and looked up at him intently.

"Would you mind if we took a walk?" J.O. asked. "There are some things I want to tell you."

"I'd love to," she replied. Stepping out the door, she pulled it closed behind her.

Just above the Idaho State University campus, atop Red Hill, stands a prominent landmark—four gleaming, white, Greek-style pillars, overlooking the campus and the city of Pocatello. Shawnee and J.O. walked toward Red Hill, making small talk as they went. He was relieved that Shawnee didn't push him or pry. He would tell her everything when he was ready.

By the time they reached the top of the Hill, the sun had set, and the entire western sky was ablaze with color. As J.O. stepped up onto the concrete platform supporting the pillars, he offered a hand to Shawnee. She stepped up beside him.

"I went to school here for years and I have never been up here." She turned to the north and let her eyes sweep over the darkening city. "This is beautiful."

J.O. stood beside her and looked out over the city. "I come up here when I want to think and can't go to the mountains. It has a great view at night."

"So I see."

J.O. moved over and sat down under the pillars. Shawnee came and sat beside him. He suddenly felt ill at ease.

"Shawnee, there are some things that I need to tell you, and I'm not exactly sure why."

She turned to look directly into his eyes. "I'm listening."

"I hardly know where to begin," he said, laughing nervously. "I drove all night and all day to get here, and now I don't know what to say."

"Let's start with this. What happened to you just before you called me that had you so shook up?"

He smiled at her. "That obvious, huh?"

She nodded, her eyes never leaving his face.

J.O. told her about the nightmare. When he was finished, she asked, "What do you suppose it meant?"

"I don't know if it meant anything."

"I think it did. I think Heavenly Father is trying to tell you something."

"Like what?"

"Well, maybe that He's there and He's getting tired of waiting for you."

J.O. looked at her and slowly grinned. "I can see why Lisa and you are such good friends. You're both outspoken."

"I'm sorry," she said. "I don't want to offend you, but I think it's the truth." She reached out and gripped his forearm. He looked down at her slender, delicate fingers. "J.O., what is the problem with you and God? Why is it such a problem to simply let your head believe what your heart is telling you?"

J.O. sighed and looked away. When he began to speak there was pain in his voice.

"About twelve years ago, my family was living in the Lemhi Valley near Salmon, Idaho. We had a nice ranch, and we were doing well. Then

Dad got cancer. Within a short time, it had spread throughout his whole body. When he was no longer able to work, the rest of us tried to fill his shoes, but it was no use. We were going under, but that wasn't the worst part by far. I watched my dad go from a strong and powerful man to a weak and sickly shell of the man he once was. I can still see him on that bed, wasting away. We had never been much of a religious family. Dad and Mom were good, honest people who lived decent lives, but they never took us to church or anything like that. When Dad got sick, I began to pray with all the belief that a young boy can muster. I prayed every night and morning, and sometimes in between, that he would get well."

He turned to face her, his voice rising. "Shawnee, I believed that my dad would get well." His voice fell again. "He never did. He died on Christmas Day. By spring, we were forced to sell the ranch. It broke my mother's heart. That ranch had been Mom and Dad's lifelong dream."

"So, you were angry with God then?" she whispered.

He nodded his head. "Yes. It was always easier after that to find reasons to believe that He wasn't there, or if He was, He didn't care about us." He smiled. "If I wanted to, I could lay out a pretty impressive argument of why there is no God."

"Considering how smart you are, I have no doubt that you could, but I notice that you're not. You're also speaking of your unbelief in the past tense, not the present. What's changed?"

"Well, that started just before I met you."

He started with the incident of the religious zealot and rehearsed all the experiences that had left him so uncertain of his convenient atheism.

A grin split his face as he continued. "You're probably the most convincing proof I've received that there must be a God."

"Me! Why?"

"The way we met, I mean at the dredge and then again the way we ran into each other in the mountains. It's like I said at the dunes, there is no way it could be an accident."

"I don't think it was either," she said, putting a hand on his arm.

"There is another reason why you make me believe that there's a God."

"What's that?"

"It's the way I feel every time I'm around you."

"How's that?" she asked quietly.

"It's hard to describe, but you remember when those clouds parted on the Middle Teton and you turned and looked at me and told me that you knew there was a God?"

"I remember," she said, laughing lightly. "I kicked myself for a week after that for being so bold."

"You were right."

Her head snapped around to stare at him.

"I can't explain it, but I knew you were right. It was just as sure as if I had always known it myself."

"Well, then—"

"I know what you're going to say," he interrupted. "Why don't I just believe and let it go at that?"

She nodded.

"Because the feeling keeps fading, and I'm not always sure anymore."

Shawnee at first said nothing, then finally asked, "So why are you telling me all this?"

He smiled again. "Because I trust you, and I think you are the one who can answer my questions."

A pained expression crossed her face that was evident to J.O., even in the darkness.

"What is it?" he asked. "Did I say something wrong?"

"No," she said quickly, "it's just that I'm not sure I can."

J.O. looked away, not liking the bitter disappointment that tasted like bile in his mouth. "I understand," he said.

He stood and walked across the platform to the edge that dropped straight off into the city below. The cool evening breeze felt like a caress on his cheek. He turned his face into it and stood stock still with his back straight, his feet apart, and his hands in his pockets.

She walked to his side and lightly gripped his upper arm with both hands. "No, I don't think you do understand," she said gently. "I'd love to help you. I'm just not sure I can answer all your questions, but that doesn't mean I don't want to try."

He seemed relieved as he turned to look down into her face. "There's one more reason why I wanted to ask you for help."

"What's that?" she asked.

"When I woke up from that dream and finally oriented myself—" he paused. "The *first* thought that popped into my head was that I had better not ignore this, or else."

"There was a second," she prompted.

"Yes. Your face came into my mind as clear as a photograph. It woke me up completely, especially with what happened next."

"J.O., please tell me. I can't stand all this suspense."

"I don't know what else to call it, but a voice seemed to speak inside my head that told me to come to you and your dad and that you would help me solve this once and for all."

||||||||||||||||||

Shawnee turned away, not wanting him to see the burning in her eyes. Her joy at that moment was incalculable. They were the very words she wanted most to hear him say. He was right. She *was* supposed to help him. He pulled her back to face him and smiled down at her. Tenderly, he brushed away the tears that spilled onto her cheeks.

"Does this mean you'll help me or that I should jump off the cliff here?" he teased as nodded his head in the direction of the steep slope two steps in front of him.

She put her hands against his chest and pushed him gently. "Of course, I'll help you," she said, laughing. "When do we start?"

"I've thought about that. I have a delivery in Salmon tomorrow that will take most of the day. I thought maybe you could come along, and we could talk."

"Sounds like fun. Conveniently, it's my day off at the hospital. What time do you want to leave?"

He looked a little sheepish. "About 6:00 a.m."

She wasn't the least bit perturbed as she looked at her watch and back up at him. "I think we'd better get some sleep then."

"I think you're probably right."

He reached for her hand and started down the trail off the hill. A burden the size of boulders seemed lifted off his shoulders.

They turned the corner and approached Shawnee's apartment. It was a perfect evening. The temperature was pleasant. A light breeze moved through the tops of the trees, filling the air with a soothing, rustling sound. The sweet smell of well-nurtured flowers wafted on the breeze.

They reached the door and stood briefly, looking at each other. Shawnee spoke first. "J.O., can I ask you a question?" She was asking as much to keep him from leaving as to satisfy her curiosity. "What does your name mean? What does *J.O.* stand for?"

A cloud of emotion seemed to pass over his face that she couldn't read. He looked down at her, as though studying her face. She realized then that the full answer to that question might not be something he liked to talk about.

"I'm sorry—" she started to say.

"Joseph Orson," he said. "It stands for Joseph Orson. My father's name was Joseph and my grandfather's name was Orson. I'm named after both of them."

"Joseph," she repeated while looking at him, as though trying the name on him to see if it fit. "I like it. It has power and dignity."

"Everyone's always called me J.O."

"Does anyone ever call you Joseph?"

"No!" he said quickly. "Only one person ever did, and that was my dad. He always called me Joseph." A faraway tone crept into his voice. "I can still hear him saying it. He always used that name with great respect, as though it was something I was to live up to."

Shawnee understood. If J.O. held anything sacred, it was the name his father had given him and the memory of his father. No wonder he was hesitant to tell anyone about it.

"Well," J.O. said firmly. "It's late, and I need to go."

He gently squeezed her hand and turned toward his Jeep. He had gone only a couple of steps when she spoke to his retreating back.

"Good night—Joseph."

He stopped in mid-stride and slowly turned around. As their eyes met, she smiled at him tenderly. After a moment, he smiled back, as though to say, *Only you can call me that.*

Near Stanley, Idaho

Chapter Twelve

NEAR STANLEY, IDAHO, AUGUST 2021

Claude felt the gentle bump as the chopper touched down just a few miles below the headquarters of the Cougar Mountain Gold Mine. A quick glance at Trent told her he was as eager as a child at Christmas. He grinned broadly, his hawk nose hanging over the smile and splitting it in half. Throwing open the cargo door, she jumped out, pulling the signs and gear with her. The blades of the chopper ground to a stop as the pilot killed the engine.

Ren Johnson materialized out of the darkness, his portly frame wrapped in tight-fitting coveralls that made him resemble an overstuffed sausage. He began helping her with the equipment. Trent jumped down beside her and pulled on his workman's coveralls.

The first traces of the impending dawn were barely visible above the steep, pine-covered mountains, but as deep in the valley as they were, it would be some time before the sun actually touched them. Wordlessly, they moved into a huddle and each held up their watches.

Johnson spoke, saying, "4:52 a.m."

They gathered up their gear and moved in the direction of the mine access road. In minutes they were settled in thick brush in their prearranged positions.

||||||||||||||||

The sound of the alarm brought J.O. straight up out of bed. His first conscious thought was of the company he would be sharing today. He dropped to the floor and did a hundred pushups. By 5:45 a.m., he had run three miles, showered, and now stood at Shawnee's doorstep with a pair of worn leather work gloves stuffed in the back pocket of faded jeans. He knocked softly. The door swung open and she stepped out to meet him, wearing jeans and a loose-fitting, button-down, cotton shirt. It was a look of unpretentious beauty—no makeup, just the real thing.

He offered her his arm. "I didn't know it was possible to look that good so early in the morning," he quipped.

"Don't look too deep," she said. "This is only a mask. My eyes are propped open with toothpicks."

They both laughed, and he helped her into the Jeep. He went around and climbed in, and she handed him a sealed drinking cup and a granola bar.

"Just in case you didn't get breakfast," she said.

He laughed out loud. "Miss James, you think of everything, don't you?"

She raised her cup of orange juice as if to toast him and said, "My mother taught me well. Always feed a man before you expect anything productive from him."

He reached and touched her cup with his. "Your mother is a very wise woman."

Within ten minutes, they were in the loaded semi and on the road to Salmon.

||||||||||||||||

The armored truck moved slowly on the rough road as it made the steady climb toward the mine.

"About time they graded this road again," growled the driver. "You'd think for all the money they make in this place, they'd pave it."

The armed passenger agreed as he artfully attempted to drink a cup of coffee rather than wear it. The truck slowed to a crawl as it traversed a narrow, one-lane bridge over a tiny mountain stream. The driver glanced at his watch. "We're right on schedule," he said to his partner.

It was 8:46 a.m. In ten minutes, they would be at the mine.

||||||||||||||||||

"They just passed the bridge," Johnson said into his radio.

"I've got them," Claude said as the truck rounded a rock outcropping and bore down on her position.

"Can you tell how many are in the truck?"

"I can only see two."

"I'm almost positive there would be three of them due to the size of the shipment." It was Lawson's voice. "The other man would be in the back."

||||||||||||||||||

The driver yawned as he pulled up in front of the mill office. Of all the runs he made, he hated this one the most because they had to get up so early. They had been here so many times even the scenery was getting old.

Minutes later, with $20 million worth of raw gold and silver ore secured in the truck, they climbed in and started down the mountain.

"How much did they say this was worth?" asked the passenger.

"Twenty-million dollars," the driver answered. "More than we have ever hauled out of here before."

Conversation dwindled to nothing as the three men in the truck became lost in their own thoughts. It would be a long, slow trip getting back home again.

155

As the truck approached the narrow bridge, the driver's head jerked at the sound of a faint pop followed by what he thought was an even fainter hissing sound.

"Did you hear that?" he asked.

"What?" his passenger said dully, interrupted from his dozing.

The driver quickly dismissed the sound as just another of the aches and pains of an old truck. "Oh, it was nothing."

As he applied the brake to cross the tiny bridge, an alarm sounded in his head. Something wasn't right. Everything was fading, spinning. . . . He couldn't see straight, and he was so tired. His last conscious thought was of trying to stop the darkness from swallowing him.

|||||||||||||||||

As the truck passed her position, Claude pointed the remote control and pushed the button. After the truck rounded the rock outcropping, she jumped out in the road and placed a bright-orange sign on the side of the road; it read, *Heavy equipment. Please wait for pilot car.* She then assumed the posture of a bored flag-woman facing another hot day of annoyed motorists.

Lawson raised his binoculars and stared at the driver as he came into view. The front wheels of the truck were just moving onto the bridge. His grinned as he saw the driver slump forward. Lawson pointed the remote control and pushed the button. The truck's engine instantly cut, and the armored truck jerked to a stop.

"It's dead," Lawson hissed into the radio. "I'm going in."

Wearing a gas mask, Lawson jumped out of the heavy brush and closed in on the truck. Using the stolen keys and codes, he entered the truck. All three occupants were unconscious.

"They're out," Lawson said into his radio.

Claude and Johnson converged on the armored truck, donning gas masks as they ran. They jumped aboard the truck as Lawson shoved the driver to the floor and took his seat. Claude extracted a syringe from her pack and plunged it into the arm of each of the sleeping men, ensuring that they wouldn't wake up for several hours. As Lawson put the truck in motion, Johnson pulled out a roll of duct tape and bound the hands and feet of each man.

The pilot of the chopper was waiting as they sped into the hidden clearing, the blades of the large craft already turning. Within minutes, the gold was in the chopper, and the unconscious guards were left bound in the truck.

"We're going to make it," Lawson said exultantly as he flopped into place. "Not a single vehicle has come down that road yet."

Claude smiled at Lawson's exuberance as she closed the doors. They were going to make it. It had been almost too easy. She felt herself pressed against the floor as the chopper leaped into the sky.

───────

"But how do you believe in a God who lets so many of His children suffer and die?" J.O. asked earnestly. "That's the one thing that just does not make sense to me. Christians claim that God is an all-powerful and loving Father. If that's true, what kind of Father lets His children be slaughtered in a holocaust or burned alive in towering twin infernos?"

Shawnee bit her lip and looked out the window of the truck. They had just passed through the little village of Leadore, Idaho, where J.O. had gone to school as a boy. It had been a wonderful morning so far. The first hour she had asked many questions about the lifestyle of a long-haul truck driver. The massive bulk and weight of the truck didn't intimidate her as she had initially feared it would. Instead, she came to enjoy the powerful rumble beneath her feet and the commanding view of the highway. The whole ambience of the big truck intrigued and delighted her. She was surprised how quiet and comfortable the cab of the Kenworth was. When she looked behind her into the big studio sleeper, she realized this was where J.O. lived when he was out on the road. It was neat and orderly. The bed was made, and the floors were clean.

The conversation had eventually shifted from her questions to his. And finally, it had settled on the subject foremost on J.O.'s mind—religion. She began to wonder if she had been wrong. Maybe she shouldn't have agreed to this. His questions were not academic curiosities. They were harder—much harder—and involved the essence of faith itself. What if she said the wrong thing?

Please, Father, she pleaded in her mind. *Give me what to say.*

As she began to speak, ideas formed in her mind. "J.O., your question assumes that God is supposed to stop all those things from happening."

"Of course. A father protects his children, doesn't he?"

"No, not always. What do you want God to do, come down and personally stop every person who is about to make a wrong choice?"

"He could."

"Of course he could, but that wouldn't be right."

"Why not?" he asked, sounding a bit impatient.

||||||||||||||||

J.O. had decided that since he had nothing to lose, he was going to speak his mind. If it proved she couldn't handle his questions and they began to frustrate her, he would back off and let it go, but so far, she had been quick on her feet and insightfully intelligent. He was impressed at her understanding and answers.

"Think about it this way. What would you do if you were a father? Would you hover over your children and make all their decisions for them? If they started to do something stupid, would you jump in and prevent them from making a mistake?"

"Sometimes I would, depending on how serious the mistake is."

"Sometimes God does too, but other times He doesn't. He has His reasons just as surely you would have reasons for raising your children the way you would."

J.O. stared straight ahead, trying to comprehend what she was saying.

"Think about it. Man is a thinking and reasoning creature. God gave us liberty and put us here to become what we want. The only way we can grow is to be allowed to choose for ourselves. Sometimes people make bad choices. How could man ever be free if his choices were controlled? If you want God to stop Nazis or terrorists, then you must also be prepared to allow God to stop you when you make a bad choice. How could you ever progress unless you could make choices and learn from your mistakes? God couldn't reward righteous people any more than He could punish wicked ones if He were making all their choices for them."

"It still seems awfully cruel to me."

"It *is* cruel and unfair from the way *we* see it, but remember, we have only a limited perspective on things in a small window of time. God sees everything at once from the vantage point of all time."

Shawnee could tell he wasn't connecting yet.

"I remember an experience a couple of years ago that might help. Emily was just a couple of years old and wasn't walking very steadily. It was late at night. The family was just going to bed when we heard this thump and an awful cry. Emily had crawled up on a chair and somehow fallen off onto the kitchen floor face first. Her teeth had been driven through her bottom lip, cutting it in half and making it into a bloody mess. I went with Dad and Mom as they took her to the emergency room. When the doctors tried to put stitches in her lip, Emily wouldn't hold still. They had to put her in a straitjacket kind of thing, and Dad sat with her head in his hands, forcing her to be still. She screamed in pain and fear, but Dad wouldn't let her go. Later, he talked about how hard it was to put her through that, even though it was necessary if Emily was going to be healed."

"I see where you're going," J.O. said. "From Emily's point of view, there was nothing good about that. She couldn't see what the rest of you could."

"That's right. She still doesn't fully understand. She still hates hospitals and doctors, but at least her lip isn't a huge, ugly scar."

J.O. seemed contemplative. "Still—why would He let so many die?"

"Is death the worst thing that can happen to a person, J.O.?"

That startled him. "What do you mean?"

"Think about it! Is death the worst thing that can happen to someone?"

"I—I don't know. I've never thought about it."

"There are things much worse than death for me."

"Like what?"

"Eternal misery and being without my family forever, living with regret and guilt burning in my soul. Those are things worse than death." After a moment's pause, she continued, "J.O., how long does death last? Only a few seconds at best, and what happens after that? Eternity! I would be willing to die the worst of deaths if it meant I could have happiness and the love of my family forever. The Nazi holocaust was a horrible thing—I agree with that—but if it costs you your faith, and thus your happiness and eternal possibilities, it will be adding a tragedy onto a tragedy. Is their dying a temporary physical death worth you dying a permanent spiritual one?"

J.O. was stunned by her words. He had asked one of his hardest questions—and she had not only handled it but had turned it back on him. He wasn't sure he fully understood what she was saying, but he knew he had been bested. He decided to momentarily change the subject.

"See that?" he said pointing to a brown road sign off to the left of the highway.

"Yes," she said, rising a little off her seat to look as they sped past.

"That's Hayden Creek. One of the most beautiful places a boy could ever grow up. About five miles up that valley is the ranch my folks used to own."

"I'd love to see it," she said.

"If there was any way to turn this thing around up there, I'd take you up and show it to you, but it's pretty close quarters."

"Do you ever go back there?"

"Not really. I went back once a couple of years ago, but it was hard. The ranch is owned by a friend of mine now. A guy named Cole Gregory. He takes pretty good care of it."

Shawnee could see the emotion of a thousand memories pass over his tanned features. "Do you think you'll ever go back to the ranch—to live, I mean?"

He glanced at her. "I'm not sure. I'm not sure if I'll ever go back. There is something about that life that certainly draws me back, but I'm not sure if—" He hesitated awkwardly. With Shawnee James at his side, he'd go back in a heartbeat. "I guess I'll just have to wait and see what the future brings."

"In the meantime, you roam the wild roads of America looking for adventure," she said with a teasing smile.

He looked over at her and let his tone mirror hers. "Absolutely! Old-time cowboys rode tired horses over dusty trails, modern truckers steer heavy rigs over asphalt roads. It's about the same."

"You jest," she said, "but I think there's more truth to that than fiction. It's a rugged lifestyle, one perfectly suited for a man who doesn't want to be tied down. Right?"

"I had a lot of options when I graduated high school. My grades were good. I could have gone to college on scholarship. I had some decent job offers."

"Then what brought you to driving a truck?"

"I know a lot of people look down on truck drivers, and I understand why, but I'm not like most of those guys. I didn't take this job because I had no other choice. I chose it because it was what I wanted. I wanted to travel. I wanted my freedom. I'm a professional driver, and I like it. Pilots fly aircraft, engineers drive trains—I drive big rigs."

|||||||||||||||

A slow-moving car appeared in front of him. J.O. reached up and flipped a switch, activating the engine brake. The engine began to rumble, and the truck slowed.

Finally, he glanced at her again. "I've thought about hanging up the keys, though—doing something else."

"And?"

"I guess I could if I had the right reason."

The tone of his voice and the smile on his face let her know there was much more to what he had just said than the words.

"Now what was that supposed to mean?" she asked.

He just grinned. "Nothing."

Could she be a rancher's wife? Shawnee's imagination suddenly catapulted her into a kaleidoscope of images of what it would be like to be this man's wife in a valley he called paradise. Before she could catch herself, a pleasant warmth stole through her entire being, like a warm bath to the soul. She basked in the dream, but after a moment, reality set in again and she shook it off. There was no way. Such little-girl fantasies didn't exist in the real world. If only they could, though. . . .

|||||||||||||||

The chopper flew low, barely above the treetops, following the sparkling blue ribbon of the Salmon River and skirting around the more populated areas of Challis and Salmon. At the confluence of the Salmon and Lemhi rivers, the chopper adjusted its course and turned south up the Lemhi River.

Claude sat quietly and watched the timber country roll beneath her like the endless footage of a monotonous movie. Johnson was studying a Forest Service topographical map in his lap.

"That's the Lemhi River down there," Johnson said, pointing down. "Just follow it to the south. Stay as low as possible. We're getting close to the Idaho National Engineering Laboratory, and it's a highly secure government installation. I don't want a fighter plane escort from Mountain Home Air Force Base."

"Roger that," the pilot said.

"So, what are you going to do with millions of dollars?" Lawson asked with boyish exuberance as he bumped Claude's leg with his. He was giddy with excitement and was trying to make conversation.

She smiled at him, like one does to indulge a prattling child, but didn't answer. Soon enough he would get his question answered—and most definitely not in the way he expected.

||||||||||||||||

While J.O. unloaded the equipment from his trailer, Shawnee walked down to the Salmon River that flowed through the center of the town of Salmon, Idaho. The sun was high in the sky, hitting the river directly from above. The intense light caused the river's surface to glitter as though a million diamonds were flowing in the current. The water seemed as clear and pure as heaven itself.

Sitting on the grassy bank, Shawnee removed her shoes and dangled her feet in the water. It was something her mother had always loved to do. The water was cold but felt good. As she splashed the water, she retreated deep into her thoughts.

What is going on inside J.O.'s head? He has peppered me with questions for almost two hours. *There's no doubt he's sincere and willing to listen.* She reached down into the water and picked up a handful of shiny river pebbles. One at a time, she began to toss them back into the water, concentrating on the plunking sound they made as they hit.

Oh, Heavenly Father, she said in her mind. *What am I doing here? Am I doing any good, or am I simply causing a much bigger problem than I'm solving? I can't help how I feel about him. If he does change, will it be because of me or because he knows it's true? I'm so confused, Father. Please help me to do the right thing.*

"Beautiful isn't it?"

Shawnee had been so engrossed in her thoughts and silent prayer that she hadn't heard J.O. come up behind her.

"Yes, it is."

He sat down in the lush grass beside her and stared out at the river, saying nothing.

"J.O., it's my turn."

"For what?"

"To ask *you* a question."

"Go for it," he said with a grin.

"Do you believe anything I've told you this morning?"

The grin slowly faded from his face. "You want an honest answer?"

"You know I do. What other kind of answer is there?"

"I'm not sure what I believe. I can't say I believe what you are saying, but at the same time I can't deny it. I need some time to think about it, I guess."

|||||||||||||||||

J.O. could tell his answer disappointed her. She turned away and stared once more out at the river. J.O. felt a twinge of pain. There was no way he wanted to hurt her, but he had made up his mind to be honest with her, regardless of the outcome. Her slender hand was resting in the grass beside her. Reaching over, he placed his hand over hers.

"Shawnee, listen. Be patient with me. I'm trying, but it's just not that easy to change a lifetime of ideas in one day."

"I know," she said. "I just don't know whether I'm helping or hurting you."

"Oh, I can answer that," he said, his grin returning. "Maybe this will calm your concerns. In all my life, no one has ever been able to answer my questions like you have. Your answers have made a lot of sense. I think I believe you. I'm just not sure." She looked relieved and grateful. "And if it makes any difference, I can promise you there is not another living soul I would talk to about this with except you."

She looked at him and smiled warmly. He stood and helped her to her feet. "We'd better get back on the road."

No sooner had they left Salmon city limits than J.O. fired off again. "So how do you know for sure that what you believe is true? How do you know that some other religion isn't the right one?"

Shawnee seemed to think a moment, then asked, "Why are you going down this road?"

He gave her a funny look at the sideways question.

"Humor me," she said with a smile.

"To get home," he said, obviously clueless.

"How do you know that home is at the end of this road?"

Now he was looking at her even more strangely. "Because it was there this morning."

"Ah," she said, "but can you say with absolute total certainty that it's still there? Do you really know for sure that something hasn't happened to it?"

"Well, no. I guess I don't know perfectly that it's there, but I'm pretty sure."

"And why is that?"

"Because I was just there this morning," he said, still struggling to keep up with her.

"What you have is faith, based on knowledge and experience, that Pocatello will be there when we get back. You are so certain of that fact that it doesn't concern you in the least whether or not the town is there, even though you have to admit that you don't know for sure."

"Okay, I see that."

"I have the same thing when it comes to God and my faith. I've had experiences that let me know that He's there and that my Church is true. I am as certain about that as you are about Pocatello."

"But how could you know that?"

Shawnee smiled. "Lisa asked me the same kind of thing the day we got into the accident. I would have to say I know because of two things. I've proved it for myself, and I've felt the Spirit."

"What do you mean you've proved it?"

"The Lord commands us to do a lot of things and then offers very specific promises if we obey. I put His promises to the test and found out that it worked time and time again. I've put God to the test, and it works just the way I was told it would. For example, I was told when I was young that if I wanted to know something, or if I needed help, that I could pray, and God would help me. Well, I did, and I found out for myself that it's true. He's answered me more times than I can count."

"But you haven't seen Him."

"I've never seen wind either, J.O., but I still know it's there. I've felt it, just like I've felt Him. God doesn't speak to our ears; He speaks to our hearts."

"What does that feel like?" he asked.

"I think you already know," she said, with a knowing smile.

"I do?"

"Sure, remember that feeling of peace and certainty that you told me you felt on the Middle Teton, and then again after the dream? God speaks to us by putting thoughts in our minds and feelings in our hearts. You've already experienced it."

"Maybe I have. If I have, I'd sure like to have it happen again."

"You can."

"How? Every time I've felt it before, it just came out of nowhere."

"The same way everyone else gets it—by prayer and faith. Have you seriously prayed and asked God for help?"

"That's the tough question isn't it? How do you pray if you're not sure you believe He's there?"

"Hasn't your company ever sent you to a place you've never been before?"

"Of course—all the time, and all over the country. Practically every time I go out, I go to someplace new."

"How did you know it was there? That's kind of risky, isn't it, driving that many miles when you don't know for sure the place is actually there?"

He smiled. "I think I see where this is going. I don't hesitate to drive hundreds of miles because I trust the people sending me, just like I should trust you and others who are telling me to go to God and pray."

"That's right," she said. Her smile looked triumphant. "People often say 'I can't believe this or that,' but if you think about it, that's not true. We believe what we choose to believe. Whether you believe in God is really a matter of your choice. It's a matter of accepting the evidence."

He stared at her for a moment, his face breaking into a wide smile.

"What?" she finally said.

He laughed. "How did you come up with all this? I can't remember the last time I ever learned so much in one day."

She didn't laugh. Although there was a smile on her face, she sounded completely serious. "I prayed, J.O.—very hard—about you, about all of this. I've been praying for days."

He became as serious as she. "It means that much to you?"

"More than you know," she said, almost so softly he couldn't hear her.

J.O. suddenly jerked in his seat. A heavy, unusual pounding sound brought his senses to full alert. In the space of a split second, his eyes scanned the dozen or more gauges of his instrument panel. Nothing was amiss. Then the source of the sound became obvious as a large helicopter came from behind and thundered over them.

"Wow," Shawnee said, "he's flying low."

"And fast too," J.O. said. "I wonder what's up with him?"

|||||||||||||||||||

"We'll be there in five minutes," Johnson called from the copilot's seat. "That's Leadore down there. Get ready."

Claude and Lawson began rounding up their gear. They felt the chopper slow and begin a gradual descent into what looked like a jungle of trees. As they neared the ground, a clearing materialized in the dense pine and fir forest. It was just wide enough to accommodate the blades of the chopper.

As the chopper touched down, there was an immediate frenzy of activity as everyone sprang into action. Johnson ran into the trees and pulled back a camouflage covering, revealing a small, ordinary-looking, moving van. He jumped in and quickly backed the van up to the open cargo door of the chopper.

In fewer than ten minutes, the dark bricks were transferred into the van.

"Check the area," Johnson barked. "Don't leave anything behind."

The chopper's pilot stripped false identification decals and stripes from the chopper's side and climbed aboard, preparing to take off. Johnson stood at the chopper door.

"Follow the route we planned. Head east as soon as you can clear the mountains. The INL is just over the mountain. Don't get any closer, or we'll all be cooked."

"I know a way around them," the pilot said confidently. "Don't worry about me."

Johnson gave a thumbs-up and turned away. "We'll be in touch," he called over his shoulder.

Johnson climbed into the driver's seat of the van. Claude sat in the passenger seat while Lawson crawled into the cargo bay with the gold. As the van pulled away, the chopper's rotors picked up speed, kicking up dust all around. It lifted straight up out of the clearing, and then, barely above the trees, turned east and picked up speed. The occupants of the van watched him gain altitude until he cleared the eastern mountains and disappeared from view.

The raucous squawk of a small walkie-talkie filled the cab of the van. "How long did you say it will it take us to get to Jackson?" Lawson asked from the back of the van.

"Probably about two hours," Johnson answered.

Gilmore Ghost Town

Claude keyed the mike on the unit she was holding. "Don't worry, they'll be ready and waiting for us when we get there. By midnight, you'll be out of the country and seeing things you never could have in Idaho." She looked over at Johnson and smiled wickedly. Johnson tipped his head back and laughed as though the joke was on Lawson.

Lawson came back on the radio. "I'm looking forward to it."

Johnson drove the van carefully down the bumpy, gravel mining road and through the old ghost town of Gilmore.

"I can see why you picked this place," Claude said with a look of disdain as she scanned the barren sagebrush landscape. "This has got to be as desolate and forsaken a place as you could find anywhere on the planet."

Johnson laughed. "Not quite the big city you're used to, is it, Babe?"

Claude's forced smile belied the seething she felt inside. She hated being called *Babe*. Fortunately, the hours she would have to listen to it and keep up this charade could be numbered on one hand.

|||||||||||||||||

"I guess there remains just one major question to be asked," J.O. said.

"What's that?" Shawnee asked.

"Say I do believe there is a God—then why do I need a church?"

"For the same reason you need a truck."

"Come again?" J.O. asked in surprise.

"We talked about how the company sends you to unknown places all the time. Well, why do they give you a truck?"

"To get the load there. There is no way I could transport a load without a truck."

His voice trailed off as he could see that once again, she had boxed him in with his own words. He continued, "The purpose of the Church is to help people find God and get back to Him. Am I right?"

"Right on," she smiled. "The Church is a bunch of people organized to help each other become perfect and save the world."

"Pretty ambitious goal, don't you think?"

"Probably, but wasn't it you who was complaining about how this world is such a cruel and unfair place? In a way, God is trying to stop all these terrible things from happening, but He's using us to do it."

By now they had dropped off Gilmore summit and were coming into the bottom land that bordered Birch Creek. As the semi rounded a corner, J.O. noticed he was rapidly bearing down on a yellow moving van. He slowed down to match its speed.

He shook his head in frustration and turned to Shawnee. "I'd give anything to be as sure about God as you are. I have a hard time accepting something I can't prove with my five senses."

"You'd give *anything*? That may be exactly what you'll have to do, J.O."

"What do you mean by that?" The words came out more sharply than he had intended.

She seemed reluctant, but said, "Sometimes God's people have paid a high price for their faith. You may have to as well."

J.O. wasn't sure he liked the ominous tone in her voice. He was still pondering what her words might mean when her voice interrupted his thoughts.

"J.O." her voice was quiet and low, "I just have to tell you one more time. It's true. There *is* a God, He is real, and He has a true Church. I hope that no matter what happens, you will pay the price to know those things for yourself."

Her words struck home like a flint to steel, and he felt the spark of warmth again. Turning his attention to her, he said, "I will, Shawnee, I—"

"J.O., look out!"

Her scream brought his eyes to the front just in time to see two cows dart out of the thick brush along the highway directly in the path of the yellow van. The van swerved and missed the first cow but not the second, slamming broadside into the large beef cow at close to sixty miles per hour.

171

The front end of the van seemed to explode on impact as its grill shattered into pieces. The hood buckled like an accordion. The cow was thrown more than fifty feet down the road and landed in a rolling heap.

J.O. had no choice but to stomp his brakes, causing the back axles of the trailer to hop and dance down the highway, leaving a dashed line of black marks on the asphalt. The van careened off the road to the right and slammed into a thick clump of willow, hitting hard and coming to an abrupt stop. J.O. skidded to a stop just a few feet short of where the van left the highway. He glanced over at Shawnee. Her eyes were wide, and her face was ashen, but she seemed okay. She was leaning forward, her hands against the dash of the truck.

Throwing open the door, J.O. vaulted to the ground. A cloud of acrid smoke from the skidding tires assailed him as he ran for the van. Upon reaching the driver's door, he yanked it open. The driver was hunched over the wheel, coughing and retching and trying to catch his breath. The woman in the passenger seat was a little dazed but otherwise seemed unhurt. She was just climbing out of the cab when Shawnee reached her.

"Are you alright?" Shawnee asked.

Surprisingly, the woman threw off her hand, rudely rebuffing her concern. Shawnee stood with a look of shock on her face as the woman walked angrily away. J.O. attempted to help the man out of the van, but as soon as he had the seatbelt off, he nearly fell out of the vehicle in his hurry. He walked around the front end of the vehicle in an obvious amount of pain, giving the van a quick inspection. Steam was already pouring out of the radiator, and oil was leaking rapidly underneath. The man began to swear. He kicked the fender, leaving another dent in the already totaled vehicle. J.O. walked over and put his arm around Shawnee.

A low moan from the injured cow caught the attention of the enraged driver. Reaching inside his coveralls, he pulled out a gun and stalked over to her. His face purple with rage, he drew down on the fatally injured cow and shot her four times.

Shocked and disgusted at the man's childish temper, J.O. started toward him, but Shawnee caught his arm. "Don't, J.O. Leave it alone."

He shook her off and continued toward the man. The man whirled at that moment and leveled his gun at J.O.'s mid-section. J.O stopped. "Mister," he said. "I'm sure you really showed that cow a thing or two—"

"Shut up!" the man ordered. "Claude, come over here and cover these two. We've got to get everything into that semi and get out of here."

The slender, dark-haired woman stepped up to within five feet of the couple and held her gun on them.

"What's going on here?" J.O. asked with surprising calmness.

"Shut up!" Claude seethed.

The driver ran to the back of the van, his bulbous body moving so fast that it would have been comical under any other circumstances. Throwing up the cargo door, he shouted inside, "Trent! Move it! We've got to get out of here before anyone else comes by."

Trent nearly fell out of the back of the van, his eyes blinking to adjust to the light.

"What happened, Johnson?" he asked, dazed.

Johnson's voice thundered. "We hit a cow, you idiot. Now move!"

Lawson jumped like a scalded cat. They forced J.O. to pull his rig forward enough that the rear of his trailer was lined up with the wrecked van. The woman then ordered him out of the cab while the two men scrambled as fast as possible to move the precious cargo.

"Turn around," the woman said, motioning for J.O. and Shawnee to turn and face the other direction. For a moment, J.O. met the woman's gaze. Her eyes were as cold, hard, and lifeless as death itself.

"That won't do much good," he said in an icy voice. "I already know what that stuff is. It's called 'dore', otherwise known as unrefined gold and silver ore."

"You're too smart for your own good, aren't you?" she snapped at him.

"Smart enough to know better than to steal gold."

The woman's expression hardened even more. "I suggest you shut your mouth before you wind up like that cow over there."

"Who'll drive the truck if I do?" he asked, deliberately trying to agitate her with his smile.

Shawnee took his arm. As he looked down into her face, he saw the unspoken request there. She was afraid, and he was making it worse.

The two men suddenly ran up. "Let's go," Johnson said, panting and sweating like a fat man in a marathon.

Claude climbed into the semi, followed by Shawnee. Lawson went next.

"Into the driver's seat," Johnson ordered J.O.

As J.O. climbed in, Johnson called out, "Cover him, Lawson, while I get in the passenger side."

J.O. climbed in and sat down. Lawson moved forward and shoved his gun up next to J.O.'s ear. J.O. knew that if he were alone, he could have taken the gun away as easily as taking scum off a pond, but he wasn't. Johnson sat down heavily in the passenger seat. Lawson settled back into the sleeper.

"Alright, drive!" Johnson ordered, his gun once more aimed at J.O. "And don't do anything to attract attention. I promise you if you cause me any grief, you'll be as dead as that cow."

J.O. looked over his shoulder into the sleeper. Shawnee was sandwiched between Claude on one side and Lawson on the other. She gave him a tentative, but reassuring smile. He turned back to the front and met Johnson's gaze, letting a look of utter contempt fill his face. These clowns might have the upper hand now, but that would soon change.

"One more thing," Johnson said, "your cell phones—give 'em to me, *now!*"

J.O. reached into his pocket and handed the man his phone. Shawnee passed hers up from the sleeper.

J.O. slipped the truck into gear and eased out onto the highway.

As he shifted into another gear, Johnson rolled down the passenger side window and dropped the phones onto the asphalt. He looked in the mirror and grunted in satisfaction as the phones rolled down the highway, shattering and shedding pieces along the road. The entire incident from start to finish had taken less than fifteen minutes, and not a single car had driven by. There were no witnesses.

||||||||||||||||||

About ten minutes outside of Idaho Falls, traveling south on Interstate 15, Johnson and the woman talked as though J.O. was a nonexistent entity.

"As I see it," Johnson said, "we have three options. We can take this truck straight there, or we can stop somewhere and have them come and meet us."

"Neither of those will work," Claude said. "The truck could be reported as missing by the time we get there. It's too big and too obvious. Besides, they can't meet us. They're completely unfamiliar with the area. So, what's your third option?"

"We'll be in Idaho Falls in a few minutes. We could drop you off to pick up a rental vehicle. I know a place in the mountains northeast of Palisades Reservoir, near the Wyoming state line, where we could wait for you. We could transfer the stuff, leave the truck, and still be in Jackson by midnight."

"That will work," she said. "Draw me a map."

Johnson reached up on the dashboard and grabbed Shawnee's Bible. Flipping it open, he ripped out one of the end pages.

J.O. glanced over his shoulder at Shawnee. Anger clouded her expression at the irreverent desecration of her scriptures.

"It would probably do you more good to read that book than use it for scratch paper," J.O. said calmly.

Johnson shot him a withering look but said nothing. Instead, he

175

shoved the book onto the floor between the seats and began sketching. Reaching into her pocket, Claude pulled out a cell phone and began making calls.

Minutes later, J.O. signaled a right-hand turn off Highway 26 into a truck stop on the north side of Idaho Falls.

"Park over there," Johnson said, pointing to an area behind the truck stop and out of the flow of traffic. "Do you have any questions about the map?" Johnson asked the woman.

"None," Claude answered. "I'll find you. My taxi is already waiting. I shouldn't be more than about forty-five minutes behind you."

Stuffing her gun into her coveralls, she climbed out and ran toward the truck stop.

"Alright," Johnson barked. "Get it out of here and head for Palisades Reservoir."

||||||||||||||||||

Tate walked in and dropped his books on the counter. His mother was standing at the stove cooking something for supper.

"Hi, Mom," he said, walking over and kissing her on the cheek.

"Hi, Tate," she said. "Hungry?"

"Very!"

He picked up his books and carried them to his bedroom. After washing his face, he went back to the kitchen and sat down at the table.

"Son, where was J.O. going today?"

"I think he just went to Salmon. Why?"

"That's what I thought. I'm positive that he told me he would be back by four o'clock at the latest."

"Oh, you know him, Mom," Tate said lightly. "Something probably went wrong, and it took longer than he thought. I'm sure he'll be back anytime."

"You're probably right. I guess I worry too much."

She turned back to her cooking and stirred the stew. She didn't believe the words she just said; she *didn't* think J.O. would be back anytime. Ruthie Steele loved her sons and had always had an uncanny ability to be in tune with them, and right now her heart told her something was wrong—very wrong!

|||||||||||||||||||

"Turn here!" Johnson ordered, brandishing his weapon.

They had just passed through the little town of Swan Valley, Idaho, and had turned northeast toward the town of Victor, Idaho, climbing steadily toward Pine Creek Pass. Darkness had begun to settle into the steep canyons. J.O. estimated they were only a couple of miles from the summit of the pass when Johnson ordered him off the main road to the right. J.O. swung the rig off the blacktop onto the tiny dirt road. The road rapidly narrowed into little more than two parallel ruts as it went deeper into the timber. J.O. geared down.

A few minutes later, a mountain stream sliced through the road. The stream's banks were high, steep, and deeply rutted where four-wheel drives had ripped through them. The bottom of the stream was gravel, and the water looked like it was two or three feet deep. J.O. idled to a stop about ten yards short of the stream and set his brakes.

"What are you waiting for?" Johnson barked impatiently. "Go through it!"

"In case you haven't noticed, friend," J.O. said with a snap to his voice, "this is an eighteen-wheeler, not a motorcycle. A rig this size can't go through things like that."

Johnson turned in his seat and raised his gun to J.O.'s head. His voice sounded like the hiss of a snake as he said, "It had better get through, or it'll be your tomb."

J.O. never acknowledged the gun with his eyes. Instead, he stared implacably at Johnson and swallowed the anger that rose anew inside. He had never been one to tolerate a bully. He had known his share of fights in his life, and almost always they had been with guys like this—guys that had what he called a "little man's complex." In other words, what they lacked in brains and social ability, they made up for by pushing other people around.

J.O. glanced back at Shawnee. She sat pressed up against the edge of the sleeper wall. Lawson sat as close as he could without sitting on top of her. He appeared to be taking delight in her discomfort. The lecherous grin on his hawk-nosed face bespoke his ugly thoughts. Shawnee saw J.O. look back, and she locked eyes with him. Even in the darkness, J.O. could see the strain there, and that shortened his patience even more. He drew a deep breath and gritted his teeth.

"Alright," he said, turning back to face Johnson, "but you'd better hang on."

J.O. dropped the truck in reverse and backed up about thirty yards. Growing up on a ranch, J.O. had learned long ago that it was better to go fast and not get stuck than it was to go slow and have to dig yourself out once you were stuck. Reaching over, he flipped a toggle switch on his console that locked his two driving axles together. He revved the engine and popped the clutch. The truck shot forward in a spray of dirt and gravel. As the engine hit its maximum rpm, J.O. snap-shifted the transmission to a higher gear and buried the accelerator. At what seemed like break-neck speed, the truck shot over the bank and bounced out into the middle of the stream, shooting a spray of water up over the cab. The force of the impact lifted J.O. up and out of his seat. Had it not been for the seat belt, his head would have slammed against the top of the cab.

The front wheels of the tractor hit the opposite bank and catapulted upward. J.O. kept his foot to the floor. The five-hundred-horsepower engine roared at full power as the eight huge driving tires dug and chewed through the streambed, trying to push their way clear. The people in the cab were tossed around like straw in a tornado. Finally, the truck cleared the stream onto the opposite bank and, with renewed traction, shot forward.

J.O. was barely cognizant of Johnson's cursing and swearing beside him. The man was fighting to keep his seat under him. Just as he righted himself, the back axles of the fifty-three-foot trailer hit the stream, nearly jerking the whole rig to an abrupt stop. Johnson was launched out his seat like a cannonball, slamming headfirst into the dashboard. Lawson tumbled out of the sleeper onto the floor between the seats in a tangled heap. J.O. reacted before he considered. Letting go of the wheel, he dove across the seats and opened the passenger door. Grabbing the dazed Johnson who was just recovering from a blow to his head, he threw him headlong out the door. Screaming all the way, Johnson landed, rolling like a half-flat beach ball.

J.O. grabbed the emergency air supply and locked the brakes on the out-of-control truck. It lurched to an abrupt stop. Lawson was thrown off balance again and fell forward into the dash console. Fighting to keep his own balance in the tight space, J.O. swung at Lawson as he flew past. The blow hit Lawson in the side of the head behind his left ear. He impacted the dashboard again and dropped to the floor, swearing like a filthy-mouthed muleskinner. J.O. threw his body on top of Lawson, pinning him to the floor.

"Shawnee," he yelled, "get out!"

Already in motion, Shawnee dove out of the sleeper across the driver's seat. On the way out she kicked Lawson in the solar plexus. She hesitated for just a moment before she shoved the door open and jumped to the ground. Momentarily distracted, J.O. didn't see Lawson's fist flying at his head. It connected with his forehead and knocked him back. J.O. shook it off and lunged forward. Lawson was reaching for his gun when J.O. pounced on top of him and drove his fist into the man's midsection. Lawson floundered and flailed like a madman trying to get at J.O. Somehow his hand found the gun, and he brought it up trying to get it at J.O. Savagely, J.O. swung with a hard right, aiming directly at the hawk nose. He connected with a crunch just as the gun fired. The explosion in such a confined space and so close to his ear was deafening. The bullet went wide and blew a .38-caliber hole through the top of the cab. Ignoring the pain and ringing in his ears, J.O. grabbed Lawson's gun hand and slammed it against the frame of the passenger seat once, then again. The gun fell free. J.O. was lunging for it when a sudden blow to the side of his head dropped him to the floor. Blackness blurred his vision as he fought to hold onto consciousness. He reached for the bunk of the sleeper to pull himself up, but it was no use; his legs buckled, and he collapsed onto the floor of the sleeper. The last thing he heard was Johnson's high-pitched voice screaming hysterically toward Shawnee.

"Get back here, girl! You come back, so help me, or I'll kill him right now!"

|||||||||||||||||

Tate and Lisa were sitting on a loveseat in the darkened room watching a movie when Ruthie walked in. She sat in a rocking chair nearby.

"Mom," Tate asked, "are you alright?"

Ruthie bit her lip as she contemplated what to say. "I'm just worried, Son. It's after ten. J.O. should have been back by now."

"I'm sure he's alright, Mom. Something probably delayed him, and he decided to spend the night up there."

"Shawnee was with him, Tate," Lisa said. "I don't think he would have done that."

"Yeah, you're right," Tate agreed. "He wouldn't, and he certainly wouldn't have kept her out this late without calling to say something."

After an uncomfortable silence, Lisa asked, "Do you have that app on your phone that allows you to track where your family and friends are?"

"I do," Tate said. "I didn't think of that." He reached into his pocket and pulled out his phone.

After studying it for a moment, he said, "It says *No location available*. Maybe he's been in touch with his company. Let me see if I can reach anybody there."

"I'll try Shawnee's parents in Idaho Falls," Lisa said. "Maybe they stopped there on their way back through."

Lisa's call quickly confirmed they were not in Idaho Falls. As she hung, up she heard Tate's one-sided dialogue.

"What! When?"

"Could there be any connection?"

"Okay, thanks. Let us know if he calls in."

Tate hung up and turned to the two women, his expression grave. "They haven't seen or heard from him either. He was supposed to have called in a long time ago. Normally they wouldn't be too concerned, except there was a major gold robbery in that same area sometime this morning."

"Oh, no!" Lisa gasped.

"They said the robbery was above Challis. Something about an armored truck heist. They're pretty sure that it has nothing to do with J.O., though, since he was two mountain ranges away near Salmon."

Ruthie walked to the TV and switched from the movie to a local channel. The familiar face of a local anchorwoman came on the screen with the printed headline of *Armored Truck Robbery* behind her. The report detailed the events of the robbery as far as they were known.

"The amount of gold stolen has been estimated at twenty million dollars," the woman intoned. "So far, authorities have no suspects or clues. Residents in the area are advised to lock their doors and report anything suspicious. More details will be given as they develop."

Tate walked over to his mother and put his arm around her shoulder. Lisa took her hand.

"J.O.'s company said they've called the State Police and notified them about J.O.," Tate continued. "No one is too concerned at this point. If he doesn't show up or call in by nine tomorrow morning, then they'll officially report him as missing, but I'm sure he's okay, Mom."

Ruthie's lips tightened into a grim smile. They could say what they wanted, but she knew better. Call it what you will, but she knew better. Her eldest son was in trouble, and she knew it.

|||||||||||||||||

J.O. awoke to see Johnson's bloated, red face staring down at him.

"Get up," the fat man ordered.

J.O. struggled to sit up while Lawson crawled out from under him and back into the sleeper. Blood was pouring from Lawson's nose. Raging and cursing like a spoiled teenager, he fumbled around, obviously looking for his gun.

J.O. struggled to his feet and sat in the driver's seat. Shawnee was standing on the running board at his side.

Lawson finally found the weapon and whirled to bring it to bear on J.O. but was brought up short in the close quarters by Johnson's gun practically under his crooked nose. "Drop that thing," Johnson ordered, "or so help me, I'll drop you."

The ominous bore of the gun less than a foot away dissolved Lawson's bravado; he sullenly turned back into the sleeper and slumped down on the bunk, using one of the blankets to sponge his nose.

"Get in here," Johnson ordered Shawnee. J.O. moved aside, and Shawnee climbed over the driver's seat and into the cab.

"Sit in the passenger seat and lock the door," he said to her.

As Shawnee took her seat, Johnson placed himself just out of reach on the floor inside the sleeper.

"Now drive," he said to J.O. "and this time keep in mind that my gun is aimed at that beautiful, blond head sitting beside you. If you so much as sneeze, I'll kill her."

J.O. turned back to the front and released the brakes. As the truck started forward, he shook his head to clear his vision. His left eye was blurry and wouldn't clear. It was then that he felt wetness on the side of his head. Reaching up, he probed the wound where Johnson had hit him. It wasn't bad—maybe only an inch long—but was just deep enough to bleed a lot. Johnson had pistol-whipped him. His anger boiled.

||||||||||||||||||

The old logging road climbed deeper into the timber and grew more and more rugged. Soon the road was little more than a deer track, so narrow that tree limbs were slapping at the truck's mirrors and brushing the tall, chromed exhaust stacks.

Shawnee sat on the edge of her seat, looking tense and anxious, as though any second she expected the truck to plummet over the steep edge and roll into the canyon below. Beads of sweat stood out on J.O.'s forehead from the intense concentration. His eyes never wavered from the road in front of him as he worked the truck around the tight switchbacks and up the steep grades. Finally, they came over a rocky rise and dropped into a small, lush, three-cornered meadow, bordered on the backside by a tiny stream.

"Shut it down and climb out the driver's door," Johnson ordered, keeping his gun on them.

J.O. brought the truck to a stop in the middle of the meadow; he and Shawnee climbed out slowly and stood together by the door. Johnson and Lawson climbed out of the truck, keeping their guns continually at the ready.

Lawson was the last to exit the truck. He had cleaned himself up, but the area around his nose and eyes was already beginning to swell and discolor. The expression on his face was as black as the bruises around his eyes.

"Move to the back of the trailer," Johnson ordered, as he gestured with the weapon.

As J.O. turned and started back, his hand brushed Shawnee's. She locked her fingers into his in a tight grip. When they reached the rear of the trailer, Johnson gestured with the weapon to the big doors. "Now, open them and get inside."

J.O. jerked the latches that secured the heavy doors. As they swung open and the faint light from a partial moon fell inside, J.O. was stunned by the amount of gold that lay scattered over the floor of the trailer. He hesitated for a moment, but as Johnson stepped menacingly toward them, he reached down and boosted Shawnee the five feet into the trailer. Then, taking her proffered hand, he too climbed in. They turned and stood together as the doors slammed shut with an echoing clang, plunging them into total darkness.

At first, they didn't move. They stood, listening. J.O. was so close that Shawnee could feel his warm breath on her forehead. His calloused hands gripped her shoulders tightly, holding her close. The voices of Lawson and Johnson moved around the end of the trailer and toward the cab of the semi.

"What are you going to do with them?" Lawson asked.

"Kill them!" Johnson nearly shouted.

"Then, why didn't you do it back there when you had a chance?" Lawson asked with obvious resentment.

Even with the voices fading out, the snap and anger of Johnson's tone was evident. "You know how to drive one of these?"

"No."

"Well, neither do I. We had to get this thing far enough back off the road that no one will find it for a few days. Soon as Claude gets here and that gold is loaded..."

The voices faded beyond recognition. Seconds later Shawnee heard the two doors of the truck cab slam shut.

"J.O., did you hear that?" Shawnee said in a hoarse whisper toward a face she couldn't see.

"I heard." The anger was plainly evident in his voice. He released his grip on her shoulders.

Her anxiety heightened as he moved away from her. She wanted him to hold her again. "What are we going to do?" she asked. "We can't just sit here and wait for them to kill us. We have to do something."

J.O. sighed wearily and slumped against the trailer wall, letting the useless anger drain away. "Yes, but what? We don't have much time. The woman will be here before long."

"Is there any way out of this thing—a trap door or something?"

"None. Some of these trailers have plexiglass skylights in them. This isn't one of them. I'm afraid the only way out is the way we came in."

"Can't we force the doors open?" Shawnee asked urgently.

"Not a chance! Those doors are inch-thick, reinforced steel, latched by heavy steel bars. You'd have a better chance cutting a hole in the wall with a pocketknife."

"There has to be some way," she said, the desperation in her voice intensifying.

"Sorry, I can't think of one right now."

A gloomy silence that matched the darkness settled over them. It lasted only a moment before J.O. spoke.

"Shawnee... I'm sorry I got you into this."

She drew in her breath, took a step toward him, and reached up in the darkness to place her fingers against his lips. "Don't say it, J.O. There was no way you could have known this would happen. It's not your fault."

When he spoke again, his voice was a barely audible whisper. "Still, I'm sorry you had to go through this."

Unexpectedly, she sank down to the floor into a sitting position and pulled him down with her.

"It's okay," she said, still holding his hands. "It's definitely been the most exciting date of my life."

He laughed lightly. "Yeah, I'll bet it has at that."

They sat in silence for a few minutes. The only sound that reached their ears was their own breathing. The air inside the trailer was stale and reeked of the stench of a thousand cargos.

Had there been enough light, J.O. would've seen the powerful emotions animating Shawnee's face as she struggled against her claustrophobia. She bit down on her lip and fought for control against the temptation to scream and go wild. Then, a thought occurred to her.

"J.O.?"

"Yes."

"Would you mind if I prayed for us?"

||||||||||||||||||

There was no mistaking the pleading in Shawnee's voice, yet J.O. hesitated. This was no time for religion. He was about to say something disparaging when he remembered the prayer in the mountains.

"If you really think it'll help, go ahead." He felt her squeeze his hands.

"Dad once told me that there was a rule: heaven will not do for man what man can do for himself, and when we have done all we can and it's not enough, we have the right to call on heaven to help us. If ever there was a time that we needed heaven's help, I think it's now. Don't you?"

"Yeah, I guess it is."

She came up to her knees and moved closer to him, still holding his hands. An unusual warmth emanated from them as he came to his knees and knelt beside her.

"Heavenly Father," she began. "Please help us. We're trapped, and they're going to kill us. We don't have much time. Please, Heavenly Father, help us find a way to escape. Help us think of a way out of here."

J.O. was touched by the sincerity of the prayer. She was, he thought, definitely her father's daughter. She had the same familiar way of speaking to God. Still, for all of her sincerity and earnestness, J.O. couldn't quiet the doubts that slammed into his mind like a pile driver. Over and over a voice inside his head screamed that it was all a lie. J.O. felt an involuntary shudder pass through his body as his mind wrestled with his heart. He wanted to believe. More than anything he wished he could believe this would help, but—

"And, Father," she continued, "in spite of our situation, we thank thee for this day and for the faith that is beginning to grow inside J.O. Help him to come to know Thee and that Thou art there for him. Help him, Father, to know that there are those who care very deeply for him."

She stopped; J.O. could hear her swallow the emotion. He held her hands more tightly, fighting back the lump that swelled in his own throat. No one had ever prayed for him with that much feeling. In fact, it occurred to him that he didn't know of anyone ever praying for him.

"We want to live and learn from this experience, Father," she continued. "May Thy will be done." She closed with amen, and a sob choked in her throat. J.O. reached for her and pulled her into his arms and held her tightly. She turned her cheek against his chest and her shoulders started shaking.

"Oh, J.O.," she sobbed. "I don't want to die. My family—"

J.O. gritted his teeth and spoke. "Shawnee, I promise you, nothing is going to happen to you if I can help it."

The emotion that drove him at that moment was the most powerful he had ever felt. What was it? It felt like the streams of many emotions were flowing into one river of intense feeling. Love and compassion filled his heart, while his mind seemed filled with light and understanding. It was suddenly clear to him what to do.

"Wait a minute," he said, his voice brightening considerably. "I have an idea. There's no way out of this trailer except by the door, but that doesn't mean we have to leave the way they want us to."

"What do you mean?" she asked, suddenly perking up.

"If we can make enough noise to get them to open the doors, I may be able to get the jump on them." He moved away from her and turned toward the back of the trailer.

"How?"

J.O. proceeded to explain the idea that was taking shape in his mind even as he spoke.

"I don't know; there are a lot of things that could go wrong."

"Sure there are, but, hey. God's on our side, remember?"

Shawnee hugged him again. "I can't believe you," she said. "You are one of a kind."

"Good thing, too," J.O. said. "The world doesn't need more people who've messed up their lives like I have."

"Now what's that supposed to mean?"

J.O. wasn't sure how to answer that. For that matter, he wasn't even sure why he had said it. *Do I really think I've messed up my life? Is a life without God a "messed-up" life?*

"Nothing," he said, trying to brush it off. "I'll tell you later. We'd better get moving."

"Just a minute, J.O."

He stopped and could feel that she was suddenly close to him.

"I—"

She cut herself off before she finished the sentence. Then, with some hesitation, she continued. "Please be careful." She went up on tiptoes and kissed him lightly.

He reached out and held her to him, burying his face in her hair. After a moment he stepped back. "Just remember—run. Don't look back. If something happens, head for that campground just over the pass, and get help."

"I will."

She stepped back and flattened herself against the side of the trailer. J.O. bent down and picked up one of the eighty-pound bricks of raw gold. With all his strength, he hurled it against the side of the trailer. The noise was deafening. He grabbed another and slammed it down on the floor. He paused for a moment, listening. The cab doors of the truck slammed shut and the sound of angry voices grew louder.

"I'll kill him," he heard Johnson muttering as he came to the back of the trailer.

J.O. grabbed another brick and threw it, then stopped and waited, listening again.

J.O. tensed. He heard the latches on the big doors move. He crouched down like a sprinter starting a race and began to count.

He leaped forward just as the one big door began to move and the first crack of moonlight shone inside. Running at near full speed, he stiff-armed the door, causing it to fly open. Johnson, who was standing directly in front of it, was hit squarely in the face and knocked off his feet, instantly unconscious. J.O.'s momentum carried him five or six feet out the door. He landed on his feet and dropped to one knee.

"Go!" he yelled up at Shawnee.

In the soft light, she leaped out of the trailer like a frightened deer sailing over his head and landed gracefully ten feet beyond the trailer. She was running at full speed even as she hit the ground.

J.O. came to his feet and started after her. Out of the corner of his eye he saw Lawson whirl and bring his gun to aim on Shawnee's fleeing back. Instantly, J.O. changed direction and barreled head-first into Lawson, knocking him to the ground. J.O. looked to see if Shawnee was clear. She was stopped at the edge of the meadow about fifty yards away and turned toward him as though uncertain of what she should do.

"Go!" he yelled, waving his arm emphatically.

His words hit her like a shot of adrenalin, and she sprang for the darkness of the trees. J.O. turned back. Lawson was in a kneeling position, his gun pointed at J.O. He knew what was coming and threw himself to the side. The gun went off, but the bullet missed cleanly. J.O. rolled several times and sprang to his feet. He lunged at Lawson, throwing his arms around the man's head and taking him hard to the ground. Cursing and ranting, Lawson rolled away and leaped up, trying to get J.O. in his sights. J.O. came to a crouch and threw himself at the loathsome wretch with a reckless fury, his fists aiming for an already swollen and crooked nose. He vaguely perceived his mistake as he saw the gun come up between them at point-blank range, but there was no stopping his momentum. The gun went off just a split second before his fist smashed into Lawson's face for the second time. The roar of the weapon so close to his ear was deafening beyond belief, but the noise was eclipsed by the sudden blow to his head. Something hit him with such force that he was instantly rendered senseless for a second time. He felt a momentary sensation of falling, but the blackness claimed him before he hit the ground.

||||||||||||||||

J.O. slowly opened his eyes, but then closed them again. Just that much effort felt as though someone was dissecting his brain with a dull knife. For a moment, he lay still, trying to orient himself.

A gentle touch on his cheek and the feeling of something wet against his head suddenly brought back his memory. The gun, Shawnee . . . He tried to sit up, but the pain in his head nearly took him out again.

Moaning, he sank back into something warm and soft. *Where am I, and what is underneath me?* He fought for consciousness.

"Easy, don't move so fast. Wait until your head clears."

The gentleness of the voice penetrated the pain and fog, and he forced his eyes open. Finally, after a moment, Shawnee's concerned face swam into a fuzzy focus.

"What—what are you doing here?" He closed his eyes again. The pain felt as though someone was tying knots in the nerves behind his eyes. "I thought I told you to run."

"You did, but . . ."

Again, he tried to sit up. With a little help from her he made it. As his head cleared further, his mind reeled with questions. *Where are Johnson and Lawson? Where is the woman? Why won't my left eye focus?*

"Johnson," he mumbled, as he struggled to get to his feet.

"It's okay, I took care of them."

He reached a wobbly upright position then turned and stared at her in amazement. "You what?"

"I took care of them."

He looked in the direction she pointed to where Lawson lay helpless on the ground, his hands bound behind his back and his feet immobilized with duct tape. He was shaking his head and writhing against the restraint, fury displayed all over his ugly face.

"How?" J.O. asked dumbly.

She looked up at him, amusement in her expression. "I couldn't leave you. I went into the trees and then stopped. I saw you tackle him the second time. I was trying to figure out a way to help you when I heard the shot. I thought he had killed you. I grabbed a branch and ran back." She pointed to a solid three-foot chunk of fir. "He didn't see me until it was too late."

J.O. smiled despite his pain. The mental image of her coming out of nowhere and furiously clubbing her lecherous tormentor with a tree branch was a sight he wished he hadn't missed.

She continued. "I remembered seeing some duct tape on the floor of your sleeper. Before he came to, I taped him up."

"What about Johnson?"

She started walking around the trailer, and J.O. followed her. "You must have hit him pretty hard with that door. As of a few minutes ago, he was still out. He's wrapped up with duct tape too."

J.O. struggled for his equilibrium. It felt as though the world was going to spin out from under him. Shawnee held his arm and steadied him.

"Easy, don't move too fast. I'm pretty sure you have a concussion."

He kept trying to walk as though he hadn't heard. As they came around the end of the trailer, he saw Johnson on the ground, trussed up, his eyes open, glaring at them with murderous intent. A deep laceration was on his discolored forehead where the door had hit him.

J.O. felt fresh blood run through his hair and onto his cheek. He reached up and probed the large bullet wound with his fingers. It was ugly and raw.

"I cleaned it as well as I could," Shawnee said, coming close to examine it again, "but we had better get you to a doctor. You've lost a lot of blood, and you're going to need some stitches."

J.O. reached into the back pocket of his faded denim jeans and pulled out a large red bandanna. He rolled it into a broad headband and tied it tightly around his head.

"I think you're going to have a bad scar," Shawnee said apologetically.

J.O. shrugged. "Match the headache." He grinned again. "I'll just tell everyone it's an old war wound."

She laughed lightly.

He straightened and sobered. "We've got to get out of here. She could be here any minute."

"What do we do?"

J.O. scanned the ground as though looking for something. He reached down and picked up Johnson's gun.

"Can you use this?"

"I think so," she said, reaching out and taking it from him.

In fewer than three seconds, J.O. knew from the way she handled it that she had been trained in the use of handguns.

"Dad taught me," she said, catching his slack-jawed expression. "He always said he didn't want wimpy daughters who were afraid of guns and couldn't drive a standard transmission."

J.O. grinned widely. "Miss James, you are amazing."

She nodded in acknowledgment and returned the smile.

J.O. reached into his pocket and pulled out a knife. He slit the tape on Johnson's feet and hauled him to a standing position. He did the same with Lawson.

"Get in the trailer, both of you," he ordered.

Johnson turned and shot him a defiant stare.

J.O. stepped forward, his temper instantly hot. "Look, you bloated sack of beef, you see this," he pointed to his bloody head. "I would like nothing better than to return the favor. Now you can either get in that trailer under your own steam, or I'll throw you in like a sack of flour."

Johnson tried to stare him down, but J.O.'s expression was so intense that he backed down and looked away. He stepped toward the trailer, and J.O. boosted him in. With his hands still tied, he rolled onto the floor and sat up.

J.O. turned back to do the same with Lawson, who moved as though he was going to follow Johnson. As he came to the rear of the trailer, he lifted a leg to be boosted in. J.O. reached to take the leg, but as he did so Lawson made an awkward move to kick him in the face. Furious, J.O. sidestepped, straightened, and swung with his right, connecting with a crack at the base of Lawson's skull. Lawson grunted and collapsed to the ground, stunned into submission. J.O. bent over and grasped Lawson by the shirt collar and the seat of his pants. Shawnee gaped in amazement at J.O.'s strength as he lifted the semi-conscious man like a bale of hay and threw him into the trailer, knocking Johnson over backward. He then slammed both doors and latched them.

When he turned around, Shawnee was grinning at him. "Not bad for a wounded man. I'd hate to see what you could do if you were really upset."

J.O. grinned. "Let's go," he said, reaching for her hand.

It took some time to turn the rig around in the tiny meadow. At one point, the trailer axles dropped into the stream, and J.O. thought he might have to unhook the trailer and leave it, but he managed to pull it free. Since J.O. now knew the road, they made better time going down the canyon than coming up. Several times he shook his head trying to get the vision in his left eye to clear, but it stubbornly remained out of focus. The pain in his head was nearly debilitating. Each sharp movement threatened unconsciousness, and it was getting worse. Shawnee seemed to sense this and watched him closely.

"Are you alright?" she asked.

"The closest law enforcement and phone is Teton Valley," J.O. said, ignoring her question. "I think we had better go there."

"We'll go right past my grandfather's ranch if we go that way," Shawnee said. "We could stop there, but I think we had better get you straight to the hospital."

He nodded. "I think we had better get these guys off our hands as quickly as possible."

"We'll call the Sheriff's department from the hospital," she said.

The headlights suddenly fell on the stream crossing.

"Here we go again," J.O. said.

This time he didn't even stop but stomped the accelerator to the floor and grabbed another gear.

"Hang on!" he shouted, just as the truck left solid ground.

The added speed and different angle got them through easier than the last time.

As they came up onto the opposite bank, J.O. looked over at Shawnee. She had a white-knuckled grip on the seat to hold herself in place. She grinned. "I wonder how those guys are doing back there?"

"I'd imagine they can probably relate with a tennis ball about now."

Shawnee laughed, but her laugh suddenly died as headlights rounded a sharp corner and appeared on the road in front of them. It was a small moving van like the one they had left on the side of the road south of Leadore, and it was coming up the canyon.

|||||||||||||||||

Ruthie Steele sat on the edge of her bed, unable to sleep. It was well past midnight now, and still there was no word of J.O. and Shawnee. She knew better than to even lay down. It was going to be a long, sleepless night. It had always been that way. Concern for family had always taken precedence over slumber. Only the utter depths of exhaustion had driven her to rest during her husband's last days. She couldn't shake the ominous feeling of dread that kept her awake now.

Help them, dear Father, she cried in her heart.

Tate and Lisa had maintained a vigil with her until close to midnight, when Lisa had announced she was going home. She had walked to the door with Tate following. Ruthie had watched curiously as the two of them conversed for a moment at the door, having what appeared to be an intense discussion. All at once, Tate had turned back to her and said, "Mom, we would like to offer a prayer for J.O. and Shawnee. Would you kneel with us?"

The request had caught Ruthie completely off guard. She knew that Tate had gone to church with Lisa a couple of times, but to now have one of her sons ask to pray with her was a first.

From the time she and her husband had seen the birth of these two boys, they had decided to let them find their own way in the world of faith and religion. She wasn't sure now that it had been the right thing to do, but at the time it had seemed more noble than to force them to accept a certain faith. Through the years, she herself had harbored a simple faith in God that was untethered to any church. She attended no worship service except the solitude of God's presence in the mountains. Prayer had been infrequent but always sincere and in her own way. To hear Tate now ask to pray brought a warmth to her soul that surprised and pleased her.

"I would love to, Tate, as long as you do the praying."

"I'm not very good at it yet, Mom," Tate had said, laughing nervously. "I'd—"

"Tate," Lisa interrupted, "I agree with your Mom. I think you should."

Tate looked from one to the other and had finally sunk to his knees on the plush carpet. The prayer Tate offered was simple yet profound and powerful in its effect on Ruthie. The feeling that had come into that quiet living room was something not of this world.

"I'd better be going," Lisa said.

"I'll walk you out to your car," Tate offered.

Lisa smiled at him. "Thank you."

Ruthie hugged Lisa. Then turning away, she brushed at the tears as she remembered the emotion she had felt in Tate's prayer. Feelings she had not felt in many years had stirred gently in her soul like a breeze through the trees. Not since the earliest days of her childhood at her great-grandfather's knee had she felt this way. He had been a Latter-day Saint, a pioneer of sorts, his family settling the Lemhi River country at the request of Brigham Young. That had been so long ago. Her grandfather and father, for reasons she did not understand, had left the Church and wanted nothing to do with religion, and they had taught their children the same. Ruthie had nothing against any religion. She just had nothing for it either. Ruthie had no religious training beyond the simplest of instincts that draws anyone to their Maker.

It had been almost fifty years since she had sat on her great-grandfather's knee and had felt his tender love and the power of his faith. That memory now seemed a faint and distant light in a world of darkness, and it warmed her soul. It stood in stark contrast against the numbing blackness of worry. Then, almost like a settling dew, she felt an overpowering prompting to pray. She pondered the feeling for a moment. It was powerfully compelling enough to quicken her breath and make her heart race. Obediently, she dropped by the bed.

"Oh, Father. I haven't done this for a long time. All I can think of to say is, I'm sorry if I haven't been all that I should." She paused, thinking of what else she wanted to say. "Father," she continued, "please help J.O. and Shawnee. I know something is wrong. Please watch over them."

She continued pouring out her heart. It felt so comforting. She hardly noticed the sound of the door as Tate came back in and climbed the stairs to his room. The words continued to flow as though decades of feelings were held in reserve for this moment. Just then, a soft rap sounded downstairs at the front door. She was instantly on her feet and pulling her bathrobe around her. As she hurried down the stairs, Tate appeared and followed her. Both knew without saying that it was not J.O. *The door was unlocked and unchained. J.O. would walk in. What if it was the police? What if they have come to tell me—*

She pushed the thought down and hurried faster to the front door. The automatic nightlight cast a faint glow over the hardwood kitchen floor, causing an eerie array of shadows as she walked. After a deep breath, she steeled herself and opened the door. Lisa stood squinting against the bright porch light.

"Lisa!" Ruthie said, surprised. "Come in, Dear. Is everything alright?"

"It is," she said. "I'm sorry to bother you so late, but I—I just didn't want to stay there alone. I hope you don't mind."

Ruthie stepped forward and pulled the frightened girl into her arms. "Mind? I should say not. Come on in. I'll fix you up a bed on the couch."

"I'm sorry to be such a baby," she said, tears welling up in her eyes.

"It's not being a baby to worry about someone you love, Lisa."

Without a word, Tate walked over and put his arms around both of them.

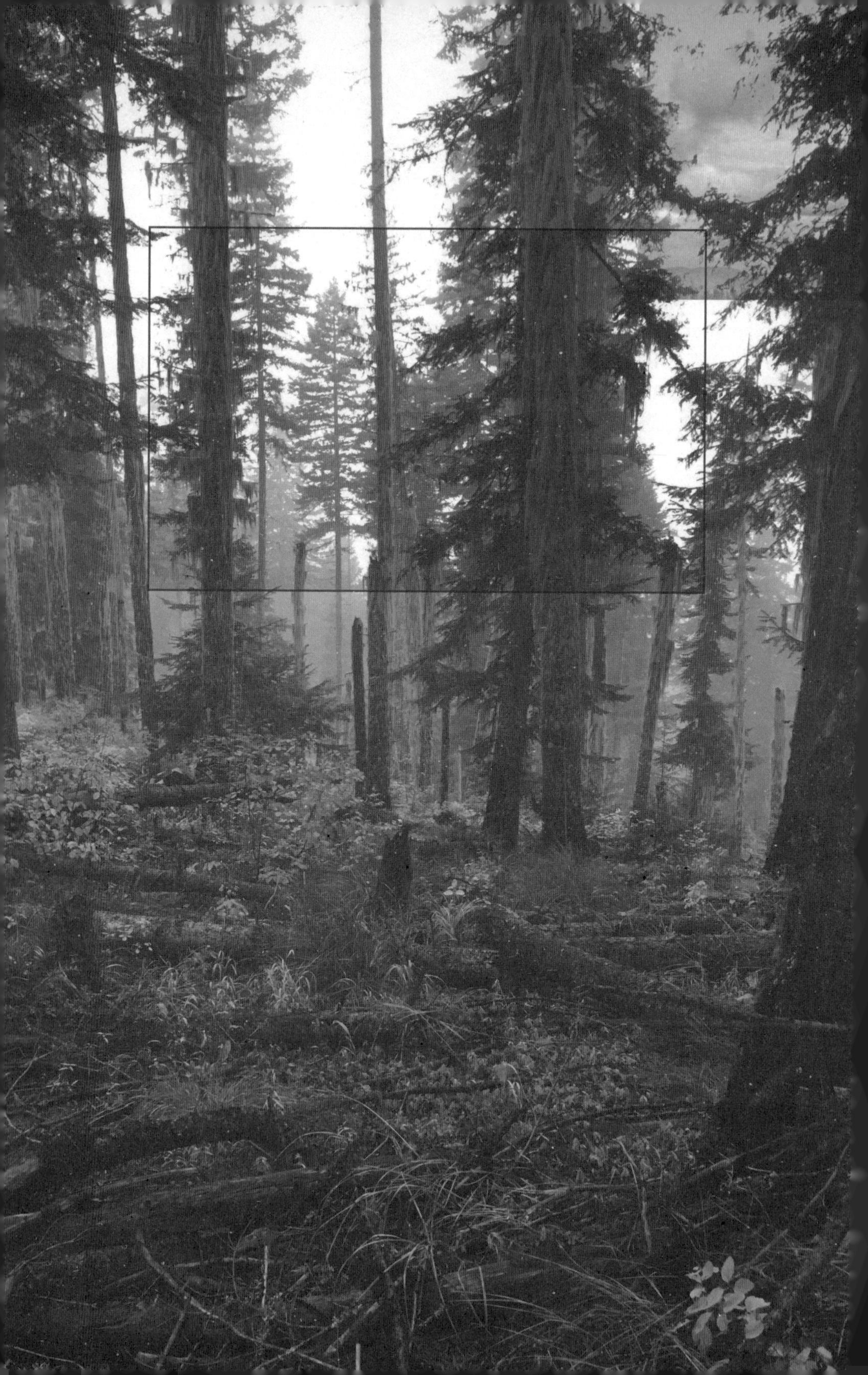

Chapter Thirteen

THE MOUNTAINS WEST OF TETON VALLEY, NEAR PINE CREEK PASS, IDAHO

J.O. brought the truck to a stop and waited. The road was too narrow for anyone to pass, and with the mountain on one side and a steep drop to the creek on the other, someone was going to have to give.

Anyone else would back up or try to pull off—but if the woman named Claude was in that van, all bets were off. The van came to within fifteen feet of the front of the truck and stopped. There was a tense, uncomfortable silence, filled only by the idling of the big diesel engine, as J.O. waited and watched for a declarative movement.

"Is it her?" Shawnee asked, leaning forward and looking out the windshield.

"It has to be," J.O. answered. "No one in her right mind would be in that kind of vehicle in these mountains."

Just then he caught a flash of movement near the driver's door of the van.

"Shawnee!" he yelled, "get down!" He grabbed her and threw her to the floor between the seats, covering her body with his own. The right side of the windshield exploded inward, shards of glass shredding the seat where Shawnee had been sitting seconds earlier. J.O. came up with Johnson's gun in his hand. He shot once through the hole in his windshield. He heard the ring of metal as it hit the van, probably the hood. The door of the van slammed shut.

J.O. scrambled into the driver's seat and rammed the truck into gear. He popped the clutch and the truck shot forward, closing in on the van in an instant. His headlights illuminated the startled expression and frantic actions of the woman as she tried to shove the vehicle into reverse and get away. She was not fast enough. The heavy truck and trailer impacted the front of the van and began pushing it backward like a heavyweight linebacker sacking a skinny quarterback. In desperation, Claude locked up all six tires on the van, but it made no difference. As the huge semi gained speed, J.O. steered it toward the edge of the road where it dropped off abruptly about twenty feet into the small stream. The van caught the steep edge and began to tip. J.O. jerked the wheel hard to the right and stomped the accelerator. The van careened off the bumper of the semi like a snowflake off a fifteen-ton snowplow. The van tipped and rolled down the embankment, coming to rest in the stream.

J.O. cast a sideward glance out the window as he went past. He saw only dust and taillights—no movement. He shifted the transmission to a higher gear and accelerated again. If Claude was alright, she would come out shooting, and he was not going to be in range when she did. If, on the other hand, she was injured, the police would take care of her.

Shawnee was up and instantly beside him, her arms around his neck hugging him. "That was incredible! Where did you learn to drive like that?"

"Back home on the ranch," he said with a grin. "Hey, I thought I told you to stay down."

"You did, but I got back up to watch the fireworks."

"Didn't your daddy ever teach you to mind?" he said, pretending to scold her.

"I'm sorry," she said, feigning a little-girl pout.

He laughed. She hugged him again, more fiercely. The relief of tension made them both almost giddy.

"I think that pretty well takes care of the bad guys, don't you?" he said, laughing.

"Does it ever!" she hugged him again and laughed with the intoxicating humor of relief. "They're all bloody and bruised. Imagine what the police are going to say when they come back to clean up this mess."

He laughed with her, the euphoria of escape making the blinding pain in his head almost bearable. "I can't believe we actually got out of that. It was a miracle!"

They both stopped at the realization of what he had just said.

When Shawnee spoke, there was softness in her voice. "It *was* a miracle, J.O.—just what we asked for." Tenderly, she reached for his right hand and held it. "I told you, J.O., God hears prayers," she leaned over closer, "and answers them!"

He smiled at her. "Maybe you're right."

"There's no *maybe* about it."

In the dim light of the cab, he looked over into her eyes. He had never seen anything so lovely.

"Yes," he murmured, "you're right!"

|||||||||||||||||||

"Turn here," Shawnee said.

J.O. wheeled the truck to the right and saw the sign marking the entrance to the Teton County Hospital. They had safely reached the highway and driven straight into Driggs, Idaho. The plan had been to call the police first, but Shawnee insisted they could do that from the hospital. He needed a doctor. The pain in his head had become so intense that he could hardly keep his eyes open. Added to that, his left eye still wouldn't focus, and he was nauseous. There was no doubt that he was suffering the effects of a concussion. Shawnee was trained, and she knew J.O. was in a precarious condition. She voiced her relief when the hospital sign

Teton Valley Hospital

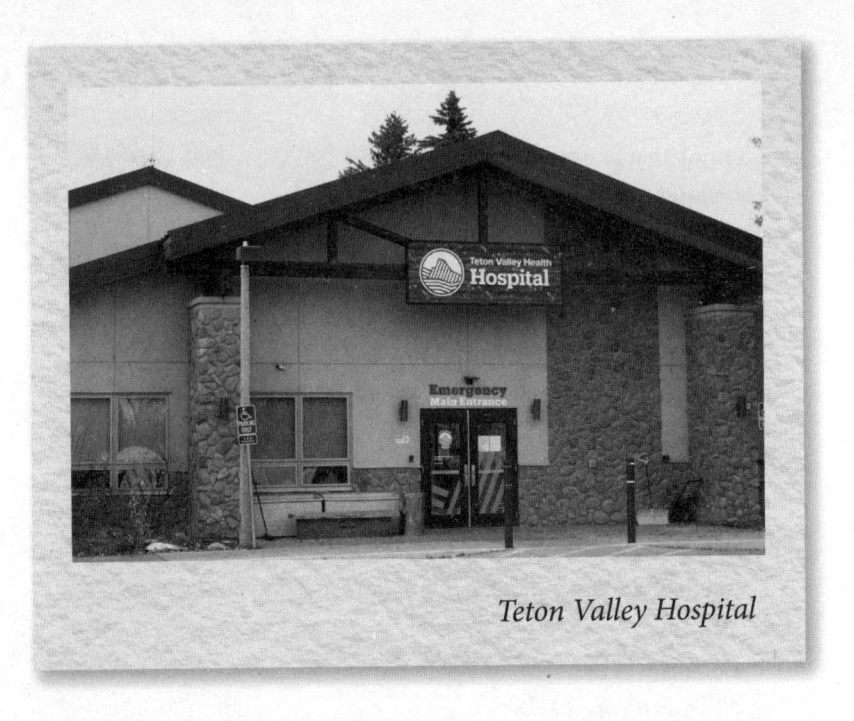

came into view and J.O. rolled the truck to a stop and set the brakes. She jumped out the passenger side and came around to help him.

"I'm alright," he protested as he started to climb to the ground.

"No, you're not," she said, taking his arm. "I've been watching you and holding my breath all the way here, hoping that you wouldn't pass out. You're in bad shape."

She steered him toward the emergency entrance some fifty yards away. They had barely rounded the front of the semi when a dark blue Ford Expedition came out of nowhere and recklessly slid to a stop between them and the hospital entrance. The two doors nearest them burst open, and two men jumped out, weapons at the ready. J.O. didn't recognize either of them. His first thought was *police*, but that was quickly dispelled as Claude came around the front of the Expedition and into view. He heard Shawnee gasp and felt her grip on his arm tighten. A large purple bruise showed on Claude's forehead, and her clothing was torn in a couple of places. Somehow, she had managed to get out of the van.

"Going somewhere?" she hissed.

J.O. glanced toward the hospital entrance. No one was there. No one was watching. He turned back to his captors.

"Evidently not," he sighed in tired resignation and lifted his hands above his head.

Shawnee was shoved roughly into the Expedition with the two men, while Claude forced J.O. into the semi at gunpoint. She ordered him to follow the Expedition. They traveled south through Victor and then began climbing Teton Pass.

"Where are we headed now?" J.O. asked.

"Top of the pass," Claude said curtly. Obviously, she didn't consider him worth wasting words on.

She didn't speak again until the Expedition reached the summit of the Pass and turned off to the right on a small, dirt road.

"Follow it," she said, with a wave of her gun.

The road was not as bad as the other had been. It wound along the top of the Teton mountain range and came out near what appeared to be a radio tower.

"Pull it over there," Claude gestured.

J.O. pulled the truck into an open grassy area alongside the Expedition. He set the brakes and looked out the front window. The mountain fell off steeply in front of him. The headlights of the truck shone out into thin air and lost all definition. The lights of the city of Jackson Hole shone from the valley floor some three thousand feet below.

"You first," Claude said, pointing to the driver's door.

J.O. backed out of the cab and stepped to the ground. Claude followed him, never taking her gun off him. Her stare was icy and full of hate. J.O. stared back, smiling blandly into the bitter expression. It satisfied him to see the anger in her expression deepen further. The angrier he could make her, the greater would be his advantage. Anger makes people irrational, even insane, which is likely why *mad* has been used as a synonym for anger. Angry people do stupid things, and that was what J.O. was counting on now. Sooner or later, her seething anger would boil over, and he would be ready.

He turned to walk, and she shoved her gun into the small of his back to prod him along. As he walked toward the rear of the trailer, he glanced at his watch. It was 3:20 a.m. He was going on twenty-two hours without sleep. The two men and Shawnee were waiting for them at the back of the trailer.

"Open it," a taller, dark-haired man with heavy eyebrows ordered.

J.O. jerked the latches and swung the heavy doors open. As the faint light fell into the trailer, Johnson and Lawson stumbled forward. They had managed to free their hands of the duct tape.

"Well, well," Claude said, "I wondered what happened to you two."

"It's about time," Johnson growled. He started forward to get out of the trailer.

He stopped short as Claude's gun came up under his nose. "Not so fast, *darling*." She seemed to spit the word out. "Let me introduce you to someone. This is my husband, Jason." she said, pointing toward the tall, dark-haired man. "And this is my brother, Marc." A slender young man with long brown hair tipped his head in a mock bow.

Johnson's face blanched as the realization hit him.

"We appreciate all your efforts to set all this up," Jason said with a derisive laugh.

Johnson looked pitiful as he sank to the floor of the trailer, his back against the wall. He looked every bit the picture of a man defeated.

"Now, if you would be so kind as to move that gold out of there," Jason said with contempt. He turned to J.O. "You, get up in there, and help them lift that gold out."

They were forced to carry the gold from the trailer and put it in J.O.'s truck. They placed bars in the exterior utility boxes, on the floor inside the truck, and throughout the sleeper. A faint pinkish glow was just beginning to illuminate the eastern horizon as they finished.

J.O. leaned against the trailer for support. His nausea and dizziness had been made worse by the exertion of lifting. Shawnee came and stood by him, taking him by the arm.

"Are you okay?" she whispered.

"Just can't get my head to clear," he said, hoarsely.

She moved closer to him as though to support him. "What do you think they are going to do now?"

"I don't know."

They didn't have long to wonder as Marc's voice called out, "Alright, driver. Turn this thing around so that the rear of the trailer is on the edge of the hill."

J.O. looked at Shawnee and shrugged. He walked to the cab while Marc brought Shawnee over to stand by him. It took a few minutes in the cramped space to turn the rig around and back it up against the edge of the mountain. Marc signaled him to stop a few feet from the edge.

"Stay in the truck," Jason ordered.

A growing feeling of dread rose in J.O. as he saw Claude and Marc force Lawson and Johnson into the back of the trailer and close the heavy doors.

"Now back it up," Jason barked.

J.O.'s eyes narrowed, and his expression hardened as he figured out what they were going to do. He didn't move.

Jason stepped up to the running board of the truck and pointed his weapon at J.O.'s head. Still, he didn't move.

"Marc!" Jason barked, without taking his eyes off J.O.

Marc's fist suddenly shot out and caught Shawnee on the cheek, knocking her off her feet.

As she lay on the ground holding her cheek, Marc stood over her and pointed his gun at her head.

"You choose," Jason said to J.O., a malevolent grin on his face.

J.O. seethed as he weighed his odds. They had him where he hated to be. If he were alone, he would take his chances, but he wasn't alone, and he would not let his actions bring her any more injury.

Without a word, he reached over and released the brakes. At the same time, he locked the driving axles together and put the truck in a low, forward gear. Keeping the clutch in and a steady pressure on the brakes, he let the rig roll backward until he felt a jerk as the axles on the trailer dropped over the steep face of the mountain. He held his breath. If he let go of the brakes or made a single error, the entire rig would plummet off the mountain and roll for several hundred feet.

Shawnee would live with the nightmare of what happened next for the rest of her life. She struggled to her feet and watched as Jason walked over to the fifth-wheel connection where the truck and trailer connected. He bent down, grabbed something, and jerked backward. The trailer rocketed back, popping the lines and wiring cables that connected it to the truck. Hissing like an angry snake, it rolled off the mountain. About a hundred feet down, the brakes on the trailer locked up. As they did so, the front of the trailer came up and flipped over in a backward somersault, slamming down on its top. The force ruptured the superstructure of the trailer, reducing it instantly to junk. It then rolled out of control for another hundred yards until it came to rest against a stand of lodgepole pine.

In the dim predawn light, Shawnee stared at the wreckage, hoping to see signs of life from the two men trapped inside. There was none.

"Goodbye, *Babe*!" Claude said with a laugh, looking down the hill.

J.O. shut off the trailer air supply valve and slowly climbed out of the truck to join the others who were looking down the hill. Jason allowed him to walk to Shawnee. He came straight to her and touched her gently on her cheek. It was already beginning to swell and discolor. As he looked into her eyes, tears welled up in hers and she placed her hand over his on her cheek. Claude's voice came from behind him.

"If it were left up to me, truck driver," she said in a low voice, "you'd be down there with them." She stared at him for a moment and then started to walk away as though going to join her husband.

J.O.'s eyes narrowed, and his teeth clenched at the threat. "Kind of tough when someone else pulls your chain, isn't it?"

She stopped and turned to face him. Her eyes became black pools of hate. She didn't have to say it, but he knew that before this was through, she would have her way with him. She would exact every last ounce of vengeance that a twisted mind can invent. J.O. didn't look away but held her gaze defiantly until the visual duel was ended by Jason calling her over.

Shawnee clutched at his arm for the first time as Claude walked away. It was as though the air was lighter now that she was gone.

"J.O., she's insane. I have never met anyone as evil and dark as she is. Even if I meet the devil, I can't imagine he would be any worse."

J.O. didn't look at Shawnee. His feet were still firmly planted, as though he were a tall tree weathering a winter blast. His back was straight, and his shoulders were squared. He nodded slightly. "Yes," he said, "and fools always make mistakes."

||||||||||||||||

The first rays of dawn would illuminate the Gros Ventre range in less than an hour. J.O. drove his truck through the quiet, darkened streets of Jackson, Wyoming. Shawnee was in the Expedition in front of him, being guarded by Jason, who was driving, and by Claude, who was sitting in the back seat beside Shawnee.

J.O. glanced over at Marc, who sat in the passenger seat of his truck. He was holding his gun on J.O. and staring at him with the same humorless grin he had worn all evening. The corners of his mouth turned up on his pretty-boy face in such a way as to give J.O. the impression that this man had few concerns in life. Not only did this man have few concerns *in* life, he had few concerns *for* life. This was a man who would kill him with a gun in one hand and a cheeseburger in the other. His soul seemed as lifeless and desolate as a high-plains winter.

As J.O. drove, he couldn't help the self-recriminations. *How could I have been so stupid as to bring Shawnee into something like this? Why didn't a loving God stop such things as this—or at least provide some warning? Was there* really *a God? Will I ever know for sure?* He felt sick inside.

He tried to shrug it off. He was too tired and in too much pain to think, let alone think rationally. He sighed and turned to look out the window at the storefronts of Jackson. They were just passing the Million Dollar Cowboy Bar. He had stood on this street in the summer when the crowds were so thick he couldn't walk a straight line down the sidewalk. The streets and sidewalks were empty now.

J.O. rubbed his left eye, hoping it would come into focus, but it only made the eye water. His head still hurt worse than any headache he had ever had, though some of the nausea had subsided. He touched the side of his head. It was swollen and tender. The bandana was dry and stiff with caked blood. He could only imagine how rough he must look.

He accelerated to keep up with the Expedition as they exited the north end of Jackson going toward Grand Teton National Park. The airport. They had to be going to the airport in Jackson. It was the only thing that made sense. These goons would have a high-priced aircraft waiting that would jet them and their stolen gold out of the country before anyone was the wiser.

J.O. felt his pulse quicken with anxiety. He was running out of time. Once the truck was no longer needed, neither was he, and he and Shawnee would be disposed of like common refuse.

He racked his aching brain for an escape. There was nothing. For all intents and purposes, he was back in the trailer with Shawnee. That thought triggered a mental image. He saw Shawnee kneeling before him on the filthy, wooden floor of the trailer and pouring out her soul to her God. Had it been because of prayer that they were still alive? In his dream, as he had been about to go over the mountain, he had called for God. When he had wanted Shawnee to breathe that day on the river, he had expressed a faith he didn't know he had. Why did the logical thinking of his head always manage to kill the innate faith of his heart? Suddenly he straightened. That was it! The thinking man was killing the feeling man. Faith sprouts in the heart. His teeth clenched and his jaw set in determination. At that moment he made a decision.

Father, are you there? he cried in his heart. *I need you. I have nowhere else to turn. Can you forgive me and help me save Shawnee? Please, Father.*

Marc stirred in his seat and sat up straighter, staring intensely at him. J.O. caught his fierce stare and momentarily held it. He had said nothing this man could have heard. If there was a devil, could it be that this incarnate son of evil sensed something divine and was discomfited by it? J.O. looked back down the highway, taking more confidence by the minute.

Father, he continued, *I have little time left. Please help.*

He stopped praying as a comforting feeling of peace and power settled on his soul. Even as the throbbing pain in his head seemed to lessen, J.O. Steele knew there was a way. Someone somewhere had heard him. He felt courage and faith for the first time in hours. He glanced over at Marc and smiled as he noticed that the smirk had disappeared from his face, replaced with a look of anger.

||||||||||||||||

J.O. saw the sign at the same time Jason signaled a left-hand turn. *Jackson Airport.*

He had been to this airport before. Celebrities went in and out of here like a revolving door. As they approached the headquarters of

Jackson Hole Aviation, J.O. looked around for any signs of someone or something to help them. The airport appeared deserted. He felt his pulse quicken. This was it. It was now or never. The Expedition pulled up to the gate. Jason gave the appropriate information to airport security, and the automated gate swung open. J.O. followed him with the truck. They turned left and moved down the apron through a long line of private aircraft parked on the ramp to a sleek Cessna Citation, gleaming brightly in the moonlight.

Marc directed J.O. to park the truck as close as possible to the aircraft's door. Once in place, he and J.O. loaded the gold into the plane. Jason climbed aboard the aircraft and started the engines.

Claude had parked the Expedition just a few feet behind the truck to block the view of anyone in the terminal. She stepped out of the Expedition and watched but forced Shawnee to get in the front seat and stay in the vehicle. When the gold was loaded, Marc said to J.O., "Get back in the truck."

They were standing about two feet apart near the passenger door of the truck. The malevolent smile had returned to Marc's face. J.O. glanced at Claude. She too was smiling. Something passed between she and her brother that sent a clear signal to J.O. The truck and Expedition would be parked in the lot like hundreds of other park-and-fly vehicles, but one occupant in each vehicle would not live to board the aircraft. Was it a voice or adrenalin? J.O. didn't know, but his fist shot out and hit Marc's gun. It launched out of his hand and skidded across the concrete. At the same moment, J.O. pivoted and with all his shoulder behind it, drove his fist into the point of Marc's delicate nose. He felt it crunch under his knuckles. There was a sharp cry of pain and Marc went down, clutching at his broken nose.

The yell brought Claude around to see. She was just getting into the Expedition. Before she could react, Shawnee kicked out with both legs and hit her in the shoulder. The force of the blow knocked the wiry

French woman off her feet and sent her sprawling on the concrete. She was instantly back on her feet, gun in hand, and as angry as a cornered panther. She fired recklessly at the Expedition, trying to hit Shawnee, but Shawnee had leaped over the seats and onto the floorboards.

J.O. started after Claude to draw her fire away from Shawnee, but Marc was on his feet, blood pouring out of his nose as he staggered forward with fists flailing like a third-grade boxer. J.O. ducked beneath the flying fists, and with a powerful uppercut he laid open the man's chin and dropped him to the ground. J.O. whirled and tried to get to Shawnee, but Claude was turning her murderous rage on him. J.O. saw it coming and threw himself to the side in a rolling somersault in front of the bumper of his truck. A bullet ricocheted off the concrete with a musical zing. Jason appeared in the door of the aircraft, holding a long-barreled handgun. He too fired at J.O.'s rolling form. J.O. ran down the length of his truck toward the Expedition, keeping low.

Suddenly, a brilliant light flooded the area and an authoritative voice barked out, "Don't move. FBI. you're under arrest!"

Marc was just staggering to his feet when three men dressed in black materialized like phantoms from out of the darkness, grabbed his arms, and yanked them behind his back. Jason drew down and fired at the agents who were wrestling with Marc. The bullet struck, but it was Marc who cried out in pain and suddenly went limp.

"Marc!" Claude screamed as the agents rolled for cover and returned fire at Jason.

Three shots rang out. Jason doubled over and was thrown backward into the plane's luxury interior.

"Jason!" Claude screamed again.

Claude hesitated only a split second and then began firing blindly in the direction of the scrambling agents, emptying her magazine like a mad woman. As she fired, she ran toward the door of the Expedition. J.O. anticipated her move and tried to cut her off. He reached the passenger door and tried to jerk it open. It was locked. He looked for Shawnee, but the dark tint of the windows blocked out the light. Where was she? Claude was almost to the driver's door. Without thinking, J.O. leaped onto the roof of the Expedition, trying to reach the driver's door before Claude did, but she was there first. She leaped inside and slammed the door. The tires of the vehicle smoked and squealed in reverse as it spun in a circle. J.O. grabbed for any kind of handhold on the roof of the Expedition. There was none.

J.O. was thrown onto the hood of the vehicle just as Claude punched it. Rolling onto his belly, he spread his legs and clung to the hood. When he looked up, he found himself eye-to-eye with Claude, her face contorted with screaming rage. As the Expedition accelerated, Claude jerked the wheel savagely from side to side, trying to dislodge him. He clung like a squirrel to a tree. He thought he caught a fleeting glance of Shawnee's blond hair in the back of the Expedition, but he couldn't look for long. His attention became riveted as Claude shoved her gun against the windshield less than three inches from his face. He let go just as the Expedition went into another wild turn. The speed and force catapulted him like a rock from a shepherd's sling. He flew off and hit the concrete at nearly thirty miles per hour, rolling and bouncing, tearing away a major portion of his already bloody shirt and parts of his shoulder. It felt like he was never going to stop rolling. As he came to a stop, he struggled to his feet, pushing down the pain, and started after the Expedition, half running, half limping. He thought he heard the agents yelling behind him and sensed they were chasing him, but he ignored them. Shawnee was in that vehicle.

There was only one exit from the airport, and that was the main gate. Claude would have to go to the end of a long line of parked aircraft and double back to the gate. J.O. changed direction, running like a wounded Olympic sprinter for the gate. He broke through the line of aircraft. The gate was less than seventy-five yards in front of him and closed. If he could reach the security controls it would stay that way, but it was going to be close. The Expedition careened around the last aircraft and turned toward the gate. J.O. reached the gate just as it began to open. *Why is it opening?* The engine of the Expedition began to roar as Claude floored it. J.O. looked about desperately, but there was nothing he could do to stop her. He jumped out of the way just as the Expedition shot through the gate and accelerated for the open road.

J.O. ran through the gate, looking about wildly. Claude was getting away, and Shawnee was with her. Then he saw it—an old Chevy pickup, vintage early seventies, was parked near the gate and idling. It had oversize tires and growled like a motor with power. He ran for it and jumped in. The tires squealed as he reversed out of the parking lot and went after Claude. The truck was old, but it was souped up and hot, probably belonging to some teenager. Snap-shifting through all the gears, he pushed the old truck to its limits, straining to keep Shawnee in his sights.

The Expedition was faster and more nimble, but he was the better driver. The taillights of the Expedition were visible as it sped toward the main road into Jackson. J.O. smashed down harder on the accelerator, willing the old war horse to go faster. It responded. His head pounded, and he felt blood trickling down the side of his head where the wound had been reopened. He ignored it and fixed his gaze on the lights. Shawnee was with that mad woman. He couldn't lose her. He wouldn't lose her!

Behind him, J.O. glimpsed the flashing lights of the agent's cars. He glanced down at the speedometer. The needle was buried. The agents would never catch up before they covered the eight miles into Jackson. They seemed to cover the distance in seconds. The Expedition's speed did not diminish in the slightest as it raced into the city center.

J.O. kept the old pickup floored as he entered Jackson, hoping mightily that there were no cars or tourists in the way.

Claude raced through Jackson's first stop light in excess of seventy miles per hour. Flashing blue lights suddenly darted out in front of her from a side street across from the Elkhorn Park. Claude mashed the brakes, causing the Expedition to slide. At the same time, she jerked the wheel to the right. The momentum lifted the Expedition up on two wheels and nearly flipped it. J.O. held his breath. By some kind of luck, the Expedition steered under the momentum and settled back onto four tires. Claude stomped it again, and it roared away down the side street. J.O. followed, sliding around the same corner, a plan forming in his mind. Claude didn't know this town like he did. There was one major route through town. If Claude made an immediate left turn, there was a chance he could get ahead of her and block the road.

"C'mon, turn that thing," he muttered through gritted teeth.

As if she heard him, the Expedition abruptly leaned hard into a left turn.

J.O. felt a rush of exhilaration. He didn't let up or turn to follow her. Instead, he went straight two more blocks. The tires of the old Chevy whined on the hot asphalt as it slid into the turn. He gunned the motor and darted two blocks south. As the nose of the pickup entered the main street, he locked up the brakes and began to slide. He looked sideways just in time to see headlights and the grill of the Expedition slam into his door with deadly force. J.O. felt the door crumple inward. His head slammed into the side window, knocking it out. Searing pain shot through his ribs, and his body was thrown across the cab. He felt nothing after that.

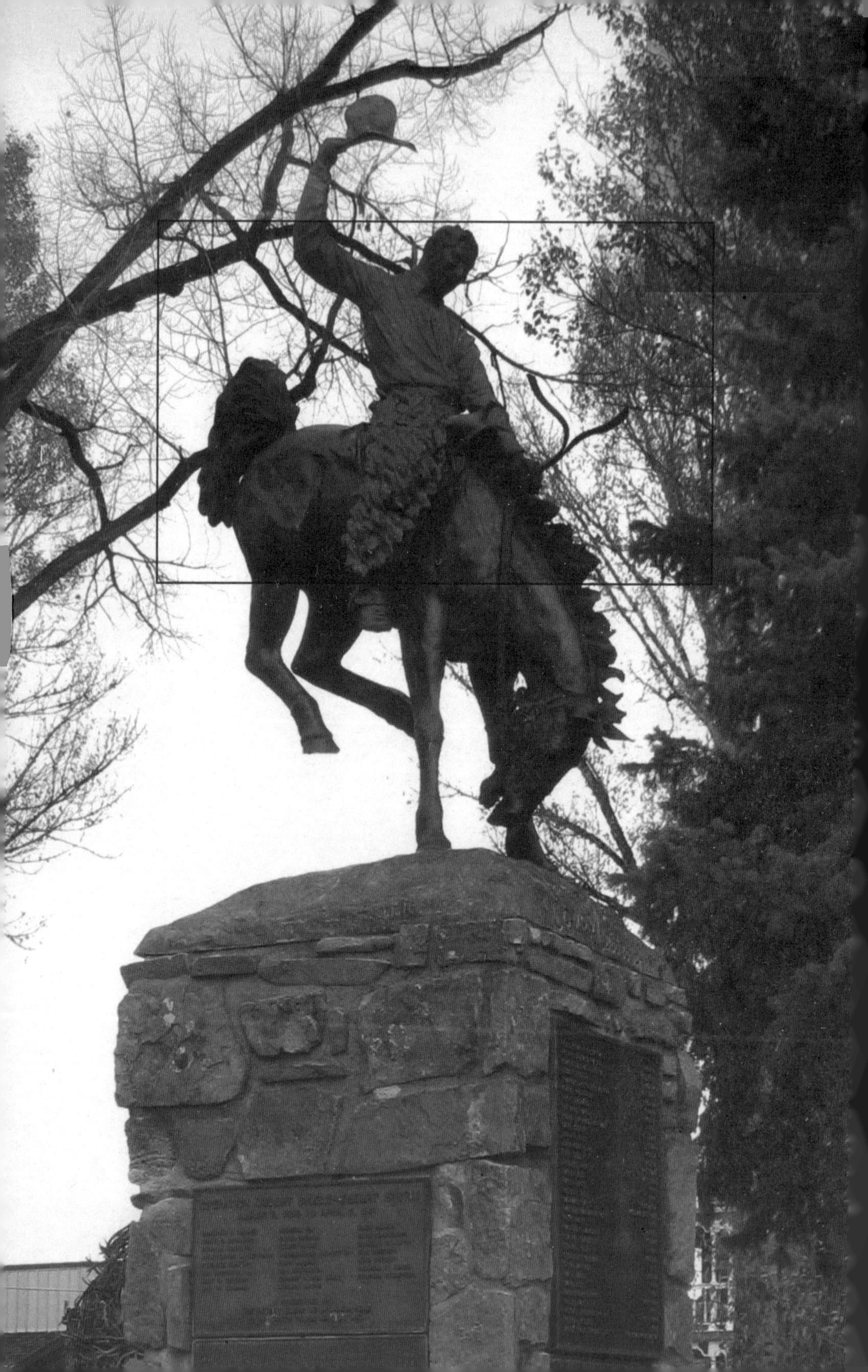

Chapter Fourteen

JACKSON HOSPITAL, AUGUST 2021

It was like coming out of a dense, soupy fog, except the darkness was over his mind and senses, not just his eyes. Slowly, J.O.'s external world began to invade his consciousness—the ambiguous murmur of voices, the sounds of movement, a sensation of feeling returning to his body. At that moment, his mind registered the pain. It was horrible. Every part of his body from the crown of his head to the ends of his toes ached. He tried to move his arm, but it wouldn't respond; neither would his legs. A feeling of panic gripped him, and he tried to cry out, but there was no sound. The word *paralyzed* pierced his mind like a flaming arrow.

No! he screamed in his mind as he pictured himself gritting his teeth and fighting against the force that held him still.

Then he sensed a slight movement in his arm. Relief washed over him. He began to concentrate on opening his eyes. It took several more minutes before he could get one eye open. The light in the room was dim, and he couldn't tell what time of day it was. He could tell he was in a hospital room, but where? Why? He closed his eyes and searched his memory for details.

Slowly it came back—the chase, the wreck, Shawnee! At the thought of her, his heart began to race. *Where is she? Did she survive the wreck? Jackson. I must be in Jackson, Wyoming.* This time when he commanded his eyes to open, they both obeyed. After a few minutes and considerable effort, he was able to turn his head and perceive that someone was sitting in a chair next to his bed. His left eye wouldn't focus, but in a few seconds the right eye finally brought the figure into focus. It was a woman. She was curled up in the chair, her legs up under her chin, apparently sleeping. He strained to make out who it was. Finally, he could focus. It was Shawnee! He tried to sit up but couldn't. Opening his mouth, he tried to say something, but only a faint, hoarse croak came from his dry throat. Frustrated, he fell back into the pillow, squeezed his eyes tightly shut, and willed his body to obey him.

Suddenly there was a sound at his side. "J.O.?" The voice was tentative and inquiring.

He opened his eyes and saw Shawnee leaning over him.

"Morning, sunshine," he said, smiling weakly.

"Oh, thank heaven," she said, pressing his hand to her lips.

"Miss me?" he rasped, teasing her.

Tears of pure relief filled her eyes and overflowed as she leaned over him and kissed him softly on the cheek and embraced him lightly. "You have no idea, Joseph," she whispered. "You have no idea!"

<hr>

"Three days," J.O. said in surprise as he sat propped against the head of his hospital bed. Shawnee, who had scarcely left his side since he woke up, sat on the edge of the bed next to him. His mother sat at the foot of the bed; Tate, Lisa, and Rick and Marie James filled the small room.

"Yes, three days," Ruthie confirmed. "You've been in a coma for three days. When they first brought you in, the doctor didn't think you were going to make it. Your head had been hit so many times, he said there was a good chance you would never wake up."

J.O. grinned weakly. "I guess my head is as hard as my name."

"It wasn't just your head," Ruthie continued. "You have two broken ribs, a broken arm, and enough sprains, bruises, and scrapes to make it look as though someone tried to run you through a hay-baler."

"Is that all?" he asked jokingly.

Tate stood with his arm around Lisa's waist. "You're really lucky you're still alive," Tate said. "The old pickup you stole was totaled. They had to cut you out of it."

"Who did it belong to?" J.O. asked sheepishly.

"Some kid who was using it for delivery work," Tate continued. Then he laughed. "Oh, he was ticked off when he saw the truck. He was going to sue. He was going to file charges. You'd think you had committed a capital offense."

"What changed his mind?" J.O. asked.

"Several things, I guess. The FBI explained the circumstances to him. I heard that the insurance company offered him more than the truck was worth, but I guess the real clincher that made him back off was that the truck wasn't insured. The city police officer investigating the accident told him to shut his trap or he would cite him for everything he could think of, and I guess he had quite a list. We haven't heard from him since."

"So how did the federal agents find us?" J.O. asked.

"The gold was bugged," Shawnee said. "It always had been. It took some time for them to get an exact fix on us, but when they did, they were right behind us. When you tackled Marc, you accelerated their plans by about five minutes. It was probably a good thing. If they had waited any longer, they would have had a worse hostage situation on their hands."

Turning slightly to look at her, J.O. studied the bruises on her cheek. Gently, he reached up and touched her cheek with the hand that carried his IV. "Speaking of that, how did you manage to come through that wreck so well?"

Shawnee looked startled for a moment. "Wreck? You mean when Claude hit you in town?"

He nodded.

Shawnee gaped at him. "You mean you thought I was in that thing?"

"You were," J.O. said, struggling to hold on to his mental equilibrium. "I saw you just as we left the plane."

"I was, but—" She paused for a moment staring at his befuddled expression. Her face softened as it suddenly became clearer. "You thought I was in that thing the whole time?"

"Yes! Why do you think I went after her in the first place?"

Shawnee leaned over and kissed him on the cheek again. Several people in the room looked down to hide the rush of emotion that swelled up. Shawnee spoke quietly. "When Claude made that last turn before the gate, I got the rear passenger door open and bailed out. I saw you running and called to you. I guess you didn't hear me." She put her arm around his shoulder and looked affectionately into his blue eyes. "I wasn't in the vehicle when Claude left the airport." J.O. sagged back into the bed and closed his eyes.

"You mean I did all that for nothing?" he said with a laugh, lifting his casted arm.

Everyone laughed lightly. "Afraid so, Son," Ruthie said.

Tate broke the ice. "If you're going to save someone, Bro, you should at least make sure they need saving." Everyone laughed again.

"Well, I think it was wonderful," Shawnee said as she put her arms around him and hugged him. "It was sweet and heroic."

Tate hooted at that.

"Whatever it was," Ruthie Steele said, "it took courage and a lot of it."

Rick James stepped forward and shook J.O.'s bandaged hand. "Thank you again for saving my daughter."

Marie came forward, bent over, and kissed him on the cheek. "That goes for me too. Thank you! And as soon as you get out of here, you have another invitation to dinner."

J.O. smiled. "I will definitely take you up on that." He glanced at Shawnee. "But this time is was more her who saved me, and in more ways than one."

Shawnee's parents glanced at her, but she shrugged her shoulders as if to say, *I don't know what he's talking about.* Everyone then looked at J.O. "I'll explain later," he said. "What about the bad guys? Did they get them?"

"Jason and Marc were both dead at the airport," Shawnee said quietly.

"What about Johnson and Lawson?" J.O. asked, afraid of the answer.

"They both survived—barely," Tate said. "They were pretty banged up, but it looks as though they'll pull through."

"Who were these people? What was this all about?"

Shawnee spoke up. "As near as we can tell, it was a double cross. Claude was the key to all of it. She was something of a grifter. She got Johnson, who worked at the gold mine, to turn. She promised him wealth and all the rest if he would give her the info on the gold. He worked at the mill and knew the mine's output. She suckered him in by pretending to have a thing for him. He fell for it. Next, they needed someone to get them access to the armored trucks. Trent Lawson was the natural. His personal life was a mess, and he was the prime dupe. They stole the gold and took it by chopper to Gilmore, where they transferred it into the van. They were then going to Jackson Pass, where they would change to a different van, meet Jason and Marc, and go on to Jackson Airport."

"Let me guess," J.O. interrupted, "Johnson and Lawson were never going to make that flight?"

"Nope," Shawnee continued. "We can only assume they got just what they were going to get all along. The whole thing would be pinned on them and Claude, and since she was a French national and now out of the country, they would never find her."

"Speaking of Claude, what about her?" J.O. asked.

The mood in the room changed perceptibly. No one would look at him. He sat up straighter. "What? Where is she?"

"She's gone, J.O." Shawnee said softly.

"Gone! What do you mean she's gone? How could she have—?"

"No one knows," Shawnee said. "After she broadsided you, she lost control and rolled the Expedition. She took out about thirty feet of very expensive storefront and came to rest upside down, mostly inside a clothing store. The police were there within minutes, but when they searched the vehicle, she was gone. They searched the area thoroughly and placed roadblocks at the edges of town, but they never found her. From the amount of blood, they think she was badly injured, but there's been no sign of her."

J.O. collapsed back into the pillow and closed his eyes. "Great!" he said with obvious exasperation. "Then it really was for nothing."

"Son," Ruthie said with concern, "are you alright?"

He opened his eyes again, but instead of acknowledging the question he turned and looked directly at Shawnee. "She'll come after us," he finally said. "You know what she was like. As sure as the wind blows in Wyoming, that crazy woman will want revenge."

Shawnee reached up and touched the heavy bandages on his head. For a moment, she said nothing, as though she were lost in her thoughts. Then she looked back at him, and with a prolonged sigh said, "I know."

What happened next would remain with all who saw it, especially her parents. Shawnee's expression seemed to change. There was no fear—no trembling dread. The quiet softness of her face was replaced with a look of fire and steely resolve. "I know," she repeated. "Let her come!"

||||||||||||||||

Three Days Earlier

The old pickup came out of nowhere. There was no time to stop or even apply a brake. Everything spun out of control at the impact. Claude felt herself being hurled forward, and her face smashed into the windshield. There was the banshee-scream of grinding metal and a sensation of spinning and rolling, and then all was quiet.

She awakened with her face pressed against the rough, wooden boardwalk. The sound of approaching sirens caused a surge of adrenalin. As she raised herself off the rough boardwalk, she felt it pull against her cheek. Her cheek had been ground into it and shredded. She jerked away and rose to her feet. Her hands shot out in front of her to steady her balance. She froze in numbed shock. The little finger on her left hand was gone. In its place was a bloody stump of mangled flesh. Bile rose in her throat and she gagged. Fighting back the urge to retch, she struggled forward.

The Expedition had flipped over onto its top. Half of it was on the boardwalk, the other half inside a store. She had been thrown out when it rolled. Only inches closer, and the vehicle would have crushed her. Panic gripped her. The wail of the sirens seemed practically on top of her. She had only seconds to get out or be caught. She saw the blue-and-red lights reflected off the nearby buildings. Half running and half crawling, she turned the corner and stumbled down the street in the direction opposite the approaching sirens and lights. Moments later, she was out of Jackson's business district and into the darker residential area. The temptation to look at her wounds was strong, but she knew if she did, shock would overtake her, and she would be caught. Willing herself to maintain control, she looked around and contemplated options.

A car rounded the corner in front of her, less than a block away. Under the faint glow of the streetlights, she could see the lights atop the car. She dived through a manicured shrub into a yard and dropped to the ground. Had the cops seen her? The car drove slowly past, searching the area with a spotlight. Claude flattened herself against the ground beneath the bushes and scarcely breathed as the car passed. Once it turned the corner out of sight, she jumped to her feet and ran. Escape was her only thought. Running to the closest car, she tried the door. It was locked. She ran a quarter block to the next car. It was unlocked, but there were no keys in it. She kept running, working her way south, checking every car as she went. Several times she saw police cars but always managed to evade them. Finally, she jerked open the door of a rusted-out Toyota. In the light of the growing dawn, she saw the keys in the ignition. With a small cry of elation, she threw herself in and turned the key. The engine caught immediately. The exhaust was worn out and the car was loud. Gritting her teeth, she idled away from the curb. Once the car was a block away, she accelerated.

In fewer than five minutes, she was out of Jackson, just seconds ahead of a police cordon, and headed south toward Hoback Junction. She glanced in the rearview mirror for pursuing blue lights; there were none. Several miles out of Jackson, she passed the Teton Mystery attraction; still no cops. Had she made it?

As she rolled into Hoback Junction, she thought she might see a roadblock. When there was no sign of any life in the sleepy little mountain village, she relaxed. At the fork in the road, she turned right, not knowing where the road led—and not caring, as long as it was away. On impulse, she leaned over and looked at the rearview mirror. The rising sun cast enough light that she was able to see her reflection. What she saw made her gasp. The face was bloody and unrecognizable. Grotesque bloody splinters of wood protruded from her once-flawless cheek. She raised the mangled left hand and looked once more at her disfigurement. Tears of white-hot rage sprang to her eyes and spilled over onto her cheeks, burning the open cuts.

"*They will pay!*" She raised her bloody left hand and fought the pain. "*Oh, how they will pay!*"

PART TWO:

The Awakening!

THE BOOK OF MORMON

ANOTHER TESTAMENT OF JESUS CHRIST

Chapter Fifteen

POCATELLO, IDAHO, LATE OCTOBER 2021

"Joshua Taylor Steele, having been commissioned of . . ."

Elder Schofield finished the baptismal prayer and lowered Tate into the water. He came up grinning widely and threw his arms around the elder. The two of them stood in a joyful embrace for a few seconds.

Lisa sat next to Shawnee. The joy on her face was as radiant as a brilliant summer sun. Shawnee had her arm around Lisa as the joy brimmed over into tears. They were both laughing and crying at the same time. J.O. reached over and put his arm around both of them, saying nothing.

He leaned back again into the hard metal chair and became momentarily lost in his thoughts. Tate had come a long way. He was converted and eager to fully embrace his new faith, as was his mother. Ruthie had needed only a gentle nudge to discover the wells of faith that were deep within her. Scripture reading and prayer had become more than commonplace around their home in the last few months. Church attendance was a given Sunday occurrence.

J.O. became suddenly self-conscious of the scar on the side of his head. His hair had grown over it, but the ugly red was still visible and caused people to stare. All his life he had been the confident one—in control of his world—but in the last few months, he felt as though his world had gotten away from him. It was as though the rug had been figuratively pulled out from under him and he was trying to pick himself up off the floor. He chided himself for feeling out of place because of a scar, but innately he knew that the scar was not the only thing that made him feel ill at ease. The scar was the symbol of all that had suddenly changed around him, and not by his choice.

Tate appeared from the dressing room and came to sit beside Lisa, who embraced him as he approached. J.O. was happy for his younger brother but angry at the same time. *Why can't things just be the way they were?* J.O. glanced around the room of the stake center. Maybe this was Tate's world now, but it wasn't his. He didn't belong here. For that matter, he couldn't figure out if he even belonged in his own home anymore.

The other missionary stood and started talking about the Holy Ghost. J.O. tuned him out. The Jackson experience had turned him inside out. His injuries were still not completely healed; his eyesight had gradually returned, but headaches still came frequently, and the broken arm was still tender. Comparatively speaking, however, his physical injuries were nothing. To say that he had been racked with doubts and questions the last few months about God, religion, faith, and the Church would have been a gross understatement. He had tried to settle it, accept it, even let himself believe it, but the old questions persisted. After Jackson, the existence of God was a given, but the method of worship—the Church—left him with doubts and questions that tore at his soul like coyotes after sheep.

Shawnee had been his ray of light. It was as though she sensed his turmoil, and though she readily answered his questions, she rarely brought the subject up. She waited for him. They had grown close, closer than he ever thought possible, but he knew at the same time he was hurting her, and that added to his anguish even more. A deep bond of love and affection had developed between them. They were the closest of friends, but the obstacle of faith created an emotional distance that kept them from being more.

The men in the room stood up and came forward to lay their hands on Tate's head. Rick James was among them. He took his place and began to act as voice in the ordinance of confirmation.

There had been flashbulb moments for J.O. when he had felt that voice whisper inside, but it had come seldom, and he was still confused. Other times it was as brilliant as a flash of lightning, but it always faded away—and when the light faded, he was the same man he had always been.

As the ordinance finished, J.O. opened his eyes. Lisa, Shawnee, Marie, and Ruthie were all crying. Powerful words had been spoken. He knew that, but he couldn't *feel* it. He felt nothing!

The benediction was offered, and everyone came forward to congratulate Tate. J.O. pasted a smile on his face and hugged his brother.

"Way to go, little brother," J.O. said, feeling like a hypocrite.

Tate pounded him on the back. "Thanks, Bro."

J.O. moved back and let the crowd have the boy of the hour. Shawnee hugged Tate and then came over to stand beside J.O. She put her arm through his and stood watching the crowd file past. After a few moments, she looked up at him. "You okay?" she asked softly.

He smiled down at her. "They're happy, aren't they?" he said, gesturing toward Tate and Lisa.

"Very much so!"

J.O. looked down at her, no longer able to stand it. "Shawnee, I have to go."

"Where?"

"I'm scheduled in a truck."

She searched his face, saying nothing. "It's still a little soon, isn't it? You're not even healed yet."

"I asked for it. I can handle it. It's an easy east coast drop-and-run. I need the space. Will you walk out with me?" he asked, reaching for her hand.

She nodded, a resigned expression on her face.

J.O. took her hand and led her out the door. Tate caught his eye as he left and waved to him. J.O. waved back, noticing the excited flush on his brother's face. Once outside in the moonlight, J.O. seemed to breathe easier.

"What is it, J.O.? What's wrong?"

"I'm sorry, Shawnee," he said quietly, looking at the ground. "I just can't do it. I can't pretend. Maybe this all works for Tate, but not for me."

For a long moment, Shawnee said nothing. Finally, she turned back to him. When she spoke, he detected pain and weariness in her voice.

"I know. I know how hard all of this has been for you. I wish I could help you, but I don't know how. All I can say, J.O., is follow your heart. Don't do what you think you should do. Do the right thing."

Her words struck him hard, bringing back that moment in Jackson when he had prayed, and his prayer had been answered. As he stood pondering her words, she lifted herself up and kissed him softly.

"I know I shouldn't say this. It's probably the last thing you need to hear, but I love you, Joseph Orson Steele, and with all my heart I pray for you."

He saw the emotion begin to rise in her, but before he could say anything, she turned and walked into the building. She had done all she could do for him. No mortal could take him any further. From here, it was all him—and God!

||||||||||||||||||

It had been a long day and an even longer trip. J.O. wanted to be home, but he still had one full day, maybe two, across Interstate 80 before he would make it home. All his years of driving had never seen him miss home as much as he had this time. He smiled to himself. Even though he had given a multitude of reasons to the dispatcher, there was really only one reason why the wanderer wanted to be home: Shawnee James.

Her image materialized on the screen of his mind. Her last words and kiss had sustained him for the three weeks he had been running up and down the eastern seaboard. He had talked to her on the phone several times, but that was not the same as being with her. She had a way of calming him and giving him hope. It was as though the ten thousand stresses of a workday vanished like morning smoke when he was with her. It was so easy to talk to her, so easy to get her to laugh. It didn't seem to matter what they were doing or where they were—they were comfortable and always had fun.

He breathed deeply and lifted the windshield visor in front of his face. For the last few hours, he had been driving almost due west. The intense sunlight coupled with a dirty windshield had made it difficult to see, but now the sun had dropped low enough on the horizon that its powerful rays were being filtered through the thick, dusty haze typical of the harvest season. The sinking light had exploded the sky into a blaze of variegated colors and hues that caught the breath and arrested the eye. He continued to stare in awestruck admiration as the sun dipped into the horizon and then finally out of sight. It struck him that one could hardly perceive the movement of the sun except at its rising and its setting, at which time it seemed to move so quickly. Within moments after the light disappeared, a gloom seemed to settle over the landscape. The colors of the sunset quickly faded, and darkness obliterated the details of the world that only moments before had been lighted.

A hated but all-too-familiar feeling of loneliness spread over J.O. like a heavy, wet blanket. He thought of Shawnee again. In a way, being away from her was like living in a world where the sun had just set—empty, cold, and unpleasant.

Did he love her? That was the question he had asked himself probably no fewer than fifty times. It wasn't easy to answer. *Can I really say I love her when I don't care about what she cares about? Can I really love her when I know that what I am and what I want is going to hurt her?*

He knew he would never intentionally hurt Shawnee. But he was smart enough to recognize that she was high-quality silk, and he was worn saddle leather. You could sew the two together, but the bond only made both fabrics coarse and cheap. It added to his darkening mood to realize that he was bringing her down, holding her back. There was something she wanted to be, and he was stopping her.

J.O. looked at his watch. He had reached his deadline and was out of driving hours allowed by law. It was time to bed down for the night. An off-ramp loomed in front of him about a mile up the road. Hitting his turn signal, he swung off to the right and brought the truck to a stop near the top of the on-ramp of the lonely country exit. The sign indicated a tiny obscure Nebraska farming village about two miles north of the freeway. He turned the key and the huge engine lurched into stillness. The immensity of a darkening world and his own pitiful nothingness within it closed in around him, making him feel even more alone. Instinctively, he reached for the medallion under his shirt. It was there, like always—and, like always, it made him feel less alone.

Maybe it was time, he thought, to hang up his keys and move on. Maybe it was time to make some radical changes in his life. He sighed. That was the hard part. He knew what Shawnee wanted of him—and she wasn't the only one. He knew her family—and Tate and Lisa, for that matter—wanted the same thing. They all wanted him to be as they were, but could he? He had to admit he didn't know, and the pressure of it was stifling and intense.

He could still see the pain in Shawnee's eyes. It haunted him—made him feel guilty. *She loves me—she told me. So, what is wrong with me? Why is God and religion such an immense hurdle for me and not for others? Why is God making me go through this? Why can't I just go along to get along, as the saying goes? Why can't I just say I believe, and let life be a bowl of peaches?*

He lowered his head into his hands and rubbed his eyes. Then, frustrated, he pushed open the driver's door and stepped out onto the running board. The cool evening air assailed his senses, and he breathed deeply. If ever there was an unthinkable lie for Joseph Orson Steele, it was pretending anything when it came to religion. There could be no "going along with it." Maybe it was his integrity or just his stubbornness, but he would make no pretense about God or religion, to Shawnee or to anyone else. Let the chips fall where they may! He dropped to the ground and did a walk-around inspection of the rig.

Five minutes later he stepped back into the truck and closed and locked the door. For a moment, he sat in the driver's seat, just staring out into the empty darkness. Finally, he turned into the sleeper, flipped on the light, and sat down heavily on the edge of his bunk, picturing himself with Shawnee going for an evening run across campus. Truth be known, that was where he wished he were right now.

His visible wounds were mostly healed now, but the wounds in his soul were still raw and seething. He knew that the state of the mind affects the health and well-being of the body—and that a mind under stress is a body under siege. Day after day he had wrestled with a catalog of questions assembled since childhood, and after nearly ten thousand miles and countless cities, he was no closer to a destination of answers than when he left home. When it all came down to it, there was only one question that mattered to him—what did Almighty God want of him? To know that, he reasoned, was to have the rest of the way laid wide open. But how was he to know that? The past months had made it crystal clear that God was not found by debate or gymnastics of the mind. No one could give God and the truth to him—at least not the truth he was searching for. Whatever path one went down, J.O. concluded, no one suddenly discovered God with questions and logic. God either revealed himself or remained forever hidden. That was it! J.O. knew he had done all he could in the search for understanding.

He was just settling onto the bed when his eyes fell on the Book of Mormon resting on an upper shelf in the sleeper. Shawnee had given it to him several months earlier. He had never read it. On an impulse, he sat up and reached for the book, opening its front cover. He read the handwritten note inside again.

> My Dear Joseph,
>
> There is no way that I can really understand what you are going through. I can only stand back and watch and pray for you. This book will answer your questions and bring a peace to your heart that nothing else can. It can change your life if you'll let it. It's true. It comes from God and will lead you to Him. Read it when you are ready.
>
> Love,
> Shawnee

    His attention was drawn back to the words *My Dear Joseph*. He smiled to himself at the name. She had given him the book shortly after their experiences in Jackson, but the words *read it when you are ready* had stopped him from going any further into the book. He had told himself he wasn't ready yet, even though he hadn't known why.

    He lowered the book and glanced around the darkened interior of the walk-in sleeper. The soundproof walls were finely upholstered in diamond, tuck-and-roll, gray fabric. The plush carpet on the floor was a luxurious dark gray. A small refrigerator sat in one corner along with a satellite-linked television and an on-board computerized GPS. His laptop computer and sound system were state-of-the-art. There was scarcely a finer rig running over the road. Less than nine feet by eight feet, the small area was clean, orderly, and right for him. It was a comfortable, quiet place, a fitting home for a wandering maverick. He breathed deeply and sunk back onto the soft bed, his eyes fixed on the roof overhead. For a long moment, he just lay there, his mind running at high speed.

Suddenly, he sat up, his eyes slowly taking in the whole of his present world. That was it! He was a maverick—one who stands apart from the crowd and chooses his own path. All his life he had refused to follow the herd, and that had generally served him well. Fads, fancies, and trends had come and gone in food, fashion, and lifestyle, seldom attracting his interest. He was and always had been a minimalist. His family and his work were about all he wanted. But now—that wasn't enough. Here he was alone—completely alone—in a dark, quiet place, in the middle of nowhere. There was no one close to him, no one to talk to, and no one to laugh with. The people he loved had no idea where he was, and he had no way to quickly get to them.

With blinding clarity, J.O. saw himself for the first time. It was as though by some extraordinary power, he was able to step away from himself and look at what he was, what he had been, and where he was going. Was this what he wanted out of life, to be like some unwanted mongrel dog sitting alongside a freeway in the middle of no man's land, unknown and unnoticed until the highway claimed his life? His eyes squeezed shut and a sickening bitterness rose in his gut. The answer was as clear as the peal of a bell: No! There had to be more to life than this—there just had to be! But what? He opened his eyes, and his gaze rested on the dark-blue book in his hand. He tore open the cover again and rifled the pages to Chapter One. The words on the page leaped out at him: "I, Nephi, having been born of goodly parents . . . "

||||||||||||||||||

Tate rang the doorbell and waited. He was early. Instinctively, he pulled the collar up on his jacket and buried his hands in its pockets. The nip of fall was in the air. It seemed colder than normal for November, but then his memory on such matters wasn't something he altogether trusted.

The door opened. When Lisa saw who it was, she jumped through the doorway and into his arms. He held her for a moment before she pulled back and kissed him firmly.

"You're early," she said.

He grinned. "What can I say? I just couldn't wait to see you."

Lisa giggled softly and hugged him again.

As they stepped together through the front door, Tate saw Shawnee standing at the stove, cooking something.

"Hi, Tate," she called cheerfully.

"Doesn't J.O. come home tonight?" There was no mistaking the tease in his voice.

Shawnee turned to face him with a mock scowl. He knew perfectly well that J.O. was coming home tonight and that she was making dinner for him. Tate walked across the room and put his arm around her shoulders. "Just kidding," he said. She poked him in the ribs with the handle of the spoon she was using. He yelped and danced away.

"Serves you right," she said. "Never tease a woman when she's cooking. She might poison you."

"I'll remember that," he said, laughing.

"Tate, I'm not quite ready yet," Lisa said. "Do you mind waiting while I finish?"

"Not at all. Take your time."

Tate sat down at the kitchen table.

"Would you like something to drink?" Shawnee asked.

"No thanks. Lisa and I are going out to eat as soon as we leave."

Shawnee nodded and turned back to what she was stirring on the stove.

"How long ago did he call you?" Tate asked.

"About forty-five minutes ago. He was just west of Soda Springs. He should be coming into town any time." She smiled at Tate. "Since your mother has meetings at the school tonight, I told him I would make dinner for him."

Tate chuckled. "I'll bet he was excited about that."

"He said it would be all he could do to keep from speeding the rest of the way home."

"I'll bet you ten dollars he buried the pedal all the way."

"I hope so," she said.

A silence seemed to settle over them for a few moments. Shawnee was busy taking some food out of the oven, and Tate watched her with open respect and admiration. Over the last several months this young woman had become one of his closest friends. He could tell her anything. She had become more like a trusted sister to him than a friend. It frustrated him what J.O. was doing to her.

"Shawnee?"

"Hmm?"

"How are things going with J.O.? I mean, really."

"They're going fine," Shawnee said with a guarded smile. "Why do you ask?"

"C'mon, Shawnee. Don't give me that. J.O. is being a bonehead."

Shawnee smirked. "You always did have a way of being so delicate and tactful."

"Okay, okay, but you know what I mean. How is it going between you two?"

Shawnee looked at him for a moment and then turned and adjusted the burners on the stove. Then, drying her hands on a towel, she came and sat down across from him.

"That's just it, Tate. They're not going anywhere. We've become very close, and we've spent a lot of time together, but something is standing between us that neither of us can get past."

"Church?"

Shawnee nodded. "Yes. He seems further away than ever. Right after Jackson, I thought things were really going to go somewhere, but then it just seemed as though the fire died, and he stopped. I don't even dare bring it up to him now."

"Well, you can bet I will," Tate said, suddenly feeling angry.

Shawnee put a hand on his arm. "No, Tate. That is the one thing you can't do. This isn't something you can force on people or threaten or coerce them into. Either J.O. finds it himself or he will never truly be converted."

"But what about the two of you?" He let the question trail off. Hopefully, she knew what he meant.

A pained expression crossed her features. "What about it? We're friends. That's all."

"That's all?" Tate probed.

"That's all," Shawnee confirmed.

"And that's the way you want it?"

Shawnee took a deep breath and studied the face of this man who was likely going to marry her best friend.

"No, Tate. That's not the way I want it. I want him to stop being so stubborn. I want him to know the gospel is true like I do. I want him to ask me to pray with him. I want him to understand me and the God that I love and be one with me. I want to be able to tell him how much I care about him and not feel like I have to hold anything back. I want to—" She stood up and moved back to the stove. "There are a lot of things I want, Tate, but right now that doesn't seem to matter."

Tate sat for a moment digesting Shawnee's words. Then he stood and walked over to Shawnee. He placed his hands on her shoulders and turned her around. Her eyes lifted to meet his.

"My brother," he said slowly, "is an idiot. If he lets you go, he's the biggest fool this world has ever known."

Shawnee smiled at the odd compliment. "Thanks, Tate. You're very kind." She gave him a quick hug. "Let's hope it doesn't come to that."

"What if he doesn't come around?" Tate asked.

"I think you already know the answer to that," she said without hesitation.

"Yeah, I do. A few months ago, I would have thought that breaking off a relationship with someone over the matter of religion would be the stupidest thing possible. If you love someone, why care what religion he is?"

"And now..." Shawnee prompted.

He moved over to the large kitchen window and looked out. "It's not stupid. That's for sure."

"And why not?"

"I'm not sure I can explain it as well as you could, but I guess it would be like hitching a mule with an ox and expecting them to pull together."

"I've never thought of myself as an ox," Shawnee said, laughing.

"You'd rather be the mule?" Tate joked.

"I think neither."

Tate grew serious again. "So, what's going to happen?"

Shawnee looked him squarely in the face. "Nothing, Tate. Nothing. I don't know why I've allowed myself to get as close as I have."

"What do you mean? Aren't you dating anyone else?"

"No."

Tate was genuinely surprised. "Why not? Hasn't anyone asked?"

"Oh, they've asked," she said, "but I've always said no or just put them off."

"Why? Why should you wait around for my muleheaded brother to get his act together? That's not right!"

"It's not that, Tate. I decided a long time ago that I wouldn't wait for J.O. I love him, but we're just friends. That's all we are, and that's all we've ever been."

"Well, then, what? I'm confused."

Shawnee laughed lightly. "You think *you're* confused?"

Tate threw his hands in the air.

Shawnee smiled at the look on his face. "If you want to know the truth—"

Shawnee was interrupted by Lisa bounding into the room. "Okay, let's go!"

Shawnee immediately turned back to the food at the stove. Tate wanted to know what she was going to say, but there was no misreading the signals she was sending. She did not want to finish the sentence. After hesitating for just a second, he stood and walked over to Lisa. "I'm ready."

"You guys have a good time," Shawnee called as they went out the door.

|||||||||||||||||

"Oh, this is beautiful," Shawnee exclaimed as they entered the canyon and started to climb.

"I hoped you would think so," J.O. said over the sound of the wind.

They had eaten a quiet and quick dinner at Shawnee's apartment, and then J.O. had suggested they go for a drive up Mink Creek Canyon to see the fall colors at sunset. He said he didn't want to do anything else. He had been in eastern Wyoming at that time the day before, and he was now going on twenty-four hours without sleep.

The Jeep still had no top on it, so they had to wear jackets, but the crisp air and the vibrant blaze of colors combined to create an exhilarating environment.

"I had no idea this looked like this up here," Shawnee said over the noise of the engine and the wind.

"Not many people do."

"Where are we going?"

"Just up to the campground."

Shawnee smiled and turned her attention back to the scenery.

J.O. knew the scenery. He had seen it before. What most captured his attention now was Shawnee. He had missed her so much it hurt. She was more beautiful than he remembered. He never tired of looking at the fine, distinct lines of her face and the way the wind captured her hair. He loved to see it whip in the breeze. That's why he hadn't yet put the top on his Jeep, despite the weather. Shawnee looked over at him and caught him admiring her. Quickly, he looked back at the road. She smiled and touched his arm.

"Thanks for bringing me up here," she said. "I really needed to see this."

"You're welcome."

He studied Shawnee out of the corner of his eye. He could tell she was trying hard to act cheerful, but all through dinner, he could tell that something heavy was on her mind. He considered telling her about his experience in Nebraska but thought better of it. *What is there to tell? Not much, yet.*

|||||||||||||||||

Minutes later, they arrived at the campground. J.O. parked the Jeep and helped Shawnee out. They walked hand in hand down the path that led to a small overlook on the point of the mountain. When Shawnee saw the rustic, covered bench among the trees, she let go of his hand and ran forward to look at it.

"Oh!" she exclaimed, "This is beautiful." She gestured to the overlook, the mountains, and the view that spread toward the north below them. "How many more of these kinds of places do you know?"

"Oh, I know a few."

She didn't miss his teasing tone of voice.

"And I suppose you make it a habit of bringing girls up here, right?"

"Oh, all the time."

He was teasing, and she knew it, but the comment cut like a hot scalpel. Her smile slipped a little and she looked away to keep him from seeing it.

"Actually," he said, sitting down beside her on the bench, "you're the only woman I've ever brought up here."

When she didn't look at him, he reached over and gently took her face in his hand and turned her toward him. She wanted to resist, but the tug was so gentle and warm on her cheek.

"What's wrong?"

"You have to ask?" It came out more bitterly than she intended.

"I can guess, but I learned a long time ago not to do that."

"It's nothing," she said, turning away again, angry at herself for being emotional. "I'm just being stupid."

|||||||||||||||||

J.O. sighed. It was time to get some things worked out. It was time for a real talk, and it was obvious she was not going to lead out. He stood, shoved his hands deep into his pockets, and walked over to the edge of the overlook, where he stood staring.

"I started reading the Book of Mormon," he announced without preamble.

"When?" There was obvious surprise in her voice.

"Two nights ago, in the middle of Nebraska."

"Why?"

He turned around to face her again. She sat on the bench looking up at him. The collar of her jacket was turned up against the increasing evening chill. Her legs were drawn up under her chin for warmth. The lowering sun cast the eminence of Scout Mountain behind her in a sharp contrast of light and shadow. The setting only made her look more beautiful to him, but it struck him how vulnerable she was at that moment. He sighed again and moved over to sit by her.

"It's hard to explain, but I think I'm going to quit driving."

A look of shock registered on her face. "Quit driving. Why?"

"It's not fun anymore," he said. "I used to love being on the road and going new places. There was never a dull moment. I loved the scenery and the trucks and the thrill of the open road. It was freedom!"

"So, what happened to change all that?"

He wanted to just blurt out "you," but there were too many ways to misread such a message. "Well, let's just say that some things have changed in my life that make me not want to be out there anymore."

"Like what?" she pressed.

He sighed with resignation. "You!"

She started to say something, but he hurried on. "Let me finish." He looked away as if gathering his thoughts and then said, "I've tried to convince myself that it would never work between us. I've kept my distance, and I've even tried to walk away." He paused and looked up at the sky. "But I can't." He turned back and took her by the shoulders. "Shawnee, let's be honest and straight up here. I care about you. I love you, and—" he hesitated as he searched her eyes—"and I think you still care about me?" It was stated as a question.

Slowly, almost imperceptibly, she nodded her head. He blew out his breath as though he had been holding it in suspense and looked out across the valley. "That's the dilemma. I can't see how this is going to work. You want a man of God, and I am not that."

"Why not?"

"I guess because I—I don't know how."

"That's easy enough to change."

"Shawnee, this isn't a game."

"And I'm not playing one, but I'm not so sure that's not what you've been doing."

"What do you mean?" he said, an edge creeping into his voice.

"J.O., I've been with you enough to know that you've felt something. You've seen prayers answered more than once, and you've even experienced things that some would call miracles. How can you say you don't know?" Before he could answer, she went on. "Not once have you come to church with me to see what it's like. Have you been praying and trying to change your life the way Heavenly Father wants you to? Do you expect God to come down and tell you Himself when you're doing nothing to help yourself? You just picked up the Book of Mormon. I gave you that book four months ago. What took you so long?"

Her intensity stung him like wind-driven hail. He started to say something, but she rode over him with even more fervor.

"What are you afraid of, J.O.? That you'll have to admit that you were wrong for so many years, or is it that you might have to change?"

Her words were like a slap in the face, and he felt the anger rising in him. Standing abruptly, he walked away and stood looking out, though he couldn't focus on anything.

"J.O.," her voice was softer now, pleading. "I do care about you, and I want to see you happy."

He whirled. "I *was* happy until—" He bit off the rest of what he was going to say.

She recoiled as though he had struck her, and then she quietly finished the sentence for him. "Until I came along, right?"

He turned back to the forested valley before him and said nothing.

Shawnee sighed. As she spoke, he could hear the pain and restrained emotion in her voice. "I guess you're right. This isn't going to work, and all I'm doing is putting us both through grief. I'm sorry."

She stood and began walking up the trail toward the Jeep. "Can I please go home now?"

They rode down the mountain in silence, both consumed with their emotions. The anger continued to swell inside him. It seemed to take him over and push him. The muscles in his jaw clenched, and his breathing became short and tense. In his heart, he knew he was acting like an idiot. This wasn't like him, but he didn't care. Something was pushing him forward, and he was too tired and spent—both physically and emotionally—to fight it. He pulled up in front of Shawnee's apartment. Silently, J.O. got out of the Jeep and walked around to let her out.

"I can see myself to the door," she said.

"No," he said tersely. "I can't let you do that."

She opened the Jeep door and he met her there. Awkwardly, they walked to the front door together. She turned the door handle on the darkened apartment and started to open the door, but then stopped and turned around.

"J.O., I'm sorry it worked out this way." She looked up into his eyes. "Good luck. I hope you find what makes you happy." Then, without anything more, she turned and went into the apartment, leaving J.O. standing on the doorstep.

||||||||||||||||

Once inside, Shawnee stood with her back against the door, listening. Her eyes were tightly closed, and her face was lifted to the ceiling. For a moment, there was no sound. Then his footsteps left the porch and started down the sidewalk.

"Goodbye, Joseph," she whispered, as the tears began to come. Suddenly, it was too much. Her hands came up and covered her face. Great sobs shook her body. Blindly, she stumbled through the kitchen and into her bedroom. As she fell across her bed, it all came out. All the restrained, confused, emotions of the last several months came out in one great rush.

"Why, Father? Why?" she cried. The sobs and pleading continued until late into the night until exhaustion took over and she fell into a deep sleep.

THE CHURCH OF
JESUS CHRIST
OF LATTER-DAY SAINTS

VISITORS WELCOME

Chapter Sixteen

LAS VEGAS, NEVADA, NOVEMBER 2021

Claude Richards walked across the expensive, deep-pile carpet of the Las Vegas penthouse to an ornately framed, full-length mirror. For a moment, she stared at herself and the ugly pink scars that had been hidden so carefully by the surgeons.

"Thank you for coming so quickly," she said cordially, turning around. "I'll get right to the point. I would like to hire you."

Sitting across the room in an overstuffed chair was a man in his early forties with iron-gray flecks in his short-cropped hair. His small, dark eyes were framed by a face that resembled worn saddle leather. Lean and hard as a steel rail, Morgan Talley looked more like a Montana cowboy than a seasoned private investigator.

"Who?" he said, simply.

"His name is Steele. J.O. Steele. I don't know where he lives or much about him, but he works for a company called Matthew's Brothers in southern Idaho. He's a truck driver. That's about all I know."

"And what am I supposed to do when I find him?"

A bemused expression settled on Claude's face. She turned and looked out the large window across the Las Vegas skyline. "I understand, Mr. Talley, that you are also an expert hunter and guide."

"That's right."

She turned back to face him. "Let's just say that you come highly recommended. I've heard it said that for the right price you'll guarantee your clients a shot at the game of their choice."

The leathery face split into a grin, exposing even, white teeth. "That has been said," he affirmed.

The faint light of a smile faded from Claude's face. Anger flashed in her eyes. Reaching down into the desk, she lifted out a large, stuffed envelope and threw it to Talley. He caught it deftly with one hand and opened it. Quickly, he counted the money. Claude watched him, satisfied that he was hers when she saw his eyes grow large with surprise.

"Find him," she said. "Set this up, and there'll be twice that much."

Talley stuffed the envelope inside his worn, denim shirt. As he stood up, he pulled a toothpick out of his shirt pocket, stuck it in his mouth, and with exaggerated emphasis bit down on it.

"Yes, Ma'am."

He nodded toward her and touched his finger to his forehead in a sort of salute and left the room. As he exited, Claude turned back to look out the window. After a moment, she brought up her left hand and turned it over. The surgeons had done their best to repair the hand and make it look as normal as possible. They had hidden the scars well, but the little finger was glaringly absent. The old familiar rage rose up at the sight of her hand. It was finally time for someone to pay!

||||||||||||||||

Ruthie Steele lifted her shoulder and locked the phone against her ear. She glanced over at Tate, noting the expectant look on his face.

"Phoenix. You're in Phoenix, Son?"

"Yes, Mother. I'm out of driving hours and I need to lay up for a while. I can't unload until Monday, so I'm going to get a motel room and take it easy."

"You'll be coming home after that, won't you?"

There was a pause on the phone. "I'm afraid not, Mom. They've scheduled me to the east coast after I leave here."

"Oh, c'mon, you've already been gone for three weeks as it is," she said in protest.

"I know, Mom. I know. I'll come back when I can."

"Son, are you okay?"

He laughed. "Mom, I'm fine. Don't worry about me. I'm a big boy. I've been out here before, remember?"

"Yes, I know, but . . ." She let it trail off. She knew that what she wanted to ask was a forbidden subject with J.O. Ruthie knew only too well that her very strong-willed son wouldn't talk about his feelings until he was ready.

"I'll call you in a couple of days, Mom. I love you."

"I love you too. Be careful."

She hung up the phone and turned to face Tate and Lisa.

"Well?" Tate asked.

"He's in Phoenix, and from there he's heading back to the east coast again. It'll be at least another two, maybe three weeks before he's home."

Tate slammed his fist down on the table. "What's the matter with him? He's running away."

"He's hurting, Tate. I haven't seen him like this since your dad died. He just needs some time."

Lisa took Tate's hand as though to calm him. "Will he be alright, Ruthie?"

"He'll be fine, dear. J.O. comes across as a happy-go-lucky, ever-cheerful kind of guy, but deep down inside, he feels and thinks very deeply. After he works this through, he'll be back to his old self again. Has Shawnee said much about what happened?"

"We took her out to lunch a couple of days ago," Tate said. "She basically told us what happened. It was what we thought. The issue was religion. She just got tired of pretending that the problem didn't exist. When she called it straight, J.O. ran the other way."

"Is she alright?" Ruthie asked.

"She will be," Lisa said. "She won't say much, but I know she's hurting. She really loves him. The experiences they had together mean a lot to her. She's like J.O., though; she acts like everything is okay, but I can tell it's not."

Ruthie sighed. "This is so hard to watch. Shawnee's such a sweetheart. Heaven help them both."

||||||||||||||||||

J.O. rolled over and opened his eyes to look at the clock in his motel room. The luminescent dial read 5:32 a.m. He rolled onto his back and groaned. It was no use. Staying in bed would only give him a headache. He might as well get up.

Slowly, he crawled out of bed, dressed in his running clothes, and walked out into the predawn Phoenix morning. It was warm. This same November morning back in Idaho would have seen temperatures cold enough to make running shorts a frigid choice. He breathed deeply and began to stretch out. After some pushups, he set his watch and started to run. He ran through the motel parking lot first to make sure his rig was secure. After satisfying his curiosity, he turned down a residential street and began to run, slowly at first. Since he had the whole day to kill, he was in no hurry.

As he ran, his mind began to wake up, and his thoughts began to process. He loved this time of the morning. It always seemed that this was when he could think the most clearly and his body seemed to perform the best. He crested the summit of a street that overlooked a lower section of the city. He thought of Shawnee and his last minutes with her on the Scout Mountain overlook. If only he hadn't made that joke about bringing girls up there all the time. If only he hadn't gotten so angry. He quickly pushed those thoughts aside; there was no sense berating himself over something he couldn't change. There was no doubt that she had been right. He was afraid. He just wasn't sure of what, though. It embarrassed him that he had acted more than a little irrational. After dropping her off, he had gone home, repacked his clothes, left his mother a note, and within the hour, he was in his truck and on his way to Boston.

Since then, he had asked the dispatcher to keep him out on the road and far away. He was grateful he hadn't quit the job as he had intended.

The first few days had been a blur. It was as though he had traveled five thousand miles in an angry fog. His thinking hadn't been clear, and his mind had been consumed with his resentment toward Shawnee, her church, and even God. The fog had carried him across the country to Boston. Then it happened.

He had been heading south along the Capitol Beltway near Washington, D.C., consumed with an illogical anger against God, blaming Him for the pain and loss he felt. Then, as clear as a pealing bell, the thought had sprung into his mind that he would never believe in God again and no church would ever claim him. Strangely enough, he had directed those thoughts to God in a sort of angry prayer. Just as the thought had entered his mind, he had rounded the corner of the beltway to see a massive, six-spired, white building rise above the trees, seeming to float on the horizon like some kind of heavenly fortress. His mouth had fallen open and his eyes had been riveted. Only when he had dangerously crossed two lanes of traffic did he wake up and direct his attention back to his driving.

He later learned that what he'd seen was the Washington D.C. Temple of The Church of Jesus Christ of Latter-day Saints. The image of the temple had remained fixed on his consciousness. The more he had thought about the effect the building had on him, the more his thinking had begun to mellow. In time, as the miles rolled away beneath him, he began to see Shawnee's point of view. She loved him. He knew she did. Yet she was willing to walk away in a moment if he posed a threat to her faith. What was it about this church that bred such quiet strength and determination? Shawnee was no shallow, glassy-eyed zealot. She was stable, calm, and rational, and she had a firm grasp on reality. She and her family utterly destroyed his stereotype of a devout religious person. She was, in every way, the kind of person he wanted to be. What made her so strong—was it her family, or was it her church? That question had driven him for the last five thousand miles. Every night on the road, and every spare moment loading and unloading, he had poured over the Book of Mormon, searching it pages for the answer. He had read it and understood the words, but its message eluded him. Nephites, Lamanites, wars—each passing day deepened his sense that he was looking at something incredible and yet couldn't see it. Somewhere there was a message, but where was it?

Last night, he had read the first few chapters of 3 Nephi until he fell asleep on the book around two in the morning. The quest was consuming him, driving him crazy. Yet it felt right. The angry fog had lifted and had been replaced with something that felt almost like adrenalin—yet stronger, deeper, and sweeter. It reached into the deepest part of his soul and drove him. It was as though the fire of an unearthly quest had kindled, and he had to know the truth. At first, he had thought about calling Shawnee and apologizing to her and asking for her help, but he had quickly rejected that idea. He had hurt her enough for long enough. Besides, what had changed? Did he know any more now than he had known before? If it was true, he had to know for himself—and he needed to come to that knowledge not because he stood to gain something from her. It had been hard to hold to that resolve. Several times he had almost weakened and called her to tell he what he was doing, but each time he had remembered the pain in her voice when she shut that door. Her goodbye was meant to be final, and likely it was. He couldn't think about that now. This had become larger—much larger—than Shawnee James. He had to know for himself, regardless of what Shawnee felt.

As he ran, his mind lifted to God in prayer. It was a new feeling that had just started a few days ago. He would just be thinking about something and would suddenly feel he was not alone. It became natural and easy to talk to God—almost a yearning.

Dear God, Heavenly Father—I need to know. Help me. The prayer was unuttered, and it was not answered by a voice or the ringing of bells, but there was always a feeling that all was well. If he knew nothing else, he knew—now, and for the first time in his adult life—that God was there. J.O. couldn't see Him, but he could certainly feel Him.

At that moment, he passed a large, brick building with immaculately landscaped grounds. A large, straight spire caught his eye and lifted his gaze. A strange sensation came over him. In the darkness he noticed a brown sign a few feet away, next to the sidewalk. He stopped and read it.

The Church of Jesus Christ of Latter-day Saints
Meeting Times 9:00 a.m. and 11:00 a.m.
All Welcome

He looked from the sign to the spire as Shawnee's voice echoed in his head. *Not once have you come to church with me to see what it's like.* A wide smile spread across his face.

I'm going to church.

Chapter Seventeen

POCATELLO, IDAHO, DECEMBER 2021

Morgan Talley pulled the immaculately waxed Ford pickup to a stop about ten feet from the bumper of the idling Matthew's Brothers semi. The driver of the semi looked around before opening the hood. Talley left the pickup running and sauntered casually over to where the driver was checking the engine. The driver stepped to meet him.

"Howdy," he drawled. "My name's Morgan Smith. I'm a friend of J.O. Steele. I understand he works for you guys, right?"

"That's right," the driver said easily.

"Is he around?"

"No, he hasn't been around for going on a month. I hear he's been running the east coast somewhere."

"I just came into town. He's an old friend from the same hometown. I'd appreciate any information you could give me that might help me find him."

"I think we can help you with that," the driver said with a grin. "Hang on just a minute." The driver crawled up in the cab and retrieved a cell phone. Within seconds, he had the dispatcher on the line. Talley waited at the door.

"Justin, this is Tony. We got a guy here at the shop that is an old friend of J.O. He's trying to get in touch with him. Can you help him?"

The driver listened for a moment, grinned, and handed the phone to Talley. Five minutes later, Talley drove away with all the information he needed.

Tate could hear his cell phone ringing across the room. He had walked out to his car to get something and forgot to pick it up. Bounding across the room, he grabbed for it.

"Hello," he said breathlessly.

"Tate? It's me."

"J.O., where are you, man?"

"I'm in San Diego, little brother, and on my way home."

"It's about time. How soon will you be here?"

J.O. chuckled softly. "It'll be a few days. Right now, I'm rolling down I–5 into San Diego to pick up a load. I should be out of town tonight and on my way back."

"Great! I'll spread the word, and we'll throw you a welcome-home party."

"Uh, Tate. There is one thing. Don't tell Shawnee."

"What! Why?"

"I think that's over, Tate. It's a long story. I'll tell you when I get there."

"I think I probably already know most of the story."

"No, trust me, Brother. There's a lot to this story that no one knows."

"What do you mean?"

"Never mind. Is she alright?"

"She's fine, all things considered. What's going on?"

"Let me ask you a question. How are things going with you and Lisa and the Church?"

"They're going great. Why do you ask?"

"And Lisa—"

"Couldn't be better. Why are you asking me all this?"

J.O. took a long, deep breath and let it out slowly. "I need your help. I've been reading the Book of Mormon ever since I left. I've almost read it twice now. I've been to church the last two Sundays, and I plan to stop in Salt Lake on the way back. I—" he hesitated. "I want to talk to some missionaries when I get home. I'll be home for about a week over Christmas. Can you arrange it?"

"Arrange it?" Tate shouted into the phone. "Are you crazy? With that kind of news, I'd drive all the way to California to get you. Wait till Mom hears about this!"

"Hold it, Brother," he said sternly. "I didn't say I was getting baptized. I said I want to talk to some missionaries. I don't want anyone to know. I'm not making any promises. There's no need to get Mother all excited."

"J.O., do you really think it's fair to not tell her?"

There was a pause on the line. "No, I guess not, but tell her not to get her hopes up."

"Did you know she's talking about going to the temple now?"

"Are you serious?" J.O. exclaimed.

Tate laughed. "Serious as heart failure. I haven't seen Mom this happy in years. And wait till I tell her this. It'll be the best Christmas present you could give her."

"Okay, okay, but be careful what you tell her, and don't tell anyone else."

"Not even Shawnee? She'll want to know."

"*Especially* Shawnee."

"But why?" Tate asked earnestly. "This could change everything."

"It changes nothing, Tate. If I join the Church, it can't be for her. It can't even *look* like it's for her. She wouldn't want it any other way. Besides, I'm not so sure she would even want to know."

Tate sighed. "J.O., sometimes you are as stubborn as a donkey and as stupid as a turkey."

J.O. laughed at the turn of phrase. "That may be, but this time I'm asking you to trust me. Don't tell her. Don't tell anyone. I need to find this on my own. The only reason I called you is, I need some help getting in touch with the missionaries."

"Okay. I'll do it. Call me when you're closer. I think I'll let you spring the news on Mom yourself."

"That's perfect! I like that."

They said goodbye, and J.O. closed the connection. He had just dropped the phone back in its dash holder when a car pulled alongside him and slowed down to match his speed. He glanced over, but the windows were tinted, and he couldn't make out the occupants. The car increased its speed and pulled into his lane in front of him. It slowed down enough that it was only twenty or so feet in front of his bumper.

"What the—" J.O. said, irritated. He started to slow down to increase the distance between the vehicles.

Suddenly a longhaired man popped up through the open sunroof, and in one swift motion heaved something back at J.O.'s truck. In a split second, J.O. registered the sudden acceleration of the car and the object flying toward him. It was a brick, coming directly toward his face!

He yanked the wheel to the left, but it made little difference. There was no way to avoid the deadly missile. Instinctively, his right arm came up to cover his face as the brick hit his windshield just to the left of center. The windshield was an instant spider web of cracks. Glass fragments sprayed the cab where the brick hit, some of which became embedded in J.O.'s arm and upper body. Ignoring the stinging pain, he fought the wheel, trying to bring the careening truck under control. As it rolled to a stop in the emergency lane, he dropped his head to the steering wheel and took a deep breath. His legs were trembling from the adrenalin rush, and the knuckles of his hands were white.

Opening the door, he got out and walked around the truck to see if there was any other damage. Heavy black skid marks marked the highway where he had jerked the wheel and again when he had tried to get the rig under control. Just then a California Highway Patrol car rolled up behind him with its lights flashing. J.O. went to meet him. The officer stepped out of his car. There was instant concern in his voice as he looked at him.

"Are you alright?"

"Yeah, I'm okay. Just a close call."

"Are you sure? You're a mess."

J.O. looked down at himself. He was covered with blood from the glass wounds in his arm, hand, and upper body. "It looks worse than it is. I'm fine."

"What happened?"

"I wish I knew. One minute I was driving, and the next minute some guy lobbed a brick through my windshield."

"Any idea who or why?"

"No." But even as he said it, the grinning specter of Claude Richards popped into his head.

|||||||||||||||||||

"Ms. Richards? This is Talley. I just called to let you know that we got the job done."

"What happened?"

"He nearly stacked the rig on its head before he got it under control," Talley said, laughing. "I guarantee we scared about ten years out of him."

There was no mirth whatsoever in Claude's voice. "Good. Follow him and keep it up. Use different people, different cars. Don't let him see you. I want you to put the absolute fear into him. I want him so paranoid that he's climbing the walls before we finish this."

"That shouldn't be too hard," Talley said, confidently. "What about the girl? Do you want her to get the same?"

"Forget the girl!" Claude snapped. "It's him I want!"

"Just as well," Talley said. "The word I hear is that they are no longer seeing each other."

Claude went on as though she hadn't heard him. "Stay with him and keep me informed. Did you say he was coming through Vegas?"

"I think so. He's heading back to Idaho through Salt Lake. The most direct route would take him through Vegas."

"Alright. Let me know the minute you're sure."

Talley had no opportunity to answer; Claude abruptly hung up.

Strange woman, he thought ruefully. *Some sort of twisted vendetta—-glad it's him and not me.*

Shawnee wrapped her coat more tightly around her and stepped out of the door of the hospital into the icy, cold night air.

Only two more days to go, and then I can get out of here.

Two weeks of vacation over the Christmas holidays seemed heavenly to contemplate. Already she planned to take the first few days at home with her family to sleep and eat, two things she had not done enough of in the last few weeks. Then she was going to break out her snowboard and hit every slope she could find between Targhee and the Salt Lake Valley. Maybe if she was lucky, she might even meet someone who was worth dating. That thought made her laugh to herself. *Who am I kidding? I'm not the least bit interested in meeting anyone, especially on a ski slope.*

Had she become cynical? She tried not to be, but inside she couldn't ignore what she felt. It had been seven weeks since that night on Scout Mountain when she had told J.O. off. In those seven weeks, she had relived with clarity every word and nuance of that conversation. What she had said and what she had done was right. She knew that, more so now than then, but why did it still hurt so much? Her goodbye to him that night hadn't seemed as permanent as it felt now. She had always been taught that when you stand up for what you think is right, everything works out and you're happy. So why wasn't she happy?

She breathed deeply and let the icy December air out slowly, watching the steam from her breath rise like smoke on a still, summer day. The night was beautiful and clear, plunging the temperatures close to zero. The storm of the day before had dropped several inches of new snow, blanketing the city in heavenly white. She loved the crunch of it under her feet. There was something pure and heavenly about a midnight-blue, crystal-clear sky overhead and the sound of fresh-fallen snow under her feet. That's why she hadn't brought her car. She could walk, and think, and feel—and hopefully not feel so alone.

The day after that fateful night on Scout Mountain she had thrown herself fully into her work. Working double shifts had sent her paychecks to the top, but her heart had stayed at the bottom. Long ago she had learned to battle loneliness and discouragement by staying busy. She was gone so much that Tate and Lisa called her "the recluse." But it hadn't worked. If she sat down for five minutes and let her mind go, it inevitably returned to the same place: a tall, sandy-haired, happy-go-lucky truck driver who loved life. She glanced at her watch. It was just after midnight. Her gaze lifted to the northern sky. There it was, the Big Dipper, high up above the North Star with its cup running out.

"Fitting," she thought, as she stared at the Big Dipper. "That cup is as empty as I am."

Lisa had told her to forget J.O. and go on. *What a laugh! How do I forget someone who risked his life more than once to save mine? How do I forget someone who gave a richness to my life I had never known before? Love is not just dismissed like some errant schoolboy who can be hauled off to the principal's office and forgotten, especially when that schoolboy came from God and captured my heart—the whole of it.* She opened her eyes and found the North Star again. In a quiet voice, she said, "I don't know where he is, Father, or what he's doing, but bless him, watch over him. Please, keep him safe and bring him home."

She closed her eyes against a pain inside that was as sharp and real as the bite of the cold. "Heavenly Father, this hurts. I can't go on like this.

I kept the commandments. I did what was right. It was not meant to be. Please, Father, take the pain away and let me go on."

Then, as gently as a falling snowflake, a voice whispered to her. It was not something she heard as much as something she felt. The impression came to her like a gentle caress: *It is enough*. And in that moment, she knew that her willingness to sacrifice love for principle had been recognized and accepted. She sensed that she had passed a great test. Tears flowed down her cheeks as the love and approval of heaven filled her soul until it felt like a fire inside. She tried to speak so she could pray further, but her voice failed her. It was the sweetest feeling she had experienced in a very long time, and she was at peace.

⁂

The waitress suddenly appeared at the table carrying a steaming plate of food.

"Here you go, Sir," she said pleasantly.

J.O. looked up. She was a pretty redhead with a big smile full of pretty, white teeth.

"Thank you," he said, pushing back his books.

She put the plate carefully down in front of him. "Is there anything else I can do for you, Sir?"

He looked up at her again and smiled. This time of the night it was unusual to meet a waitress who was so cheerful, especially at a truck stop. "No, I don't think so. Thank you."

"Well, if you need anything, let me know. My name is Kim." She pointed to her nametag.

"I'll do that; thanks, Kim." J.O. smiled at her. He had the distinct feeling that she was flirting.

Kim moved away, and J.O. turned his attention to his food. It was good, but he wasn't eating because he was hungry—he just needed to stoke the furnace. The food was reasonably good, but tonight it might as well have been cardboard with gravy on it. His mind was on other things. Something funny was going on. After getting his truck repaired and leaving San Diego, he had connected with I-15 northbound, headed for Las Vegas. About twenty miles north of the city, a car had come out of nowhere and started following him so close that he could scarcely see it in his mirrors. It was not uncommon for cars to tailgate on long trips. Somehow, they thought it saved them gas by being pulled along in his tailwind. He had paid the car little attention, and it had followed him for another ten miles.

All at once, a full-size passenger van had come out of nowhere and pulled alongside until it matched his speed. J.O. had been instantly wary. He had increased his speed. The van had too, as had the car behind him. He had slowed down; so had they. There was no way he could outrun them. The two cars harassed him for the next fifteen miles, pulling in front of him and suddenly hitting the brakes, forcing him to slow down, or driving alongside him and forcing him into the emergency lane. He was constantly going to extremes to keep from running over them.

Finally, he had had enough. He had just gotten his speed back up to seventy when the van had swerved over to crowd him. This time he was ready, and he had pulled the wheel to the left. The steel front corner of his trailer had torn down the side of the van like a hot knife through butter. The driver had pulled away and had instantly cut his speed, as had the car behind him. He had traveled on to Las Vegas without further incident, but his nerves were on edge. It had been his intention to bed down for the night in Vegas, but he was too wired. Something was going on. He could feel it. This wasn't just the coincidental nonsense of bored teenagers. But if it was Claude, how had she been able to find him out here?

He had stopped at this casino on the south side of Vegas, intending to fuel up, get some food, and get back on his way. If someone was after him, he was going to make it cost them, even if it was only sleep.

J.O. finished his food. Kim came back to ask him if he wanted dessert. Somewhat less than subtly, she told him she would be off duty in forty-five minutes. He ignored the hint as gently as he could. To ease the rejection, he slipped her an extra-large tip and a note thanking her for being so cheerful.

While the clerk processed his credit card, J.O. stood looking out over the sea of slot machines and bleary-eyed gamblers. He was just turning back to the cashier when he saw something out of the corner of his eye that instantly sent his heart rate into orbit. Across the casino, about fifty feet away, stood a woman with one arm resting on a slot machine. She was slight of build with dark hair and dark complexion. And she was looking directly at him.

It was Claude!

J.O. started forward, but the clerk said, "Sign here, Sir." He quickly signed the receipt and picked up his card. When he looked back around, she was gone. He started toward where he had seen her but stopped. If it *was* her, following her would surely lead him to a trap. He turned and walked out of the casino, went straight to his truck, and climbed in. As he started the engine and released the brakes, a thought struck him. *Check the truck.*

It had always been a safety habit when he made stops like this to do a quick walk-around inspection before he got back on the road. There was seldom anything wrong, but it was an important habit for a driver to have, and he had kept it.

No. I need to get out of here.

The little voice inside spoke again. *Check the truck.* J.O. figured the force of a long-ingrained habit was talking to him. For a moment, he sat and argued with himself. Finally, he reached over and reset the brakes. He opened the door and grabbed his tire mallet. The truck was parked in the darkened back corner of the parking lot. There were trucks on all sides of him, most shut down for the night, with drivers sleeping in them. If someone wanted to jump him, this would be the place to do it. He tightened his grip on the mallet and walked around the truck, bumping each of the tires as he went. He came around the front of the truck, casting a fleeting glance at the front tires, lights, and fuel tanks as he went. Everything was in order.

He opened the cab door, reached for the handle, and started to step up when he froze in place. An unsettling image formed in his mind. Carefully he lowered himself back down and ducked beneath the door to look at the left front tire of the rig. What he saw almost made him ill. He moved closer. The tire was cut. Someone had axed the tire where the tread and sidewall met. It was deep, but not enough to flatten the tire. J.O. hung his head and, for a second, closed his eyes. The cut was just deep enough and low enough that he would have driven away without seeing it—and as soon as the tire got hot enough, it would have blown out. To blow a steering tire on a car is dangerous enough, but to blow one on a loaded semi-truck at high speed can be, and often is, disastrous.

Images of horrible accidents caused by blown front tires flashed through his mind. He straightened and looked around. It was flawlessly clear what the strange events of the last few days meant. They were trying to scare him, to psyche him out. It was Claude's demented way of inflicting mental torture on him before she moved in for the kill. She was the cat. He was the mouse, and the game had begun. His fists balled into rocks at his sides. If they expected him to run to a corner and cry, they were sorely mistaken. Let them go ahead and start the fight. That was fine with him. But, God willing, he was going to end it. He glanced back at the tire and then up at the sky. A measure of peace came over him as he found the North Star and took his bearings. It was just after midnight.

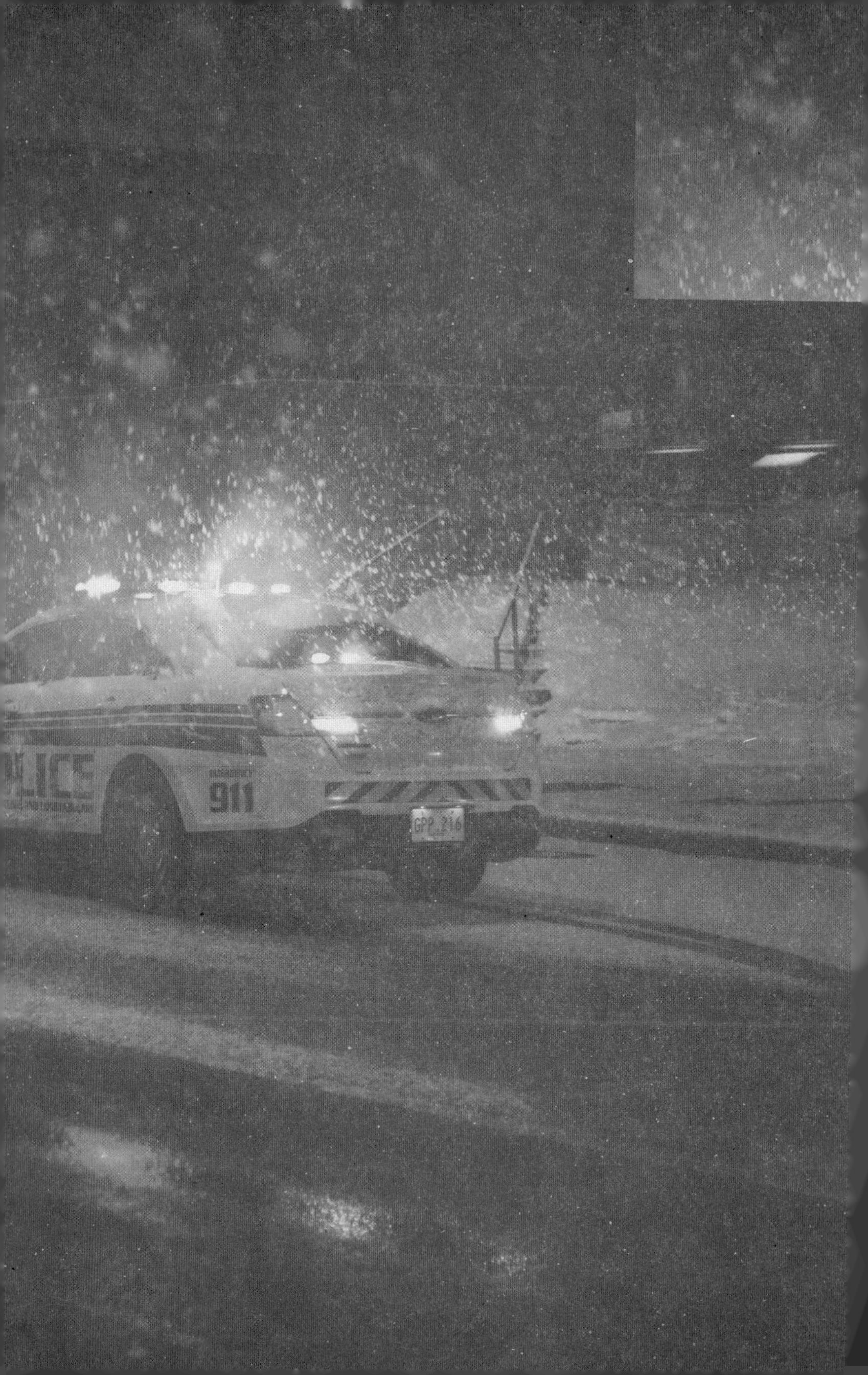
911
GPP 216

Chapter Eighteen

SALT LAKE CITY, UTAH, DECEMBER 23, 2021

J.O. walked out of the shipping office carrying the bills for his new load. His eyes instantly inspected the entire rig, truck, trailer, everything. Nothing had happened since the axed tire in Vegas two nights earlier, but his nerves were on edge, and he was ready to get off the road. Since the incident with the tire, he had hardly let the truck out of his sight; if he left it for more than five minutes, he had been careful to inspect the rig from end to end before he drove it. If they wanted to spook him, they had succeeded well. In a little more than three hours, he would be back home on his own turf, where he could figure out how to fight on his own terms. Opening the cab door, he threw the clipboard with the bills up into the driver's seat and grabbed the tire mallet for another inspection.

The load he had picked up in San Diego had been delivered here in Salt Lake. Strapped to the deck of his flatbed trailer now were three excavation tractors—called Bobcats—to be delivered in Idaho Falls two days after Christmas. Each one was held in place with safety straps and chains. They were not huge pieces of machinery, but large enough that he didn't want one of them bouncing off in the middle of Salt Lake traffic. Carefully, he checked each strap and chain one more time to make sure each was tight. Satisfied that everything was in order, he climbed into the truck and headed for the freeway. It occurred to him that he was hungry. He saw a small convenience store on the left and pulled over to the curb so he could run inside for a soda and bag of chips. The clerk was as slow checking out his purchases as if he were frozen in December ice. J.O. kept casting worried glances out the large front windows toward the truck. It made him nervous to be away from the rig, but at least it was in full view.

Finally, the drowsy clerk finished. J.O. grabbed the small sack and trotted out to the truck. Seconds later he was on the freeway and headed north toward Idaho. As he drove past the city center, he looked off to the right and saw the lights of the Salt Lake Temple just coming on. An involuntary shudder of awe ran through him at the sight of the magnificent structure. All his life he had heard about this temple and seen pictures of it. Maybe now it was time to see it for himself.

Traffic moved slowly, especially through North Salt Lake and Bountiful, but all things considered, he was making good time. Suddenly, a dark-blue SUV came out of nowhere and darted around in front of him. J.O. rose up straighter in his seat. Such a maneuver was normal enough in heavy traffic, especially in Salt Lake, but the last few days had made him wary. Tightening his grip on the steering wheel, he shifted his foot to the brake to slow down and put some distance between him and the SUV. His foot had just touched the brake when the brake lights of the SUV flashed on and it braked hard, almost locking up its wheels. It was too close. There was no way J.O. could stop in time.

"No!" J.O. yelled through gritted teeth as he rose up out of his seat and stomped his own brakes to the floor. The action caused his rig to lurch violently forward. In one whirlwind moment, the brake lights of the SUV went out, and the vehicle shot forward just in time to avoid being crushed by the loaded Kenworth. A loud pop and a crunch sounded from somewhere behind him. A rapid glance in his mirror told him the source: the strap on the last Bobcat snapped, and as it did, the machine lurched forward into the one in front of it and then raised up, teetering off balance. J.O. watched with a sick feeling as the machine rolled off the deck of the flatbed trailer and landed upside down on the asphalt. The Bobcat was instantly reduced to a three-ton ball of scrap cannonballing down the freeway at fifty miles per hour. Pieces of red-painted steel were catapulted high in the air, and sparks flew as it bounced and rolled across one lane of traffic and struck a car in the rear end, causing it to spin out of control and strike another car. The Bobcat kept going, rolling toward the median. Another car slammed on its brakes to avoid the tractor but couldn't stop, slamming into it. That car was then hit from behind by another car and spun off into the median. The impact on the tractor sent it rolling off into the median, where it came to a rest, hardly distinguishable for what it was.

J.O. coasted to a stop. He dared not hit his brakes for fear another machine might come loose. He rolled to a stop in the emergency lane, set his flashers, and bailed out. The sight that met his eyes was awful. Six cars were smashed and strewn about the freeway. It was a mess. He ran to the first car. The lone occupant was struggling to open a jammed driver's side door. He was okay. The driver of the second car was already out standing in the emergency lane, rubbing the back of his neck. J.O. breathed something of a sigh of relief as one by one each of the people in the wrecked cars climbed out and got off the freeway. They had aches and pains, but at least no one seemed critically injured. Northbound traffic had come to a complete stop—all lanes were blocked.

Two emotions bubbled to the surface. The first was a stupefying sense of helplessness that there was nothing he could do to fix the problem he had just caused. The second was a seething, indignant rage. This was no accident. Claude and her goons had caused this. As his emotions battled for dominance, the fury won.

||||||||||||||||

The Utah Highway Patrol took charge of the scene within minutes. Wreckers were called, and traffic was directed on its way. The scene looked like something out of a highway nightmare. It seemed like hundreds of red, yellow, and blue flashing lights were reflecting in the darkness off the snow and all the surrounding buildings. J.O. assisted wherever he could, directing traffic, helping wreckers, and calming stricken motorists. Almost an hour after the crash, the last wrecked car was towed away. A large, brown-uniformed officer walked toward J.O., carrying a report book in his hand.

"Care to tell me how this happened?" he asked sternly. J.O. immediately detected the accusing tone in the man's voice.

J.O. told the officer exactly what happened. As he spoke, the officer wrote his report.

"And the dark-blue SUV?"

"It didn't stop," J.O. said.

The officer looked up from his report book. The expression on his face spoke volumes. J.O. knew exactly what the man was thinking: *Sure, Buddy, blame it on someone else. Why don't you just tell me straight? You took off without checking your load. You were following too close to another car, and when he hit his brakes, you slammed on yours and dumped your load on the freeway.*

A thought occurred to J.O. "Officer, would you come here for a moment?"

J.O. walked over to his truck in the emergency lane. The officer followed. J.O. knew what he would find even before he got there. The chain binders that had held the tractor were lying on the deck of the trailer. They had been intentionally unlocked. J.O. bent over, retrieved the end of the broken heavy-gauge nylon strap, and held it up in front of the officer's face. The man's eyes widened perceptibly and then narrowed in a comprehending scowl. The strap had been cleanly cut, almost all the way through.

Chapter Nineteen

IDAHO FALLS, CHRISTMAS DAY 2021

Shawnee sighed contentedly. The day had been wonderful, more therapeutic than any medicine on earth. Just walking through the front door had been like coming out of a killer storm into the warmth and security of home and hearth. It felt so good to be home again. It felt so good to roll on the floor and play with her brothers and sisters and their new toys. Her mother had been an angel, ministering to her every need and spoiling her in a way she had never done before. It was as though she sensed the deep, unspoken need of her oldest child.

It was late, after 10:00 p.m. They had just had family prayer, and Shawnee was trying to persuade Emily to put away her new toys and go to bed.

"Come on, Emily. I'll put your doll right here in bed with you. Now get your pajamas on and go to bed."

"But, Nawnee, I'm not tired."

"You're going to be, sweetheart, if you don't get to bed. Besides, you wouldn't want Santa Claus to come and take that doll away because you were being naughty now, would you?"

That did it. Emily was instantly cooperative. In minutes, she had her teeth brushed and was ready for bed.

"Would you like help with your prayers?" Shawnee asked.

"I can do it," Emily said with mild indignance, "but don't leave."

Shawnee smiled as she knelt beside Emily. Her little sister might be old enough to say her own words now, but she was not so old that she didn't still need adult confirmation and praise for a job well done.

"Heavenly Father," Emily began. "Thank you for Christmas. Thank you for the presents I got, and thank you for letting Nawnee be home again. Please bless the missionaries and the prophet and all our family. Help us to be good and not fight."

The sweetest feeling of warmth and love came over Shawnee as she listened to her little sister lisp out her simple prayer. Tenderly, she reached over and put her arm around Emily's tiny shoulder as the little one continued to pray. But Emily's next words stunned Shawnee: "And Heavenly Father, please bless J.O. that he will be okay and come to our home soon. In the name of Jesus Christ, amen."

As soon as the prayer was finished, Emily hopped to her feet and threw her arms around Shawnee. "I love you, Nawnee."

"I love you too, Emily."

Emily scrambled into bed and reached for her doll, pulling it close. As Shawnee tucked the covers in around her, Emily spoke again. "Nawnee, when is J.O. going to come again?"

"I don't know, Emily. Probably never."

"Why?" Emily cried in alarm.

Shawnee searched for the right words, but there just weren't any that would make sense to a four-year-old. "I don't know. I guess because . . ." she stopped, letting the words trail off. There was no way to answer her. "I don't know, Emily," she finished lamely. "Maybe someday he will come again."

"I hope so," she said, as she snuggled down into her covers. "I miss him."

Shawnee bent over and kissed her on the forehead. "I do too, Emily. I do too." And she meant it.

"Dad, Mom, can we talk for a moment?" Shawnee asked as she came into the kitchen where her parents were sitting.

"Sure, Honey," her mother said, "Come and sit down. Would you like something to drink?"

Shawnee smiled appreciatively at her mother. "No thanks, Mom. I'm fine."

"What's on your mind, Dear?" her dad asked.

Quickly she related what had happened minutes before with Emily's prayer.

"Does she always pray like that?" she asked.

Her parents looked at each other and then back at her. "No," her mother said. "I've never heard her bring it up."

"Neither have I," her dad added. "It was probably triggered by having you home again. She talks about you all the time when you're gone."

Shawnee smiled. "I miss her too. I miss all of them. I never appreciated how wonderful it is to have a big family until I was away from them."

"Does that mean you like us, then?" her father teased.

"Dad," Shawnee protested, even as her mother dug him in the ribs.

Then, growing more serious, Shawnee continued. "This last year has been incredible for me. I can't believe how much I've learned."

"Like what?" her mother asked.

"Like how much the Church means to me—and my testimony, and all of you."

Shawnee could see tears at the corners of her mother's eyes, but she rushed on. "It was so wonderful to come home again yesterday. I've been gone from home for more than four years now, but I've never missed the family as much as I have in the last few months."

"Why do you suppose that is?" her dad asked.

"Probably because all this stuff with J.O. has caused me to really evaluate what's most important to me."

"And what have you concluded?" her dad pressed.

"That this is real happiness." She spread her arms wide as if to encompass the entire household. "All that any person could ever want in terms of happiness, joy, love, and peace is right here." She looked directly at her mother, who was openly weeping. "Thank you for being the most wonderful parents anyone could ever have. Thank you for teaching me what you did. You were right. It is all true! I just want you to know. You were right."

Her father reached across the table and put his large hands over hers. "You're welcome, my dear. Fortunately for us, not everyone has a daughter as easy to raise as you were."

Shawnee smiled at that. "I'm glad you can say that now."

Her mother broke in. "Can I ask you a question?" Without waiting for an answer, she went on. "What *did* happen with J.O.?"

Shawnee sighed and shook her head. Briefly she told them of her last encounter with him and of the final goodbye.

"Have you seen him since?" her father asked.

"No. According to Tate, he got in his truck that very night and has been gone ever since. He's been all over the United States in the last few weeks."

Both parents seemed to consider what she said. Neither of them spoke. "Dad," Shawnee continued, "did I do the right thing by confronting him? In some ways he was so close. He told me he had just started reading the Book of Mormon and that he was tired of driving and was going to quit. Maybe I ruined everything." She closed her eyes and tipped her head back in frustration. "What if I drove him away from the truth?"

"You take too much on yourself, Shawnee. Don't forget that J.O. is a big boy and he can make his own decisions. Joining the Church will ultimately be a decision he has to make. Would you have wanted to him to join the Church because of you?"

Shawnee instantly recoiled. "No! But what if I drove him away from it?"

"Let me share something with you that might help," her dad said. "Do you remember the parable of the lost sheep in Luke 15?"

Shawnee nodded, searching the catacombs of her memory for the details of the story.

"Most of us remember the part about the shepherd going after the lost sheep, and the big party when he comes back, but there is a part there that I think adds deep significance to the parable. The shepherd, who is obviously the Savior, leaves the ninety and nine safe and secure and goes *into* the wilderness after the lost one. Think about the significance of a lone sheep in the wilderness. You know from Grandpa's ranch that sheep have no natural defenses and many natural predators. A sheep doesn't have a chance of survival out there. But the verse records that the shepherd stays out there *until* he finds the lost one."

Shawnee looked up from the page of the Bible that her mother had retrieved off the counter. Her eyes locked with her father's as he continued. "You see, Shawnee, He won't come home without that lamb. He'll stay there until he finds him. Even if that lamb," he paused, "happens to be running all over the United States in a truck. It makes no difference. The staff of this Shepherd reaches a very long way. He'll get him back."

Shawnee smiled at her dad and shook her head. "I love talking to you. How come you got so smart after I left home?"

Rick laughed.

"Can I ask you another question?"

He nodded.

"You know how J.O. and I met. This has been bothering me for a long time. I'm sure it was no accident that we met when we did and the way we did. It was just too crazy to be a coincidence. And all the things that happened to the two of us with the wreck and the Tetons and the kidnapping and all that. So many miracles and incredible things happened, and he changed so much."

Both her parents were nodding.

"Then . . . why? Why would Heavenly Father bring him into my life only to have it end the way it did? It makes no sense, and it seems so cruel."

Now it was her dad's turn to take a deep breath. He glanced at his wife, who said with the look in her eyes that this was his question to answer.

"That's a tough one. I don't know the answer."

"But, Dad. That's not good enough. I have to know!"

"Why, Dear?" her mother broke in. "Why is it so important?"

"Because . . ." she hesitated, frustrated at her lack of words. "Because the same feelings that told me that meeting J.O. was right and from God are the same kind of feelings that tell me that the Church is true. So how could it end the way it did if it were from God?"

"Shawnee," her dad said soothingly, "calm down. You're forcing this question into a box it doesn't belong in."

Shawnee was puzzled as she looked at her father.

"Isn't it possible that Heavenly Father wanted you to meet J.O. when you did, the way you did, and then wanted it to end when it did and the way it did?"

She drew back in her chair as she considered his words.

He went on. "Who ever said that God's will always has to feel good and be a pleasant experience?" After a pause, he continued, "And another thing—I think you're missing something important about faith."

"What's that?"

"Remember what it says in Alma 32:21? 'Faith is not to have a *perfect knowledge* of things. Therefore, if ye have faith, ye hope for things which are *not seen*, which are true.' I'm as sure as you are that meeting J.O. was no accident. I was there. It was strange to say the least. And I liked him. He's a good young man. There's something special about him. I believe the Lord has something in mind for him, but the fact that it ended the way it did between the two of you does not make your meeting or experiences any less true or right. Have some faith, Shawnee. Some day you will have a perfect knowledge of why everything happened the way it did—but for now, trust the Lord. He knows what He's doing. You were a great blessing to J.O."

Shawnee's head tipped back, and she stared at the ceiling, deep in thought. After a moment, she looked back at her parents and smiled. "You're right. I haven't been exercising a whole lot of faith lately. Mostly I've been murmuring and feeling sorry for myself."

"That's understandable, Dear," her mother said. "When you love someone, you can't just cancel those feelings like an unwanted credit card."

Shawnee looked sharply at her mother. "Love?"

Her mother smiled. "Yes, love! You loved him, and you still do. Since we're being honest here and laying it all out on the table, we might as well cover this ground too. You love him, and if I am any judge of the way he looked at you when he was here, he loves you too."

"Love," Shawnee said. "If he loved me, then why didn't he change?"

"Have you ever thought that maybe he was thinking the same thing?" her mother asked. "If she really loved me, why didn't she let this church thing go?"

"But . . ." Shawnee protested weakly.

"Whether you meant to or not, you were asking that young man to change his whole life, to instantly develop a whole new set of values and attitudes. How would you feel and what would you do if someone came to you with the same kind of thing?"

Shawnee slumped in her chair; she felt like she had been punched in the stomach. She had never thought of it quite like that.

"Don't get me wrong," her mother continued. "I'm not saying you did the wrong thing by telling him what you did. Maybe it was what he needed to hear. But be careful expecting him or anyone else to change their whole life according to your specifications and timetable. You grew up in the Church and probably don't recognize that to come from where he is to a way of life like ours is a stark and radical adjustment on every level."

"I think," her dad broke in, "that the love and example you gave him will eventually make a difference. It may be slow at first, but as time goes on it will cause his heart to swell and open to the gospel. I believe he'll change into exactly what you want him to be, with enough time."

"You really think so, Dad?" Shawnee asked, feeling a glimmer of hope.

"I do, Dear. He's a good man."

"I don't know why it matters, though. I'll probably never see him again, but I hope you're right. Oh, I hope you're right."

Shawnee stood up, signaling that she was going to bed. She stepped to her father and threw her arms around his neck and hugged him fiercely. "I love you, Daddy!"

"I love you too, Sweetie."

Shawnee then hugged her mother. "I love you too, Mother. Thanks for taking such good care of me."

"You're welcome, Dear. It's a privilege."

As Shawnee walked out of the kitchen, her parents stood side by side with their arms around each other, watching her go.

"It's not over yet," Rick James whispered softly.

His wife looked up at him. "What do you mean?"

"I think those two are going to see each other again. There's something to this that's bigger than all of us. I'm not sure what it is or how it will happen, but I can feel it."

Marie James squeezed her husband's waist harder. "I think you're right. I hope you're right."

///////////////////

In the two days since J.O. had been home, Ruthie had done all she could to satisfy J.O.'s voracious appetite. It was as though he had been fasting the whole time he had been gone and was now trying to make up for lost time. That morning she had prepared the largest Christmas dinner she had ever fixed for her boys. She looked across her kitchen table and counter to see that very little of it remained. Lisa had been with them but hadn't eaten that much. J.O. had eaten like a starving man.

Ruthie sighed. She could satisfy his hunger for food, but not his hunger for answers. He had met with the missionaries every night since his return and had absolutely pummeled them with questions. Their discussions had taken the whole of every evening. Nothing had been allowed to pass unexamined. It was as though he wanted to know everything at his first sitting. She was sure the missionaries were feeling like they had gone ten rounds with a prize fighter, but they kept coming back, eager and with cheerful countenances.

The door opened, and J.O. walked in, breathing heavily.

"Have a good run, Dear?"

He gave her a thumbs-up sign and a smile, panting so hard he couldn't speak.

"Better get showered. The missionaries will be here in about thirty minutes."

He moved off toward his bedroom. She heard the door shut. That was the other thing that was bothering her. J.O. seemed as restless as a cat on the prowl. He had been running twice a day, harder than she had ever known him to. He wouldn't relax. He was constantly keyed up and going. He wouldn't even sit to watch television. In the two days since he had been home, he had made every household repair on her list and was looking for more. Every other time he had come home, he had been exhausted and ready to sleep, but not this time. He was as active and jittery as a man slamming energy drinks.

She walked to the counter and began fixing a turkey sandwich for him. He would be hungry when he came out. The explanations he offered for his behavior were cheerful, one-sentence answers, more evasive than explanatory. He was never rude; he just didn't want to talk about it.

Except for the Church, that is—and when it came to that, he wanted to know everything. He had seemed startled to learn that he had a pioneer heritage.

"Why didn't you ever tell me these things?" he asked in an almost accusing tone.

"Because I knew very little about it myself—and besides, your father and I decided that we'd let you boys find religion on your own. We didn't want to push you into it."

The look of hurt on his face had seared her soul. She was sure now that decision so many years ago had been wrong. *Not only was our decision wrong, but it has cost my sons dearly. With the reawakening of my faith and the interest of both my sons, perhaps now all the baggage of the past could be dropped. Is it too late for my boys to find what I have rediscovered?* She had hoped and prayed for the last several nights that it was not.

The abrupt knock at the door startled her out of her thoughts. Wiping her hands on her apron, she went to the door and opened it.

"Come in, elders. We're waiting for you."

"Thanks, Sister Steele. Did you have a good Christmas?" Elder Schofield asked.

Ruthie liked Elder Schofield. He was shorter in stature and of medium build. He was going bald and had a smattering of freckles over his cheeks. It was obvious he was older than most missionaries—she guessed twenty-two or twenty-three. He seemed to have a good command of the scriptures. Not only was he the one who fielded most of J.O.'s questions, but he seemed to relish the challenge while his companion, Elder Merkley, was usually content just to listen.

"It was wonderful. How about you?"

Elder Schofield patted his stomach. "We've been eating all day."

Elder Merkley sat down with a groan. "I'm not going to eat for a week."

She laughed. "Well, in that case, I guess you wouldn't be interested in a sandwich, would you?"

Both elders gave her an exaggerated, pained look.

"Maybe after J.O. gets through with you you'll want a piece of pie. We'll wait till later."

"Hey, elders!" J.O. said, coming into the room and toweling his hair. "How was Christmas?"

"Great! It was a white Christmas for us."

Seeing the uncomprehending expression on J.O.'s face, Elder Schofield went on. "A *white Christmas* means we had a baptismal service earlier today. A man we were teaching decided to give his baptism to his wife as her Christmas present."

"Oh, that's so sweet," Ruthie said.

"It was one of neatest experiences of my mission," Elder Schofield said. "The Spirit was really strong."

"Why do you wear white when you get baptized?" J.O. asked.

"It's a symbol of purity," Elder Merkley said.

"We're going to talk about that tonight, J.O. That is," he stopped and winked at Ruthie, "if we get that far."

Just then Tate and Lisa walked in holding hands.

"Sorry we're late," Tate said. "A lady got stuck against a curb downtown in the snow. We stopped and pushed her out."

"Probably just showing off all those muscles for Lisa," J.O. said to the elders.

Tate grabbed a dinner roll off the counter and pitched it at his brother. J.O. caught it with one hand and laughed. "As a matter of fact," Lisa said, laughing, "I was pretty impressed. I had no idea he was such a strong, handsome gentleman." She sidled up to him.

"Alright, alright. Enough already," Tate growled, his face flaming.

Ruthie smiled. It was so good to have her boys together and all the family at home. J.O. added so much humor when he was here, and Lisa seemed so natural in the niche that was hers.

Soon they were all seated in the comfortable living room of the townhome around a warm fireplace. J.O. was sitting on the floor on the plush carpet, with his back against the large, overstuffed sofa, the place he always preferred to be. His new scriptures were open on the floor around him and he was intently staring at Elder Merkley, who was teaching.

"Why is faith so important?" J.O. suddenly interrupted.

This had been his way. His questions were as short and direct as the bark of a drill sergeant.

"Well," Elder Merkley stammered, "it's the first principle of the gospel."

"I know that, but why?"

"Everyone has a hero, J.O.," Elder Schofield broke in. "To have faith in the Lord means that He becomes your hero, and you'll follow and obey Him. All the way to heaven."

J.O.'s mind replayed discussions he and Shawnee had had about faith. "Is Christ the only way?" he blurted out. "What about the billions of people who have never known Him? Are they lost?"

"No," Elder Schofield said. "If God is loving and perfect, how could He turn His back on so much of the human race? He couldn't, and He doesn't. All those who have died without knowing Him have that chance to have someone teach them beyond the grave, just like we're teaching you."

J.O. felt an excitement shoot through him as his soul resonated with the principle. "That means Dad . . ." He turned and looked at his mother, and a knowing look passed between them.

"He was close when he died, J.O.," Ruthie said. "He spoke of God and heaven a lot just before he passed away. He had many questions, just like you."

J.O. fingered the medallion under his shirt. *The polar star! Is this the polar star?*

"Listen to your heart, J.O.," Elder Schofield said, suddenly very intense and serious. "You know what we're saying is true. You've known it all along. Why are you holding back?"

J.O.'s eyes narrowed as irritation swept over him, but he forced it away. His reaction to this question had cost him dearly once. He wouldn't let it happen again. *What is holding me back?* He blew out his breath and looked down at the floor. The only sound in the room was the crackling of the fire. Every eye was fixed on him. Tate was tense and anxious, uncertain how J.O. would react to being hit so directly. This could be it.

"Elder, I've been around religious people all my life, and when it comes down to it, they are just like everyone else—no better, and in some cases, a whole lot worse. The most religious people seem to be the most annoying. If you really want to know the truth, I keep asking myself, do I really want to be a religious fanatic like them, and the answer keeps coming back, no!"

"What about Shawnee and her family?" Tate asked. "Is that what you think of them?"

The room became even more charged with tension, since Shawnee was a subject that no one had dared broach with him. J.O. looked directly at Tate, who held his gaze with fixed determination. For a moment, everyone held their breath. Finally, J.O. spoke. "No. She and her family are the one example that tell me it's possible to be religious without being a pain in the world's backside."

Elder Schofield laughed. "Don't worry. The most Christlike people are the easiest ones to love. But let's stop for a minute. Are you saying that you've never cared much for religious people, and that's why you don't want to be one?"

"Yeah, that, and religious people have always seemed so . . ." he hesitated, looking for the right way to say it, "well, I don't want to offend you."

Elder Schofield laughed. "Go ahead, offend me, if you think you can."

"Well, they always seem so blind and stupid when it comes to wrestling with life's questions. They just seem so gullible and simple. It's as though all they're interested in is getting people to join their church so that they have more numbers than the next Church."

Elder Schofield rubbed his chin. "Well, I have to say, I've been out here for a long time, and that's the first time I've ever heard that one."

"I'm sorry," J.O. quickly said, "I didn't want to offend you." But even as he said it, he felt a strange sense of exhilaration. It was as though for the first time he was able to explain why religion bothered him: why God had become a sore spot. Strangely enough, however, it was as though his arguments were like a shoddy piece of merchandise that he was finally able to examine up close and realize its poor quality.

"J.O.," Elder Schofield said, the intensity back in his voice, "let's cut to the chase here. What really matters here, truth or show?"

"Truth!" J.O. said without hesitation.

"Alright, then, forget about the show and the appearances. Forget about every other religious person in the world. The question is, is this church true and of God, or is it not true? Are we liars . . . ," he paused, "or are we messengers from the Lord?"

"But they all claim to be the true messengers."

"So, is it impossible to know, then?" Elder Schofield asked.

Ruthie watched in amazement. She had never seen Elder Schofield like this. There was a power that seemed to emanate from him. He was bearing down on J.O. with undeniable intensity but ultimate gentleness. He was handling her strong-willed son as though he were a petulant toddler.

J.O. looked up at the ceiling and closed his eyes. When he opened them there was pain in his expression. "Elder Schofield, I hope not. I've thought long and hard about this. I *want* to know. Don't tell me that I have to spend my life guessing."

Elder Schofield seemed to pounce on that. "You don't have to guess. Listen to your heart. There is a voice that speaks inside that is undeniable. As a missionary, I can influence and, to a measure, control your five senses. I can speak and you can hear. I can cook and you can taste. I can wave my arm and you can see. But this other voice is beyond man's ability to control. It speaks in your mind and in your heart, and by gentle whisperings, it lets you know the truth." He stopped and looked at intently at J.O. "You've felt that voice before, haven't you?"

Slowly, J.O. nodded.

Elder Schofield's voice dropped almost to a whisper. "Look at me, Brother. Look me in the eye and listen to your heart. Are we telling you the truth, or are we lying to you?"

Silence gripped the room, and no one breathed. Then something seemed to settle over the room. No one could see it, but it was obvious all could feel it. Ruthie and Lisa had tears in their eyes.

"It's true," J.O. said at last.

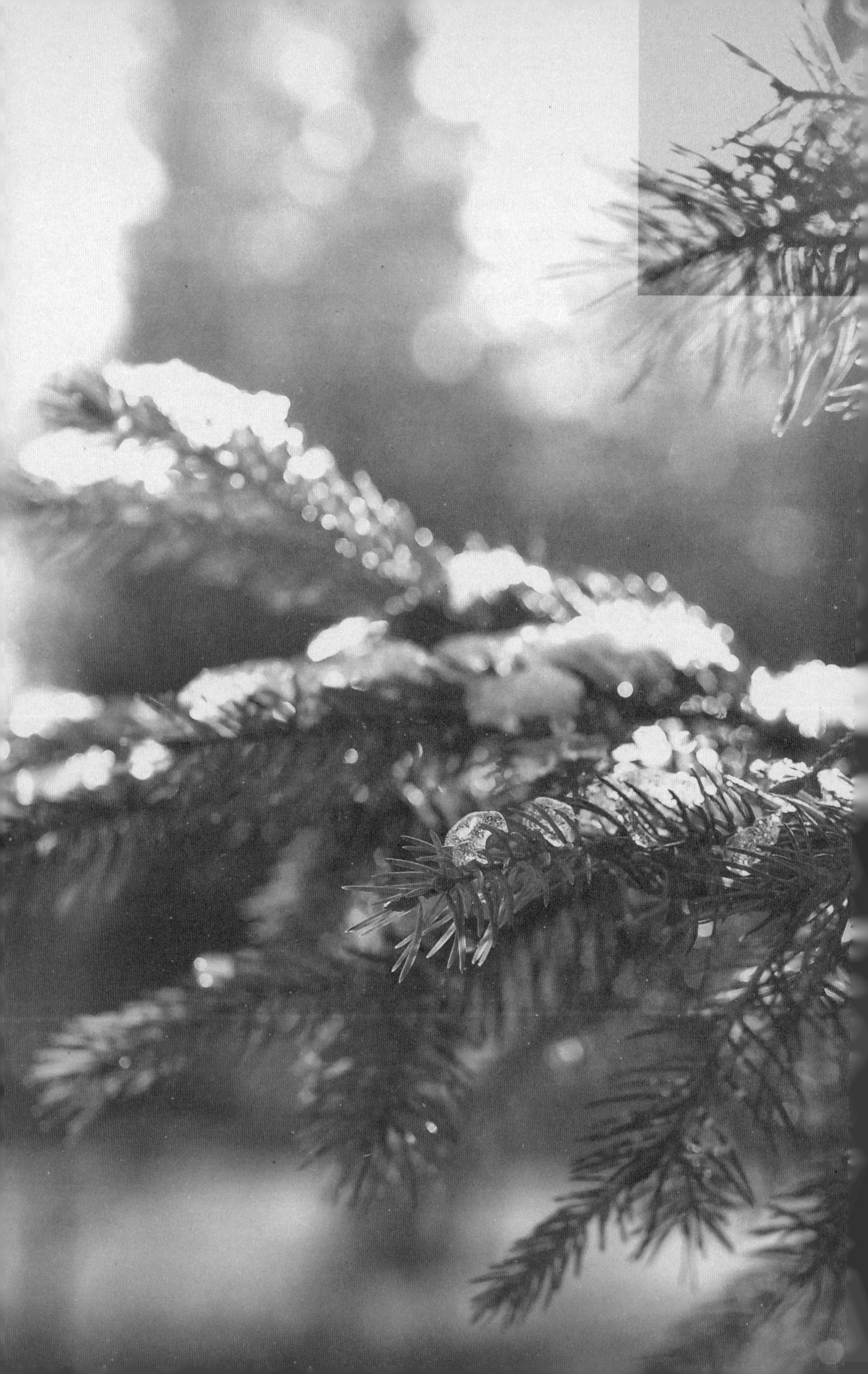

Chapter Twenty

POCATELLO, IDAHO, DECEMBER 28, 2021

"Okay, so what do we get?" J.O. asked. "What are you guys in the mood for?"

"Pizza," Lisa said. "Let's get some pizza and do a movie and stay here for the evening."

"Pizza it is!" J.O. said with a flourish. "You okay with that, Bro?"

"Yup!"

"You'd be okay with puppy chow as long as Lisa was serving it."

Tate grinned and put his arm around Lisa. "True that!"

J.O. laughed and opened the door to his Jeep. "You okay with some pizza tonight, Mom?"

Ruthie smiled and waved her hand as if to say *whatever*. They had persuaded her to let them do "the cooking" tonight. Reluctantly, she had agreed, knowing what they would come back with. She watched as they pulled out of the driveway and started away, the sound of their laughter still reaching her. The last few days had been some of the happiest she could remember. It was as though they had been living under a pall for many years without realizing it, and now the clouds seemed to be lifting and the brilliance of the sun was all around them.

She turned and walked back into the house. It was the missionaries and the gospel that were making the difference. There was a light and peace that came with them and remained once they were gone. She could not remember a time when she felt so much at peace inside. It was as though she was whole and at full strength once more. Even J.O. was different. He seemed to be the one on whom the gospel was having the most profound impact. He spent hours searching the scriptures, making notes, and writing questions for the missionaries. They had come every night for a little while to spend time with them. She smiled to herself as she replaced a sofa pillow. Last night they had asked J.O. to prepare himself to be baptized on the seventh of January. His response had been, "Why wait? I've been to church from one end of this country to the other. I've read the Book of Mormon two and a half times through. I've almost finished the lessons. Why don't we do it on January first and start the year off right?"

Elder Schofield's grin had spread so wide you could have tied it behind his ears in a bow. "January first it is!" he had exclaimed and stood up and shook J.O.'s hand vigorously.

Her smile faded slightly as another thought crossed Ruthie's mind. After the missionaries left, Lisa had asked, "J.O., are you going to invite Shawnee to the baptism?"

A thoughtful expression had filled his features before he had sighed deeply. "I don't think so, Lisa."

"Why?"

"There are two reasons. First, I don't think she wants anything to do with me, and second, I wouldn't want her to get the idea that I was doing this just to get her back. If I asked her to come it would be like I was saying, 'Okay I'm a Latter-day Saint now. I did what you wanted. Can we go out again?' No, thanks," he had said with a wave of his hand. "*I know I'm doing this for me*, but I want there to be no doubts in everyone else's mind that I'm doing this for me, not her."

Lisa had bit down on her lip. It seemed she had something to say but could see there was no fighting him. His mind was made up.

After J.O. had left the room that night to go to bed, Lisa had spoken up. "He's wrong about one thing." Ruthie and Tate turned and stared in surprise at her. "Shawnee still loves him."

"You didn't tell me that," Tate had said.

"Would it have done any good?" Lisa had asked. "She's still having a hard time. I know she wants to ask me about him every time I come home, but she won't."

"Have you told her about what's going on?" Tate had asked.

"No. J.O. didn't want us to, remember?"

"She'll find out soon enough," Ruthie had said sagely. "You know she will."

That was last night. Ruthie walked into J.O.'s bedroom. A small, framed picture of a lovely, long-haired, young woman standing atop the Tetons was sitting on his dresser. She picked up Shawnee's picture. *Call it mother's intuition or whatever you want, but this young woman is meant for my son. I am more sure of that now than ever.*

<hr>

Tate held the door for Lisa and J.O. as they walked out of the restaurant. J.O. carried two large pizzas.

"Mmm, that smells good," J.O. said, breathing in deeply.

"No snitchin'," Tate said.

"Snitchin'? What's that?" Lisa asked.

"Stealing," Tate said. "I've never yet seen J.O. go out for pizza but what it was half gone before it ever got home."

"So? I was hungry!" J.O. said, laughing.

"Well, then, you'd better let me guard the pizza—otherwise Ruthie won't get any," Lisa said to Tate as they neared the Jeep.

"Fine with me," J.O. said.

They were just approaching the Jeep when four men dressed in black materialized out of the darkness from beyond the parking lot. They walked toward them carrying clubs and chains.

"Going somewhere?" one of them sneered.

J.O. turned without taking his eyes off the men and set the pizzas on the hood of the Jeep. He took a step away from the vehicle and toward the men. "Lisa, get in the Jeep," he said quietly.

Lisa moved to the opposite side of the Jeep from the four men. Tate appeared at his side, standing shoulder to shoulder with him. "What do you want?" Tate asked, his voice a low growl.

"A piece of you!" one of the men said, slapping a three-foot chunk of pipe against the palm of his hand.

"Come and get it," J.O. said calmly with a slight smile on his face.

The leader faltered, and the three men with him shot him an uncertain glance. It was as though they hadn't expected any opposition, and now they were uncertain what to do. J.O. picked up on the body language. They had expected him to run. He rocked forward on the balls of his feet in readiness. The leader stared at him for a moment and then ratcheted up his courage and continued moving forward. The others followed him. The thugs stopped about five feet away and stood staring in intimidating silence. J.O. held their gaze and slowly popped each of the knuckles on his right hand. Each pop sounded as distinct as a gunshot in the frigid night air.

The leader suddenly lunged forward, swinging the pipe. J.O. dropped to the asphalt and kicked the leader in the knees. One knee popped and hyper-extended backward. The man went down, clutching at his knee and screaming in pain. At the same moment, another of the men threw a fist at Tate. Tate had studied some martial arts. He blocked the swing neatly and laid the man out with a stiff, hard jab to the nose. The man bent over, bleeding and gasping. J.O. rolled back to his feet just as another of the men stepped up and swung a length of chain at him. It whizzed over his head like a scythe as he ducked and rolled. Tate whirled as the fourth man charged him, but he couldn't avoid him, and the two of them fell to the icy asphalt with the man on top of him. Like a cat, Tate twisted onto his back and with cupped hands popped the man in the ears, breaking both his eardrums. The man screamed and fell to the side, rolling in agony.

"Tate, watch out!" J.O. yelled.

Tate looked in time to see the lone thug with the chain winding up to swing at him. He tried to roll away, but there was not enough time. The chain came down across his back with a crack. Tate grunted with pain and went down. The man with the broken nose was up again and wild with rage. He was coming at J.O., but the man with the chain was going to swing again at Tate, who was trying to roll away. J.O. sidestepped the charge and in two jumps, closed from behind on the man with the chain just as he was going to swing. J.O. brought his hands together in a rock-hard ball and slammed them down like a club on the back of the man's neck. He fell to the ground with a grunt and didn't move.

The broken-nosed man jumped to face the two brothers. He pulled a knife with an unusually long blade from a sheath at his leg.

The bruiser with the broken knee was trying to regain his feet. He cried out, "Pete, don't! We were only supposed to scare him, not kill anybody!"

"Shut up!" The man roared. "I want 'em!"

Bellowing like an angry bull, he came at Tate. Tate backed away from him until he was against the Jeep. The man swung savagely with the knife, but Tate caught his arm. The larger man threw his weight into the knife and inched closer. Tate deflected it, and it swung downward and sliced his thigh. The shock of the wound caused Tate to momentarily weaken. An angry, throaty bellow came from the man's throat.

"Tate!" Lisa's scream of alarm momentarily distracted the man with the knife. J.O. leaped over the last man he had downed and charged the knifeman from the side, knocking him away from Tate and into the Jeep. Tate spun away, clear of the knife. The man bounced off the Jeep, turning as he did so toward J.O. He swung the knife. It sliced the front of J.O.'s coat cleanly. Before the man could recover from his swing, J.O. hit him with a lightning punch, carrying all the power and fury he could muster. It caught the man squarely in the left side of the head just above the ear. The force of the blow slammed the man's head back into the Jeep, where it struck the roll bar with a metallic clang. He went down, unconscious before he hit the ground.

||||||||||||||||||

Tate lay on the gurney in the Pocatello Regional Medical Center emergency room. Lisa stood by his side, holding his hand, her face pale and drawn. A large white bandage swathed Tate's thigh.

"The pain is going to be pretty bad for the next few days, Son," the doctor said. "Here's a prescription that should take the edge off of it."

"Thanks," Tate said, his voice laced with fatigue and pain.

"I'll want to see you in a few days to make sure the stitches are holding and that there's no infection."

The doctor walked out. Ruthie came over and picked up Tate's other hand. "How are you feeling, Dear?"

"Like I got in a fight with a chainsaw," he said as he winced and sat up. J.O. came over from where he had been sitting in a chair, silent and withdrawn.

"Need some help?" he asked.

"No, I think I'm okay. The leg feels like it'll hold me."

"With thirty-some stitches and the amount of blood you lost, let's not take chances," Lisa said, as she came up at his side and lifted his arm up over her shoulder.

J.O. came up on the other side, and they steadied him as he stood up. A nurse approached with a wheelchair, and they eased him into it. Together they went into the waiting area of the emergency room. A uniformed police officer was waiting there.

"Any idea why those men attacked you?" he asked.

"None," Tate said. "I've never seen any of them before."

"Did they try to rob you?"

"No. They never demanded our wallets or anything," Tate said. "It was like they just wanted to pick a fight for no reason."

"And you say you had never seen any of them before?"

"Never," Lisa and Tate said in unison. "J.O., did you recognize them?" Tate asked.

"No," he answered quietly.

"Well, we have them in custody. If we learn anything, and I'm sure we will, we'll be in touch."

"Thanks, Officer," Tate said.

Ruthie came over to J.O. and took his arm. Her face wore an expression of deep concern. "J.O., are you sure you're alright?" She looked down at the gash in the front of his coat that ran across the level of his navel.

"I'm fine," he said, smiling at his mother. "All he got was fabric."

Ruthie stared up into her son's face, convinced there was something else he was not telling her.

|||||||||||||||||||||

J.O. looked down in the darkness at the luminescent display on his sports watch. It was after two in the morning. Lisa had gone back to her apartment. Shawnee was coming back from Idaho Falls tonight. His own family had long since gone to bed. J.O. sat fully dressed on the edge of his bed, his mind racing at high speed. The words *we were only supposed to scare him, not kill him* replayed on a repeating loop in his mind. The vermin had been Claude's animals. She had sent them for one reason and one reason only—to continue her game. Anger rolled over him like a high tide. That was it! Tonight was enough. It had been bad enough to jeopardize *his* life, but when they endangered the lives of innocent people, especially those of his family, that was going too far. Tate had come very close to being killed tonight.

The problem facing J.O. now was what he should do. If he told his family, they would worry about a problem they couldn't do anything about—especially his mother, who tended to worry too much anyway. Had he done the right thing in not telling the police? But what could they do if they knew? There was no way they could get to Claude. Surely Claude expected him to tell the police. Did she seem the least bit worried that the police would be a problem for her? Besides, if there was any connection to Claude, the cops would probably get it out of her hired muscle.

So, what should he do now? Even before he got home with the truck on that last run, he had decided that he was not going back out on the road until this was over. There was too much risk. It was only a matter of time before she struck again, and this time it might be the end of the game. But if he stayed here in Pocatello, the chances were high that someone else in the family might be hurt as well. If he left, he would be better equipped to fight on his own terms.

The question that flamed his nerves now was whether he should tell anyone where he was going and why. If he told his mother or Tate where he was going, they would come after him and put themselves in danger again. If he told them what his suspicions were about Claude, they would try to protect him, and he would have the same problem. Moreover, there was always the possibility that Claude could use his family to get to him. If his family didn't know where he was or why he was there, it reduced the risk of them being hurt. They would never forgive him, but at least they would be okay. It was all a high-stakes gamble.

He stood, wincing with pain, and walked to his dresser. He lifted the small, framed picture of Shawnee in the Tetons and the copy of the Book of Mormon she had given him. He held one in each hand and thought for a moment. What should he do? He set both on the dresser and lifted the front of his shirt. A long, shallow cut ran across his midsection. It wasn't deep, but it was long, and it stung.

Too close. Any deeper, and I would understand how a trout feels.

The exertion of working through his thoughts had taken hours. He had to do something and do it quick. He sensed that Claude was closing in. There were still many questions and many what-ifs that he couldn't answer. There wasn't time. If Claude had tracked him to his home, he had to move fast. Tonight! No delays!

ALMA 55:34–56:12

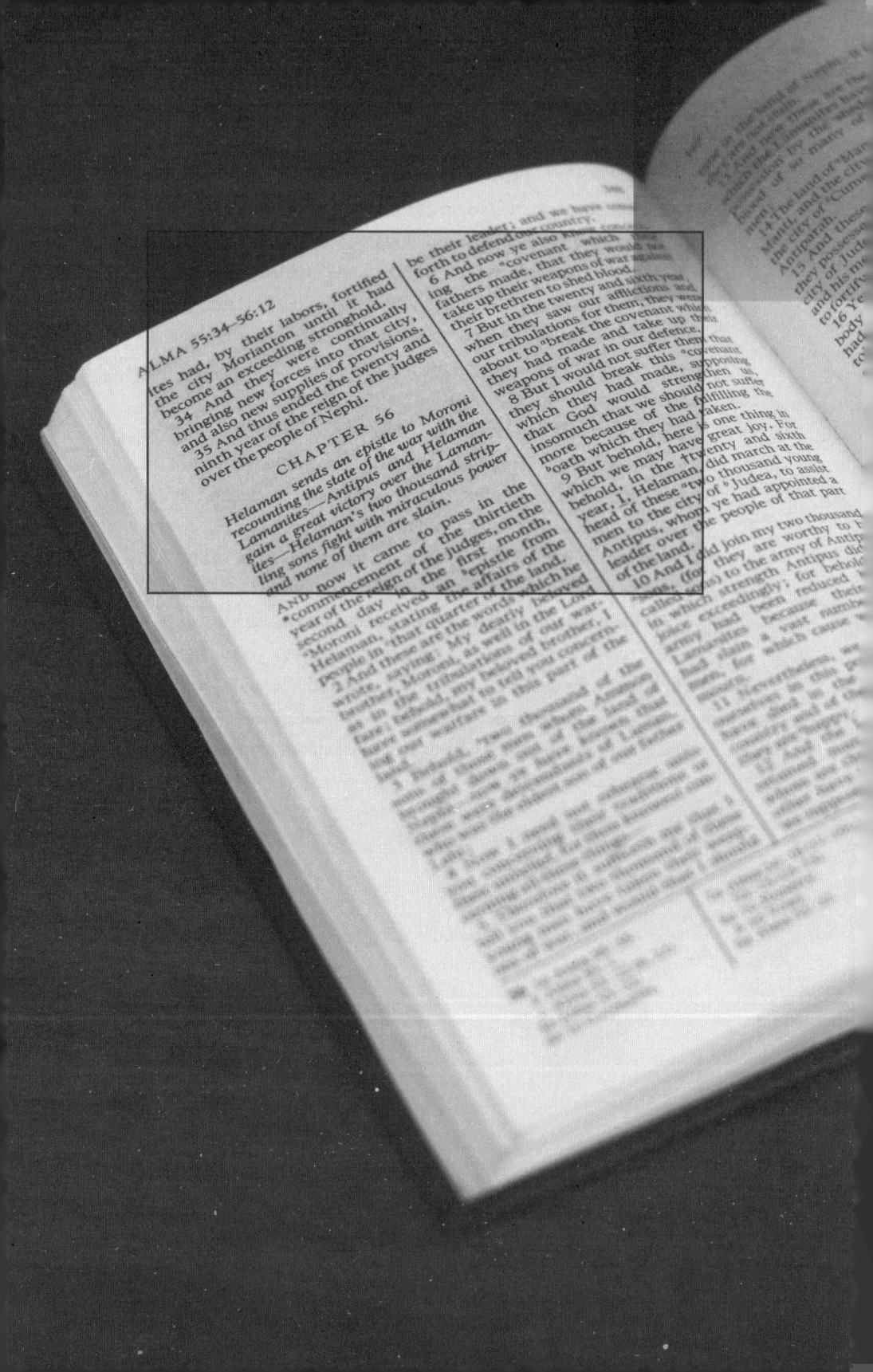

ites had, by their labors, fortified the city Morianton until it had become an exceeding stronghold.

34 And they were continually bringing new forces into that city, and also new supplies of provisions.

35 And thus ended the twenty and ninth year of the reign of the judges over the people of Nephi.

CHAPTER 56

Helaman sends an epistle to Moroni recounting the state of the war with the Lamanites—Antipus and Helaman gain a great victory over the Lamanites—Helaman's two thousand stripling sons fight with miraculous power and none of them are slain.

AND now it came to pass in the commencement of the thirtieth year of the reign of the judges, on the second day in the first month, Moroni received an *epistle from Helaman, stating the affairs of the people in that quarter of the land.

2 And these are the words which he wrote, saying: My dearly beloved brother, Moroni, as well in the Lord as in the tribulations of our war; behold, my beloved brother, I have somewhat to tell you concerning our warfare in this part of the land.

be their leader; and we have covenanted with them to defend their country.

6 And now ye also know concerning the *covenant which their fathers made, that they would not take up their weapons of war against their brethren to shed blood.

7 But in the twenty and sixth year, when they saw our afflictions and our tribulations for them, they were about to *break the covenant which they had made and take up their weapons of war in our defence.

8 But I would not suffer them that they should break this *covenant which they had made, supposing that God would strengthen us, insomuch that we should not suffer more because of the fulfilling the *oath which they had taken.

9 But behold, here is one thing in which we may have great joy. For behold, in the twenty and sixth year, I, Helaman, did march at the head of these *two thousand young men to the city of *Judea, to assist Antipus, whom ye had appointed a leader over the people of that part of the land.

10 And I did join my two thousand sons (for they are worthy to be called sons) to the army of Antipus, in which strength Antipus did rejoice exceedingly; for behold, his army had been reduced by the Lamanites because their

Chapter Twenty-One

POCATELLO, IDAHO, DECEMBER 29, 2021, 7:15 A.M.

The front door suddenly opened, and Lisa walked in. Tate and Ruthie sat at the kitchen table with a piece of paper in front of them. Tate stood and took her in his arms. He buried his face in her hair. Lisa held him tightly. He was obviously very upset.

"What's happened?" Lisa asked.

"Sit down, Lisa," Ruthie said gently.

As she sat, Ruthie handed her a single white sheet of paper. She began to read.

Dear Mom and Tate,

I know this is not going to make any sense, but if there was ever a time in my life that I needed you to trust me, it's now. Some things are happening right now that make it necessary for me to leave. They came out of nowhere. I didn't plan on it, but I have to deal with it. Don't try to find me, and don't worry if I'm not in contact for a while. I'll be back as soon as I can.

Neither you nor Tate have done anything to cause me to leave. It's something else entirely unrelated to you. It has nothing to do with the Church. I plan on being baptized just as soon as I get back. Tell the missionaries I'm sorry, but not to worry. They were awesome, and I will keep the faith.

I love you dearly,
J.O.

P.S. Alma 56

Lisa looked up from the letter, an expression of confusion on her face. "Why?" she said.

"Who knows?" Tate said angrily, slamming his fist down on the table. "Who knows what goes through his crazy head?"

"Tate!" Ruthie said sharply. "That isn't going to help. He asked us to trust him."

"Trust him!" Tate cried, rising to his feet. "Has he given us any reason in the last few weeks to trust him? First, he does what he does to Shawnee. Then he runs off like some angry child and doesn't come home for two months. And then," his voice was rising in pitch, "he gets this close to baptism, and boom, off he goes again."

"It's not like that, Tate," Ruthie said. "I'll admit that J.O. hasn't been himself since that kidnapping last summer, but I think you're judging him unfairly. Look at how he acted when he came home for Christmas. He wasn't kidding about the Church. You saw how sincere he was—how happy he was. If he's leaving now, there's got to be good reason."

Tate looked like he was about to make another angry comment when Lisa cut him off. "Your mom's right, Tate. J.O. wouldn't do this unless there was a very good reason. Question is, what's the reason?"

"Does it have anything to do with Shawnee?" Tate asked, calming somewhat. "Has he been in contact with her at all?"

"I don't think so," Lisa said. "I talked to her last night until after midnight. I didn't get the impression J.O. had been in contact with her at all."

"Did you tell her about J.O.'s decision to be baptized?" Tate asked.

"No. I didn't think I should. After what he said about joining the Church for the right reasons, I figured I'd better keep quiet." She hesitated a moment and addressed her next comments to Ruthie. "She still loves him, though. She asked about him."

Ruthie smiled at that announcement.

"So, where is he?" Tate persisted, back in control of his storming emotions. "Where is he headed in his big truck now?"

"Couldn't we call his dispatcher and find out?" Lisa asked, a little uncertain.

Tate looked down at his watch. "That's a great idea. I'll call them right now."

He picked up the phone and dialed the number. "Hello, Justin. This is Tate Steele, J.O.'s brother. I was just wondering—could you tell me where J.O. was heading this morning?"

Ruthie and Lisa watched as Tate became silent while he listened to Justin on the other end of the line. They were startled when Tate suddenly said, "He *what*? When? Do you know why?" There was a long pause as Tate listened. When he finally hung up and turned around, the two women were staring fixedly at him.

"J.O. quit this morning," he said abruptly.

"What?" both women cried.

"Why?" Ruthie asked.

"Justin said that J.O. had several strange accidents on this last trip. A brick was thrown through his window in California that nearly caused him to wreck. After that, someone axed one of his tires in Las Vegas, and he discovered it just in time. Then, in Salt Lake he lost a piece of machinery off his trailer in heavy traffic and caused a six-car pile-up."

"And he didn't say a word about it to me. No wonder he was acting so funny when he first got home," Ruthie exclaimed. "It's a wonder he wasn't climbing the walls."

"Why do you think he didn't tell us?" Lisa asked.

"You have to know him, Lisa," Ruthie said. "When he was a little boy, he once saw me cry because I was so worried about him. Since then, he has always tried to protect me. The world could be falling down around his ears, and you would never know it. Right or wrong, he'll carry all the weight of the world squarely on top of his own two shoulders, just like his dad did, to keep the ones he loves from worrying about him. The worst part is that you never know he's doing it. He's tougher than old leather, and it's an art with him to shrug off difficulties as though they don't exist. He was never a boy to want or need sympathy. I love him for his strength," she concluded, "but would like to kick his backside when he does something like this."

Despite the gravity of the situation, Lisa smiled. "What do you suppose has happened, then?"

"I'm thinking it must have something to do with what happened last night," Tate said.

"That's what I thought when I first found the letter," Ruthie said. "I thought there was something J.O. wasn't telling us last night. Now I'm almost sure of it."

"What?" Tate asked.

"I have no idea," Ruthie answered, "but there is this." She held up a bloody gray undershirt. They all stared fixedly at it. Ruthie continued. "I found it this morning stuffed in the bottom of his wastebasket." She spread it out showing where it was sliced open across the front. Lisa gasped. "So that knife did get him."

Ruthie nodded. "I can only hope that it's not too serious."

"So where would he go?" Lisa added, turning back to Tate. "Did the company know?"

"No. They said J.O. asked for ten days off for the holidays when he first got home. They gave it to him. Then this morning he just called up and quit; said he had made some decisions in his life."

"Decisions?" Ruthie mused. "About what, I wonder?"

"Well, we know he made decisions about the Church," Tate said, "but I can't see how that would cause him to do this. It has to have something to do with last night or those accidents."

"Do you suppose he's in some kind of trouble with the law?" Lisa asked tentatively.

"I don't think so," Tate replied evenly. "J.O. has a deep respect for the law, and if he's one thing, he's honest to a fault. No, I think it's something else."

"Tell us again what happened with the accidents on this last trip," Ruthie said, her brows furrowed in deep concentration.

Tate repeated what the dispatcher had told him. "There weren't many details given over the phone, but he did tell me that J.O. had filled out extensive reports for insurance purposes. I'm sure there's plenty of detail there."

Ruthie exhaled. "Okay, this much is obvious: he's in some kind of trouble, or he wouldn't have left. Even the tone of the note sounds like there is a problem. The question is, where did he go?"

"What about this," Lisa said, holding up the note and pointing at something.

"P.S. Alma 56," she quoted. "What's in Alma 56?"

Tate went to his bedroom and came out with his copy of the Book of Mormon. Carefully he read the chapter aloud to his mother and Lisa. When he finished, he closed the book and looked at them.

"What were we supposed to get from that?" Lisa asked.

"I don't know," Tate said. "Probably that verse about not doubting because their mothers knew it."

"Maybe, Tate, but I'm not so sure," Ruthie said.

"What then?"

"Alma 56 is about war and fighting and keeping the faith," she continued. "Obviously, it means something to J.O., or he wouldn't have made reference to it."

The three of them settled into a contemplative silence. After a few moments, Ruthie spoke again. "I don't want to worry you, but I think he's in serious trouble of some kind. If I know my son, it's something that would worry me a great deal if I knew what it was. If he doesn't call in the next few days, I'll know it's bad."

Lisa reached across the table and grasped Ruthie's hand. "What do we do?"

Ruthie looked at Lisa. "We pray, and then—"

"And then we go after him," Tate said, interrupting and finishing his mother's sentence. "I'll find him." He gritted his teeth and looked out the window. His voice resonated with determination. "I'll find him."

302

Chapter Twenty-Two

HAYDEN CREEK VALLEY, LEMHI, IDAHO, JANUARY 7, 2022

T. Jamison Thorpe kicked the last few pieces of hay off the back of the beat-up old ranch truck. It sailed out about ten feet and struck a healthy Hereford cow in the face. She followed it to the ground and began to devour it.

He breathed deeply the scent of the hay and the high mountain air. It was good to be home again. Since the time that Jim, as his friends called him, had accepted a call to be a member of the temple presidency of the Idaho Falls Temple, he had been home very little. It was as though he lived in the house of the Lord, and he loved that. He and Susan kept a small condominium in Idaho Falls during the week and returned home on occasional Sundays and Mondays. The day-to-day operations of the ranch had largely fallen to his two sons, Seth and Josh.

Forty years earlier, he and Susan had entered this valley with an old pickup, a horse trailer, and five dollars in his pocket. By the grace of God and the work ethic of a pioneer, they had carved out one of the most prosperous cattle ranches in the state—and at a time when so many were going bankrupt. He missed it, but long ago he and his sweetheart had covenanted to answer the call whenever and wherever it came. Over the years he had been a bishop, a stake president, and everything in between.

"Do you want to go back, Dad?" Seth called from the cab.

"No, drive on up through the herd, Son, and let me look at them."

Seth turned the truck around and started back through the long line of mother cows that would start calving any day. With the trained eye of a seasoned cattleman, Jim visually scanned each cow for signs of sickness or injury.

This life had been good to him. It was Thomas Jefferson who had once remarked that the men of the soil were the best of men. He wasn't sure about that, but there was something about a life close to the soil that kept a man close to his God. His faith had blossomed as he had trusted in the Lord to temper the elements during winter calving or send rain for the hay crop in drought years. The law of the harvest was true. By a thousand experiences through the years, he could testify that as a man sowed in this life, so would he reap in this one and the next. There was no free lunch in ranching or in the things of the Spirit. Hard work was as much a part of the religion of Christ for Jim Thorpe as was ranching.

They reached the end of the herd, and Seth stopped the truck and got out. Jim looked to the north where his property bordered on the old Steele place. In the gathering darkness he made out a lone figure, stripped to his shirt sleeves, fixing a corner brace on the fence.

"Who's that?" Jim asked.

"That's the new hand Cole Gregory picked up a week or two ago to help with winter calving."

"Looks like a worker."

Seth snorted. "A worker? You have no idea, Dad. That guy works harder than any man I've ever seen. Every time I come out here, he's doing something. I don't know where Cole found him, but if I could double his wages and get him to work for us, I'd consider myself lucky."

"Who is he?"

"I don't know. Cole didn't tell me, and the guy's never stopped to socialize so I could find out."

"I want to meet him," Jim said as he jumped down from the truck bed and started to the fence.

"Evenin'," Jim said as he strode up behind the young man.

The tall, broad-shouldered young man straightened from the wire-puller he was working and turned around to face his visitors.

"Sorry to bother you," Jim said, "but we wanted to get acquainted. My name's Thorpe, Jim Thorpe." He stuck out his hand. The young man's face split into a wide grin, and he stretched out his hand in return.

"Good to see you again, Mr. Thorpe. It's been a long time."

Jim stopped and stared at him. There was something very familiar about this rugged young man.

"Do I know you?" Jim asked in bewilderment.

"I think you do," the young man laughed. "But it's been a while."

Jim peered more closely, the wrinkles at the corners of his eyes deepening considerably. Suddenly, his countenance changed. "J.O.? J.O. Steele?"

"The same. I'm surprised you remember."

Now it was J.O.'s turn to be caught off guard as the older man suddenly pulled hard on his right hand and drew him into an affectionate bear hug. When he pulled back, there was a look of genuine pleasure on the old man's face.

"It has been a long time, Son. It's good to see you again. How are your mother and brother?"

"They're fine. Mom's teaching school down in Pocatello, and Tate's finishing a degree in business from Idaho State."

"That's great." Jim turned slightly, gesturing toward Seth. "You remember my son, Seth."

"I do," J.O. said. "Best athlete Leadore High School ever had, or so I heard."

"Not quite," Seth said, modestly, "but I tried hard. Good to see you again, J.O. What brings you all the way up here?"

"Oh, things were getting pretty complicated down in the city," J.O. said quickly. "I decided to come up here to get away from it all for a while. Cole needed a hand for calving, and I needed something to do, so here I am."

Jim heard the nonchalance in J.O.'s voice, but he also caught the strain behind it. The decades he had served as a priesthood leader listening to people's problems told him this kid was in some kind of trouble.

"You going to be around very long?" Jim asked.

J.O. shrugged. "Don't know. Guess I'll just have to see how things go with Cole."

"The old place look familiar?" Jim asked, gesturing over the ranch.

J.O. turned and looked to the north over the place that his parents had once owned. "It does. It's good to be home again."

Jim put his arm around J.O.'s shoulders. "It's good to see you again, Son. We'll let you get back to work." He dropped his arm and started to turn away when a little voice inside whispered to him. He stopped and turned back around. "J.O., why don't you come over for supper tomorrow night? Susan would love to see you again."

J.O. stood speechless for a moment, caught completely off guard. When he finally found his voice, he said, "I'd love to, Mr. Thorpe. What time?"

"Jim. Just call me Jim, and six o'clock on the dot."

"I'll be there."

Jim and Seth walked back to the old truck, and J.O. went back to mending fence. As Seth drove down the hill toward the ranch house, Jim became lost in his thoughts. He was carried back some twelve years to that day when he first learned that his good friend and neighbor, Joe

Steele, was dying of cancer. A gnawing feeling of regret that Jim hadn't felt in years bubbled to the surface. All those years ago he had tried so hard to get his friend to take an interest in the gospel, but there had never been the right opportunity to bring it up, and the hard-working young cowboy had never asked. That is, until the doctors told him he had less than six months to live. A hunger seemed to awaken in Joe even as his body wasted away to a skeleton. Jim had been with him the day before he died. There had been a fire of recognition and acceptance in Joe's eyes as Jim had told him of eternal families and the work for the dead. His friend had believed him, he knew that, but it had been too late. Joe had died the next day, most of his questions never answered.

Maybe if I had only tried harder, he thought again, as he had so many times in the last twelve years.

His efforts to help Ruthie had also been in vain. Grief had so overpowered her that she had been barely coherent. He had done all he could to help her hang on to the ranch, but in the end, it had been swindled away from her. One day, after returning from a meeting in Salmon, he had discovered they had packed up and left, leaving most everything behind. He had never known where they went. So many times, the Steele family had crossed his mind, and each time there had been a will to repent and apologize to the Almighty.

Jim turned and looked out the window of the truck back to the north. Maybe the good Lord was now giving him a chance to complete his repentance, and this time he would do it right!

||||||||||||||||||

"Lisa, how'd you like to go to a movie tonight?" Shawnee asked as she passed through the darkened living room and saw Lisa watching television.

It was unusual enough to see her normally effervescent roommate sitting still, but watching TV? Something must be wrong.

"No, thanks," Lisa replied dully, "Tate will be here in a few minutes. We're going out for the evening."

"Okay," Shawnee said, forcing cheerfulness into her voice as she turned away. She couldn't help the stab of pain that she felt. Lisa had Tate, and she had no one. Moreover, all this with J.O. had not only broken her heart, it had taken her best friend away as well. She missed Lisa, who spent practically every waking minute with Tate.

Lisa was suddenly at her elbow. "Shawnee, I'm sorry. I didn't mean it that way. It's just that—" she broke off.

"It's okay," Shawnee said smiling. "I understand. If I were in your shoes, I would do the same thing. My only question is, when is he going to make this more permanent?" She had meant it as a tease, but Lisa didn't rise to it. Something about the look on her friend's face seemed out of place.

Shawnee cocked her head as though to look into Lisa's eyes. "Lisa, what's wrong? Is everything okay with Tate?"

Lisa nodded her head but was interrupted before she could answer by the doorbell. She turned and walked to the door. Tate stepped inside and shook the fresh-fallen snow off his shoulders.

"Hi," he said cheerfully to Lisa. "Hi, Shawnee."

"Hi, Tate," she returned.

There seemed a momentary awkwardness in the room. "Is everything okay?" Tate asked. "Am I interrupting something?"

Shawnee was about to brush it off when Lisa spoke. "Tate, I think Shawnee needs to know."

Startled, Shawnee looked from Lisa to Tate and back again. Lisa's hands were placed firmly on her hips. "This has gone on long enough!" Tate looked as though he was weighing something in his mind, and then he spoke. "You're right," he said with a deep sigh. "I think we should have told her a long time ago."

"Told me what?"

"Sit down, Shawnee," Tate said, gesturing toward the living room sofa. "This may take a while."

When they were all seated, Tate began. "J.O. has never been the same since last summer when you two were kidnapped by those gold thieves. Something happened that's been heavy on his mind ever since."

The face of Claude Richards instantly flashed into Shawnee's mind.

"After the two of you parted company," he continued, "he disappeared on the road. He went all over the country. Just before Christmas time he called and said he was on his way home. Then he really blew me away. He asked first about you, then he told me he wanted to take the missionary lessons when he got back."

Shawnee sat bolt upright. Her eyes grew large. "He did?" she asked exultantly.

"He did," Tate confirmed, smiling at her excitement. "He got home just before Christmas. He finished all the discussions in the week or so that he was home. The missionaries were at our home every night. You've never seen someone so eager and willing to learn. He went to church with us and everything."

Shawnee settled back into the sofa, letting the joy sweep through as her imagination conjured up a picture of J.O. sitting in church.

"It seems," Tate said, continuing, "that something must have happened while he was gone, because he read the Book of Mormon twice and went to church all over the country. By the time he got home, he was converted."

"He asked for baptism," Lisa said, joining in.

"He was going to be baptized on New Year's Day," Tate said.

"Was?" Shawnee asked, feeling a knot settle in the pit of her stomach.

"He disappeared about ten days ago," Tate said, looking down at the floor. "We have no idea where or why. He left us a note asking us to trust him, but he didn't explain why he was leaving or where he was going. We haven't heard from him since."

"We would have told you all this a lot sooner," Lisa said apologetically, "but he didn't want us to. He didn't want us to tell you about him and the Church."

"He was afraid," Tate added quickly, "that you and others would get the wrong idea about *why* he was joining the Church."

"The wrong idea?" Shawnee cried, her emotions a combination of shock and frustration. "What wrong idea can someone get about joining the Church, Tate?"

"You'll have to ask J.O. to get the full story on that one," he said, "but I can understand a little bit. He said that if he told you about him taking the missionary lessons and joining the Church, it would look like he was only doing it to get you back and that he wasn't really sincere."

Shawnee considered that. "I guess I can see his point. Was he ever going to tell me?"

"I don't know. We never got that far."

"Shawnee," Lisa said, "J.O. is serious about the Church. He's changed. I saw it for myself. I wish you could have seen him."

"I wish I could've too," Shawnee said, wistfully.

"You should have heard him pray," Tate said, a smile breaking his face. "It was like he was really trying to talk to someone who was just on the other side of the room. It was the neatest thing to listen to."

Shawnee remembered their prayer in the back of a semi-trailer when they were prisoners. Her eyes were suddenly burning.

Tenderly, Lisa took her hand. "Maybe I shouldn't tell you this, but I think he still loves you, Shawnee. I can tell."

Shawnee smiled at her friend through moist eyes, amazed that such simple words could affect her so deeply. She wanted to speak but didn't trust her voice.

"He does," Tate confirmed. "I think he's been waiting to get all this sorted out before he came to you."

"I wish he would have let me help him through it," Shawnee said.

Tate shrugged. "That's J.O. He may be about as happy-go-lucky as they come, but he's the strongest, most independent man I know. If he says the Church is true, then it's true, and he'll defend that for the rest of his life."

Shawnee considered that for a moment. She had yearned to hear what she was hearing now. Knowing how J.O. felt about her and about the Church seemed to lift an incalculable burden off her heart. Yet J.O. wasn't here, and it was not him declaring these feelings. The joy she felt was shadowed by a lurking sense of uneasiness.

"So why did he leave?" she asked.

"That's where the story gets complicated," Tate said. "His dispatcher told me that on his way home just before Christmas, J.O. had three very mysterious 'accidents' that evidently weren't accidents. In San Diego, someone threw a brick through his windshield as he was driving on the freeway. In Las Vegas, someone took an axe to one of his front tires. Fortunately, he discovered it in time."

"Then in Salt Lake," Lisa finished for him, "someone cut the straps on his load, and part of it fell off in traffic and caused a major pile-up."

An awful feeling of dread seemed to crawl up Shawnee's spine. As each new piece of information assailed her, one name flashed in her mind like a monotonous computer cursor: CLAUDE!

"Then the night before he disappeared," Tate went on, "we went downtown to get some pizza. Four guys came out of nowhere and jumped us. The fight was ugly. I got my leg opened up by a knife." He pointed to his injured thigh.

"Was that the night I got back?" Shawnee asked.

"Yes," Lisa said, "I wanted to tell you about it, but I was afraid I would just worry you for nothing."

"Did the police learn anything from the four guys in the fight?" Shawnee asked.

"Nothing of any help. Some stranger paid them five hundred bucks to pick a fight and rough us up," Tate said. "That's all we got."

Shawnee walked across the room and turned back to face Lisa and Tate. When she began to speak, her eyes were blazing, and there was anger in her voice. "I feel like I've been walking around with all the world laughing at me through a one-way window. Is there anything else I should know while we're at it?"

"I don't blame you for being frustrated," Tate said. "But no. That's all there is. At least as far as we know."

"So, any clues where he went?" Shawnee asked.

"No, he quit his job, so we know he's not out on the road. We're pretty sure his leaving has something to do with those accidents and that fight. As for where he went, your guess is as good as mine. He left one thing on his note that was supposed to mean something, but we can't figure it out."

"What was that?"

"Alma 56," Tate said simply.

Chapter Twenty-Three

LAS VEGAS, NEVADA, LATE JANUARY 2022

"Ms. Richards?"

"Yes."

"This is Talley. I found him."

"Where is he?"

"He's holed up on a ranch in the mountains of central Idaho. It's a place called Lemhi."

"Can we get to him?"

"It's remote, but easy to get to. There's hardly anybody for miles back in there."

"Perfect!" Claude said. "It's time to bring this little game to an end, Mr. Talley. What's the closest airport?"

"Just fly into Idaho Falls, and I'll meet you there. It's about three hours north of there."

"I'll book the first flight I can tonight. I'll let you know when I'm arriving. Meet me."

"Got it," Talley said. "I'll be there."

"And Talley..."

"Yes?"

"This is the hunt. I want all the equipment necessary for a kill. Understood?"

"Yes, Ma'am," Talley said as a smile spread across his face.

J.O. stuffed the last of the calf medicine in his saddlebags and stepped up into the saddle. The long-legged sorrel danced nervously in a circle.

"Easy, boy," J.O. soothed. "If you have that much energy after working all day, maybe I should work you harder."

He gave a little slack to the reins, and the sorrel stepped toward the barn and a warm stall. As he rode through the herd, J.O. studied the cows, looking for the tell-tale signs of a cow that would calve that night. If he found one, he would take her down to the calving sheds, where there was better shelter and warm bedding straw. It amazed him how much all the things his dad had taught him years before had come back to him.

Unconsciously, his hand dropped to the saddle carbine that was tucked in the scabbard on the saddle. His eyes drifted from the cows and surveyed the surrounding hills. Nothing was out of place, and no cows seemed to be due. He rode on toward the barn, keeping an ever-wary eye as he went. Claude was coming. He had left just enough clues. It was only a matter of time. He couldn't afford to get lax.

After unsaddling the sorrel, combing him down, and giving him feed for the night, J.O. began walking up the worn path to the cabin. It had been almost two weeks since he had arrived. In many ways, they had been some of the most wonderful days in the last twelve years of his life. The old place brought back memories. Every building, corner, and stream carried a connection to his past. At times it seemed as though his father was there with him, holding his little-boy hand once again and teaching him how a man handles life.

When he had left home in the middle of that whirlwind night, he had second-guessed himself all the way up here, but the minute Cole had opened the front door of the old house and welcomed him in, the sense of familiarity had washed over him like a refreshing spring breeze. These were his roots, and, logical or not, it was right to be here.

Cole Gregory and his wife, Janie, were the same age as J.O. They had all been classmates in school. Cole had branched away from his dad, who owned a ranch down the valley a few miles. After scraping hard and working smart, he and Janie had bought the old Steele place after a California outfit with romantic notions had run it into the ground. Cole and Janie had worked hard and brought the place back to productivity. There had never been enough money to hire another hand, and during calving season it was particularly difficult, as cows needed help night and day. When J.O. had walked in and said he would work for room and board, they had been overjoyed, and Janie had hugged the breath out of him. Of course, they wanted to know why he was there, and J.O. had leveled with them, telling them about Claude and his suspicions. The reaction of his old friends had been just what he expected it to be—feisty indignation and a willingness to fight. Maybe these valleys of the mountains didn't contain the most sophisticated people on earth, but they nurtured some of the toughest and most honest. Fighting the elements or devils incarnate—it made no difference to them.

J.O. topped the small hill above the calving barns and lingered for a moment behind a spreading pine tree. The cabin sat about seventy-five yards away near the head of the valley, flanked on two sides by pine forest. To the north, pastures continued for several hundred yards before giving way to rising elevation and thick timber. They were at the end of the road. If anybody were to come at him, he would see them coming for more than a mile as they climbed the canyon. The only other way to get to him was to cross over two canyons of rugged mountain country to the east. It could be done, but it would be rough.

J.O. let his eyes sweep over the old cabin. The fresh snow that had fallen that day made it evident that no one had been here in the last several hours. Everything seemed to be as he had left it that morning when he had left to work with the cows. He lingered a moment longer. Claude should have been here before now. Maybe he'd buried his trail too deep, or maybe she'd given up. His eyes narrowed in a scowl, and he stepped back onto the path. No; instinct told him she'd come.

The fresh snow crunched under his feet as he approached the cabin, saddle carbine gripped in his right hand. Cautiously, he approached the front door and shoved it open. It was clear.

Cole and Janie had wanted to board him in the house with their family, but he had flatly refused. There was the old settler's cabin on the north end of the ranch at the head of the canyon. J.O.'s dad had kept it up and used it as a calving cabin in the winter. It had fallen into disrepair in the last few years, becoming not much more than a storage shed. There was no electricity and no running water—and never had been. An ancient cast-iron fireplace at one end of the cabin provided more than ample warmth for the small interior. J.O. had insisted on coming here, where he could be close to the cows and away from Cole's family, for their own safety. He had spent most of the first two days cleaning and making the old cabin livable again. It had been a labor of love. While he worked, he had relived his childhood. Every pleasant thought of his father and this place had flooded through his memory. Even things he had forgotten were brought back to him as places and images stimulated his memory. A deep sense of closure that he had never felt before had settled into him. The pain of his father's death had vanished, replaced with a feeling that he could only describe as contentment. His father had lived on this land, and now that J.O. was here, he was with his dad.

J.O. stepped inside the cabin. The temperature outside was close to zero, but the cabin was warm and inviting. The fire he had built that morning had burned down to coals that still faintly glowed in the fireplace.

He and his father had spent more than one winter night here watching over mother cows and fighting to keep the newborn calves alive. It was not a condominium nor a luxury resort in Sun Valley, but it was rustic and comfortable. He pulled off his coat and hung it on a wooden peg stuck in the log wall near the door. Old, worn, wooden floors made a hollow thump under his boots as he crossed the room to the fireplace and placed some split pine on the fire. The flames sprang up immediately and lit the cabin. J.O. walked to the ancient rough-hewn log table and lit the kerosene lantern. Soft, yellow light illuminated the cabin's interior.

The lonely nights spent in this relic of history had been more therapeutic than any doctor or treatment could ever be. Every night, after working until there was not enough light to see, he had come back here and fixed himself a simple supper. Then, with his Book of Mormon, he had curled up near the fire and read and prayed by lantern light until he had drifted into an exhausted sleep. Outside, one of Cole's cow dogs had slept near the door, allowing J.O. to sleep confidently inside.

Claude was never far from his consciousness, but neither was the Spirit of God. J.O. could feel himself changing. It was like the stretching of muscles he never knew he had. The feeling was wonderful. He wasn't sure what was happening, but he liked it.

J.O. placed the rifle on the table and walked toward the washbasin. It was almost 5:30 p.m. and nearly dark in the deep canyon. The Thorpes were expecting him for dinner in less than an hour. He had just enough time to get cleaned up and down to their place.

|||||||||||||||||||

Shawnee walked into the apartment and set her bag on the kitchen counter. It had been a long day at work. The storms had brought icy roads and more than the normal number of accident victims into the hospital. She had gone out on life-flight three times in the last twelve hours. She was exhausted. As expected, Lisa was gone, probably studying at the library with Tate. The apartment seemed empty and lonely. Crossing into the living room, she turned on the stereo. Music filled the room, adding an inviting warmth to the otherwise desolate apartment.

Returning to the kitchen, she pulled a microwave dinner out of the freezer and cooked it. With a book in one hand and a fork in the other, she sat down to eat, scarcely noticing the cardboard flavor of the soupy, lukewarm food. Despite the intensity of her work, it had been a battle all day to keep her mind on what she was doing. The tall, rugged truck driver had continually pushed his way into her thoughts. Where was he? Was Claude after him? That was the biggest concern. If Claude was after him, no wonder he hadn't told his family. But he couldn't take her on alone. Claude would have help, and they would be professional. J.O. wouldn't stand a chance. That was what worried her.

She set the book down. She had just read the same paragraph three times and still couldn't remember what it said. The taste of the food also registered, and she pushed it away as well. Fasting suddenly seemed more appealing. A glance at her watch reminded her how late it was and that she was tired. She wrapped the food up and put it away, thinking to herself that she would eat it later but knowing she wouldn't.

She walked into the living room and sat down on the sofa. The apartment seemed so bleak and cold. How wonderful it would be to be home with her family at that moment. There was love and peace there, greater than all the wealth of the world. It was what she wanted, what she was living for. When she was married with her own children, she wouldn't live in a cold, lonely apartment.

The idea was troubling to her more than comforting. Thoughts like that made her depressed under the present circumstances. She stood up and shook off the train of thought she had been entertaining. It always led down the same track to the same destination: discouragement and despair. And that was the last thing she needed now.

She walked into the bedroom, her thoughts turning again to J.O. Finding out how he felt about the Church and her had brought a joy and thrill to her that still had not dissipated. *What they said just had to be true—but where was he, and why did he leave if he felt that way? Claude! It had to be Claude. What else could it be?* The thought of Claude revived the anger and determination to fight she had once felt. Her eyes fell on the Book of Mormon resting on her nightstand. Remembering the P.S. in J.O.'s letter, she picked it up and opened to Alma 56. In a matter of a few minutes, she had read through the chapter. Her first thought as to why J.O. had given the chapter as a clue focused on verse 48, "we do not doubt our mothers knew it." Carefully, she read the chapter again, but her thoughts were unfocused, and it was difficult to concentrate. She found her eyes growing heavy. Frustrated at her own weakness, she tried again, but with similar results.

Finally, she gave up, deciding that it would have to wait for the clearer mind of morning. Closing the book, she got ready for bed, turned out the lamp, and knelt beside her bed. In prayer she poured out her heart to Heavenly Father, asking Him to help her and to bless J.O.

"Father," she pleaded, "if it is Thy will, let me help him."

Deep compassion unexpectedly welled up in her as she prayed. If only there was some way she could find him—help him.

"Oh, Father. Isn't there something I can do? I'm sure it's Claude, and if it is, it is as much my fight as it is his." Her tone changed to earnest pleading. "Help me find him!" Tears trickled gently down her cheeks as she paused, listening. Nothing came.

She concluded the prayer and opened her eyes and looked around. The room seemed as black as her mind. Standing up, she walked to the window and opened the curtains, hoping to see the light of the moon, but heavy clouds darkened the night sky. It had begun to snow and was coming down in huge flakes.

Slipping into bed, she stared at the ceiling, thinking about J.O., the chapter, Claude. Slowly, gradually, sleep started to overtake her, and her eyes closed. Her mind seemed to lock in on a distant thought that gradually faded away into welcome oblivion. She was nearly out when a thought penetrated the euphoria. Her eyes popped open, and she sat upright in bed. It all clicked into place. Her mind filled with light, and any semblance of sleep was gone.

War. A stripling, a youth. Being pursued. Into the wilderness. Turning to fight. Fighting with faith to protect his family and friends. Not doubting because of his mother. Miraculous deliverance. She threw back the covers and leaped out of bed, grabbing for her Book of Mormon. This time she devoured the chapter, comprehending as though an angel were giving her a guided tour through the chapter. It was all there, and it fit like a hand inside a glove. *Wilderness. To what wilderness would J.O. go to fight?* An image materialized in her mind of a small brown sign in the Lemhi River Valley that read *Hayden Creek*. It was the place J.O. had shown her last summer. How was it that he had referred to that place? "One of the most beautiful places a boy could ever grow up . . . the ranch my folks used to own."

A chill raced up her spine as she thought of J.O. alone in a mountain wilderness being pursued by a modern enemy who was bent on his destruction. Shawnee whirled toward her closet. There was no time to waste. Pulling on a pair of jeans and a woolen shirt, she ran out of the apartment, grabbing her car keys as she went.

───────────

Ruthie reached for the remote and shut the television off. A welcome hush came over the room. She thought most prime-time programming was an insult to intelligence, and the news seemed to leave an after-taste of hopelessness and despair. Reaching for a book, she decided to read until she was tired enough to go to bed. She had barely opened the book and found her place when an urgent knock came at the door.

Ruthie was surprised as she opened the door and Shawnee was standing there.

"Shawnee! Come in, Dear."

"Ruthie, I'm so sorry to bother you this time of night."

Ruthie could sense the young woman's nervousness and knew Shawnee was uncertain if she was even welcome in this home. Ruthie's heart filled with compassion, and she took Shawnee by the hand and drew her into the softly lighted living room.

"Don't you worry about that. Come in here where it's warm. Can I get you something warm to drink?"

"No, thank you." There was a moment of silence, and then Shawnee went on.

"I . . . I know where he is," she said quickly.

"Who? J.O.?"

"Yes. I know where he is. It came to me tonight."

"Where?"

"I think he's gone back to Hayden Creek, to the ranch you used to own."

"The ranch. Why would he go there?"

"You remember in Alma 56 that it talked about the stripling warriors being chased and hunted, and how they turned to fight in the wilderness, and the Lord protected them because of their faith?"

"I don't know the story very well, but yes, I remember it."

It was obvious to Shawnee that Ruthie was following what she was saying, but the connection had not yet been made.

"You remember those accidents that J.O. had on this last trip—the windshield, the tire, and the straps?"

"Yes, but—"

"Do you remember last summer, there was one of those gold thieves who was never caught?"

Ruthie jumped as though she had been struck. Her deep brown eyes grew wide with understanding. "The woman—the one who lost her husband."

"Yes, Claude Richards."

"You don't think she's after J.O., do you?" Ruthie asked, the horror evident in her voice.

321

Shawnee didn't answer but watched as the older woman processed the information.

"That has to be it. I had forgotten all about her." Ruthie came to her feet. "Shawnee, I think you're right. Our ranch is owned by a young man who was one of J.O.'s close friends in school. His name is Cole Gregory. If J.O. felt like he needed a place to stand and fight, that is exactly where he would go. He knows those mountains like the back of his hand." Ruthie walked rapidly into the kitchen and grabbed her cell phone. She hit a speed dial code.

"Tate," she said tersely. "Where are you?" She listened for a moment and then spoke again. "How fast can you get home? I think we've found J.O., and there's trouble."

She ended the conversation and hung up the phone.

"He and Lisa should be here within ten minutes," she said, turning back to Shawnee. "They were just leaving the library."

Seven minutes later, Tate and Lisa burst into the house, holding hands and breathless. "Where is he?" Tate panted. He stopped short when he saw Shawnee.

"Shawnee," he said in confusion. "What—?"

Ruthie took him by the arm and led him to the sofa. "Sit down, Son, and let me explain."

Tate allowed himself to be led to the sofa, and Lisa went with him. Once they were seated, Ruthie turned back to Shawnee.

"Shawnee, why don't you tell them what you told me?"

Shawnee told the story and explained her conclusions. Tate became more agitated the longer she spoke.

"If what you're saying is true," he burst out, "then why in heaven's name didn't he tell us, or go to the cops or something?"

"Think about it," Ruthie broke in. "Would it help anything to tell us? All we would do is worry and try to protect him, and what would that accomplish? Nothing. It might even make things worse. And the police—

what could they do? If they can't find Claude now, how are they going to protect him from her?" She shook her head. "No, I don't like what J.O.'s done either, but I can see why he's done it. It's my guess he's trying to protect us and save his own life."

Tate shot to his feet, his voice strained to the breaking point. "If you think I'm going to sit here while my brother becomes target practice for some crazy . . . " His voice choked off and he turned away.

Ruthie stepped to his side. "I didn't say you should stay here, Tate. Go after him. Pray and ask the Lord to help you."

Tate looked down into the kind, wise face of his mother, two long streaks of tears running down his cheeks. "Tonight!" he said with quiet fierceness.

"Tonight, Son. As soon as you can." Tears were in her eyes now.

Tate started to turn away when a voice behind him stopped him. "I'm going with you," Shawnee said.

"No—" Tate started to protest.

Suddenly in his face, Shawnee interrupted him. "I'm going, Tate," she said fiercely, "with or without you. I'm going. I'm a part of this. I was there." The emotion rose in her voice. "This is my fight as much as it is J.O.'s. I know that woman, and if she's after him, there's no way I'm going to leave him up there to fight her alone. Do you *understand*?" She almost shouted it at him.

For a moment nothing was said. Tate looked into Shawnee's stormy eyes, and she held his gaze, defying him to deny her. Tate glanced briefly at his mother and then back to Shawnee. "We'll leave as soon as I can get the gear together," he said finally.

"Tate!" Lisa said pleadingly.

Tate came to her and took her in his arms. "No, Lisa. Please don't come. Stay here. Stay here where I know nothing will happen to you."

Lisa broke into sobs and threw herself against Tate. He held her tightly, stroking her hair. "I love you," he said, tenderly. "It'll be alright."

She looked up at him. "I love you too!" she pressed her face into his chest again.

"You'd better hurry," Ruthie said. "Earlier this evening they upgraded the winter storm warning to a severe blizzard warning. They are expecting winds above forty-five miles per hour and several feet of snow."

Tate briefly locked eyes with everyone in the room, took a deep breath, then turned on his heel and walked out of the room.

|||||||||||||||||||

Conversation during dinner had been light and casual. The Thorpes were gracious hosts. As he walked into their home, J.O. couldn't help but notice the picture of the Idaho Falls Temple over the fireplace mantle and the luxurious leather-bound copy of the Book of Mormon lying on the living room table. He vaguely remembered they were members of the Church.

"Let's go into the living room and sit down," Jim said. "I want to hear all about your family and what's been happening since you left the valley."

They moved into the cozy living room and sat on facing sofas in front of the fireplace. Susan Thorpe kept an excellent home, though it was not adorned with as much high-priced finery as big-city furniture stores might provide. The furniture, the art, and the carpet all bespoke the simple life of humble country people. There was a warm and inviting atmosphere in the home that reminded J.O. of what he had felt in the James home months earlier.

"So," Jim began, as he settled into the sofa. "I remember you saying something about Pocatello. Tell us what's happened to your family in the last twelve years."

"Like I said, after we sold the ranch, we moved to Pocatello. Mom went back to school and is now an elementary school teacher. She loves it."

Susan Thorpe smiled. "I can see her doing that. She was one of the best young mothers I ever saw. Every boy should be as blessed as you and Tate."

J.O. smiled at the kindly, silver-haired woman. "I kind of think so too."

"What about Tate?" Jim continued.

"He's finishing a degree in business. He plans to go out and make a million dollars by the time he's thirty. I'm afraid," J.O., said with a grin, "that he'll probably make it. He seems to be the one who has all the brains in the family."

Jim and Susan both laughed.

"I take it your mother never remarried?" Jim asked.

J.O.'s grin faded. "No, and I don't know if she ever will. She and Dad had something pretty special."

"They did," Jim agreed. "I remember when they came to the valley as newlyweds. They were as much in love as any two people I've ever met. It seemed like they spent every waking minute together. Even after you boys came along, she still found ways to go to the fields and help him."

"I remember your parents going out in the evening to change the irrigation water," Susan said with a chuckle. "They had both of you boys in the pickup sandwiched between them so you couldn't get out. It was the cutest sight to see you two little white-haired boys bouncing up and down across the fields."

J.O. was warmed through by the recollections they were sharing. He found himself yearning to hear more about the idyllic life of his childhood.

"Your dad," Jim continued, "was one of the hardest-working men I ever knew. He practically built that place from the ground up. If he hadn't passed away when he did, I'm sure he would have been a rich man by now."

J.O. smiled and shrugged.

"So, what about you?" Susan asked. "What's been happening in your life?"

J.O.'s crooked grin appeared. "Well, I guess I'm the black sheep in the family. I'm the only one who's still a shiftless bum." The Thorpes laughed again. "I did okay in high school—sports and grades and all that—but when I graduated, college just didn't suit me. I went for a year but didn't like it. I eventually dropped out and went on the road as a long-haul truck driver. Been doing that ever since."

"A truck driver," Jim said, surprised. "Do you enjoy that?"

"I used to," J.O. said with a sigh, "then some things happened that made it not quite so appealing anymore."

"Do I dare ask what?" Susan asked with a smile.

"It's kind of a long story," he said.

Jim grinned. "We've got all night, Son. Let's hear it."

Warmed by their genuine interest, J.O. was surprised at his own desire to share a story with them that no one other than God knew the full extent of. "I guess I could summarize it as two things that completely changed my way of thinking. The first was someone I met, and the second was—" he hesitated, not knowing if he really wanted to go there. He drew a deep breath. "The second was the Church."

"The Church?" Jim asked, surprised. "You mean The Church of Jesus Christ of Latter-day Saints?"

J.O. nodded.

Jim exhaled loudly and looked quickly at his wife then back to J.O. "You've got my full attention now, J.O. You're going to have to tell me this story."

J.O. told them about the unusual events of the last summer and his more-than-coincidental meeting with Shawnee in the wreck and in the Tetons. He described in detail his bitterness because of his father's death and the agnosticism that followed. He told them everything. Something compelled him to reveal it all—all, that is, except Claude.

"I know the Church is true," he concluded. "It hasn't come easy, but I know there's a God who loves me, and that the Book of Mormon is not a piece of fiction. It comes from God." He breathed deeply and shrugged his shoulders. "There's a lot that I still don't understand, but those are some things I do know."

There was the briefest lull in the conversation, long enough for everyone to perceive that the feeling in the room had changed noticeably. It was warmer and more comfortable. J.O. recognized it as the feeling that had been present when he had told the James family the story of Shawnee's rescue. The missionaries had taught him that the feeling was the influence of the Holy Ghost. It was a feeling one could come to love. If there was a natural high, this was it. J.O. sensed he could tell these two kindly souls anything worthy or wicked about him and they would still love him.

Susan Thorpe was visibly moved. Tears were coursing down her cheeks as she rose out of her chair and came over to embrace him. J.O. stood, accepted the embrace, and returned it. After only a moment, Jim stood and joined them. "I think maybe there's something else you ought to know, J.O."

"What's that?"

Jim motioned toward the sofas again. When they had all sat down, Jim began. "Just before your father died, he came to know the same things you've found. The Spirit whispered to him of the truthfulness of the gospel, but by then he was too weak and sick to do anything about it. He died the next day."

J.O. leaned forward toward Jim, a look of shock on his face. "You mean Dad believed?"

"He did, and told me so," Jim confirmed. "I still remember him testifying to me that he had found his polar star, at last."

J.O. started as though he had been struck. "Polar star?" he repeated. An incredulous expression came over his features. Jim and Susan caught the look and watched as J.O. reached into his shirt and pulled out the medallion. He lifted it off and stretched it out toward them. Jim leaned forward to take it. He and Susan examined it, noting the pattern of stars etched on its surface. They looked up together, curiosity written on their faces. "The Big Dipper?" they queried.

"And the North Star," J.O. confirmed. "I was at Dad's bedside the moment he died. The last thing he told me was to find the polar star."

"Have you found it?" Jim asked, almost reverently.

J.O. nodded slowly. "I believe I have, Sir."

"J.O., I think there's something else you should know," Susan cut in. "Has your mother ever told you about your pioneer ancestors?"

"She told me a little bit, that they were some of the first settlers in this area back in the 1800s, but that's about it."

"Your great-great-grandfather was sent here by Brigham Young in 1855. He was a man of much strength and faith. He was one of the first white men in this valley. When Shoshones attacked the Saints and drove them out, your grandfather went and then came back."

"You mean—" J.O. couldn't find the words. It was as though his whole heritage was being revealed to him in a single night. "My history really was in the Church?"

"Not only in the Church, but the backbone of the Church in this valley for decades." Jim raised his hands up as if to sweep the valley. "The entire name of the Lemhi valley, river, and mountains comes from King Limhi in the Book of Mormon. This is as much the land of the Saints as is Utah, J.O., thanks in part to your family."

J.O. blew out his breath. "I feel like a guy who just woke up after being in a coma for twenty years," J.O. said. "I think I've been missing a few things."

Jim laughed. "I can see why you would feel that way." He became more serious. "But you need to know, Son, you come from a hardy stock of pioneers that were people of the land and the Lord. If these mountains feel like home to you, it's probably because it's in your blood and because your ancestors are still here."

J.O. shook his head in wonder as chills raced up his spine. "That explains a few things." He glanced down at his watch. "I am so glad I came here tonight. Thanks . . . both of you . . . for all you've done. I probably had better be going. I've got cows to check on." He stood and moved to the front door. The Thorpes went with him.

"There's one more thing, J.O.," Jim said, as he opened the door. "I was just wondering, what do you think that polar star is that you and your dad were looking for?"

J.O. reached in his shirt again and pulled out the medallion. Turning it over in his hand, he was deep in thought. "I think it's the Lord Jesus Christ and His gospel," he finally answered. "They're constant and unchanging, and from them any man anywhere can find his bearings."

Jim nodded his head in confirmation, obviously pleased. "That, my boy, is the greatest of all knowledge that a man can know in this life or the next. Now that you know it, be careful. The evil one will do everything in his power to stop you, but hold on. Never let go of this truth, and it will never let go of you."

J.O. reached to shake hands with the older man. Thorpe grabbed the hand and pulled J.O. into a fierce bear hug. "Thank you," J.O. said with a grunt.

"No, thank *you*," Jim said.

Susan Thorpe hugged him again. "I hope we'll see you again."

"You will," J.O. said, and he turned out into the storm.

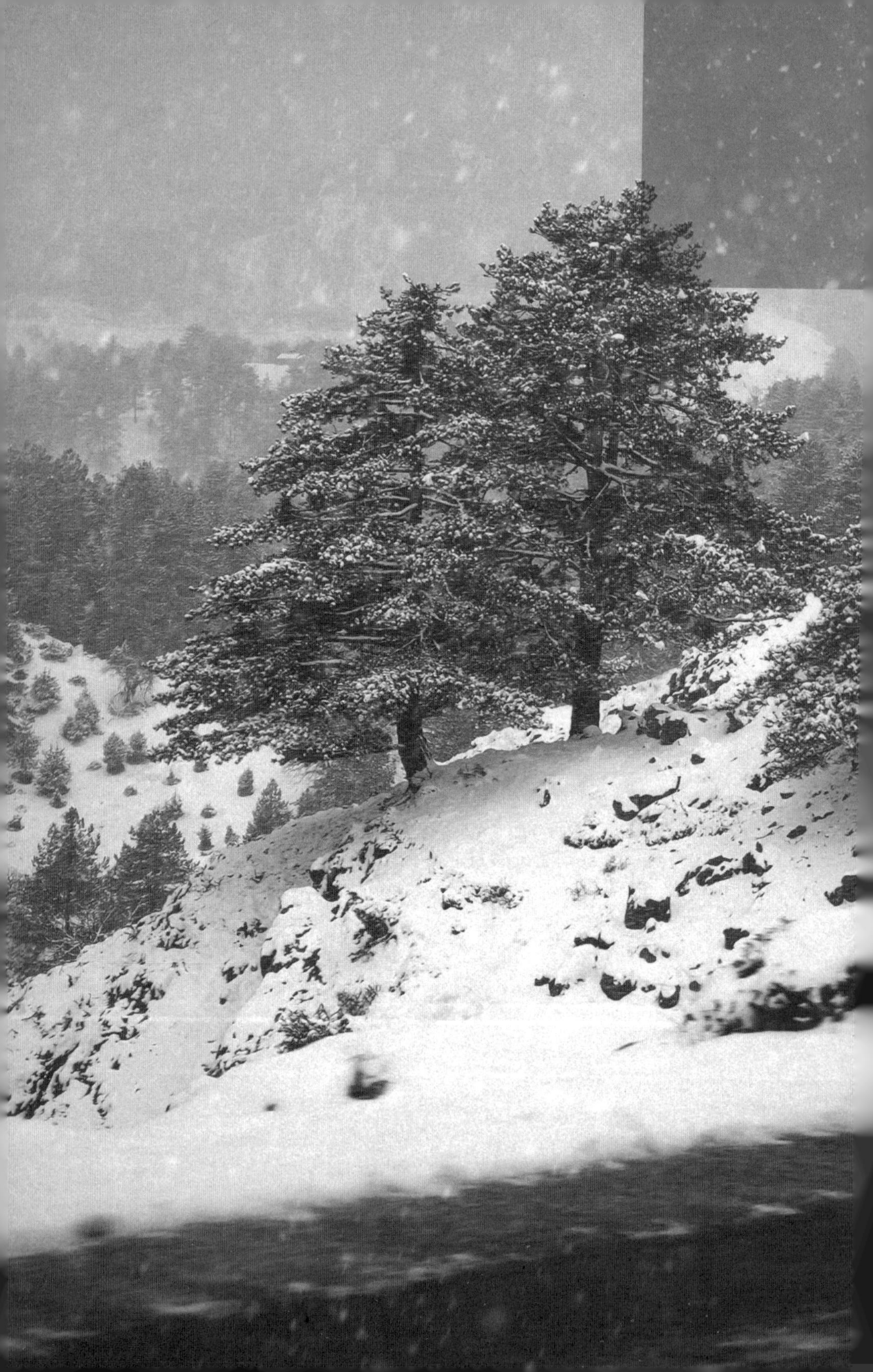

Chapter Twenty-Four

GILMORE, IDAHO, LATE JANUARY 2022

Those experienced with the road would call it a *white-out*. Snow seemed to come straight at the windshield before curling upward and rising over the cab at the last second. It tended to lift the eyes away from the road and disorient the driver. As the intensity increased, the snow swirled in every direction at once in front of the headlights, causing the senses to reel. It wasn't long before nothing was visible beyond the hood of the vehicle. The wind howled at thirty miles per hour with gusts approaching fifty.

"How much further is it?" Claude asked, the impatience evident in her voice.

"Quite a ways," Talley answered, not taking his eyes from the icy road in front of him. "We're coming up on Gilmore Summit. Who knows how long it will take us after that."

Claude swore and stared once more into the storm.

Talley had picked her up in Idaho Falls just a short time before. No sooner had she landed than all planes had been grounded because of the storm. Now, the farther north they traveled, the worse the storm became. It had become a raging blizzard, increasing in intensity as the night wore on. Talley found his eyes growing tired. He frequently looked away and focused on something else just to restore a sense of accurate depth perception.

The snow was so thick and the roads so bad that Talley could manage only a scant twenty miles per hour. He kept rolling down his windows and looking out the side to be sure he was still on the road.

He wasn't too worried. Though he didn't know this country well, he had hunted here a couple of times. His calm came from long years of experience that had taught him to prepare well for mountain terrain and the unpredictable elements. The four-wheel-drive SUV was well-stocked for survival and more if they got stranded.

He smiled to himself. Two snow machines, late model and top of the line in power, were waiting for him at Lemhi. Steele was holed up well, but not so well that he couldn't dig him out. Talley had done his homework, and knew just how to get to J.O.

Talley narrowed his tired eyes and squinted into the storm, causing the weathered wrinkles of his forehead to deepen considerably. All evidence of road lines was gone. Instinctively, he edged closer to the middle of the road and rolled down his window once more to see if he could tell where he was. Suddenly, two headlights materialized out of the darkness coming straight for him.

"Look out!" Claude yelled.

Talley jerked the wheel to the right, sending the SUV into a slide. It careened off the side of the road, flattening a marker post as it slid to a stop facing back the way it had come.

Talley and Claude watched as the black mass of a tractor-trailer rig shot past them in the darkness, completely out of control. The driver had evidently slammed on the brakes at the sight of headlights coming straight for him. As they watched, the trailer slid sideways to pass the tractor. A moment later, the trailer passed the truck. It folded up like a boy's pocketknife, lifted into the air, and slammed down on its side, blocking the entire road. For a moment, Talley and Claude sat in stunned silence, struggling to comprehend what had just happened. Talley recovered first and started to open his door.

"Forget him," Claude barked. "Get us out of here."

Talley's eyes narrowed, but he made an instant decision not to cross her. He slammed his door, flipped a switch for the four-wheel drive, and drove out of the drift and back onto the road, headed north.

////////////////

Tate and Shawnee had just left Interstate-15 near Sage Junction when they saw flashing lights through the thickly swirling snow. As they coasted to a stop, a uniformed state policeman approached their window. Tate rolled it down.

"I'm sorry, folks," he said, "but if you are headed toward Salmon, the road is closed."

"For how long?" Tate asked.

"That's hard to say," the officer responded, his back hunched against the wind. "A truck is on its side up there, and the conditions are so bad we're having trouble getting wreckers and snowplows through. They should have everything cleared up shortly, but I wouldn't recommend going through unless you absolutely have to."

Shawnee felt a clutch of fear grab at her insides. They *had* to get through.

"Believe me, Officer," Tate said, "we wouldn't be out here on a night like this if it weren't a matter of life and death. We have to go through."

"You do so at your own risk."

"I understand, Officer. Thank you."

"You can wait here in your car or go into the weigh station where it's warm. I'll let you know when the road is clear."

Tate rolled up the window and looked at his watch. It was 2:10 a.m. He looked over at Shawnee. "Are we crazy for doing this?"

"Do you think so?" she returned.

Tate thought a moment and then the line of his jaw set in determination. "No!"

||||||||||||||||||

J.O. stopped for a moment at the front door of the cabin, switched off his large flashlight, and looked out at the snow. He had just come from checking on the cows in the calving barns. Huge flakes were falling gently out of the sky. Already more than six inches had fallen, giving everything a fresh coat of pure white powder. There was a pleasing coolness as the flakes landed on his cheek and melted. It was the storm that Cole had warned him about earlier in the day. Several feet of snow along with high winds were expected. The snow was falling, but the wind was scarcely even a breeze. He looked at his watch. It was almost 2:30 a.m.

Lingering a moment longer, he savored the quiet stillness and the peace of the falling snow. It would be hard to leave here. He opened the door and stepped into the snug warmth of the cabin. Dropping his flashlight on the table, he lit the lantern, placed some wood on the fire, and got ready to lie down for a few more hours of sleep. At 5:30 a.m. he would go out again. There was a first-calf heifer that would probably need some help.

He sat for a moment on the edge of his bunk, still conscious of the stillness. There were no sounds of traffic and trains and busy civilization—only complete peace and silence. Reaching over, he took Shawnee's picture off the antique nightstand near his bed. If it weren't for some unfinished business, perhaps he wouldn't leave here at all. His heart was here, but it was elsewhere as well. He replaced the picture, blew out the lamp, and lay down. As he felt himself sinking into slumber, he imagined the gentle flakes of pure snow settling to the ground and blanketing the valley in glistening white, just like he remembered as a boy. He burrowed deeper under the heavy, denim, patched quilt. Tonight, he was safe. In a storm like this there was no way Claude would come after him. His thoughts drifted to Shawnee. It was her face that filled his mind as sleep carried him away.

J.O. stepped off the horse and dropped the reins on the ground. His boots made a crunching sound in the fresh snow as he walked toward the lean-to.

Years ago, his father had built several of the sturdy structures on the upper end of his winter pastures to provide shelter for the young calves. Once cows calved, they were turned out of the calving barns into the open pastures. J.O. had kept the lean-tos full of clean bedding straw. During storms like this, the mother cows brought their tiny calves into the shelters and bedded them down. At least twice a day, J.O. rode through the herd, checking each lean-to for sick calves. The lean-to where he now stood was situated at the edge of the timber with its back against the howling wind and its front facing into the trees.

The snow had fallen all through the night, but it was hard to determine exactly how much there was because of the wind that had picked up. The snow was coming horizontally, piling up in huge drifts on the leeside of the lean-tos and fences.

J.O. walked around the corner of the lean-to and peered in, his eyes adjusting to the diminished light. The calf that was burrowed down into the straw didn't look well. He started forward. It had been a busy morning so far. At 5:30 he had gone out and helped the heifer deliver her calf. By the time he had finished, it was daylight. The gauntness of his stomach had reminded him how much weight he had lost in the last two weeks and that he was hungry, but he decided to come out and check the rest of the herd before he went back to eat.

The small black calf saw him coming and made a feeble attempt to escape. J.O. caught him just outside the lean-to and held him between his legs. Expertly, he slipped a large pill into the calf's mouth and massaged its throat to help it swallow. Finished, he was just about to release the frail creature when it jerked violently out of his hands and sprawled on the ground. The simultaneous crack of a rifle was the next thing he registered. A spreading red stain appeared on the dead calf's neck. Gunshot!

J.O. reacted instantly, bolting around the corner of the lean-to toward his horse. A second shot splintered wood two inches behind his hip pocket. With the lean-to now between him and the killers, he had momentary shelter, but if he stayed here, he was trapped like a rat in a bucket. His horse danced nervously, smelling the blood and hearing the shots. J.O. made up his mind instantly. He scooped the reins, grabbed the saddle horn, and yelled at the horse. It broke into a run even before J.O. was mounted. Holding on to the saddle horn, J.O. clung to the side of the running horse, using its body as protection. The killers would see the running horse with no rider and wonder where he was. When J.O. was sure their attention had left the fleeing horse, he dropped both feet to the ground, still holding on to the saddle horn. The momentum catapulted him up and into the saddle. As soon as he had his seat, he dropped low over the horse, making himself as small a target as possible. The rifle cracked again.

"Go, boy!" he shouted in the big horse's ear.

The gelding reached for more and went harder. Another shot cracked, and he felt the big horse momentarily break stride, but he quickly recovered. The shots were coming from the timber to the east. J.O. estimated that in another hundred yards the timber, swirling snow, and uneven terrain would make him invisible. Urging the horse even faster, he raced up the valley, and in a few seconds vanished like a phantom into the storm.

|||||||||||||||||

Claude cursed as the shot missed its mark and hit the calf. *I was less than seventy-five yards away; how could I have missed?* She fired again, but Steele was quicker than a darting fox. He disappeared around the other side of the lean-to. She lowered the rifle a fraction just as the horse exploded into a run from behind the lean-to. Claude shifted and brought the weapon up to the horse. Her head came up. The horse had no rider. Where was Steele? She lowered the rifle and looked around in confusion. Taking a step forward, she froze when Talley cried out, "Look!"

Claude stared in disbelief. Where once there had been an empty saddle on a running horse, she could now see Steele hunkered down over the horse's neck. Talley shouldered his rifle. Claude savagely knocked the barrel down. "He's mine," she yelled.

She threw the rifle to her shoulder and fired without aiming. The bullet struck a tree a few yards behind the horse. Desperately, she fired again, but to no avail. Steele was gone, swallowed by the storm.

|||||||||||||||||

J.O. looked back over his shoulder. Knowing that he was out of sight, he slowed the gelding and raised himself up in the saddle. From the first day he arrived, he had planned for this. He guided the gelding through the narrowing canyon and dense forest, picking a course and laying a trail that would be easy to follow. He bent forward and looked at the big gelding's chest. That last shot had grazed him. It wasn't deep but it was open and raw and continued to bleed lightly.

After almost two miles, he reined in the lathered horse and stopped to listen. Not surprisingly, the sound of distant snow machines carried to his ears over the wind. He glanced around quickly. The snow was deep and still coming fast. It would be impossible to outrun them. His horse couldn't go much further, and no matter where he went on foot, they would track him. He was the fox, and the hounds were hot on his trail.

"Keep coming, Claude," he said into the wind.

Reining the horse around, he nudged him, and the powerful quarter horse lunged forward, fighting through the deep snow and racing further up the canyon.

|||||||||||||||||

Claude stopped and studied the horse's tracks, which led up the canyon. They were plain and unmistakable. The snow depth was somewhere around three and a half feet, making the going easy for a snow machine but hard for the horse. Beside her, Talley lifted the visor of his helmet and grinned at Claude. Steele was a fool. Obviously in a panic, he was keeping to the valley floor, exactly where the snow was the deepest.

"Let's go!" Claude yelled over the wind.

Talley snapped his visor down and throttled his machine. He leaped out ahead, keeping his eyes on the snow and tracks in front of him. Claude raced about thirty feet behind in his same track, running parallel to a small stream. They swept up over a small, bare knoll, and Talley opened the throttle down the other side. Claude did likewise. Just as they entered a small stand of trees, Talley was suddenly lifted off the snow machine and flung backward into the snow like a rag doll. The hood and windshield of the machine were ripped off as well as it struck a nylon lariat stretched tight between two trees. There was no time to stop. Claude leaped off her speeding machine and landed rolling. She gasped as the soft, cold snow hit her in the face, filling her mouth and eyes.

When she stopped rolling, Claude jumped to her feet. Her machine had hit the lariat, but it had only shattered the windshield. The machine was still drivable. It had lost momentum after she was thrown off, and it had stopped against a tree. Cursing, she ran for the machine, passing Talley, who was face down in the snow. She heaved and jerked until her machine was free. Gunning the machine, she spun in a circle and picked up the tracks. Steele evidently wasn't as panicked as she had thought. Pulling her rifle out of its scabbard, she laid it across her lap. Steele couldn't be too far ahead, and he wouldn't go far in this snow. She moved through the trees as fast as she dared, keeping a wary eye out for ropes.

She hadn't gone far when she saw where a thick tangle of deadfall had forced Steele to cross the stream into a large, open meadow. Cautiously, Claude followed, her eyes sweeping the terrain in front of her. As she came around a cluster of large rocks, her heart leaped as she saw Steele and his horse through the blizzard just entering the trees about 150 yards uphill. He looked back over his shoulder, saw her, and appeared to spur his spent horse forward. Claude gunned the machine and leaped forward across the open meadow in fast pursuit. Fifty yards later, she realized her mistake too late as the ground suddenly dropped out from under her.

|||||||||||||||||||

Tate and Shawnee pulled up in front of the old ranch house nestled in the huge trees that grew along the creek. The roads had finally been cleared sometime after 4:00 a.m., and they had been allowed to leave, but not before the officer had again warned them against going on.

"Road's open now," he had said, "but the storm is bad, and it's worse up on Gilmore. Visibility is terrible."

"We understand, Sir," Tate had said, "but this is a matter of life and death—and not ours. We've got to go through!"

He had peered at them curiously, debating whether to inquire as to why these two were so insane as to be out on a night like this.

"Well, go ahead then," he had said gruffly, probably expecting that in a few hours he would get a call to come and fish them out of a ditch somewhere.

His warning hadn't been an idle one. The road was a solid sheet of ice with several inches of snow laid over it. In places, the drifts were as high as the bumper of Tate's Subaru, and they had no choice but to speed up and bust through. Several times the visibility was reduced so much that Tate and Shawnee both had to look out the side windows just to keep the car on the road. What should have taken fewer than three hours to drive had taken them closer to six, but they had made it and they were safe.

Shutting off the engine, Tate leaned back and ran both hands down his face and back up through his hair. He looked totally spent.

"You alright?" Shawnee asked.

"Yeah," Tate said, "just a little tired."

They approached the front door and knocked. A young woman in her late twenties opened the door; two gorgeous little girls were clutching her legs.

"Yes?"

Tate grinned. "Janie?"

Janie's eyes narrowed as she peered at him and struggled for recognition. Then her countenance lit up. "Tate!"

||||||||||||||||||

J.O. was looking over his shoulder and saw the large, sleek snow machine plunge into the steep-sided gully and disappear. Pulling on the reins and throwing his weight back, he brought the lathered quarter horse to a sliding stop. At a touch of the reins, the animal spun around and was instantly going just as hard the other way.

J.O. heard the momentary race of the engine and then a crunch as it was silenced on the rocks at the bottom. He was almost to the ravine when he pulled back on the reins, jerked the saddle carbine out of its scabbard, and vaulted off the sliding horse. Carefully, he looked over the edge.

Claude was lying about ten feet down the embankment, mostly

buried in deep snow, and not moving. Her wrecked machine was on its side in the ravine's bottom. It was twisted junk. J.O. stood for a moment and watched, making certain her actions weren't a trap. When Claude slowly began to move, J.O. slid down the embankment, picked up her rifle, and pulled her up out of the snow to her feet. For a moment, she struggled to orient herself. When she finally became cognizant of her surroundings, she turned and fixed him with an expression that was one of ugly rage and hate. Lashing out with her right arm, she attempted to throw off his hand. To his surprise, she screamed in agony and dropped to her knees in the snow. The arm she had thrown out was grossly misshapen and twisted. As he watched, the sleeve of her parka became soaked in red. The arm was broken—a compound fracture.

J.O. stood for a moment watching her as she clutched the arm and gasped for breath against the debilitating pain.

"Claude," he said calmly. "Let me help you."

"Shut up!" she yelled.

J.O. turned and walked back to the horse, lifting his reins. "Suit yourself."

He stepped up in the saddle. "We're several miles from any help. In your condition, you'll either bleed to death or be frozen stiff long before you reach help." He turned the horse and started to ride away.

"Wait," Claude called after him weakly, self-preservation calling louder than revenge.

J.O. reined the horse around and stopped. Claude pulled herself to her feet, but as she did so, she staggered back a step and collapsed, unconscious.

|||||||||||||||||

Morgan Talley lay in the snow, the icy wetness burning his cheek. His tolerance for pain had always been astounding to all who knew him, but this was beyond anything he had ever known. It felt like his insides were on fire. He was breathless, and the pain in his sides convinced him that several ribs were broken. Slowly he rolled over, spasms of agony shooting through him. The waterproof parka had kept most of his body dry, but the shock of his injuries made him shiver as though he was in the advanced stages of hypothermia.

Long years in the outdoors told him that if he stayed where he was, he would be frozen stiff before nightfall. His body screamed in protest as he slowly forced himself to his feet. A gasp escaped his lips as he tried to straighten up. It felt as though the bones of his broken ribs were grating together and lacerating his vitals. The pain forced his breathing into short little gasps, barely enough to sustain consciousness.

He stood for a moment, hunched over, waiting for his head to clear. The snow machine lay a few yards beyond him on its side. It was going nowhere. He examined the rope that had caught him across the middle of the chest at thirty miles per hour. It was a tough nylon lariat, the sort that cattleman use to handle heavy stock. No wonder it hadn't broken.

From the tracks in the snow and the extra pieces of shattered plexiglass scattered around, he concluded that the rope had also caught Claude's machine. He scanned the surrounding area. Claude was nowhere in sight. He listened for the sound of her machine, but only the noise of the howling blizzard wind reached him.

"Left me to die," he growled under his breath.

Staggering through the snow to his wrecked machine, he pulled his rifle out of its scabbard and chambered a shell. The effort made blackness swim before his vision. He stood with eyes closed and concentrated on pulling as much air as possible into his lungs. Suddenly, a cough ripped through his chest, causing him to double over in excruciating pain. Slowly, he straightened, his eyes awash with tears.

"Gotta move!" he mumbled to himself.

Talley turned and started moving down the valley toward the ranch, forcing his thoughts away from the fact that he had several miles to go and he was in no condition to walk even several feet.

||||||||||||||||

While Claude was unconscious, J.O. splinted and wrapped her broken arm, using duct tape from his saddlebags. The bleeding was heavy, but he managed to slow it enough that he was sure she would be alright until they got back to the ranch. She regained consciousness as he was finishing. Angrily, she tried to pull away. Stubbornly, J.O. held the arm.

"Listen to me," he snapped. "I'm trying to save your miserable life. You fight me one more time and I'll leave you up here to become a popsicle for the coyotes." He emphasized the last phrase with a tightening of his grip on the injured arm that made her wince.

Her gaze became a baleful stare, but she didn't move again. When he finished with the arm, he helped her pull the parka back on and zip it up.

"We've got to get out of here as fast as possible," J.O. said. "This storm is not letting up, and the longer we wait, the harder it will be to get out of here. You're not going to walk far in your condition, but can you stay in the saddle?"

Claude slowly nodded, knowing that her cooperation now meant her survival.

J.O. held the reins of the horse and picked up Claude's petite frame. He lifted her gently into the saddle. Unable to reach the stirrups, she clamped her legs tightly to the horse's side and, with her good hand, held on to the saddle horn.

"I'm keeping the reins," he said. "Don't be stupid and try to get away. It won't work."

Claude nodded but said nothing, her expression still one of intense hatred. With his rifle in one hand and the reins in the other, J.O. started down the canyon.

||||||||||||||||||

Talley walked only a few hundred yards before he nearly collapsed. An innate sense told him he was in a desperate situation. The temperature was close to zero, if not below, and the wind chill dropped it even more. The blizzard was only getting worse, and visibility was dropping. It wasn't a matter of escaping the law anymore. It was a matter of sheer survival. Exhausted, he leaned against a tree, fighting back the sense of panic. Suddenly a flash of color and movement in the trees caught his eye. He rubbed his caked and frozen eyebrows. It was Steele leading his horse with . . . he peered closer through the driving snow. Claude! Claude was on the back of the horse.

Exultant, Talley melted behind the tree, out of sight, and waited. He had a chance after all.

||||||||||||||||||

J.O.'s breathing was labored as he fought his way through the snow. *Was this the right thing to do? Trying to save this crazy woman might get us both killed. Maybe I should have left her in the snow and rode hard for help.* Even as the thought crossed his mind, he rejected it. The ambulance and the sheriff were nearly sixty miles away and grounded. She would have been dead long before they reached her. *But she had tried to kill me. Wasn't that justification enough for leaving her to the elements?* No! He had to save her despite herself, even if it cost him his own life in the effort. He could never just leave her and let her die.

All at once, the clarity of his own thoughts struck him and words he didn't know came clearly into his mind.

Father, forgive them, for they know not what they do.

It was as though his mind expanded and filled with light as he comprehended the Savior's love. They had hated Him without a shred of cause, and had hunted Him relentlessly, but He had loved them anyway.

No. Us! He loves us, even when we hate Him. Like I did for so many years. He never gave up on me. He died saving me, the one who hated him.

In an instant, all the remaining bitterness and anguish of twelve years melted away. All the burning questions were swept away into insignificance. The only thing that mattered anymore was the love of God that burned so hot within him he could scarcely breathe. Reaching up, he felt the medallion against his chest.

The love and life of the Savior. The Polar Star.

The realization struck him that his quest was over. He had found what his dad had charged him to find. There could be no going back now. His old life was gone, forever!

As a cruel irony, a snow-covered figure stepped out from behind a tree at that very moment with a rifle leveled at his midsection.

Talley stepped forward, the rifle wavering in his hands. "I'll take that horse," he said in a low voice.

Seeing her chance, Claude rammed her heels into the horse's flanks. The big animal reared up in surprise and leaped forward, his shod foot raking down the back of J.O.'s right leg, ripping the pants, tearing the muscles, and shredding the skin. J.O. was thrown to the side by the horse's chest and knocked sprawling in the snow. Talley saw the charging horse and fell back off-balance against a tree stump, jerking the trigger on the rifle at the same moment. Searing pain shot through Talley's chest as the fall shoved his broken ribs into his lungs. He went down into the snow gasping for breath that would never come again.

The rifle exploded practically under the horse's nose. The bullet went high and obliterated the saddle horn that Claude grasped with her one good hand. Her scream pierced the wind as the horse leaped sideways. Claude fell to the side, but her foot slid down and hung up in the stirrup. The panicked horse snorted in terror and broke into a run, shying sideways at the terrifying object flapping against its side. Less than a hundred yards later, Claude's foot tore free of the stirrup, but the mangled foot would never be repaired, as the pounding hooves of the horse had already snuffed out her life.

|||||||||||||||||

Shawnee's pulse quickened as the familiar sight of J.O.'s Jeep came into view. The thought that she would be seeing him again in just a few minutes brought a mixture of fear and excitement. Would he welcome her or turn her away? Did he want to see her again? Shawnee took a deep breath to calm her racing heart. So many questions. . . .

Cole stopped his pickup and the three of them climbed out. "He's probably down at the barn, but let's check the cabin anyway."

"J.O.," Cole called, as he opened the cabin door. Tate and Shawnee followed him inside.

"He's not here," Cole said, turning around, "and judging from the tracks outside, he hasn't been here since early this morning."

"Do you think you can find him?" Tate asked anxiously.

"There's not a whole lot of places he can be," Cole answered. "He's probably with the cows."

Cole and Tate stepped out the door while Shawnee walked over to J.O.'s neatly made bunk in the corner. Her glance took in the whole of the rustic old cabin with its glowing coals in the fireplace. In a glance, she could see why he had come here. Something about this place just seemed like J.O. Steele. She stepped closer and noticed a small, framed picture standing beside a copy of the Book of Mormon, near the head of J.O.'s bed. Lifting it, she felt her throat tighten as she saw her own image. He had kept her picture by his bed. That had to mean something. Replacing the picture, she picked up the Book of Mormon. It was the one she had given him. There were markings all through it, revealing that it was a well-used book.

"Coming, Shawnee?" Tate stuck his head back in the cabin looking for her.

"Yes. I'm coming," she said, pulling the zipper of her parka to the top and stepping out into the blizzard.

Together the three of them walked toward the calving barn down near the creek.

"Hmm," Cole said, after walking through the barn. "I wonder where he is?"

"Is he out there in the pasture somewhere" Tate asked, the tension evident in his voice.

"Must be," Cole answered. "The big sorrel's gone. So he must be up there somewhere doctoring calves."

"Can we get up there?"

"It's a walk, but we should be able to get far enough to see if he's there."

Shawnee didn't like the prickle of fear that crept up her spine.

"Is there any other way into this valley?" she asked. "Could somebody sneak in here another way?"

"No," Cole said. "That road is the only way in here. The only other way is by horse, over a lot of rough country."

"Or snow machine," Tate said.

"That's possible," Cole agreed, "at least this time of year."

Shawnee looked out the open barn door at the surrounding hills. Cole spoke behind her.

"I'm sure he's alright, Shawnee. The chances of them sneaking up on J.O. in this canyon are slim to none."

"Not in a storm like this," she responded. "He would never hear them coming."

They stepped through the door and turned into the wind. A large red horse suddenly materialized out of the storm, running full speed across the pasture toward the barn. Cole stepped to meet it. It shied away, its eyes wide with fright. In a few minutes, he had captured the frightened animal and was trying to calm it down. Shawnee stepped to other side of the lathered horse and stroked its neck. Her eyes met Cole's.

"This is J.O.'s horse," Cole said, his voice tight. "Something's wrong."

Shawnee felt sick inside. She glanced upward and saw the shattered saddle horn. "Cole, look at this!"

Cole examined the horn, then quickly pulled the saddle off the horse.

"What happened to it?" Tate asked as Cole inspected it more closely.

"I'm not sure," Cole said, "but if I didn't know better, I'd say that damage was done with a high-powered rifle. Look at this hole in the leather and these burn marks."

They leaned forward and examined what his pointing finger indicated. Shawnee felt a clutch at her heart at the mention of *rifle*.

"He's been hit!" Cole exclaimed, bending down under the horse's neck. Blood streamed down the horse's right leg from a horizontal gash in his chest. The horse flinched as Cole probed the wound. "That's a

348

bullet wound if I ever saw one," he said, straightening. "Someone's taken a shot at him."

The three of them stood staring at each other in awful silence while the icy snow swirled around them and the wind howled like demon banshees. Shawnee was the first to speak. "You have another horse and saddle?"

"Yeah," Cole said, "there's a young black one that J.O. was working. He's rough, but he's workable. Why?"

"Help me get him!" Shawnee cried over her shoulder as she whirled back into the barn.

"What! You're not riding out there," Cole shouted, following her. "That's crazy. You can't even see fifty yards in this storm."

Shawnee whirled, her anger overflowing, and came back in his face. "That's right," she snapped, "and he's out there in it. Now you either help me saddle that horse or get out of my way."

Cole rocked back on his heels in surprise. After a moment he looked over at Tate, who met his gaze and slowly nodded his head. "Let her go. She knows horses, and she's a nurse. Who better to go after him?"

Minutes later, they had caught and saddled the horse. The young black humped his back when the cinch was tightened on the saddle. Shawnee had seen that look in a young horse's eye before. There was going to be a fight before this was through. Cole set the stirrups while Tate stuffed the saddlebags with emergency supplies. He also wrapped more supplies in an old blanket and tied it on the saddle behind her.

Shawnee found an old pair of Janie's boots in the barn that fit her. She put them on and strapped on a pair of well-used spurs.

"I'm going to follow the tracks before they disappear," she said, zipping up her coat and pulling on her gloves.

She stepped up into the saddle and felt the black tense his muscles.

"They're heading toward National Forest property," Cole said pointing. "Build a big fire when you find him. We'll go to Thorpes' for the snow cat and be right behind you."

349

Tate came forward and reached up for her hands. Their eyes met. He was unable to hold back his emotions as tears filled his eyes. "Find him! Find my brother," he said, his voice pleading.

"I will," Shawnee said around the lump in her own throat.

Shawnee turned the horse out of the corral and nudged him forward. In response, the colt dropped his head and began to buck—hard, stiff, crow-hops. Shawnee wanted to scream at the stubborn animal. Every precious moment she spent fighting this horse meant J.O. was that much longer afoot in a killer storm. Savagely, she whipped the extra-long bridle reins over both sides of the horse's rump. The reins cracked like pistol shots. At the same moment she rammed the rowels of her spurs as deep into his ribs as her heels would go. The startled horse grunted in pain and leaped forward into a run, all thoughts of fight forgotten.

|||||||||||||||||

J.O. groaned and rolled to a sitting position. He had gone face-first into some rose shrubbery, and his frosted face was scratched and bleeding. He turned and watched as his horse disappeared into some trees, stampeding down the valley. It was gone, and he wasn't likely to catch it again. He felt the pain in his leg. The horse had caught him from behind, tearing away most of his jeans from the thigh down. Large, purple swelling showed on the calf of his leg, and blood oozed from cuts and scrapes that ran the length of his lower leg. He forced himself to stand, but his leg would bear no weight. The increasing tightness of his boot told him that his ankle and foot were swelling rapidly.

Glancing around, he saw some color lying in the snow about twenty yards away. He broke off a branch from a fallen tree and used it as a crutch to support him as he hobbled over. The man was lying on his back in the snow, eyes frozen open in agony. J.O. didn't recognize him. There was no need to check for a pulse.

J.O. sat down on a fallen log and assessed his situation. He was several miles from the ranch in a blizzard with sub-zero windchill and an injured leg. All his supplies had been in his saddlebags. He wore only light work clothing. If his situation were any more critical, he would already be dead. He knelt by the dead man and checked his pockets. They were empty. Evidently, his attackers had carried nothing with them but what they needed to kill him.

He stood, bearing his weight on one leg, and looked around. It was well past noon, and the blizzard showed no signs of stopping. J.O. shivered. He was already cold and wet. If he sat still, he would freeze. He had no matches, nor did he have any tinder with which to start a fire. His only option for warmth was his own body. Either he started walking, or they would find him frozen next spring. Gamely, he picked up his body and his attitude and started hobbling down the valley.

Distances were nearly impossible to gauge, but J.O. calculated that he had gone about a mile when he collapsed on a log to rest, soaked from the waist down. Sweat streamed off his forehead from the exertion of fighting through the deep snow with one good leg and a crude, ill-fitting crutch. The pain had gotten worse when several times he had tried to keep from falling by throwing his weight to the bad leg. It had given out from under him every time. He closed his eyes and breathed deeply against the pain.

J.O. knew his situation was severe, but he refused to let his mind entertain defeat. Warmth and a doctor were both hours away. Nothing he could do would change that except walking. Grimly, he opened his snow-encrusted eyes and stared into the storm. The wind howled like a demon from hell through the tall conifers above him, and the snow lashed at him. It was as deep as his thighs in places and piling up deeper. Clenching his jaw in determination, J.O. used his crutch to pull himself to his feet.

"You're not going to take me," he hurled defiantly into the storm as he started forward again.

A few yards later, he came to a place where he had no choice but to cross the stream. The water was only about waist deep, but to step into that water in this weather would be suicide. Looking around, he saw what looked like a log buried beneath the deep snow, fallen across the creek about thirty yards upstream. Hobbling to it, he used his crutch to get up on the log and start across. He was midway across, about six feet from the opposite bank, when the dead, rotting tree cracked and sagged. J.O. felt the log disintegrate under him. Desperately, he lunged forward for the opposite bank, but fell instead into the icy black water, going completely under. The shock tore his breath away. Gasping and choking, he struggled to pull himself out of the water. He managed to grab a low tree branch and heave himself out by the sheer strength of his arms. He collapsed onto the bank, breathing heavily.

For a moment, he was tempted to lie there and let the numbing pain win, but he knew that if he did, he would die. Deep in his mind, the question presented itself to him: *"Do you want to live?"*

How many times have I wondered and wished that if I died, I would be with my dad again somewhere in another life? Is this my opportunity? Should I let go and go to Dad?

Lying in the snow, J.O. spoke aloud. "Father in Heaven . . ."

As he uttered the words, his mind was flooded with memories—images of his family, of Shawnee, and of the missionaries. Then suddenly out of the swirling snow, his father stood before him, tall and powerful, just as he remembered. He was smiling, and though he said nothing, J.O. was given to understand that he was not to give up—not to surrender to the cold. The vision was gone in a moment, but it was enough. Courage and determination hit him like a shot of adrenalin. Using a nearby tree, he fought the unbearable pain, and once more pulled himself to his feet. His crutch had been lost in the stream. He attempted to break off another limb to use, but the tree was green. Dragging himself forward, J.O. made his way to another fallen tree and broke off a limb. His legs were stiff and seemed nearly detached from his brain. He commanded them to move, but they would not respond. His soaked clothing began to freeze on the outside, making his movements even more stiff and sluggish. Even his mind seemed clouded and slow, as though in a drunken stupor.

He thrust his crutch forward and shifted his weight to take a step. As he did so, the branch snapped. J.O. tried to compensate by catching himself with his bad leg, but it didn't move. He fell forward onto a rock, the broken stick ramming him sharply in the ribs. Searing pain went through his upper body, and he writhed in the snow. A moment later, he told himself to get up, but his body wouldn't move. His mind swirled like the snow around him.

"Get up," he screamed at himself, but his broken body refused to respond. Then, the awful pain was gone as a warm, inviting blackness overtook him. He had no choice. He gave himself up to it and was gone.

|||||||||||||||||||

Shawnee's eyes watered from the wind-driven snow that peppered her face as she rode into the face of the storm. She leaned lower over the horse's neck, urging him forward as she sheltered herself from the biting wind. The sorrel's tracks were easy to follow in the deep snows of the open winter pasture, but when she finally entered the forest, the heavy cloud cover and blizzard combined with the forest canopy made it as dark as twilight. The gloom forced her to slow down and lean closer to see the trail.

When the tracks came close to the small stream at the bottom of the valley, she saw what looked like the remnants of fresh snow machine tracks. That could mean only one thing. Her pulse quickened in panic and she urged the horse faster, leaning lower to see the tracks. The snow and wind increased as she climbed into higher country, making the tracks more difficult to find and follow. She continually scanned the trail ahead and off to the side for any signs of life. The thought crossed her mind that this was unfamiliar country, and she was a long way from civilization in the worst storm she had ever seen. Would she survive herself, let alone find J.O.?

She pushed the thought away with a prayer. "Help me, O Father. I have to find him. Help me, please."

There was no sound that reached her ears or her heart except the howling wind. The black horse was walking now, plodding forward into the wind with his head down. The tracks were all but obliterated except in a few places where the trees sheltered them from the wind, and these were few and far between.

Shawnee stood in the stirrups and studied the terrain ahead, hoping to guess where the trail would lead next. It had been several minutes since she had last seen any clear sign. She was moving on instinct now, and the possibility of losing the tracks panicked her.

Her own body was becoming cold and stiff from inaction in the saddle. Her hands and feet ached terribly. The horse pulled slightly to the right and started into a sheltering stand of trees nearer the stream. Shawnee's mind was so consumed with her own thoughts that she scarcely noticed the self-serving action of the horse. It was almost dark in the thick trees. Suddenly, the horse snorted and shied away from something off to his right. His abrupt action nearly unseated her, and she grabbed for the saddle horn to stay on. The horse snorted again and danced away from the frightening object.

Shawnee peered through the snow and darkness to see what had frightened him. At first, she couldn't see it, but then a flash of blue stood out against the snow. Leaping off the horse, her legs nearly buckled under her. She tied the horse to a high tree limb and hobbled over to see what lay in the snow. When she was about ten feet away, she recognized that it was a man lying partially buried in the snow. Shawnee gasped and lunged forward, falling on her knees and scraping the snow away. When she turned him over, her heart dropped. It was J.O. His outer clothing, what little there was, was frozen stiff. His hair was also frozen. She glanced down and saw the shredded jeans and the torn and bloody leg. *Am I too late?* Tearing at the frozen clothing, she searched for a pulse. It was there.

Faint, but there! She knew from her training that his core temperature had dropped dangerously and that she had to warm him or he would be dead within minutes.

She ran back to the horse and pulled off the saddle. Grabbing the saddle blanket and the other blanket that Tate had wrapped supplies in, she ran back to J.O. Her fingers throbbed as she pulled off J.O.'s soaked coat and wrapped the warm saddle blanket around his torso. Once he was wrapped as warmly as she could manage, she dug through the saddlebags and found dry paper and a large supply of matches.

Fire. She had to start a fire. Her father had taught her that the best place to get dry wood in winter weather was to use shavings from a dead standing tree. Using a large hunting knife she found in the saddlebags, Shawnee dug out some dry inner tree bark and cut some shavings, which she used to build a small fire. When the tiny flame caught and began to grow, she knew they had a chance. Working quickly, she gathered a large supply of twigs and semi-dry branches to feed the fire as it grew. A search through the saddlebags produced a tin drinking cup, which she filled with snow and placed near the fire.

J.O.'s body had to be warmed quickly, but not too quickly. She remembered reading a book that described a way to do this. Shawnee knelt and pulled J.O.'s limp form closer to the fire. As she worked his wet shirt off his body, she studied his rugged features. He was more tanned and leaner than she remembered. Her eyes fell upon the small medallion around his neck. She lifted it and read the inscription.

Bending over, she kissed him softly. "I love you, Joseph. Please don't die."

She pulled off her own coat and pulled him to her. Putting her arms around his frigid body, she pulled him close and wrapped every dry coat and blanket she could find around them until they were completely bundled together. At first his chilled body caused her teeth to chatter, but gradually the nearby fire and her own body warmth overpowered the chill.

"Come on, J.O.," she coaxed in his ear, "wake up."

As time slowly passed, she massaged his torso, touched his face, and rocked him, continually trying to wake him up. As it began to get dark, the wind stopped howling and the storm seemed to blow itself out. An eerie calm settled over the little camp as night fell. A couple of times she got up and fed the fire with more wood, building it up as high as she dared in the thick trees, but then immediately went back and lay close to J.O.

How long she had sat there she didn't know. All alone in a wilderness, with a helpless, injured man on a night as dark as hell itself, scared her beyond description. She couldn't give in to it, though. She forced her mind away from her fears. The firelight created dancing shadows on the now-still trees. The only sound that reached her ears in the blackness was the faint sound of the nearby stream. The hard ground was making her muscles ache, but she didn't move. *Where are Tate and Cole? Have they gone up the wrong canyon and can't find me?* It was a thought too terrible to consider.

J.O.'s pulse seemed stronger now, but still, he didn't wake up. *Was I too late? Is the damage irreversible?* Closing her eyes, she drew his unconscious body closer, as though she could will her life force into him.

A sound carried on the breeze. Shawnee raised her head and strained to make it out. It came again—louder. Coyotes! It was a pack of hungry coyotes on the move. Though she knew they would not likely bother her, still, they were predators, and she was alone and unprotected.

The words of a hymn came into her mind, and she began to sing softly.

As she continued singing, a calming peace and presence settled over her. She found herself no longer afraid. It surprised her when she looked up and saw a few stars twinkling through the dispersing cloud cover. As she watched, the clouds widened further until she realized that she was staring up at the Big Dipper and the North Star.

"It's there, J.O.—the Polar Star—it's there," she whispered fiercely. "Come back to me!"

There was no sign of life except the now-regular beating of his heart. Pressing her cheek against his, she continued to rock him and sing one sacred hymn after another as they came to her mind.

Finally, she heard an engine growling its way up the canyon. Minutes later, Cole and Tate jumped out of the snow cat and ran to her, followed by an older, white-haired man.

As the older man approached, Shawnee didn't recognize him, yet there was something familiar about him.

"Can you give him a blessing?" she pleaded earnestly. "I can't wake him up."

The man smiled understandingly and without a word placed his hands on J.O.'s head. His voice was deep and clear. "Joseph Orson Steele, by the authority of the Melchizedek Priesthood and in the name of our Savior, I command you to be whole and return to those who love you."

He spoke other words, but Shawnee scarcely heard them. His hands shifted, causing one of them to brush her cheek. His touch was electric, creating a sensation of warmth that coursed through her entire body. He finished the blessing and lifted his hands. He rested his hand on Shawnee's cheek.

"He'll be alright, child. There's no need to worry."

He stepped back and spoke to the others. "Let's get him in the cat where it's warm."

Shawnee unrolled the coat and blankets. Cole and Tate lifted J.O. into the back seat of the snow cat. Shawnee climbed in after him and held him close to steady him.

Moments later, they were turned around and moving back down the valley toward civilization. The cat rocked from side to side over the rough terrain. Shawnee pulled J.O. closer and wrapped the blanket more tightly. Suddenly, she felt a movement. His arm jerked slightly. Shawnee pulled back and looked at his face in the dim light, hardly daring to hope.

A low moan escaped his lips and he struggled to hold his head up.

"He's awake," she cried. "He's awake!"

Tate turned around and stared from the front seat, tears glistening in his eyes. "Thank God," he whispered.

Consciousness slowly returned, and J.O. raised his head. Confusion crossed his features as he recognized who was sitting by him. "Shawnee?"

Tate laughed jubilantly from the front seat. "Yes, it's her, and don't you ever let her go again."

"Tate . . . what . . . how?" J.O. stammered, trying to get his foggy mind to clear.

"It's okay, Son," Jim Thorpe called from the front seat. "You just relax. There'll be time for questions later."

J.O. lifted his head, blinked to clear his vision, and looked into Shawnee's eyes. She met his gaze. A smile slowly spread over her face. Feebly, he smiled back. He didn't resist when she wrapped the blankets around him and pulled him into her arms. His head rested on her shoulder.

Shawnee held him close, and though no one in the cab heard a word, Shawnee poured out her gratitude to the Almighty with power and real intent.

A few minutes later, J.O. raised himself up again and looked at her.

"Shawnee," he said. All evidence of disorientation and confusion was gone now, and though there was pain in his face, his voice was clear.

"Yes?"

"There's something I have to say in case I never draw another breath." He paused as though gathering strength, and then continued.

"I *know*! I found what I was looking for."

Despite the strength of his voice, she heard a crack in it. Her eyes burned and a great sob welled up inside.

"And," he concluded, "I love you! Please forgive me!"

His arms came around her, and she buried her face against his neck. "I love you too, Joseph. Oh, I love you too. There's nothing to forgive."

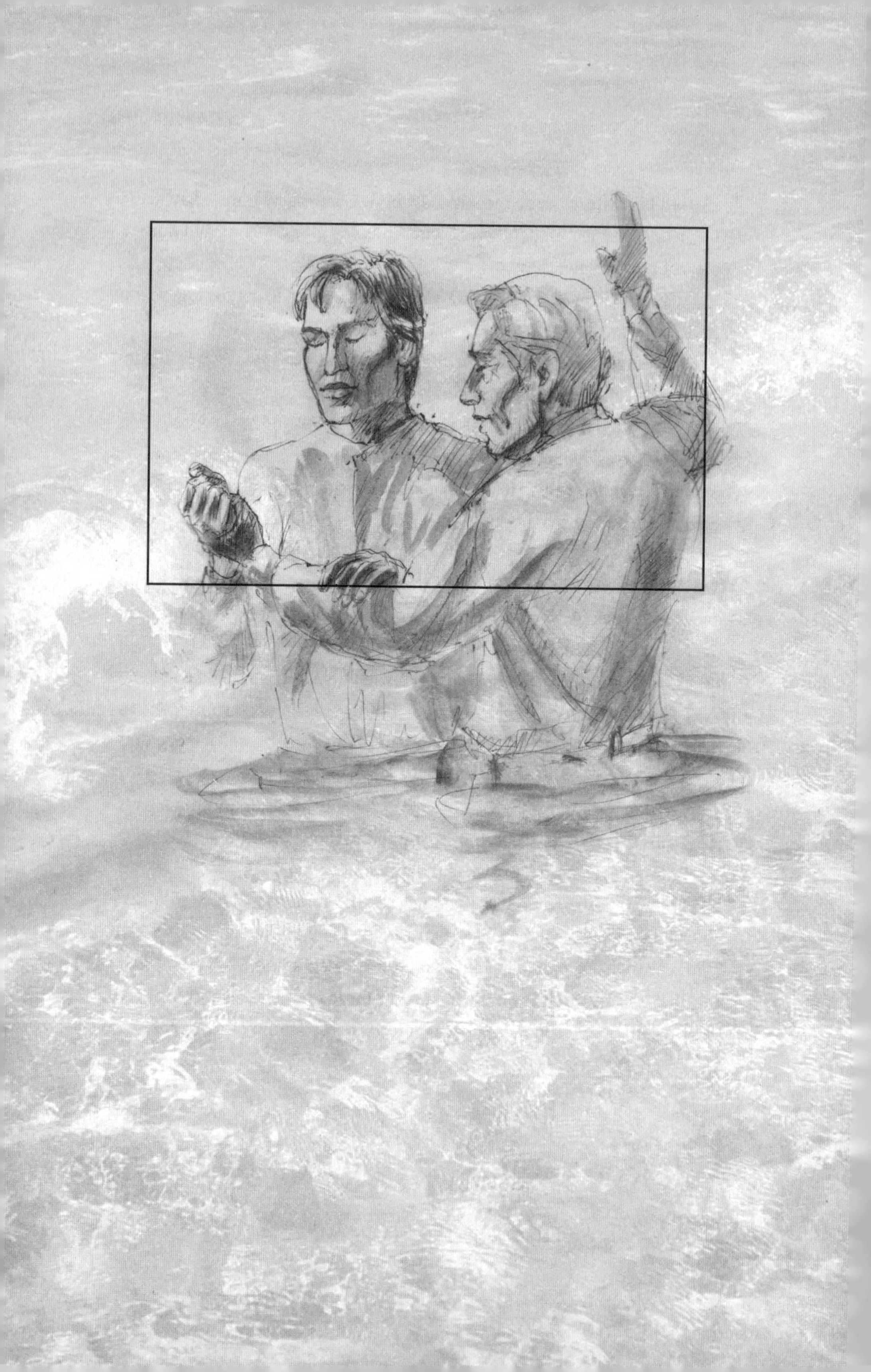

Chapter Twenty-Five

ALAMEDA LDS STAKE CENTER, POCATELLO, IDAHO
FEBRUARY 7, 2022

Slowly, Joseph Orson Steele descended the steps into the waist-deep warm water of the baptismal font. T. Jamison Thorpe waited for him, dressed in white. The older man stuck out his hand and pulled J.O. closer, moving him into position.

J.O. looked up into the anxious mix of faces that packed the room, searching for just one. He found her on the front row, smiling radiantly, her blue eyes filled with unmistakable joy. He smiled up at her, clutched something at his chest, and winked. Her smile grew even larger, and she winked back. Around his neck and under his shirt he wore a new medallion. On one side, it showed a picture of the Big Dipper and the North Star over the Tetons. On the other side, it was inscribed with the words, *I am the light and the life of the world. 3 Nephi 11:11.* Shawnee had given him the gift only moments before.

"You ready, Son?" Jim asked.

"Yes."

Jim raised his arm to the square and in a commanding voice declared, "Joseph Orson Steele, having been commissioned of Jesus Christ, I baptize you in the name of the Father, and of the Son, and of the Holy Ghost. Amen."

J.O. felt himself being lowered into the water. As it closed over him, it was as though he was being enveloped in a heavenly white cloud that seemed to suspend his body and lift his soul. Jim drew him out of the water. J.O. opened his eyes and saw immediately the light overhead. A pure joy, more powerful than he had ever known, coursed through him like a purging fire, and he knew, for the first time in his life, that he was right before his God.

An expression of joy on his face, President T. Jamison Thorpe placed his hands on J.O.'s shoulders and held him for a moment at arm's length, tears running down his weathered, old cheeks.

"The prodigal has returned," he said as he pulled him tightly into a father's embrace. "Welcome home, Son! Welcome home."

Epilogue

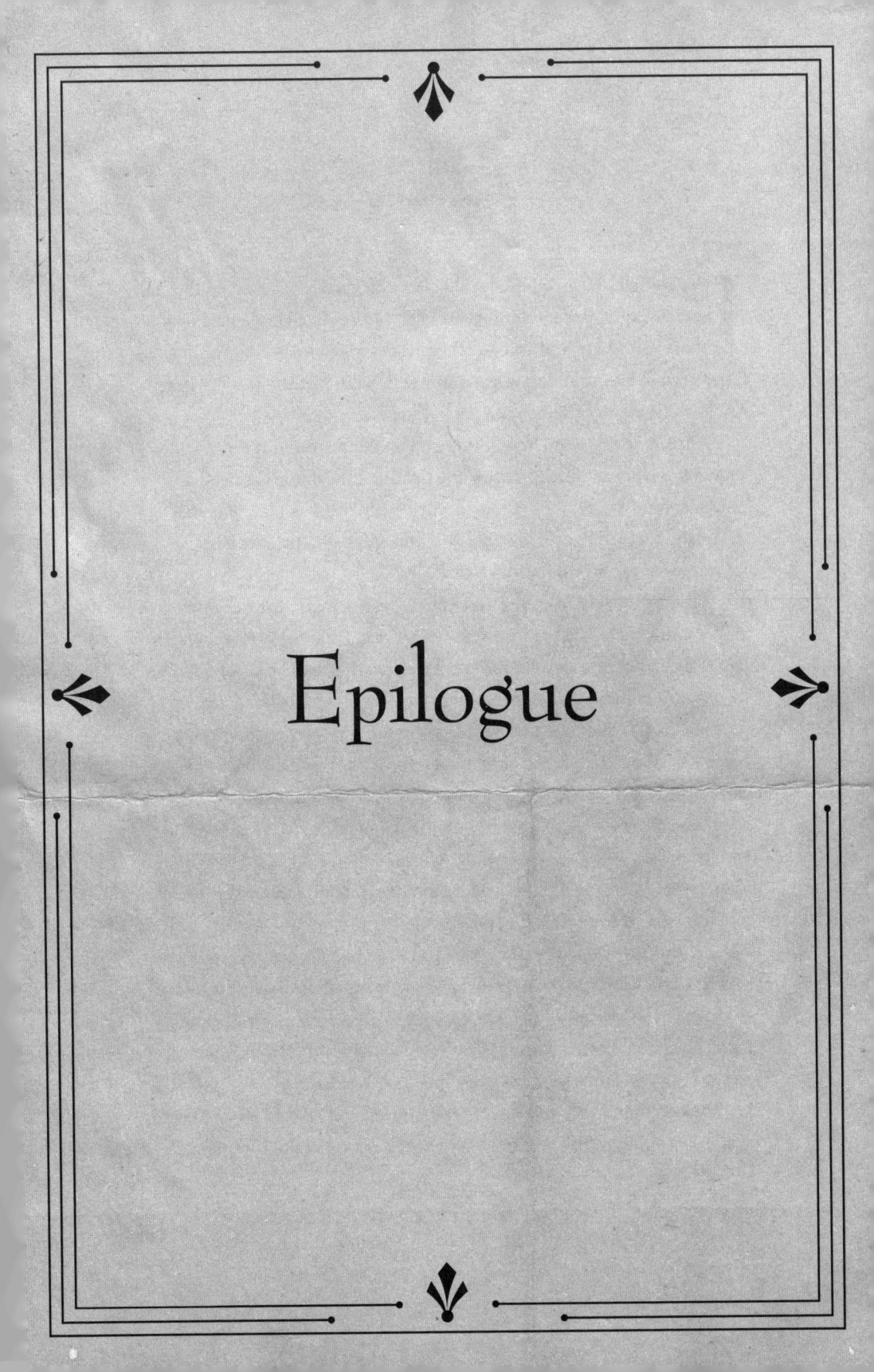

Jake Tolman downshifted the old chevy pickup as it started up the east side of Parley's Summit, east of Salt Lake City. He glanced over at his wife, Amy, and smiled. Their baby girl, Coby, was squirming and crying, letting all the world know with force that she was not happy. Amy was trying to calm her and get her to take a bottle.

"This is so pretty up here," Amy said, looking around at the mountainscape and finally getting the babe and the bottle connected. "How awesome would it be if someday we could live in a place like this?"

Jake laughed lightly. "I'm not sure that guys who plan on being a forest ranger can afford to live up here."

"That's probably true," she said, "but we can dream, can't we?" She smiled and gave him that adorable look that made him fall in love with her two years before. She was the absolute love of his life, and he never got over the sense of gratitude he felt to have her and their beautiful daughter.

The 1972 Chevrolet pickup they were driving was old and tired, but it was giving it all it had climbing up the Pass. The ancient cab-over camper in its bed and the fifteen-foot borrowed boat and trailer secured to the bumper increased the strain on the old mechanical warhorse. It was older than Jake and Amy combined, but still ran. Jake had bought it as a derelict junker in high school and poured enough money and sweat into it to keep it from its last demise in a scrapyard.

With a three-day weekend, Jake and Amy had decided to go camping and fishing, driving from Salt Lake City, where they were both students at the University of Utah, to Strawberry Reservoir southeast of Park City. It had been a glorious break and loads of fun, but now they had to get back. Summer classes resumed in the morning.

The pickup finally topped Parley's Summit and started off the west side. Jake shifted the transmission into high gear as the old '72 began to pick up speed. He didn't even notice the sign off to the right warning of the steep grade ahead. In just a few hundred yards the heavy-laden pickup was going so fast that Jake had to push down hard on the brakes. The truck slowed, but as soon as he released the brakes, the truck quickly picked up speed again; again, he stepped down hard on the brakes. This time, he held them there. By now the old rig was far down the mountain below the runaway truck ramps.

Then with a grip of fear, Jake noticed that the truck was accelerating in spite of his pressure on the brakes. He stepped down harder, but there was no response. He stomped down, the petal sinking almost to the floor; the truck barely slowed. Full-on panic then seized him. He looked into the side mirror and saw white smoke billowing out from under the rear of the pickup.

"Amy," he cried in terror. "I can't stop. The brakes are gone."

"What!" she cried, shooting up straight and looking over at him. "Jake, what are we going to do?"

"I don't know," he said, fighting with the wheel and laying on the horn. "I could try running it off the road, but there's nowhere to go."

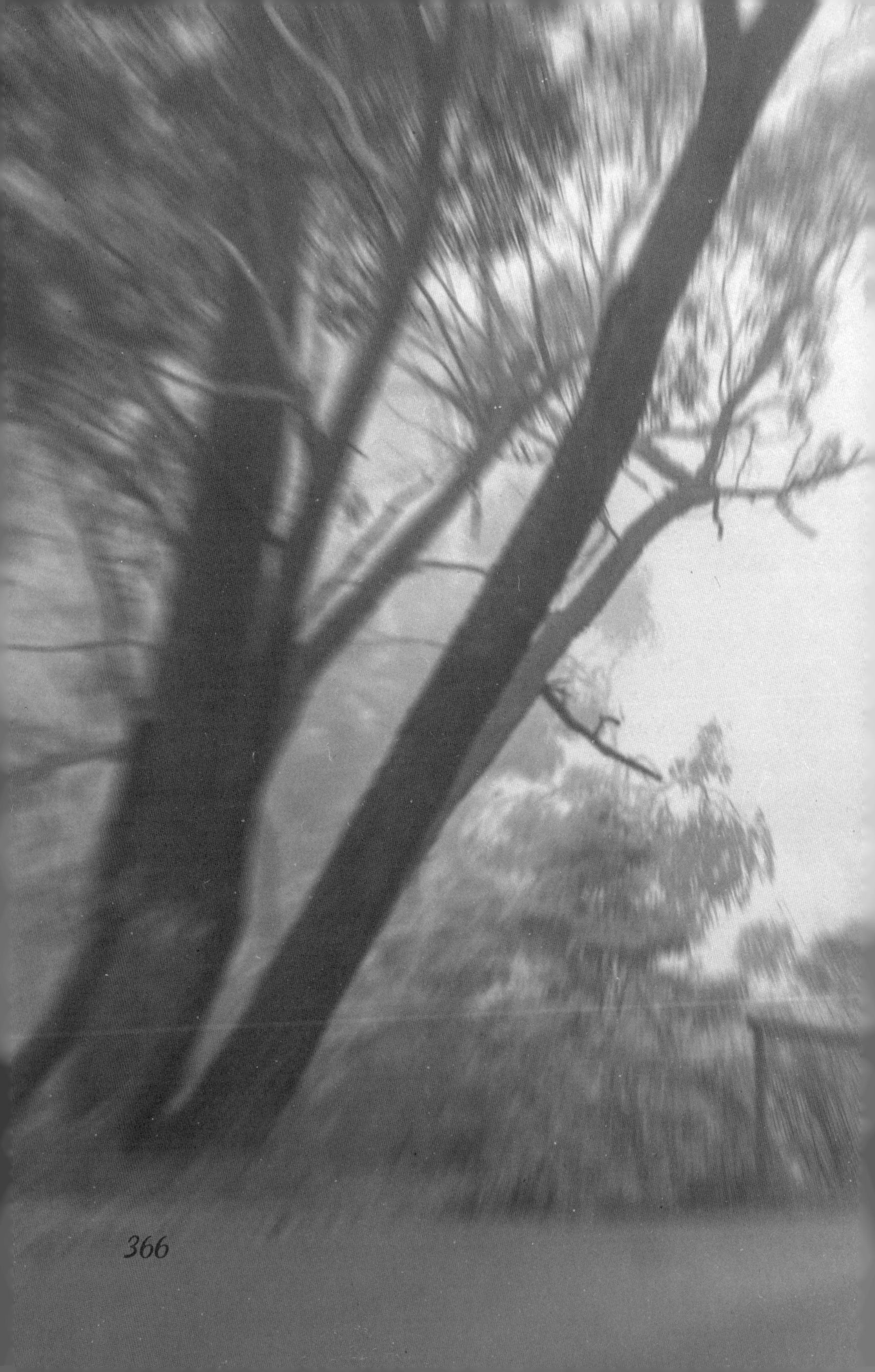

"Get out of the way!" he yelled at the cars in front of him, violently waving his arm. Cars swerved to avoid the old truck.

Just then the road curved. Jake swung as wide as he could and took the pickup into the turn. The centrifugal force and the worn-out, overloaded suspension caused the truck to lift dangerously as though it would tip over. Jake looked ahead and saw another curve coming. The old truck continued to accelerate.

"Amy, we're not going to make it. I can't make that curve."

Amy screamed in terror and clutched her baby to her chest. "Oh, Jake!"

At that moment, a long, sleek, black truck with no trailer, unlike anything Jake had ever seen, passed them and pulled in directly in front of them.

"Just hold on and keep it steady," a deep reassuring voice crackled over Jake's CB radio. "We've got you."

Not comprehending, Jake tried to reach for the mic to answer, but it took both hands on the wheel to control the careening pickup. To his astonishment, he saw large, padded bumpers raise up from beneath the rig in front of him and lock into place on its rear. At the same moment, the brake lights of the mysterious truck flashed on. The distance between the two vehicles closed rapidly. Amy screamed again, thinking they were going to crash, but the driver of the big truck expertly feathered the brakes, and the two vehicles came together with only a bump.

Jake felt the pickup slow rapidly. Now comprehending the driver's intent, he shouted exultantly to his wife, "We're going to be okay. He's got us. We're slowing down, sweetheart!"

Seconds later, with their speed safely reduced, the driver

367

ahead steered them onto the shoulder and rolled to a stop. Jake heard the air brakes set up on the unbelievable rig in front of him. Jake shut off the engine and rammed the transmission into first gear. Dropping his hands from the wheel, he heaved a sigh of relief.

"Are you okay?" he asked, reaching tenderly for his wife.

"We're fine," she said through her tears. "Thank you for saving us."

"It wasn't me," he said, jerking his head toward the black truck. "It was them."

They both stepped out of the pickup and walked to the side of the road. For the first time they noticed a large, beautiful mural painted on the back of the truck. It showed a wild horse with a long, flowing mane and tail running across a mountain landscape. Just then a tall, lean man with wind-blown sandy hair and rugged features walked around the front of the black truck. He wore boots, jeans, and a tee-shirt. The passenger door opened, and a woman stepped out to join him. She was striking, with long, blond hair falling loosely past her shoulders. She was similarly dressed in faded jeans and a white half-sleeve cotton blouse. The man reached for her hand and their fingers locked tightly and affectionately together. They walked up to Jake and Amy.

"Are you alright?" the man asked. Jake recognized the deep voice as the one from the radio. Before he could answer, the woman broke hands with the man and walked to Amy. She reached out and took Amy's proffered hand. "Are *you* okay?" she asked tenderly.

"Oh, yes." Amy cried, all the emotions suddenly flooding out. "Thank you." The woman stepped closer and took mother and baby in her arms.

"Who are you?" Jake burst out, "and what kind of a truck is that?"

The man grinned and looked over his shoulder at the truck and then back to Jake.

"My name is J.O., and this beautiful lady is Shawnee. The truck is a very long story for another day."

The End